120

Rowland G. Rodman,

April 14/09 —
M. D. R —
California

SEPTIMUS

By the Same Author

THE MORALS OF MARCUS ORDEYNE

THE BELOVÉD VAGABOND

AT THE GATE OF SAMARIA

A STUDY IN SHADOWS

THE WHITE DOVE

IDOLS

DERELICTS

THE USURPER

WHERE LOVE IS

THE DEMAGOGUE AND LADY PHAYRE

SHE LAUGHED, ALTHOUGH SHE DETESTED HIM.

(page 7)

SEPTIMUS

BY
WILLIAM J. LOCKE

Illustrations by James Montgomery Flagg

NEW YORK
JOHN LANE COMPANY
MCMIX

SET UP, ELECTROTYPED AND PRINTED BY
PUBLISHERS PRINTING COMPANY, NEW YORK

RUTGER BLEECKER JEWETT

CARO SEPTIMI
AUCTORISQUE AMICO HIC LIBER
SEPTIMI INSCRIBITUR

LIST OF ILLUSTRATIONS

SEPTIMUS

CHAPTER I

"I LOVE Nunsmere," said the Literary Man from London. "It is a spot where faded lives are laid away in lavender."

"I'm not a faded life, and I'm not going to be laid away in lavender," retorted Zora Middlemist.

She turned from him and handed cakes to the Vicar. She had no desire to pet the Vicar, but he was less unbearable than the Literary Man from London whom he had brought to call on his parishioners. Zora disliked to be called a parishioner. She disliked many things in Nunsmere. Her mother, Mrs. Oldrieve, however, loved Nunsmere, adored the Vicar, and found awe-inspiring in his cleverness the Literary Man from London.

Nunsmere lies hidden among the oaks of Surrey, far from the busy ways of men. It is heaven knows how many miles from a highroad. You have to drive through lanes and climb right over a hill to get to it. Two old Georgian houses covered with creepers, a modern Gothic church, two much more venerable and pious-looking inns, and a few cottages settling peacefully around a common form the village. Here and there a cottage lurks up a lane. These cottages are mostly inhabited by the gentle classes. Some are really old, with great oak beams across the low ceilings, and stone-flagged kitchens furnished with great open fireplaces where you can sit and get scorched and covered with smoke. Some are new, built in imitation of the old, by a mute, inglorious Adam, the village carpenter. All have long casement windows, front gardens in which grow stocks and phlox and sunflowers and hollyhocks and roses; and a red-tiled path leads from the front gate to the entrance porch. Nunsmere is very quiet and restful. Should a roisterer cross the common singing a song at half-past nine at night, all Nunsmere hears it and is shocked—if not frightened to the extent of bolting doors and windows, lest the dreadful drunken man should come in.

In a cottage on the common, an old one added to by the local architect, with a front garden and a red-tiled path, dwelt Mrs. Oldrieve in entire happiness, and her daughter in discontent. And this was through no peevish or disagreeable traits in Zora's nature. If we hear Guy Fawkes was fretful in the Little-Ease, we are not pained by Guy Fawkes's lack of Christian resignation.

When the Vicar and the Literary Man from London had gone, Zora threw open the window and let the soft autumn air flood the room. Mrs. Oldrieve drew her woolen shawl around her lean shoulders.

"I'm afraid you quite snubbed Mr. Rattenden, just when he was saying one of his cleverest things."

"He said it to the wrong person, mother. I'm neither a faded life nor am I going to be laid away in lavender. Do I look like it?"

She moved across the room, swiftly, and stood in the slanting light from the window, offering herself for inspection. Nothing could be less like a faded life than the magnificent, broad-hipped, full-bosomed woman that met her mother's gaze. Her hair was auburn, her eyes brown with gold flecks, her lips red, her cheeks clear and young. She was cast, physically, in heroic mold, a creature of dancing blood and color and warmth. Disparaging tea-parties called her an Amazon. The Vicar's wife regarded her as too large and flaring and curvilinear for reputable good looks. She towered over Nunsmere. Her presence disturbed the sedateness of the place. She was a wrong note in its harmony.

Mrs. Oldrieve sighed. She was small and colorless. Her husband, a wild explorer, a tornado of a man, had been killed by a buffalo. She was afraid that Zora took after her father. Her younger daughter Emmy had also inherited some of the Oldrieve restlessness and had gone on the stage. She was playing now in musical comedy in London.

"I don't see why you should not be happy here, Zora," she remarked, "but if you want to go, you must. I used to say the same to your poor, dear father."

"I've been very good, haven't I?" said Zora. "I've been the model young widow and lived as demurely as if my heart were breaking with sorrow. But now, I can't stand it any longer. I'm going out to see the world."

"You'll soon marry again, dear, and that's one comfort."

Zora brought her hands down passionately to her sides.

"Never. Never—do you hear, mother? Never. I'm going out into the world, to get to the heart of the life I've never known. I'm going to live."

"I don't see how you are going to 'live,' dear, without a man to take care of you," said Mrs. Oldrieve, on whom there occasionally flashed an eternal verity.

"I hate men. I hate the touch of them—the very sight of them. I'm going to have nothing more to do with them for the rest of my natural life. My dear mother!" and her voice broke, "haven't I had enough to do with men and marriage?"

"All men aren't like Edward Middlemist," Mrs. Oldrieve argued as she counted the rows of her knitting.

"How am I to know that? How could anyone have told that he was what he was? For heaven's sake don't talk of it. I had almost forgotten it all in this place."

She shuddered and, turning to the window, stared into the sunset.

"Lavender has its uses," said Mrs. Oldrieve.

Here again it must be urged on Zora's behalf that she had reason for her misanthropy. It is not cheerful for a girl to discover within twenty-four hours of her wedding that her husband is a hopeless drunkard, and to see him die of delirium tremens within six weeks. An experience so vivid, like lightning must blast something in a woman's conception of life. Because one man's kisses reeked of whisky the kisses of all male humanity were anathema.

After a long spell of silence she came and laid her cheek against her mother's.

"This is the very last time we'll speak of it, dear. I'll lock the skeleton in its cupboard and throw away the key."

She went upstairs to dress and came down radiant. At dinner she spoke exultingly of her approaching freedom. She would tear off her widow's weeds and deck herself in the flower of youth. She would plunge into the great swelling sea of Life. She would drink sunshine and fill her soul with laughter. She would do a million hyperbolic things, the mention of which mightily confused her mother. "I, my dear," said the hen in the fairy tale, "never had the faintest desire to get into water." So, more or less, said Mrs. Oldrieve.

"Will you miss me very dreadfully?" asked Zora.

"Of course," but her tone was so lacking in conviction that Zora laughed.

"Mother, you know very well that Cousin Jane will be a more sympathetic companion. You've been pining for her all this time."

Cousin Jane held distinct views on the cut of underclothes for the deserving poor, and as clouds disperse before the sun so did household dust before her presence. Untidiness followed in Zora's steps, as it does in those of the physically large, and Cousin Jane disapproved of her thoroughly. But Mrs. Oldrieve often sighed for Cousin Jane as she had never sighed for Zora, Emily, or her husband. She was more than content with the prospect of her companionship.

"At any rate, my dear," she said that evening, as she paused, candle in hand, by her bedroom door, "at any rate I hope you'll do nothing that is unbecoming to a gentlewoman."

Such was her benison.

Zora bumped her head against the oak beam that ran across her bedroom ceiling.

"It's quite true," she said to herself, "the place is too small for me, I don't fit."

What she was going to do in this wide world into whose glories she was about to enter she had but the vaguest notion. All to her was the Beautiful Unknown. Narrow means had kept her at Cheltenham and afterwards at Nunsmere, all her life. She had met her husband in Ipswich while she was paying a polite visit to some distant cousins. She had married him offhand, in a whirl of the senses. He was a handsome blackguard, of independent means, and she had spent her nightmare of a honeymoon at Brighton. On three occasions, during her five-and-twenty years of existence, she had spent a golden week in London. That was all she knew of the wide world. It was not very much. Reading had given her a second-hand acquaintance with the doings of various classes of mankind, and such pictures as she had seen had filled her head with dreams of strange and wonderful places. But otherwise she was ignorant, beautifully, childishly ignorant—and undismayed.

What was she going to do? Sensitive and responsive to beauty, filled with artistic impulses, she could neither paint, act, sing, nor write pretty little stories for the magazines. She had no special gift to develop. To earn her living in a humdrum way she had no need. She had no high Ibsenite notions of working out her own individuality. She had no consuming passion for reforming any section of the universe. She had no mission—that she knew of—to accomplish. Unlike so many of her sex who yearn to be as men and go out into the world she had no inner mandate to do anything, no ambition to *be* anything. She was simply a great, rich flower, struggling through the shade to the sunlight, plenty of sunlight, as much sunlight as the heavens could give her.

The Literary Man from London happened to be returning to town by the train that carried Zora on the first stage of her pilgrimage. He obtained her consent to travel up in the same carriage. He asked her to what branch of human activity she intended to devote herself. She answered that she was going to lie, anyhow, among the leaves. He rebuked her.

"We ought," said he, "to justify our existence."

She drew herself up and flashed an indignant glance at him.

"I beg your pardon," he apologized. "You do justify yours."

"How?"

"You decorate the world. I was wrong. That is the true function of a beautiful woman, and you fulfill it."

"I have in my bag," replied Zora slowly, and looking at him steady-eyed, "a preventive against sea-sickness; I have a waterproof to shelter me from rain; but what can I do to shield myself against silly compliments?"

"Adopt the costume of the ladies of the Orient," said the Literary Man from London, unabashed.

She laughed, although she detested him. He bent forward with humorous earnestness. He had written some novels, and now edited a weekly of precious tendencies and cynical flavor.

"I am a battered old man of thirty-five," said he, "and I know what I am talking about. If you think you are going to wander at a loose end about Europe without men paying you compliments and falling in love with you and making themselves generally delightful, you're traveling under a grievous hallucination."

"What you say," retorted Zora, "confirms me in my opinion that men are an abominable nuisance. Why can't they let a poor woman go about in peace?"

The train happened to be waiting at Clapham Junction. A spruce young man, passing by on the platform, made a perceptible pause by the window, his eyes full on her. She turned her head impatiently. Rattenden laughed.

"Dear lady," said he, "I must impart to you the elements of wisdom. Miss Keziah Skaffles, with brain cordage for hair, and monoliths for teeth, and a box of dominoes for a body, can fool about unmolested among the tribes of Crim Tartary. She doesn't worry the Tartars. But, permit me to say it, as you are for the moment my disciple, a beautiful woman like yourself, radiating feminine magnetism, worries a man exceedingly. You don't let him go about in peace, so why should he let you?"

"I think," said Zora, as the train moved on, "that Miss Keziah Skaffles is very much to be envied, and that this is a very horrid conversation."

She was offended in her provincial-bred delicacy. It was enough to make her regard herself with repulsion. She took up the fashion paper she had bought at the station— was she not intending to run delicious riot among the dressmakers and milliners of London?—and regarding blankly the ungodly waisted ladies in the illustrations, determined to wear a wig and paint her face yellow, and black out one of her front teeth, so that she should not worry the Tartars.

"I am only warning you against possible dangers," said Rattenden stiffly. He did not like his conversation to be called horrid.

"To the race of men?"

"No, to yourself."

She laughed scornfully. "No fear of that. Why does every man think himself irresistible?"

"Because he generally is—if he wants to be," said the Literary Man from London.

Zora caught her breath. "Well of all——" she began.

"Yes, I know what you're going to say. Millions of women have said it and eaten their words. Why should you—beautiful as you are—be an exception to the law of life? You're going out to suck the honey of the world, and men's hearts will be your flowers. Instinct will drive you. You won't be able to get away from it. You think you're going to be thrilled into passionate raptures by cathedrals and expensive restaurants and the set pieces of fashionable scenery. You're not. Your store of honey will consist of emotional experiences of a primitive order. If not, I know nothing at all about women."

"Do you know anything about them?" she asked sweetly.

"More than would be becoming of me to tell," he replied. "Anyhow," he added, "that doesn't matter. I've made my prophecy. You'll tell me afterwards, if I have the pleasure of seeing you again, whether it has come true."

"It won't come true," said Zora.

"We shall see," said the wise man.

She dashed, that afternoon, into her sister's tiny flat in Chelsea. Emily, taken by surprise, hastily stuffed to the bottom of her work-basket a man's silk tie which she was knitting, and then greeted Zora affectionately.

She was shorter, slimmer, paler than her sister: of a certain babyish prettiness. She had Mrs. Oldrieve's weak mouth and gentle ways.

"Why, Zora, who would have thought of seeing you? What are you doing in town?"

"Getting hats and frocks—a trousseau of freedom. I've left Nunsmere. I'm on my own."

Her eyes sparkled, her cheeks were flushed. She caught Emily to her bosom.

"Oh, darling! I'm so happy—a bird let out of a cage."

"An awful big bird," laughed Emily.

"Yes, let out of an awful small cage. I'm going to see the world, for the first time in my life. I'm going to get

out of the cold and wet—going South—to Italy—Sicily—
Egypt—anywhere."

"All by yourself?"

"There'll be Turner."

"Turner?"

"Ah, you don't know her. My new maid. But isn't it
glorious? Why shouldn't you come with me, darling? Do.
Come."

"And throw up my engagement? I couldn't. I should
love it, but you don't know how hard engagements are to
get."

"Never mind. I'll pay for everything."

But Emily shook her fluffy head. She had a good part,
a few lines to speak and a bit of a song to sing in a successful musical comedy. She looked back on the two years'
price she had paid for that little bit of a song. It was
dearer to her than anything—save one thing—in life.

"I can't. Besides, don't you think a couple of girls fool-
ing about alone look rather silly? It wouldn't really be
very funny without a man."

Zora rose in protest. "The whole human race is man-
mad! Even mother. I think everybody is detestable!"

The maid announced "Mr. Mordaunt Prince," and a
handsome man with finely cut, dark features and black
hair parted in the middle and brushed tightly back over the
head, entered the room. Emmy presented him to Zora,
who recognized him as the leading man at the theater where
Emmy was playing. Zora exchanged a few polite commonplaces with the visitor and then took her leave. Emmy
accompanied her to the front door of the flat.

"Isn't he charming?"

"That creature?" asked Zora.

Emmy laughed. "In your present mood you would find fault with an archangel. Good-bye, darling, and take care of yourself."

She bore no malice, having a kind heart and being foolishly happy. When she returned to the drawing-room the man took both her hands.

"Well, sweetheart?"

"My sister wanted to carry me off to Italy."

"What did you say?"

"Guess," said the girl, lifting starry eyes.

The man guessed, after the manner of men, and for a moment Emmy forgot Zora, who went her own way in pursuit of happiness, heedless of the wisdom of the wise and of the foolish.

CHAPTER II

FOR five months Zora wandered over the world—chiefly Italy—without an experience which might be called an adventure. When the Literary Man from London crossed her mind she laughed him to scorn for a prophetic popinjay. She had broken no man's heart, and her own was whole. The tribes of Crim Tartary had exhibited no signs of worry and had left her unmolested. She had furthermore taken rapturous delight in cathedrals, expensive restaurants, and the set pieces of fashionable scenery. Rattenden had not a prophetic leg to stand on.

Yet she longed for the unattainable—for the elusive something of which these felicities were but symbols. Now the wanderer with a haunting sense of the Beyond, but without the true vagabond's divine gift of piercing the veil, can only follow the obvious; and there are seasons when the obvious fails to satisfy. When such a mood overcame her mistress, Turner railed at the upsetting quality of foreign food, and presented bicarbonate of soda. She arrived by a different path at the unsatisfactory nature of the obvious. Sometimes, too, the pleasant acquaintances of travel were lacking, and loneliness upset the nice balance of Zora's nerves. Then, more than ever, did she pine for the Beyond.

Yet youth, receptivity, imagination kept her buoyant. Hope lured her on with renewed promises from city to city. At last, on her homeward journey, he whispered the magic name of Monte Carlo, and her heart was aflutter in anticipation of wonderland.

She stood bewildered, lonely, and dismayed in the first row behind the chairs, fingering an empty purse. She had been in the rooms ten minutes, and she had lost twenty louis. Her last coup had been successful, but a bland old lady, with the white hair and waxen face of sainted motherhood, had swept up her winnings so unconcernedly that Zora's brain began to swim. As she felt too strange and shy to expostulate she stood fingering her empty purse.

The scene was utterly different from what she had expected. She had imagined a gay, crowded room, wild gamblers shouting in their excitement, a band playing delirious waltz music, champagne corks popping merrily, painted women laughing, jesting loudly, all kinds of revelry and devilry and Bacchic things undreamed of. This was silly of her, no doubt, but the silliness of inexperienced young women is a matter for the pity, not the reprobation, of the judicious. If they take the world for their oyster and think, when they open it, they are going to find pearl necklaces ready-made, we must not blame them. Rather let hoary-headed sinners envy them their imaginings.

The corners of Zora Middlemist's ripe lips drooped with a child's pathos of disillusionment. Her nose delicately marked disgust at the heavy air and the discord of scents around her. Having lost her money she could afford to survey with scorn the decorous yet sordid greed of the crowded table. There was not a gleam of gaiety about it. The people behaved with the correct impassiveness of an Anglican congregation. She had heard of more jocular funerals.

She forgot the intoxication of her first gold and turquoise day at Monte Carlo. A sense of loneliness—such as a solitary dove might feel in a wilderness of evil bats—oppressed her. Had she not been aware that she was a remarkably attractive woman and the object of innumerable glances, she would have cried. And twenty louis pitched into unprofitable space! Yet she stood half fascinated by the rattle of the marble on the revolving disc, the glitter of the gold, the soft pat of the coins on the green cloth as they were thrown by the croupier. She began to make imaginary stakes. For five coups in succession she would have won. It was exasperating. There she stood, having pierced the innermost mystery of chance, without even a five-franc piece in her purse.

A man's black sleeve pushed past her shoulder, and she saw a hand in front of her holding a louis. Instinctively she took it.

"Thanks," said a tired voice. "I can't reach the table."

She threw it, *en plein*, on Number Seventeen; and then with a start, realizing what she had done, she turned with burning cheeks.

"I *am* so sorry."

Her glance met a pair of unspeculative blue eyes, belonging to the owner of the tired voice. She noted that he had a sallow face, a little brown mustache, and a shock of brown hair, curiously upstanding, like Struwel Peter's.

"I am *so* sorry," she repeated. "Please ask for it back. What did you want me to play?"

"I don't know. It doesn't matter, so long as you've put it somewhere."

"But I've put it *en plein* on Seventeen," she urged. "I ought to have thought what I was doing."

"Why think?" he murmured.

Mrs. Middlemist turned square to the table and fixed her eyes on the staked louis. In spite of the blue-eyed man's implied acquiescence she felt qualms of responsibility. Why had she not played on an even chance, or one of the dozens, or even a *transversale?* To add to her discomfort no one else played the full seventeen. The whole table seemed silently jeering at her inexperience.

The croupiers had completed the payments of the last coup. The marble fell with its sharp click and whizzed and rattled around the disc. Zora held her breath. The marble found its compartment at last, and the croupier announced:

"*Dix-sept, noir, impair et manque.*"

She had won. A sigh of relief shook her bosom. Not only had she not lost a stranger's money, but she had won for him thirty-five times his stake. She watched the louis greedily lest it should be swept away by a careless croupier —perhaps the only impossible thing that could not happen at Monte Carlo—and stretched out her arm past the bland old lady in tense determination to frustrate further felonious proceedings. The croupier pitched seven large gold coins across the table. She clutched them feverishly and turned to deliver them to their owner. He was nowhere to be seen. She broke through the ring, and with her hands full of gold scanned the room in dismayed perplexity.

At last she espied him standing dejectedly by another table. She rushed across the intervening space and held out the money.

"See, you have won!"

"Oh, Lord!" murmured the man, removing his hands from his dinner-jacket pockets, but not offering to take his winnings. "What a lot of trouble I have given you."

"Of course you have," she said tartly. "Why didn't you stay?"

"I don't know," he replied. "How can one tell why one doesn't do things?"

"Well, please take the money now and let me get rid of it. There are seven pieces of five louis each."

She counted the coins into his hand, and then suddenly flushed scarlet. She had forgotten to claim the original louis which she had staked. Where was it? What had become of it? As well try, she thought, to fish up a coin thrown into the sea. She felt like a thief.

"There ought to be another louis," she stammered.

"It doesn't matter," said the man.

"But it does matter. You might think that I—I kept it."

"That's too absurd," he answered. "Are you interested in guns?"

"Guns?"

She stared at him. He appeared quite sane.

"I remember now I was thinking of guns when I went away," he explained. "They're interesting things to think about."

"But don't you understand that I owe you a louis? I forgot all about it. If my purse weren't empty I would repay you. Will you stay here till I can get some money from my hotel—the Hôtel de Paris?"

She spoke with some vehemence. How could the creature expect her to remain in his debt? But the creature only passed his fingers through his upstanding hair and smiled wanly.

"Please don't say anything more about it. It distresses me. The croupiers don't return the stake, as a general rule, unless you ask for it. They assume you want to back your luck. Perhaps it has won again. For goodness' sake don't bother about it—and thank you very, very much."

He bowed politely and moved a step or two away. But Zora, struck by a solution of the mystery which had not occurred to her, as one cannot grasp all the ways and customs of gaming establishments in ten minutes, rushed back to the other table. She arrived just in time to hear the croupier asking whom the louis on seventeen belonged to. The number had turned up again.

This time she brought the thirty-six louis to the stranger.

"Dear me," said he, taking the money. "It is very astonishing. But why did you trouble?"

"Because I'm a woman of common sense, I suppose."

He looked at the coins in his hand as if they were shells which a child at the seaside might have brought him, and then raised his eyes slowly to hers.

"You are a very gracious lady." His glance and tone checked an impulse of exasperation. She smiled.

"At any rate, I've won fifty-six pounds for you, and you ought to be grateful."

He made a little gesture of acknowledgement. Had he been a more dashing gentleman he might have expressed his gratitude for the mere privilege of conversing with a gracious lady so beautiful. They had drifted from the outskirts of the crowded table and found themselves in the thinner crowd of saunterers. It was the height of the Monte Carlo season and the feathers and diamonds and rouge and greedy eyes and rusty bonnets of all nations confused the sight and paralyzed thought. Yet among all the women of both worlds Zora Middlemist stood out remarkable. As Septimus Dix afterwards explained, the rooms that evening contained a vague kind of conglomerate woman and Zora Middlemist. And the herd of men envied the creature on whom she smiled so graciously.

2

She was dressed in black, as became a young widow, but it was a black which bore no sign of mourning. The black, sweeping ostrich plume of a picture hat gave her an air of triumph. Black gloves reaching more than halfway up shapely arms and a gleam of snowy neck above a black chiffon bodice disquieted the imagination. She towered over her present companion, who was five foot seven and slimly built.

"You've brought me all this stuff, but what am I to do with it?" he asked helplessly.

"Perhaps I had better take care of it for you."

It was a relief from the oppressive loneliness to talk to a human being; so she lingered wistfully in conversation. A pathetic eagerness came into the man's face.

"I wish you would," said he, drawing a handful from his jacket pocket. "I should be so much happier."

"You can hardly be such a gambler," she laughed.

"Oh, no! It's not that at all. Gambling bores me."

"Why do you play, then?"

"I don't. I staked that louis because I wanted to see whether I should be interested. I wasn't, as I began to think about the guns. Have you had breakfast?"

Again Zora was startled. A sane man does not talk of breakfasting at nine o'clock in the evening. But if he were a lunatic perhaps it were wise to humor him.

"Yes," she said. "Have you?"

"No. I've only just got up."

"Do you mean to say you've been asleep all day?"

"What's the noisy day made for?"

"Let us sit down," said Zora.

They found one of the crimson couches by the wall vacant, and sat down. Zora regarded him curiously.

"Why should you be happier if I took care of your money?"

"I shouldn't spend it. I might meet a man who wanted to sell me a gas-engine."

"But you needn't buy it."

"These fellows are so persuasive, you see. At Rotterdam last year, a man made me buy a second-hand dentist's chair."

"Are you a dentist?" asked Zora.

"Lord, no! If I were I could have used the horrible chair."

"What did you do with it?"

"I had it packed up and despatched, carriage paid, to an imaginary person at Singapore."

He made this announcement in his tired, gentle manner, without the flicker of a smile. He added, reflectively——

"That sort of thing becomes expensive. Don't you find it so?"

"I would defy anybody to sell me a thing I didn't want," she replied.

"Ah, that," said he with a glance of wistful admiration, "that is because you have red hair."

If any other strange male had talked about her hair, Zora Middlemist would have drawn herself up in Junoesque majesty and blighted him with a glance. She had done with men and their compliments forever. In that she prided herself on her Amazonianism. But she could not be angry with the inconclusive being to whom she was talking. As well resent the ingenuous remarks of a four-year-old child.

"What has my red hair to do with it?" she asked pleasantly.

"It was a red-haired man who sold me the dentist's chair."

"Oh!" said Zora, nonplussed.

There was a pause. The man leaned back, embracing one knee with both hands. They were nerveless, indeterminate hands, with long fingers, such as are in the habit of dropping things. Zora wondered how they supported his knee. For some time he stared into vacancy, his pale-blue eyes adream. Zora laughed.

"Guns?" she asked.

"No," said he, awaking to her presence. "Perambulators."

She rose. "I thought you might be thinking of breakfast. I must be going back to my hotel. These rooms are too hot and horrible. Good night."

"I will see you to the lift, if you'll allow me," he said politely.

She graciously assented and they left the rooms together. In the atrium she changed her mind about the lift. She would leave the Casino by the main entrance and walk over to the Hôtel de Paris for the sake of a breath of fresh air. At the top of the steps she paused and filled her lungs. It was a still, moonless night, and the stars hung low down, like diamonds on a canopy of black velvet. They made the flaring lights of the terrace of the Hôtel and Café de Paris look tawdry and meretricious.

"I hate them," she said, pointing to the latter.

"Stars are better," said her companion.

She turned on him swiftly.

"How did you know I was making comparisons?"

"I felt it," he murmured.

They walked slowly down the steps. At the bottom a

FOR SOME TIME HE STARED INTO VACANCY, HIS PALE-BLUE
EYES ADREAM.

(page 20)

carriage and pair seemed to rise mysteriously out of the earth.

" 'Ave a drive? Ver' good carriage," said a voice out of the dimness. Monte Carlo cabmen are unerring in their divination of the Anglo-Saxon.

Why not? The suggestion awoke in her an instant craving for the true beauty of the land. It was unconventional, audacious, crazy. But, again, why not? Zora Middlemist was answerable for her actions to no man or woman alive. Why not drink a great draught of the freedom that was hers? What did it matter that the man was a stranger? All the more daring the adventure. Her heart beat gladly. But chaste women, like children, know instinctively the man they can trust.

"Shall we?"

"Drive?"

"Yes—unless—" a thought suddenly striking her— "unless you want to go back to your friends."

"Good Lord!" said he, aghast, as if she were accusing him of criminal associations. "I have no friends."

"Then come."

She entered the carriage. He followed meekly and sat beside her. Where should they drive? The cabman suggested the coast road to Mentone. She agreed. On the point of starting she observed that her companion was bareheaded.

"You've forgotten your hat."

She spoke to him as she would have done to a child.

"Why bother about hats?"

"You'll catch your death of cold. Go and get it at once."

He obeyed with a docility which sent a little tingle of exaltation through Mrs. Middlemist. A woman may have an inordinate antipathy to men, but she loves them to do her bidding. Zora was a woman; she was also young.

He returned. The cabman whipped up his strong pair of horses, and they started through the town towards Mentone.

Zora lay back on the cushions and drank in the sensuous loveliness of the night—the warm, scented air, the velvet and diamond sky, the fragrant orange groves—the dim, mysterious olive trees, the looming hills, the wine-colored, silken sea, with its faint edging of lace on the dusky sweep of the bay. The spirit of the South overspread her with its wings and took her amorously in its arms.

After a long, long silence she sighed, remembering her companion.

"Thank you for not talking," she said softly.

"Don't," he replied. "I had nothing to say. I never talk. I've scarcely talked for a year."

She laughed idly.

"Why?"

"No one to talk to. Except my man," he added conscientiously. "His name is Wiggleswick."

"I hope he looks after you well," said Zora, with a touch of maternal instinct.

"He wants training. That's what I am always telling him. But he can't hear. He's seventy and stone-deaf. But he's interesting. He tells me about jails and things."

"Jails?"

"Yes. He spent most of his time in prison. He was a professional burglar—but then he got on in years. Besides, the younger generation was knocking at the door."

"I thought that was the last thing a burglar would do," said Zora.

"They generally use jemmies," he said gravely. "Wiggleswick has given me his collection. They're very useful."

"What for?" she asked.

"To kill moths with," he replied dreamily.

"But what made you take a superannuated burglar for a valet?"

"I don't know. Perhaps it was Wiggleswick himself. He came up to me one day as I was sitting in Kensington Gardens, and somehow followed me home."

"But, good gracious," cried Zora—forgetful for the moment of stars and sea—"aren't you afraid that he will rob you?"

"No. I asked him, and he explained. You see, it would be out of his line. A forger only forges, a pickpocket only snatches chains and purses, and a burglar only burgles. Now, he couldn't burgle the place in which he was living himself, so I am safe."

Zora gave him sage counsel.

"I'd get rid of him if I were you."

"If I were you, I would—but I can't," he replied. "If I told him to go he wouldn't. I go instead sometimes. That's why I'm here."

"If you go on talking like that, you'll make my brain reel," said Zora laughing. "Do tell me something about yourself. What is your name?"

"Septimus Dix. I've got another name—Ajax—Septimus Ajax Dix—but I never use it."

"That's a pity," said Zora. "Ajax is a lovely name."

He dissented in his vague fashion. "Ajax suggests somebody who defies lightning and fools about with a spear. It's a silly name. A maiden aunt persuaded my mother to give it to me. I think she mixed it up with Achilles. She admired the statue in Hyde Park. She got run over by a milkcart."

"When was that?" she inquired, more out of politeness than interest in the career of Mr. Dix's maiden aunt.

"A minute before she died."

"Oh," said Zora, taken aback by the emotionless manner in which he mentioned the tragedy. Then, by way of continuing the conversation:—

"Why are you called Septimus?"

"I'm the seventh son. All the others died young. I never could make out why I didn't."

"Perhaps," said Zora with a laugh, "you were thinking of something else at the time and lost the opportunity."

"It must have been that," said he. "I lose opportunities just as I always lose trains."

"How do you manage to get anywhere?"

"I wait for the next train. That's easy. But there's never another opportunity."

He drew a cigarette from his case, put it in his mouth, and fumbled in his pockets for matches. Finding none, he threw the cigarette into the road.

"That's just like you," cried Zora. "Why didn't you ask the cabman for a light?"

She laughed at him with an odd sense of intimacy, though she had known him for scarcely an hour. He seemed rather a stray child than a man. She longed to befriend him— to do something for him, motherwise—she knew not what. Her adventure by now had failed to be adventurous. The spice of danger had vanished. She knew she could sit beside this helpless being till the day of doom without fear of molestation by word or act.

He obtained a light for his cigarette from the cabman

and smoked in silence. Gradually the languor of the night again stole over her senses, and she forgot his existence. The carriage had turned homeward, and at a bend of the road, high up above the sea, Monte Carlo came into view, gleaming white far away below, like a group of fairy palaces lit by fairy lamps, sheltered by the great black promontory of Monaco. From the gorge on the left, the terraced rock on the right, came the smell of the wild thyme and rosemary and the perfume of pale flowers. The touch of the air on her cheek was a warm and scented kiss. The diamond stars drooped towards her like a Danaë shower. Like Danaë's, her lips were parted. Her eyes strained far beyond the stars into an unknown glory, and her heart throbbed with a passionate desire for unknown things. Of what nature they might be she did not dream. Not love. Zora Middlemist had forsworn it. Not the worship of a man. She had vowed by all the saints in her hierarchy that no man should ever again enter her life. Her soul revolted against the unutterable sex.

As soon as one realizes the exquisite humbug of sublunary existence he must weep for the pity of it.

The warm and scented air was a kiss, too, on the cheek of Septimus Dix; and his senses, too, were enthralled by the witchery of the night. But for him stars and scented air and the magic beauty of the sea were incarnate in the woman by his side.

Zora, as I have said, had forgotten the poor devil's existence.

CHAPTER III

WHEN they drove up to the Hôtel de Paris, she alighted and bade him a smiling farewell, and went to her room with the starlight in her eyes. The lift man asked if Madame had won. She dangled her empty purse and laughed. Then the lift man, who had seen that light in women's eyes before, made certain that she was in love, and opened the lift door for her with the confidential air of the Latin who knows sweet secrets. But the lift man was wrong. No man had a part in her soul's exultation. If Septimus Dix crossed her mind while she was undressing, it was as a grotesque, bearing the same relation to her emotional impression of the night as a gargoyle does to a cathedral. When she went to bed, she slept the sound sleep of youth.

Septimus, after dismissing the cab, wandered in his vague way over to the Café de Paris, instinct suggesting his belated breakfast, which, like his existence, Zora had forgotten. The waiter came.

"*Monsieur désire?*"

"Absinthe," murmured Septimus absent-mindedly, "and —er—poached eggs—and anything—a raspberry ice."

The waiter gazed at him in stupefaction; but nothing being too astounding in Monte Carlo, he wiped the cold perspiration from his forehead and executed the order.

The unholy meal being over, Septimus drifted into the square and spent most of the night on a bench gazing at the Hôtel de Paris and wondering which were her windows.

When she mentioned casually, a day or two later, that her windows looked the other way over the sea, he felt that Destiny had fooled him once more; but for the time being he found a gentle happiness in his speculation. Chilled to the bone, at last, he sought his hotel bedroom and smoked a pipe, meditative, with his hat on until the morning. Then he went to bed.

Two mornings afterwards Zora came upon him on the Casino terrace. He sprawled idly on a bench between a fat German and his fat wife, who were talking across him. His straw hat was tilted over his eyes and his legs were crossed. In spite of the conversation (and a middle-class German does not whisper when he talks to his wife), and the going and coming of the crowd—in spite of the sunshine and the blue air, he slumbered peacefully. Zora passed him once or twice. Then by the station lift she paused and looked out at the bay of Mentone clasping the sea—a blue enamel in a setting of gold. She stood for some moments lost in the joy of it when a voice behind her brought her back to the commonplace.

"Very lovely, isn't it?"

A thin-faced Englishman of uncertain age and yellow, evil eyes met her glance as she turned instinctively.

"Yes, it's beautiful," she replied coldly; "but that is no reason why you should take the liberty of speaking to me."

"I couldn't help sharing my emotions with another, especially one so beautiful. You seem to be alone here?"

Now she remembered having seen him before—rather frequently. The previous evening he had somewhat ostentatiously selected a table near hers at dinner. He had watched her as she had left the theater and followed her to the lift door. He had been watching for his opportunity and now thought it had come. She shivered with sudden anger, and round her heart crept the chill of fright which all women know who have been followed in a lonely street.

"I certainly am not alone," she said wrathfully. "Good morning."

The man covered his defeat by raising his hat with ironic politeness, and Zora walked swiftly away, in appearance a majestic Amazon, but inwardly a quivering woman. She marched straight up to the recumbent Dix. The Literary Man from London would have been amused. She interposed herself between the conversing Teutons and awakened the sleeper. He looked at her for a moment with a dreamy smile, then leaped to his feet.

"A man has insulted me—he has been following me about and tried to get into conversation with me."

"Dear me," said Septimus. "What shall I do? Shall I shoot him?"

"Don't be silly," she said seriously. "It's serious. I'd be glad if you'd kindly walk up and down a little with me."

"With pleasure." They strolled away together. "But I *am* serious. If you wanted me to shoot him I'd do it. I'd do anything in the world for you. I've got a revolver in my room."

She laughed, disclaiming desire for supreme vengeance.

"I only want to show the wretch that I am not a helpless woman," she observed, with the bewildering illogic of the sex. And as she passed by the offender she smiled down at her companion with all the sweetness of intimacy and asked him why he carried a revolver. She did not point the offender out, be it remarked, to the bloodthirsty Septimus.

"It belongs to Wiggleswick," he replied in answer to her question. "I promised to take care of it for him."

"What does Wiggleswick do when you are away?"

"He reads the police reports. I take in *Reynolds* and the *News of the World* and the illustrated *Police News* for him, and he cuts them out and gums them in a scrap book. But I think I'm happier without Wiggleswick. He interferes with my guns."

"By the way," said Zora, "you talked about guns the other evening. What have you got to do with guns?"

He looked at her in a scared way out of the corner of his eye, child-fashion, as though to make sure she was loyal and worthy of confidence, and then he said:

"I invent 'em. I have written a treatise on guns of large caliber."

"Really?" cried Zora, taken by surprise. She had not credited him with so serious a vocation. "Do tell me something about it."

"Not now," he pleaded. "Some other time. I'd have to sit down with paper and pencil and draw diagrams. I'm afraid you wouldn't like it. Wiggleswick doesn't. It bores him. You must be born with machinery in your blood. Sometimes it's uncomfortable."

"To have cogwheels instead of corpuscles must be trying," said Zora flippantly.

"Very," said he. "The great thing is to keep them clear of the heart."

"What do you mean?" she asked quickly.

"Whatever one does or tries to do, one should insist on remaining human. It's good to be human, isn't it? I once knew a man who was just a complicated mechanism of brain encased in a body. His heart didn't beat; it clicked and whirred. It caused the death of the most perfect woman in the world."

He looked dreamily into the blue ether between sea and sky. Zora felt strangely drawn to him.

"Who was it?" she asked softly.

"My mother," said he.

They had paused in their stroll, and were leaning over the parapet above the railway line. After a few moments' silence he added, with a faint smile:—

"That's why I try hard to keep myself human—so that, if a woman should ever care for me, I shouldn't hurt her."

A green caterpillar was crawling on his sleeve. In his vague manner he picked it tenderly off and laid it on the leaf of an aloe that grew in the terrace vase near which he stood.

"You couldn't even hurt that crawling thing—let alone a woman," said Zora. This time very softly.

He blushed. "If you kill a caterpillar you kill a butterfly," he said apologetically.

"And if you kill a woman?"

"Is there anything higher?" said he.

She made no reply, her misanthropical philosophy prompting none. There was rather a long silence, which he broke by asking her if she read Persian. He excused his knowledge of it by saying that it kept him human. She laughed and suggested a continuance of their stroll. He talked disconnectedly as they walked up and down.

The crowd on the terrace thinned as the hour of déjeuner approached. Presently she proclaimed her hunger. He murmured that it must be near dinner time. She protested. He passed his hands across his eyes and confessed

SHE SAILED MAJESTICALLY PAST THE WRETCH, FOLLOWED MEEKLY
BY SEPTIMUS.

(page 31)

that he had got mixed up in his meals the last few days. Then an idea struck him.

"If I skip afternoon tea, and dinner, and supper, and petit déjeuner, and have two breakfasts running," he exclaimed brightly, "I shall begin fair again." And he laughed, not loud, but murmuringly, for the first time.

They went round the Casino to the front of the Hôtel de Paris, their natural parting place. But there, on the steps, with legs apart, stood the wretch with the evil eyes. He looked at her from afar, banteringly. Defiance rose in Zora's soul. She would again show him that she was not a lone and helpless woman at the mercy of the casual depredator.

"I'm taking you in to lunch with me, Mr. Dix. You can't refuse," she said; and without waiting for a reply she sailed majestically past the wretch, followed meekly by Septimus, as if she owned him body and soul.

As usual, many eyes were turned on her as she entered the restaurant—a radiant figure in white, with black hat and black chiffon boa, and a deep red rose in her bosom. The maître d'hôtel, in the pride of reflected glory, conducted her to a table near the window. Septimus trailed inconclusively behind. When he seated himself he stared at her silently in a mute surmise as the gentlemen in the poem did at the peak in Darien. It was even a wilder adventure than the memorable drive. That was but a caprice of the goddess; this was a sign of her friendship. The newness of their intimacy smote him dumb. He passed his hand through his Struwel Peter hair and wondered. Was it real? There sat the goddess, separated from him by the strip of damask, her gold-flecked eyes smiling frankly and trustfully into his, pulling off her gloves and disclosing, in almost disconcerting intimacy, her warm wrists and hands. Was he dreaming, as he sometimes did, in broad daylight, of a queer heaven in which he was strong like other men and felt the flutter of wings upon his cheek? Something soft was in his hand. Mechanically he began to stuff it up his sleeve. It was his napkin. Zora's laugh brought him to earth—to happy earth.

It is a pleasant thing to linger *tête-à-tête* over lunch on the terrace of the Hôtel de Paris. Outside is the shade of the square, the blazing sunshine beyond the shadow; the fountain and the palms and the doves; the white gaiety of pleasure houses; the blue-gray mountains cut sharp against the violet sky. Inside, a symphony of cool tones: the pearl of summer dresses; the snow, crystal, and silver of the tables; the tender green of lettuce, the yellows of fruit, the soft pink of salmon; here and there a bold note of color— the flowers in a woman's hat, the purples and topazes of wine. Nearer still to the sense is the charm of privacy. The one human being for you in the room is your companion. The space round your chairs is a magic circle, cutting you off from the others, who are mere decorations, beautiful or grotesque. Between you are substances which it were gross to call food: dainty mysteries of coolness and sudden flavors; a fish salad in which the essences of sea and land are blended in cold, celestial harmony; innermost kernels of the lamb of the salted meadows where must grow the Asphodel on which it fed, in amorous union with what men call a sauce, but really oil and cream and herbs stirred by a god in a dream; peaches in purple ichor chastely clad in snow, melting on the palate as the voice of the divine singer after whom they are named melts in the soul.

It is a pleasant thing—hedonistic? yes; but why live on

lentils when lotus is to your hand? and, really, at Monte Carlo lentils are quite as expensive—it is a pleasant thing, even for the food-worn wanderer of many restaurants, to lunch *tête-à-tête* at the Hôtel de Paris; but for the young and fresh-hearted to whom it is new, it is enchantment.

"I've often looked at people eating like this and I've often wondered how it felt," said Septimus.

"But you must have lunched hundreds of times in such places."

"Yes—but by myself. I've never had a——" he paused.

"A what?"

"A—a gracious lady," he said, reddening, "to sit opposite me."

"Why not?"

"No one has ever wanted me. It has always puzzled me how men get to know women and go about with them. I think it must be a gift," he asserted with the profound gravity of a man who has solved a psychological problem. "Some fellows have a gift for collecting Toby jugs. Everywhere they go they discover a Toby jug. I couldn't find one if I tried for a year. It's the same thing. At Cambridge they used to call me the Owl."

"An owl catches mice, at any rate," said Zora.

"So do I. Do you like mice?"

"No. I want to catch lions and tigers and all the bright and burning things of life," cried Zora, in a burst of confidence.

He regarded her with wistful admiration.

"Your whole life must be full of such things."

"I wonder," she said, looking at him over the spoonful of pêche Melba which she was going to put in her mouth,

3

"I wonder whether you have the faintest idea who I am and what I am and what I'm doing here all by myself, and why you and I are lunching together in this delightful fashion. You have told me all about yourself—but you seem to take me for granted."

She was ever so little piqued at his apparent indifference. But if men like Septimus Dix did not take women for granted, where would be the chivalry and faith of the children of the world? He accepted her unquestioningly as the simple Trojan accepted the Olympian lady who appeared to him clad in grace (but otherwise scantily) from a rosy cloud.

"You are yourself," he said, "and that has been enough for me."

"How do you know I'm not an adventuress? There are heaps of them, people say, in this place. I might be a designing thief of a woman."

"I offered you the charge of my money the other night."

"Was that why you did it? To test me?" she asked.

He reddened and started as if stung. She saw the hurt instantly, and with a gush of remorse begged for forgiveness.

"No. I didn't mean it. It was horrid of me. It is not in your nature to think such a thing. Forgive me."

Frankly, impulsively, she stretched her hand across the table. He touched it timidly with his ineffectual fingers, not knowing what to do with it, vaguely wondering whether he should raise it to his lips, and so kept touching it, until she pressed his fingers in a little grip of friendliness, and withdrew it with a laugh.

"Do you know, I still have that money," he said, pulling a handful of great five-louis pieces from his pocket. "I can't spend it. I've tried to. I bought a dog yesterday but he wanted to bite me and I had to give him to the hotel porter. All this gold makes such a bulge in my pocket."

When Zora explained that the coins were only used as counters and could be changed for notes at the rooms, he was astonished at her sapience. He had never thought of it. Thus Zora regained her sense of superiority.

This lunch was the first of many meals they had together; and meals led to drives and excursions, and to evenings at the theater. If she desired still further to convince the wretch with the evil eyes of her befriended state, she succeeded; but the wretch and his friends speculated evilly on the relations between her and Septimus Dix. They credited her with pots of money. Zora, however, walked serene, unconscious of slander, enjoying herself prodigiously. Secure in her scorn and hatred of men she saw no harm in her actions. Nor was there any, from the point of view of her young egotism and inexperience. It scarcely occurred to her that Septimus was a man. In some aspects he appealed to her instinctive motherhood like a child. When she met him one day coming out of one of the shops in the arcade, wearing a newly bought Homburg hat too small for him, she marched him back with a delicious sense of responsibility and stood over him till he was adequately fitted. In other aspects he was like a woman in whose shy delicacy she could confide. She awoke also to a new realization— that of power. Now, to use power with propriety needs wisdom, and the woman who is wise at five-and-twenty cannot make out at sixty why she has remained an old maid. The delightful way to use it is that of a babe when he first discovers that a stick hits. That is the way that Zora, who was not wise, used it over Septimus. For the first time in her life she owned a human being. A former joy in the possession of a devoted dog who did tricks was as nothing to this rapture. It was splendid. She owned him. Whenever she had a desire for his company—which was often, as solitude at Monte Carlo is more depressing than Zora had realized—she sent a page boy, in the true quality of his name of *chasseur*, to hunt down the quarry and bring him back. He would, therefore, be awakened at unearthly hours, at three o'clock in the afternoon, for instance, when, as he said, all rational beings should be asleep, it being their own unreason if they were not; or he would be tracked down at ten in the morning to some obscure little café in the town where he would be discovered eating ices and looking the worse for wear in his clothes of the night before. As this meant delay in the execution of her wishes, Zora prescribed habits less irregular. By means of bribery of chambermaids and porters, and the sacrifice of food and sleep, he contrived to find himself dressed in decent time in the mornings. He would then patiently await her orders or call modestly for them at her residence, like the butcher or the greengrocer.

"Why does your hair stand up on end, in that queer fashion?" she asked him one day. The hat episode had led to a general regulation of his personal appearance.

He pondered gravely over the conundrum for some time, and then replied that he must have lost control over it. The command went forth that he should visit a barber and learn how to control his hair. He obeyed, and returned with his shock parted in the middle and plastered down heavily with pomatum, a saint of more than methodistical meekness. On Zora declaring that he looked awful (he was indeed inconceivably hideous), and that she preferred Struwel Peter after all, he dutifully washed his head with soda (after grave consultation with the chambermaid), and sunned himself once more in the smiles of his mistress.

Now and then, however, as she was kind and not tyrannical, she felt a pin-prick of compunction.

"If you would rather do anything else, don't hesitate to say so."

But Septimus, after having contemplated the world's potentialities of action with lack-luster eye, would declare that there was nothing else that could be done. Then she could rate him soundly.

"If I proposed that we should sail up the Andes and eat fried moonbeams, you would say 'yes.' Why haven't you more initiative?"

"I'm like Mrs. Shandy," he replied. "Some people are born so. They are quiescent; other people can jump about like grasshoppers. Do you know grasshoppers are very interesting?" And he began to talk irrelevantly on insects.

Their intercourse encouraged confidential autobiography. Zora learned the whole of his barren history. Fatherless, motherless, brotherless, he was alone in the world. From his father, Sir Erasmus Dix, a well-known engineer, to whose early repression much of Septimus's timidity was due, he had inherited a modest fortune. After leaving Cambridge he had wandered aimlessly about Europe. Now he lived in a little house in Shepherd's Bush, with a studio or shed at the end of the garden which he used as a laboratory.

"Why Shepherd's Bush?" asked Zora.

"Wiggleswick likes it," said he.

"And now he has the whole house to himself? I suppose he makes himself comfortable in your quarters and drinks your wine and smokes your cigars with his friends. Did you lock things up?"

"Oh, yes, of course," said Septimus.

"And where are the keys?"

"Why Wiggleswick has them," he replied.

Zora drew in her breath. "You don't know how angry you make me. If ever I meet Wiggleswick——"

"Well?"

"I'll talk to him," said Zora with a fine air of menace.

She, on her side, gave him such of her confidences as were meet for masculine ears. Naturally she impressed upon him the fact that his sex was abhorrent to her in all its physical, moral, and spiritual manifestations. Septimus, on thinking the matter over, agreed with her. Memories came back to him of the men with whom he had been intimate. His father, the mechanical man who had cogs instead of corpuscles in his blood, Wiggleswick the undesirable, a few rowdy men on his staircase at Cambridge who had led shocking lives—once making a bonfire of his pyjamas and a brand-new umbrella in the middle of the court —and had since come to early and disastrous ends. His impressions of the sex were distinctly bad. Germs of unutterable depravity, he was sure, lurked somewhere in his own nature.

"You make me feel," said he, "as if I weren't fit to black the boots of Jezebel."

"That's a proper frame of mind," said Zora. "Would you be good and tie this vexatious shoestring?"

The poor fool bent over it in reverent ecstasy, but Zora was only conscious of the reddening of his gills as he stooped.

This, to her, was the charm of their intercourse: that he never presumed upon their intimacy. When she remembered the prophecy of the Literary Man from London, she laughed at it scornfully. Here was a man, at any rate, who regarded her beauty unconcerned, and from whose society she derived no emotional experiences. She felt she could travel safely with him to the end of the earth.

This reflection came to her one morning while Turner, her maid, was brushing her hair. The corollary followed: "why not?"

"Turner," she said, "I'll soon have seen enough of Monte Carlo. I must go to Paris. What do you think of my asking Mr. Dix to come with us?"

"I think it would be most improper, ma'am," said Turner.

"There's nothing at all improper about it," cried Zora, with a flush. "You ought to be ashamed of yourself."

CHAPTER IV

At Monte Carlo, as all the world knows, there is an Arcade devoted to the most humorously expensive lace, diamond and general vanity shops in the universe, the Hôtel Métropole and Ciro's Restaurant. And Ciro's has a terrace where there are little afternoon tea-tables covered with pink cloths.

It was late in the afternoon, and save for a burly Englishman in white flannels and a Panama hat, reading a magazine by the door, and Zora and Septimus, who sat near the public gangway, the terrace was deserted. Inside, some men lounged about the bar drinking cocktails. The red Tzigane orchestra were already filing into the restaurant and the electric lamps were lit. Zora and Septimus had just returned from a day's excursion to Cannes. They were pleasantly tired and lingered over their tea in a companionable silence. Septimus ruminated dreamily over the nauseous entanglement of a chocolate éclair and a cigarette while Zora idly watched the burly Englishman. Presently she saw him do an odd thing. He tore out the middle of the magazine,—it bore an American title on the outside,— handed it to the waiter and put the advertisement pages in his pocket. From another pocket he drew another magazine, and read the advertisement pages of that with concentrated interest.

Her attention was soon distracted by a young couple, man and woman, decently dressed, who passed along the terrace, glanced at her, repassed and looked at her more attentively, the woman wistfully, and then stopped out of earshot and spoke a few words together. They returned, seemed to hesitate, and at last the woman, taking courage, advanced and addressed her.

"*Pardon, Madame*—but Madame looks so kind. Perhaps will she pardon the liberty of my addressing her?"

Zora smiled graciously. The woman was young, fragile, careworn, and a piteous appeal lay in her eyes. The man drew near and raised his hat apologetically. The woman continued. They had seen Madame there—and Monsieur —both looked kind, like all English people. Although she was French she was forced to admit the superior generosity of the English. They had hesitated, but the kind look of Madame had made her confident. They were from Havre. They had come to Nice to look after a lawsuit. Nearly all their money had gone. They had a little baby who was ill. In desperation they had brought the remainder of their slender fortune to Monte Carlo. They had lost it. It was foolish, but yet the baby came out that day with nine red spots on its chest and it seemed as if it was a sign from the *bon Dieu* that they should back nine and red at the tables. Now she knew too late that it was measles and not a sign from the *bon Dieu* at all. But they were penniless. The baby wanted physic and a doctor and would die. As a last resource they resolved to sink their pride and appeal to the generosity of Monsieur and Madame. The woman's wistful eyes filled with tears and the corners of her mouth quivered. The man with a great effort choked a sob. Zora's generous heart melted at the tale. It rang so stupidly true. The fragile's creature's air was so pathetic. She opened her purse.

"Will a hundred francs be of any use to you?" she asked in her schoolgirl French.

"Oh, Madame!"

"And I, too, will give a hundred to the baby," said Septimus. "I like babies and I've also had the measles." He opened his pocketbook.

"Oh, Monsieur," said the man. "How can I ever be sufficiently grateful?"

He held out his hand for the note, when something hit him violently in the back. It was the magazine hurled by the burly Englishman, who followed up the assault by a torrent of abuse.

"*Allez-vous-ong! Cochons! Et plus vite que ça!*" There was something terrific in his awful British accent.

The pair turned in obvious dismay. He waved them off.

"Don't give them anything. The baby hasn't any red spots. There isn't a baby. They daren't show their noses in the rooms. *Oh je vous connais. Vous êtes George Polin et Celestine Macroù. Sales voleurs. Allez-vous-ong ou j'appelle la police.*"

But the last few words were shouted to the swiftly retiring backs of the pathetic couple.

"I've saved you two hundred francs," said the burly Englishman, picking up his magazine and tenderly smoothing it. "Those two are the most accomplished swindlers in this den of thieves."

"I can't believe it," said Zora, half hurt, half resentful. "The woman's eyes were full of tears."

"It's true," said her champion. "And the best of it is that the man is actually an accredited agent of Jebusa Jones's Cuticle Remedy."

He stood, his hands on his broad hips, regarding her with

the piercing eyes of a man who is imparting an incredible but all-important piece of information.

"Why the best of it?" asked Zora, puzzled.

"It only shows how unscrupulous they are in their business methods. A man like that could persuade a fishmonger or an undertaker to stock it. But he'll do them in the end. They'll suffer for it."

"Who will?"

"Why, Jebusa Jones, of course. Oh, I see," he continued, looking at the two perplexed faces, "you don't know who I am. I am Clem Sypher."

He looked from one to the other as if to see the impression made by his announcement.

"I am glad to make your acquaintance," said Septimus, "and I thank you for your services."

"Your name?"

"My name is Dix—Septimus Dix."

"Delighted to meet you. I have seen you before. Two years ago. You were sitting alone in the lounge of the Hôtel Continental, Paris. You were suffering from severe abrasions on your face."

"Dear me," said Septimus. "I remember. I had shaved myself with a safety razor. I invented it."

"I was going to speak to you, but I was prevented." He turned to Zora.

"I've met you too, on Vesuvius in January. You were with two elderly ladies. You were dreadfully sunburnt. I made their acquaintance next day in Naples. You had gone, but they told me your name. Let me see. I know everybody and never forget anything. My mind is pigeon-holed like my office. Don't tell me."

He held up his forefinger and fixed her with his eye.

"It's Middlemist," he cried triumphantly, "and you've an Oriental kind of Christian name—Zora! Am I right?"

"Perfectly," she laughed, the uncanniness of his memory mitigating the unconventionality of his demeanor.

"Now we all know one another," he said, swinging a chair round and sitting unasked at the table. "You're both very sunburnt and the water here is hard and will make the skin peel. You had better use some of the cure. I use it myself every day—see the results."

He passed his hand over his smooth, clean-shaven face, which indeed was as rosy as a baby's. His piercing eyes contrasted oddly with his chubby, full lips and rounded chin.

"What cure?" asked Zora, politely.

"What cure?" he echoed, taken aback, "why, *my* cure. What other cure is there?"

He turned to Septimus, who stared at him vacantly. Then the incredible truth began to dawn on him.

"I am Clem Sypher—Friend of Humanity—Sypher's Cure. Now do you know?"

"I'm afraid I'm shockingly ignorant," said Zora.

"So am I," said Septimus.

"Good heavens!" cried Sypher, bringing both hands down on the table, tragically. "Don't you ever read your advertisements?"

"I'm afraid not," said Zora.

"No," said Septimus.

Before his look of mingled amazement and reproach they felt like Sunday-school children taken to task for having skipped the Kings of Israel.

"Well," said Sypher, "this is the reward we get for spending millions of pounds and the shrewdest brains in the country for the benefit of the public! Have you ever considered what anxious thought, what consummate knowledge of human nature, what dearly bought experience go to the making of an advertisement? You'll go miles out of your way to see a picture or a piece of sculpture that hasn't cost a man half the trouble and money to produce, and you'll not look at an advertisement of a thing vital to your life, though it is put before your eyes a dozen times a day. Here's my card, and here are some leaflets for you to read at your leisure. They will repay perusal."

He drew an enormous pocketbook from his breast pocket and selected two cards and two pamphlets, which he laid on the table. Then he arose with an air of suave yet offended dignity. Zora, seeing that the man, in some strange way, was deeply hurt, looked up at him with a conciliatory smile.

"You mustn't bear me any malice, Mr. Sypher, because I'm so grateful to you for saving us from these swindling people."

When Zora smiled into a man's eyes, she was irresistible. Sypher's pink face relaxed.

"Never mind," he said. "I'll send you all the advertisements I can lay my hands on in the morning. Au revoir."

He raised his hat and went away. Zora laughed across the table.

"What an extraordinary person!"

"I feel as if I had been talking to a typhoon," said Septimus.

They went to the theater that evening, and during the first entr'acte strolled into the rooms. Except the theater the Casino administration provides nothing that can allure the visitor from the only purpose of the establishment. Even the bar at the end of the atrium could tempt nobody not seriously parched with thirst. It is the most comfortless pleasure-house in Europe. You are driven, deliberately, in desperation into the rooms.

Zora and Septimus were standing by the decorous hush of a *trente et quarante* table, when they were joined by Mr. Clem Sypher. He greeted them like old acquaintances.

"I reckoned I should meet you sometime to-night. Winning?"

"We never play," said Zora.

Which was true. A woman either plunges feverishly into the vice of gambling or she is kept away from it by her in-born economic sense of the uses of money. She cannot regard it like a man, as a mere amusement. Light loves are somewhat in the same category. Hence many misunderstandings between the sexes. Zora found the amusement profitless, the vice degraded. So, after her first evening, she played no more. Septimus did not count.

"*We* never play," said Zora.

"Neither do I," said Sypher.

"The real way to enjoy Monte Carlo is to regard these rooms as non-existent. I wish they were."

"Oh, don't say that," Sypher exclaimed quickly. "They are most useful. They have a wisely ordained purpose. They are the meeting-place of the world. I come here every year and make more acquaintances in a day than I do elsewhere in a month. Soon I shall know everybody and everybody will know me, and they'll take away with them to Edinburgh and Stockholm and Uruguay and Tunbridge Wells—to all corners of the earth—a personal knowledge of the cure."

"Oh—I see. From that point of view——" said Zora.

"Of course. What other could there be? You see the advantage? It makes the thing human. It surrounds it with personality. It shows that 'Friend of Humanity' isn't a cant phrase. They recommend the cure to their friends. 'Are you sure it's all right?' they are asked. 'Of course it is,' they can reply. '*I know the man, Clem Sypher himself*.' And the friends are convinced and go about saying they know a man who knows Clem Sypher, and so the thing spreads like a snowball. Have you read the pamphlet?"

"It was most interesting," said Zora mendaciously.

"I thought you'd find it so. I've brought something in my pocket for you."

He searched and brought out a couple of little red celluloid boxes, which he handed to Septimus.

"There are two sample boxes of the cure—one for Mrs. Middlemist and one for yourself, Mr. Dix. You both have a touch of the sun. Put it on to-night. Let it stay there for five minutes; then rub off with a smooth, dry towel. In the morning you'll see the miracle." He looked at Septimus earnestly. "Quite sure you haven't anything in the nature of an eruption on you?"

"Good Lord, no. Of course not," said Septimus, startled out of a dreamy contemplation of the two little red boxes.

"That's a pity. It would have been so nice to cure you. Ah!" said he, with a keen glance up the room. "There's Lord Rebenham. I must enquire after his eczema. You won't forget me now. Clem Sypher. Friend of Humanity."

He bowed and withdrew, walking kindly and broad-shouldered through the crowd, like a benevolent deity, the latest thing in Æsculapiuses, among his devotees.

"What am I to do with these?" asked Septimus, holding out the boxes.

"You had better give me mine, or heaven knows what will become of it," said Zora, and she put it in her little chain bag, with her handkerchief, purse, and powder-puff.

The next morning she received an enormous basket of roses and a bundle of newspapers; also a card, bearing the inscription "Mr. Clem Sypher. The Kurhaus. Kilburn Priory, N. W." She frowned ever so little at the flowers. To accept them would be to accept Mr. Sypher's acquaintance in his private and Kilburn Priory capacity. To send them back would be ungracious, seeing that he had saved her a hundred francs and had cured her imaginary sunburn. She took up the card and laughed. It was like him to name his residence "The Kurhaus." She would never know him in his private capacity, for the simple reason that he hadn't one. The roses were an advertisement. So Turner unpacked the basket, and while Zora was putting the roses into water she wondered whether Mr. Sypher's house was decorated with pictorial advertisements of the cure instead of pictures. Her woman's instinct, however, caused the reflection that the roses must have cost more than all the boxes of the cure she could buy in a lifetime.

Septimus was dutifully waiting for her in the hall. She noted that he was more spruce than usual, in a new gray cashmere suit, and that his brown boots shone dazzlingly, like agates. They went out together, and the first person who met their eyes was the Friend of Humanity sunning himself in the square and feeding the pigeons with bread crumbs from a paper bag. As soon as he saw Zora he emptied his bag and crossed over.

"Good morning, Mrs. Middlemist. Good morning, Mr.

Dix. Used the cure? I see you have, Mrs. Middlemist. Isn't it wonderful? If you'd only go about Monte Carlo with an inscription 'Try Sypher's Cure!' What an advertisement! I'd have you one done in diamonds! And how did you find it, Mr. Dix?"

"I—oh!" murmured Septimus. "I forgot about it last night—and this morning I found I hadn't any brown boot polish—I——"

"Used the cure?" cried Zora, aghast.

"Yes," said Septimus, timidly. "It's rather good," and he regarded his dazzling boots.

Clem Sypher burst into a roar of laughter and clapped Septimus on the shoulder.

"Didn't I tell you?" he cried delightedly. "Didn't I tell you it's good for everything? What cream could give you such a polish? By Jove! You deserve to be on the free list for life. You've given me a line for an ad. 'If your skin is all right, try it on your boots.' By George! I'll use it. This is a man with ideas, Mrs. Middlemist. We must encourage him."

"Mr. Dix is an inventor," said Zora. She liked Sypher for laughing. It made him human. It was therefore with a touch of kindly feeling that she thanked him for the roses.

"I wanted to make them blush at the sight of your complexion after the cure," said he.

It was a compliment, and Zora frowned; but it was a professional compliment—so she smiled. Besides, the day was perfect, and Zora not only had not a care in the wide world, but was conscious of a becoming hat. She could not help smiling pleasantly on the world.

An empty motor car entered the square, and drew up near by. The chauffeur touched his cap.

4

"I'll run you both over to Nice," said Clem Sypher. "I have to meet my agent there and put the fear of God into him. I shan't be long. My methods are quick. And I'll run you back again. Don't say no."

There was the car—a luxurious 40 h. p. machine, upholstered in green; there was Clem Sypher, pink and strong, appealing to her with his quick eyes; there was the sunshine and the breathless blue of the sky; and there was Septimus Dix, a faithful bodyguard. She wavered and turned to Septimus.

"What do you say?"

She was lost. Septimus murmured something inconclusive. Sypher triumphed. She went indoors to get her coat and veil. Sypher admiringly watched her retreating figure—a poem of subtle curves—and shrugging himself into his motor coat, which the chauffeur brought him from the car, he turned to Septimus.

"Look here, Mr. Dix, I'm a straight man, and go straight to a point. Don't be offended. Am I in the way?"

"Not in the least," said Septimus, reddening.

"As for me, I don't care a hang for anything in the universe save Sypher's Cure. That's enough for one man to deal with. But I like having such a glorious creature as Mrs. Middlemist in my car. She attracts attention; and I can't say but what I'm not proud at being seen with her, both as a man and a manufacturer. But that's all. Now, tell me, what's in your mind?"

"I don't think I quite like you—er—to look on Mrs. Middlemist as an advertisement," said Septimus. To speak so directly cost him considerable effort.

"Don't you? Then I won't. I love a man to speak straight to me. I respect him. Here's my hand." He

wrung Septimus's hand warmly. "I feel that we are going
to be friends. I'm never wrong. I hope Mrs. Middlemist
will allow me to be a friend. Tell me about her."

Septimus again reddened uncomfortably. He belonged
to a class which does not discuss its women with a stranger
even though he be a newly sworn brother.

"She mightn't care for it," he said.

Sypher once more clapped him on the shoulder. "Good
again!" he cried, admiringly. "I shouldn't like you half
so much if you had told me. I've got to know, for I know
everything, so I'll ask her myself."

Zora came down coated and veiled, her face radiant as a
Romney in its frame of gauze. She looked so big and
beautiful, and Sypher looked so big and strong, and both
seemed so full of vitality, that Septimus felt criminally insignificant. His voice was of too low a pitch to make itself
carry when these two spoke in their full tones. He shrank
into his shell. Had he not realized, in his sensitive way,
that without him as a watchdog—ineffectual spaniel that
he was—Zora would not accept Clem Sypher's invitation,
he would have excused himself from the drive. He differ-
entiated, not conceitedly, between Clem Sypher and himself. She had driven alone with him on her first night at
Monte Carlo. But then she had carried him off between
her finger and thumb, so to speak, as the Brobdingnagian
ladies carried off Gulliver. He knew that he did not count
as a danger in the eyes of high-spirited young women. A
man like Sypher did. He knew that Zora would not have
driven alone with Sypher any more than with the wretch
of the evil eyes. He did not analyze this out himself, as
his habit of mind was too vague and dreamy. But he knew
it instinctively, as a dog knows whom he can trust with his

mistress and whom he cannot. So when Sypher and Zora, with a great bustle of life, were discussing seating arrangements in the car, he climbed modestly into the front seat next to the chauffeur, and would not be dislodged by Sypher's entreaties. He was just there, on guard, having no place in the vigorous atmosphere of their personalities. He sat aloof, smoking his pipe, and wondering whether he could invent a motor perambulator which could run on rails round a small garden, fill the baby's lungs with air, and save the British Army from the temptation of nursery-maids. His sporadic discourse on the subject perplexed the chauffeur.

It was a day of vivid glory. Rain had fallen heavily during the night, laying the dust on the road and washing to gay freshness the leaves of palms and gold-spotted orange trees and the purple bourgainvillea and other flowers that rioted on wayside walls. All the deep, strong color of the South was there, making things unreal: the gray mountains, fragile masses against the solid cobalt of the sky. The Mediterranean met the horizon in a blue so intense that the soul ached to see it. The heart of spring throbbed in the deep bosom of summer. The air as they sped through it was like cool spiced wine.

Zora listened to Clem Sypher's dithyrambics. The wine of the air had got into his head. He spoke as she had heard no man speak before. The turns of the road brought into sight view after magic view, causing her to catch her breath: purple rock laughing in the sea, far-off townlets flashing white against the mountain flank, gardens of paradise. Yet Clem Sypher sang of his cure.

First it was a salve for all external ills that flesh is heir to. It spared humanity its heritage of epidermatous suffer-

HE WAS JUST THERE, ON GUARD.

(page 52)

ing. It could not fail. He reeled off the string of hideous diseases with a lyrical lilt. It was his own discovery. An obscure chemist's assistant in Bury St. Edmunds, he had, by dint of experiments, hit on this world-upheaving remedy.

"When I found what it was that I had done, Mrs. Middlemist," said he solemnly, "I passed my vigil, like a knight of old, in my dispensary, with a pot of the cure in front of me, and I took a great oath to devote my life to spread it far and wide among the nations of the earth. It should bring comfort, I swore, to the king in his palace and the peasant in his hut. It should be a household word in the London slum and on the Tartar steppe. Sypher's Cure could go with the Red Cross into battle, and should be in the clerk's wife's cupboard in Peckham Rye. The human chamois that climbs the Alps, the gentle lunatic that plays golf, the idiot that goes and gets scalped by Red Indians, the missionary that gets half roasted by cannibals—if he gets quite roasted the cure's no good; it can't do impossibilities—all should carry Sypher's Cure in their waistcoat pockets. All mankind should know it, from China to Peru, from Cape Horn to Nova Zembla. It would free the tortured world from plague. I would be the Friend of Humanity. I took that for my device. It was something to live for. I was twenty then. I am forty now. I have had twenty years of the fiercest battle that ever man fought."

"And surely you've come off victorious, Mr. Sypher," said Zora.

"I shall never be victorious until it has overspread the earth!" he declared. And he passed one hand over the other in a gesture which symbolized the terrestrial globe with a coating of Sypher's Cure.

"Why shouldn't it?"

"It shall. Somehow, I believe that with you on my side it will."

"I?" Zora started away to the corner of the car, and gazed on him in blank amazement. "I? What in the world have I to do with it?"

"I don't know yet," said Sypher. "I have an intuition. I'm a believer in intuitions. I've followed them all my life, and they've never played me false. The moment I learned that you had never heard of me, I felt it."

Zora breathed comfortably again. It was not an implied declaration.

"I'm fighting against the Powers of Darkness," he continued. "I once read a bit of Spenser's 'Faërie Queene.' There was a Red Cross Knight who slew a Dragon—but he had a fabulous kind of woman behind him. When I saw you, you seemed that fabulous kind of woman."

At a sharp wall corner a clump of tall poinsettias flamed against the sky. Zora laughed full-heartedly.

"Here we are in the middle of a Fairy Tale. What are the Powers of Darkness in your case, Sir Red Cross Knight?"

"Jebusa Jones's Cuticle Remedy," said Sypher savagely.

CHAPTER V

THAT was Clem Sypher's Dragon—Jebusa Jones's Cuticle Remedy. He drew so vivid a picture of its foul iniquity that Zora was convinced that the earth had never harbored so scaly a horror. Of all Powers of Evil in the universe it was the most devastating.

She was swept up by his eloquence to his point of view, and saw things with his eyes. When she came to examine the poor dragon in the cool light of her own reason it appeared at the worst to be but a pushful patent medicine of an inferior order which, on account of its cheapness and the superior American skill in distributing it, was threatening to drive Sypher's Cure off the market.

"I'll strangle it as Hercules strangled the dog-headed thing," cried Sypher.

He meant the Hydra, which wasn't dog-headed and which Hercules didn't strangle. But a man can be at once unmythological and sincere. Clem Sypher was in earnest.

"You talk as if your cure had something of a divine sanction," said Zora. This was before her conversion.

"Mrs. Middlemist, if I didn't believe that," said Sypher solemnly, "do you think I would have devoted my life to it?"

"I thought people ran these things to make money," said Zora.

It was then that Sypher entered on the exordium of the speech which convinced her of the diabolical noisomeness of the Jebusa Jones unguent. His peroration summed up the contest as that between Mithra and Ahriman.

55

Yet Zora, though she took a woman's personal interest in the battle between Sypher's Cure and Jebusa Jones's Cuticle Remedy, siding loyally and whole-heartedly with her astonishing host, failed to pierce to the spirituality of the man—to divine him as a Poet with an Ideal.

"After all," said Sypher on the way back—Septimus, with his coat-collar turned up over his ears, still sat on guard by the chauffeur, consoled by a happy hour he had spent alone with his mistress after lunch, while Sypher was away putting the fear of God into his agent, during which hour he had unfolded to her his scientific philosophy of perambulators—"after all," said Sypher, "the great thing is to have a Purpose in Life. Everyone can't have my Purpose"— he apologized for humanity—"but they can have some guiding principle. What's yours?"

Zora was startled by the unexpected question. What was her Purpose in Life? To get to the heart of the color of the world? That was rather vague. Also nonsensical when so formulated. She took refuge in jest.

"I thought you had decided that my mission was to help you slay the dragon?"

"We have to decide on our missions for ourselves," said he.

"Don't you think it sufficient Purpose for a woman who has been in a gray prison all her life—when she finds herself free—to go out and see all that is wonderful in scenery like this, in paintings, architecture, manners, and customs of other nations, in people who have other ideas and feelings from those she knew in prison? You speak as if you're finding fault with me for not doing anything useful. Isn't what I do enough? What else can I do?"

"I don't know," said Sypher, looking at the back of his

gloves; then he turned his head and met her eyes in one of his quick glances. "But you, with your color and your build and your voice, seem somehow to me to stand for Force—there's something big about you—just as there's something big about me—Napoleonic—and I can't understand why it doesn't act in some particular direction."

"Oh, you must give me time," cried Zora. "Time to expand, to find out what kind of creature I really am. I tell you I've been in prison. Then I thought I was free and found a purpose, as you call it. Then I had a knockdown blow. I am a widow—I supposed you've guessed. Oh, now, don't speak. It wasn't grief. My married life was a six-weeks' misery. I forget it. I went away from home free five months ago—to see all this"—she waved her hand—"for the first time. Whatever force I have has been devoted to seeing it all, to taking it all in."

She spoke earnestly, just a bit passionately. In the silence that followed she realized with sudden amazement that she had opened her heart to this prime apostle of quackery. As he made no immediate reply, the silence grew tense and she clasped her hands tight, and wondered, as her sex has done from time immemorial, why on earth she had spoken. When he answered it was kindly.

"You've done me a great honor in telling me this. I understand. You want the earth, or as much of it as you can get, and when you've got it and found out what it means, you'll make a great use of it. Have you many friends?"

"No," said Zora. He had an uncanny way of throwing her back on to essentials. "None stronger than myself."

"Will you take me as a friend? I'm strong enough," said Sypher.

"Willingly," she said, dominated by his earnestness.

"That's good. I may be able to help you when you've found your vocation. I can tell you, at any rate, how to get to what you want. You've just got to keep a thing in view and go for it and never let your eyes wander to right or left or up or down. And looking back is fatal—the truest thing in Scripture is about Lot's wife. She looked back and was turned into a pillar of salt."

He paused, his face assumed an air of profound reflection, and he added with gravity:

"And the Clem Sypher of the period when he came by, made use of her, and plastered her over with posters of his cure."

The day she had appointed as the end of her Monte Carlo visit arrived. She would first go to Paris, where some Americans whom she had met in Florence and with whom she had exchanged occasional postcards pressed her to join them. Then London; and then a spell of rest in the lavender of Nunsmere. That was her programme. Septimus Dix was to escort her as far as Paris, in defiance of the proprieties as interpreted by Turner. What was to become of him afterwards neither conjectured; least of all Septimus himself. He said nothing about getting back to Shepherd's Bush. Many brilliant ideas had occurred to him during his absence which needed careful working out. Wherefore Zora concluded that he proposed to accompany her to London.

A couple of hours before the train started she dispatched Turner to Septimus's hotel to remind him of the journey. Turner, a strong-minded woman of forty—like the oyster she had been crossed in love and like her mistress she held

men in high contempt—returned with an indignant tale.
After a series of parleyings with Mr. Dix through the me-
dium of the hotel *chasseur*, who had a confused comprehension of voluble English, she had mounted at Mr. Dix's en-
treaty to his room. There she found him, half clad and in
his dressing-gown, staring helplessly at a wilderness of cloth-
ing and toilet articles for which there was no space in his
suit cases and bag, already piled mountain high.

"I can never do it, Turner," he said as she entered.
"What's to be done?"

Turner replied that she did not know; her mistress's
instructions were that he should catch the train.

"I'll have to leave behind what I can't get in," he said
despondently. "I generally have to do so. I tell the hotel
people to give it to widows and orphans. But that's one
of the things that make traveling so expensive."

"But you brought everything, sir, in this luggage?"

"I suppose so. Wiggleswick packed. It's his professional training, Turner. I think they call it 'stowing the
swag.'"

As Turner had not heard of Wiggleswick's profession,
she did not catch the allusion. Nor did Zora enlighten her
when she reported the conversation.

"If they went in once they'll go in again," said Turner.

"They won't. They never do," said Septimus.

His plight was so hopeless, he seemed so immeasurably
her sex's inferior, that he awoke her contemptuous pity.
Besides, her trained woman's hands itched to restore order
out of masculine chaos.

"Turn everything out and I'll pack for you," she said
resolutely, regardless of the proprieties. On further in-
vestigation she held out horrified hands.

He had mixed up shirts with shoes. His clothes were rolled in bundles, his collars embraced his sponge, his trees, divorced from boots, lay on the top of an unprotected bottle of hair-wash; he had tried to fit his brushes against a box of tooth-powder and the top had already come off. Turner shook out his dress suit and discovered a couple of hotel towels which had got mysteriously hidden in the folds. She held them up severely.

"No wonder you can't get your things in if you take away half the hotel linen," and she threw them to the other side of the room.

In twenty minutes she had worked the magic of Wiggleswick. Septimus was humbly grateful.

"If I were you, sir," she said, "I'd go to the station at once and sit on my boxes till my mistress arrives."

"I think I'll do it, Turner," said Septimus.

Turner went back to Zora flushed, triumphant, and indignant.

"If you think, ma'am," said she, "that Mr. Dix is going to help us on our journey, you're very much mistaken. He'll lose his ticket and he'll lose his luggage and he'll lose himself, and we'll have to go and find them."

"You must take Mr. Dix humorously," said Zora.

"I've no desire to take him at all, ma'am." And Turner snorted virtuously, as became her station.

Zora found him humbly awaiting her on the platform in company with Clem Sypher, who presented her with a great bunch of roses and a bundle of illustrated papers. Septimus had received as a parting guerdon an enormous package of the cure, which he embraced somewhat dejectedly. It was Sypher who looked after the luggage of the party. His terrific accent filled the station. Septimus regarded him with envy. He wondered how a man dared order foreign railway officials about like that.

"If I tried to do it they would lock me up. I once interfered in a street row."

Zora did not hear the dire results of the interference. Sypher claimed her attention until the train was on the point of starting.

"Your address in England? You haven't given it."

"The Nook, Nunsmere, Surrey, will always find me."

"Nunsmere?" He paused, pencil in hand, and looked up at her as she stood framed in the railway carriage window. "I nearly bought a house there last year. I was looking out for one with a lawn reaching down to a main railway track. This one had it."

"Penton Court?"

"Yes. That was the name."

"It's still unsold," laughed Zora idly.

"I'll buy it at once," said he.

"*En voiture*," cried the guard.

Sypher put out his masterful hand.

"Au revoir. Remember. We are friends. I never say what I don't mean."

The train moved out of the station. Zora took her seat opposite Septimus.

"I really believe he'll do it," she said.

"What?"

"Oh, something crazy," said Zora. "Tell me about the street row."

In Paris Zora was caught in the arms of the normal and the uneventful. An American family consisting of a father, mother, son and two daughters touring the continent do not generate an atmosphere of adventure. Their name was Callender, they were wealthy, and the track beaten by the golden feet of their predecessors was good enough for them. They were generous and kindly. There was no subtle complexity in their tastes. They liked the best, they paid for it, and they got it. The women were charming, cultivated and eager for new sensations. They found Zora a new sensation, because she had that range of half tones which is the heritage of a child of an older, grayer civilization. Father and son delighted in her. Most men did. Besides, she relieved the family tedium. The family knew the Paris of the rich Anglo-Saxon and other rich Anglo-Saxons in Paris. Zora accompanied them on their rounds. They lunched and dined in the latest expensive restaurants in the Champs Elysées and the Bois; they went to races; they walked up and down the Rue de la Paix and the Avenue de l'Opéra and visited many establishments where the female person is adorned. After the theater they drove to the Cabarets of Montmartre, where they met other Americans and English, and felt comfortably certain that they were seeing the naughty, shocking underside of Paris. They also went to the Louvre and to the Tomb of Napoleon. They stayed at the Grand Hotel.

Zora saw little of Septimus. He knew Paris in a queer, dim way of his own, and lived in an obscure hotel, whose name Zora could not remember, on the other side of the river. She introduced him to the Callenders, and they were quite prepared to receive him into their corporation. But he shrank from so vast a concourse as six human beings; he seemed to be overawed by the multitude of voices, unnerved by the multiplicity of personalities. The unfeathered owl blinked dazedly in general society as the feathered

one does in daylight. At first he tried to stand the glare
for Zora's sake.

"Come out and mix with people and enjoy yourself,"
cried Zora, when he was arguing against a proposal to join
the party on a Versailles excursion. "I want to you enjoy
yourself for once in your life. Besides—you're always so
anxious to be human. This will make you human."

"Do you think it will?" he asked seriously. "If you
do, I'll come."

But at Versailles they lost him, and the party, as a party,
knew him no more. What he did with himself in Paris
Zora could not imagine. A Cambridge acquaintance—
one of the men on his staircase who had not yet terminated
his disastrous career—ran across him in the Boulevard
Sévastopol.

"Why—if it isn't the Owl! What are you doing?"

"Oh—hooting," said Septimus.

Which was more information as to his activities than he
vouchsafed to give Zora. Once he murmured something
about a friend whom he saw occasionally. When she asked
him where his friend lived he waved an indeterminate hand
eastwards and said, "There!" It was a friend, thought
Zora, of whom he had no reason to be proud, for he prevented further questioning by adroitly changing the conversation to the price of hams.

"But what are you going to do with hams?"

"Nothing," said Septimus, "but when I see hams
hanging up in a shop I always want to buy them. They
look so shiny."

Zora's delicate nostrils sniffed the faintest perfume of a
mystery; but a moment afterwards the Callenders carried her off to Ledoyen's and Longchamps and other in-

dubitable actualities in which she forgot things less tangible. Long afterwards she discovered that the friend was an old woman, a *marchande des quatre saisons* who sold vegetables in the Place de la République. He had known her many years, and as she was at the point of death he comforted her with blood-puddings and flowers and hams and the ministrations of an indignant physician. But at the time Septimus hid his Good Samaritanism under a cloud of vagueness.

Then came a period during which Zora lost him altogether. Days passed. She missed him. Life with the Callenders was a continuous shooting of rapids. A quiet talk with Septimus was an hour in a backwater, curiously restful. She began to worry. Had he been run over by an omnibus? Only an ever-recurring miracle could bring him safely across the streets of a great city. When the Callenders took her to the Morgue she dreaded to look at the corpses.

"I do wish I knew what has become of him," she said to Turner.

"Why not write to him, ma'am?" Turner suggested.

"I've forgotten the name of his hotel," said Zora, wrinkling her forehead.

The name of the Hôtel Quincamboeuf, where he lodged, eluded her memory.

"I do wish I knew," she repeated.

Then she caught an involuntary but illuminating gleam in Turner's eye, and she bade her look for hairpins. Inwardly she gasped from the shock of revelation; then she laughed to herself, half amused, half indignant. The preposterous absurdity of the suggestion! But in her heart she realized that, in some undefined human fashion, Septimus

Dix counted for something in her life. What had become of him?

At last she found him one morning sitting by a table in the courtyard of the Grand Hotel, patiently awaiting her descent. By mere chance she was un-Callendered.

"Why, what——?"

The intended reproval died on her lips as she saw his face. His cheeks were hollow and white, his eyes sunken. The man was ill. His hand burned through her glove. Feelings warm and new gushed forth.

"Oh, my *dear* friend, what is the matter?"

"I must go back to England. I came to say good-bye. I've had this from Wiggleswick."

He handed her an open letter. She waved it away.

"That's of no consequence. Sit down. You're ill. You have a high temperature. You should be in bed."

"I've been," said Septimus. "Four days."

"And you've got up in this state? You must go back at once. Have you seen a doctor? No, of course you haven't. Oh, dear!" She wrung her hands. "You are not fit to be trusted alone. I'll drive you to your hotel and see that you're comfortable and send for a doctor."

"I've left the hotel," said Septimus. "I'm going to catch the eleven train. My luggage is on that cab."

"But it's five minutes past eleven now. You have lost the train—thank goodness."

"I'll be in good time for the four o'clock," said Septimus. "This is the way I generally travel. I told you." He rose, swayed a bit, and put his hand on the table to steady himself. "I'll go and wait at the station. Then I'll be sure to catch it. You see I must go."

"But why?" cried Zora.

5

"Wiggleswick's letter. The house has been burnt down and everything in it. The only thing he saved was a large portrait of Queen Victoria."

Then he fainted.

Zora had him carried to a room in the hotel and sent for a doctor, who kept him in bed for a fortnight. Zora and Turner nursed him, much to his apologetic content. The Callenders in the meanwhile went to Berlin.

When Septimus got up, gaunt and staring, he appealed to the beholder as the most helpless thing which the Creator had clothed in the semblance of a man.

"He must take very great care of himself for the next few weeks," said the doctor. "If he gets a relapse I won't answer for the consequences. Can't you take him somewhere?"

"Take him somewhere?" The idea had been worrying her for some days past. If she left him to his own initiative he would probably go and camp with Wiggleswick amid the ruins of his house in Shepherd's Bush, where he would fall ill again and die. She would be responsible.

"We can't leave him here, at any rate," she remarked to Turner.

Turner agreed. As well abandon a month-old baby on a doorstep and expect it to earn its livelihood. She also had come to take a proprietary interest in Septimus.

"He might stay with us in Nunsmere. What do you think, Turner?"

"I think, ma'am," said Turner, "that would be the least improper arrangement."

"He can have Cousin Jane's room," mused Zora, knowing that Cousin Jane would fly at her approach.

"And I'll see, ma'am, that he comes down to his meals regular," said Turner.

"Then it's settled," said Zora.

She went forthwith to the invalid and acquainted him with his immediate destiny. At first he resisted. He would be a nuisance. Since his boyhood he had never lived in a lady's house. Even landladies in lodgings had found him impossible. He could not think of accepting more favors from her all too gracious hands.

"You've got to do what you're told," said Zora, conclusively. She noticed a shade of anxiety cross his face. "Is there anything else?"

"Wiggleswick. I don't know what's to become of him."

"He can come to Nunsmere and lodge with the local policeman," said Zora.

On the evening before they started from Paris she received a letter addressed in a curiously feminine hand. It ran:

"DEAR MRS. MIDDLEMIST:

"I don't let the grass grow under my feet. I have bought Penton Court. I have also started a campaign which will wipe the Jebusa Jones people off the face of the earth they blacken. I hope you are finding a vocation. When I am settled at Nunsmere we must talk further of this. I take a greater interest in you than in any other woman I have ever known, and that I believe you take an interest in me is the proud privilege of

"Yours very faithfully,

"CLEM SYPHER."

"Here are the three railway tickets, ma'am," said Turner,

who had brought up the letter. "I think we had better take charge of them."

Zora laughed, and when Turner had left the room she laughed again. Clem Sypher's letter and Septimus's ticket lay side by side on her dressing-table, and they appealed to her sense of humor. They represented the net result of her misanthropic travels.

What would her mother say? What would Emmy say? What would be the superior remark of the Literary Man from London?

She, Zora Middlemist, who had announced in the market place, with such a flourish of trumpets, that she was starting on her glorious pilgrimage to the Heart of Life, abjuring all conversation with the execrated male sex, to have this ironical adventure! It was deliciously funny. Not only had she found two men in the Heart of Life, but she was bringing them back with her to Nunsmere. She could not hide them from the world in the secrecy of her own memory: there they were in actual, bodily presence, the sole trophies of her quest.

Yet she put a postscript to a letter to her mother.

"I know, in your dear romantic way, you will declare that these two men have fallen in love with me. You'll be wrong. If they had, *I shouldn't have anything to do with them*. It would have made them *quite impossible*."

The energy with which she licked and closed the envelope was remarkable but unnecessary.

CHAPTER VI

THINGS happen slowly at Nunsmere—from the grasping of an idea to the pace of the church choir over the hymns. Life there is no vulgar, tearing two-step, as it is in Godalming, London, and other vortices of human passions, but the stately measure of a minuet. Delights are deliberate and have lingering ends. A hen would scorn to hatch a chicken with the indecent haste of her sister in the next parish.

Six months passed, and Zora wondered what had become of them. Only a few visits to London, where she had consorted somewhat gaily with Emmy's acquaintances, had marked their flight, and the gentle fingers of Nunsmere had graduated the reawakening of her nostalgia for the great world. She spoke now and then of visiting Japan and America and South Africa, somewhat to her mother's consternation; but no irresistible force drove her thither. She found contentment in procrastination.

It had also been a mild amusement to settle Septimus Dix, after his recovery, in a little house facing the common. He had to inhabit some portion of this planet, and as he had no choice of spot save Hackney Downs, which Wiggleswick suggested, Zora waved her hand to the tenantless house and told him to take it. As there was an outhouse at the end of the garden which he could use as a workshop, his principal desideratum in a residence, be obeyed her readily. She then bought his furniture, plate, and linen, and a complicated kitchen battery over whose uses Wiggleswick scratched a bewildered head.

"A saucepan I know, and a frying-pan I know, but what you're to put in those things with holes in them fairly licks me."

"Perhaps we might grow geraniums in them," said Septimus brightly, after a fit of musing.

"If you do," said Zora, "I'll put a female cook in charge of you both, and wash my hands of you."

Whereupon she explained the uses of a cullender, and gave Wiggleswick to understand that she was a woman of her word, and that an undrained cabbage would be the signal for the execution of her threat. From the first she had assumed despotic power over Wiggleswick, of whose influence with his master she had been absurdly jealous. But Wiggleswick, bent, hoary, deaf, crabbed, evil old ruffian that he was, like most ex-prisoners instinctively obeyed the word of command, and meekly accepted Zora as his taskmistress.

For Septimus began happy days wherein the clock was disregarded. The vague projects that had filled his head for the construction of a new type of quick-firing gun took definite shape. Some queer corner of his brain had assimilated a marvelous knowledge of field artillery, and Zora was amazed at the extent of his technical library, which Wiggleswick had overlooked in his statement of the salvage from the burned-down house at Shepherd's Bush. Now and then he would creep from the shyness which enveloped the inventive side of his nature, and would talk with her with unintelligible earnestness of these dreadful engines; of radial and initial hoop pressures, of drift angles, of ballistics, of longitudinal tensions, and would jot down trigonometrical formulæ illustrated by diagrams until her brain reeled; or of his treatise on guns of large caliber just written and now in the printers' hands, and of the revolution in warfare these astounding machines would effect. His eyes would lose their dreamy haze and would become luminous, his nervous fingers would become effectual, the man would become transfigured; but as soon as the fervid fit passed off he would turn with amiable aimlessness to his usual irrelevance. Sometimes he would work all night, either in his room or his workshop, at his inventions. Sometimes he would dream for days together. There was an old-fashioned pond in the middle of the common, with rough benches placed here and there at the brink. Septimus loved to sit on one of them and look at the ducks. He said he was fascinated by the way they wagged their tails. It suggested an invention: of what nature he could not yet determine. He also formed a brotherly intimacy with a lame donkey belonging to the sexton, and used to feed him with *pâté de joie gras* sandwiches, specially prepared by Wiggleswick, until he was authoritatively informed that raw carrots would be more acceptable. To see the two of them side by side watching the ducks in the pond wag their tails was a touching spectacle.

Another amenity in Septimus's peaceful existence was Emmy.

Being at this time out of an engagement, she paid various flying visits to Nunsmere, bringing with her an echo of comic opera and an odor of *Peau d'Espagne*. She dawned on Septimus's horizon like a mischievous and impertinent planet, so different from Zora, the great fixed star of his heaven, yet so pretty, so twinkling, so artlessly and so obviously revolving round some twopenny-halfpenny sun of her own, that he took her, with Wiggleswick, the ducks, and the donkey, into his close comradeship. It was she who had ordained the carrots. She had hair like golden thistledown, and the dainty, blonde skin that betrays every motion of the blood. She could blush like the pink tea-rose of an old-fashioned English garden. She could blanch to the whiteness of alabaster. Her eyes were forget-me-nots after rain. Her mouth was made for pretty slang and kisses. Neither her features nor her most often photo-graphed expression showed the tiniest scrap of what the austere of her sex used to call character. When the world smiled on her she laughed: when it frowned, she cried. When she met Septimus Dix, she flew to him as a child does to a new toy, and spent gorgeous hours in pulling him to pieces to see how he worked.

"Why aren't you married?" she asked him one day.

He looked up at the sky—they were on the common—an autumn stretch of pearls and purples, with here and there a streak of wistful blue, as if seeking the inspiration of a reason.

"Because no one has married me," he replied.

Emmy laughed. "That's just like you. You expect a woman to drag you out of your house by the scruff of your neck and haul you to church without your so much as ask-ing her."

"I've heard that lots of women do," said Septimus.

Emmy looked at him sharply. Every woman resents a universal criticism of her sex, but cannot help feeling a twinge of respect for the critic. She took refuge in scorn.

"A real man goes out and looks for a wife."

"But suppose he doesn't want one?"

"He must want a woman to love. What can his life be without a woman in it? What can anybody's life be without some one to care for? I really believe you're made of sawdust. Why don't you fall in love?"

Septimus took off his hat, ran his fingers through his up-standing hair, re-covered his head, and looked at her help-lessly.

"Oh, no! I'm booked. It's no use your falling in love with me."

"I wouldn't—presume to do such a thing," he stammered, somewhat scared. "I think love is serious. It's like an invention: sometimes it lies deep down inside you, great and quiet—and at other times it racks you and keeps you from sleeping."

"Oho!" cried Emmy. "So you know all about it. You *are* in love. Now, tell me, who is she?"

"It was many years ago," said Septimus. "She wore pigtails and I burned a hole in her pinafore with a toy cannon and she slapped my face. Afterwards she married a butcher."

He looked at her with his wan smile, and again raised his hat and ran his hand through his hair. Emmy was not convinced.

"I believe," she said, "you have fallen in love with Zora."

He did not reply for a moment or two; then he touched her arm.

"Please don't say that," he said, in an altered tone.

Emmy edged up close to him, as they walked. It was her nature, even while she teased, to be kind and caressing.

"Not even if it's true? Why not?"

"Things like that are not spoken of," he said soberly. "They're only felt."

This time it was she who put a hand on his arm, with a charming, sisterly air.

"I hope you won't make yourself miserable over it. You see, Zora is impossible. She'll never marry again. I do hope it's not serious. Is it?" As he did not answer, she continued: "It would be such—such rot wasting your life over a thing you haven't a chance of getting."

"Why?" said Septimus. "Isn't that the history of the best lives?"

This philosophic plane was too high for Emmy, who had her pleasant being in a less rarified atmosphere. "To want, to get, to enjoy," was the guiding motto of her existence. What was the use of wanting unless you got, and what was the use of getting unless you enjoyed? She came to the conclusion that Septimus was only sentimentally in love with Zora, and she regarded his tepid passion as a matter of no importance. At the same time her easy discovery delighted her. It invested Septimus with a fresh air of comicality.

"You're just the sort of man to write poetry about her. Don't you?"

"Oh, no!" said Septimus.

"Then what do you do?"

"I play the bassoon," said he.

Emmy clapped her hands with joy, thereby scaring a hen that was straying on the common.

"Another accomplishment? Why didn't you tell us? I'm sure Zora doesn't know of it. Where did you learn?"

"Wiggleswick taught me," said he. "He was once in a band."

"You must bring it round," cried Emmy.

But when Septimus, prevailed on by her entreaties, did

appear with the instrument in Mrs. Oldrieve's drawing-room, he made such unearthly and terrific noises that Mrs. Oldrieve grew pale and Zora politely but firmly took it from his hands and deposited it in the umbrella-stand in the hall.

"I hope you don't mind," she said.

"Oh, dear, no," said Septimus mildly. "I could never make out why anybody liked it."

Seeing that Septimus had a sentimental side to his character, Emmy gradually took him into her confidence, until Septimus knew things that Zora did not dream of. Zora, who had been married, and had seen the world from Nunsmere Pond to the crater of Mount Vesuvius, treated her sister with matronly indulgence, as a child to whom Great Things were unrevealed. She did not reckon with the rough-and-tumble experiences of life which a girl must gain from a two years' battle on the stage. In fact, she did not reckon with any of the circumstances of Emmy's position. She herself was too ignorant, too much centered as yet in her own young impulses and aspirations, and far too serene in her unquestioning faith in the impeccability of the Oldrieve family. To her Emmy was still the fluffy-haired little sister with caressing ways whom she could send upstairs for her work-basket or could reprimand for a flirtation. Emmy knew that Zora loved her dearly; but she was the least bit in the world afraid of her, and felt that in affairs of the heart she would be unsympathetic. So Emmy withheld her confidence from Zora, and gave it to Septimus. Besides, it always pleases a woman more to tell her secrets to a man than to another woman. There is more excitement in it, even though the man be as unmoved as a stockfish.

Thus it fell out that Septimus heard of Mordaunt Prince, whose constant appearance in Emmy's London circle of friends Zora had viewed with plentiful lack of interest. He was a paragon of men. He acted like a Salvini and sang like an angel. He had been far too clever to take his degree at Oxford. He had just bought a thousand-guinea motor car, and—Septimus was not to whisper a word of it to Zora—she had recently been on a three-days' excursion with him. Mordaunt Prince said this and Mordaunt Prince said that. Mordaunt paid three guineas a pair for his brown boots. He had lately divorced his wife, an unspeakable creature only too anxious for freedom. Mordaunt came to see her every day in London, and every day during their absence they corresponded. Her existence was wrapped up in Mordaunt Prince. She traveled about with a suit-case (or so it appeared to Septimus) full of his photographs. He had been the leading man at the theater where she had her last engagement, and had fallen madly, devotedly, passionately in love with her. As soon as the divorce was made absolute they would be married. She had quarreled with her best friend, who had tried to make mischief between them with a view to securing Mordaunt for herself. Had Septimus ever heard of such a cat? Septimus hadn't.

He was greatly interested in as much of the story as he could follow—Emmy was somewhat discursive—and as his interjectory remarks were unprovocative of argument, he constituted himself a good listener. Besides, romance had never come his way. It was new to him, even Emmy's commonplace little romance, like a field of roses to a town-bred child, and it seemed sweet and gracious, a thing to dream about. His own distant worship of Zora did not strike him as romantic. It was a part of himself, like the hallowed memory of his mother and the conception of his devastating guns. Had he been more worldly-wise he would have seen possible danger in Emmy's romance, and insisted on Zora being taken into their confidence. But Septimus believed that the radiant beings of the earth, such as Emmy and Mordaunt Prince, from whom a quaint destiny kept him aloof, could only lead radiant lives, and the thought of harm did not cross his candid mind. Even while keeping Emmy's secret from Zora, he regarded it as a romantic and even dainty deceit.

Zora, seeing him happy with his guns and Wiggleswick and Emmy, applauded herself mightily as a contriver of good. Her mother also put ideas into her head.

From the drawing-room window they once saw Emmy and Septimus part at the little front gate. They had evidently returned from a walk. She plucked a great white chrysanthemum bloom from a bunch she was carrying, flicked it laughingly in his face, and stuck it in his buttonhole.

"What a good thing it would be for Emmy," said Mrs. Oldrieve, with a sigh.

"To marry Septimus? Oh, mother!"

She laughed merrily; then all at once she became serious.

"Why not?" she cried, and kissed her mother.

Mrs. Oldrieve settled her cap. She was small and Zora was large, and Zora's embraces were often disarranging.

"He is a gentleman and can afford to keep a wife."

"And steady?" said Zora, with a smile.

"I should think quite steady," said Mrs. Oldrieve, without one.

"And he would amuse Emmy all day long."

"I don't think it is part of a husband's duty, dear, to amuse his wife," said Mrs. Oldrieve.

The sudden entrance of Emmy, full of fresh air, laughter, and chrysanthemums, put an end to the conversation; but thenceforward Zora thought seriously of romantic possibilities. Like her mother, she did not entirely approve of Emmy's London circle. It was characterized by too much freedom, too great a lack of reticence. People said whatever came into their minds, and did, apparently, whatever occurred to their bodies. She could not quite escape from her mother's Puritan strain. For herself she felt secure. She, Zora, could wander unattended over Europe, mixing without spot or stain with whatever company she listed; that was because she was Zora Middlemist, a young woman of exceptional personality and experience of life. Ordinary young persons, for their own safe conduct, ought to obey the conventions which were made with that end in view; and Emmy was an ordinary young person. She should marry; it would conduce to her moral welfare, and it would be an excellent thing for Septimus. The marriage was therefore made in the unclouded heaven of Zora's mind. She shed all her graciousness over the young couple. Never had Emmy felt herself enwrapped in more sisterly affection. Never had Septimus dreamed of such tender solicitude. Yet she sang Septimus's praises to Emmy and Emmy's praises to Septimus in so natural a manner that neither of the two was puzzled.

"It is the natural instinct that makes every woman a matchmaker. She works blindly towards the baby. If she cannot have one directly, she will have it vicariously. The sourest of old maids is thus doomed to have a hand in the perpetuation of the race."

Thus spake the Literary Man from London, discoursing generally—out of earshot of the Vicar and his wife, to whom he was paying one of his periodical visits—in a corner of their drawing-room. Zora, conscious of matchmaking, declared him to be horrid and physiological.

"A woman is much more refined and delicate in her motives."

"The highly civilized woman," said Rattenden, "is delightfully refined in her table manners, and eats cucumber sandwiches in the most delicate way in the world; but she is obeying the same instinct that makes your lady cannibal thrust raw gobbets of missionary into her mouth with her fingers."

"Your conversation is revolting," said Zora.

"Because I speak the truth? Truth is a Mokanna."

"What on earth is that?" asked Zora.

The Literary man sighed. "The Veiled Prophet of Khorasan, Lalla Rookh, Tom Moore. Ichabod."

"It sounds like a cypher cablegram," said Zora flippantly. "But go on."

"I will. Truth, I say, is a Mokanna. So long as it's decently covered with a silver veil, you all prostrate yourselves before it and pretend to worship it. When anyone lifts the veil and reveals the revolting horror of it, you run away screaming, with your hands before your eyes. Why do you want truth to be pretty? Why can't you look its ghastliness bravely in the face? How can you expect to learn anything if you don't? How can you expect to form judgments on men and things? How can you expect to get to the meaning of life on which you were so keen a year ago?"

"I want beauty, and not disgustfulness," said Zora.

"Should it happen, for the sake of argument, that I wanted two dear friends to marry, it is only because I know how happy they would be together. The ulterior motive you suggest is repulsive."

"But it's true," said Rattenden. "I wish I could talk to you more. I could teach you a great deal. At any rate I know that you'll think about what I've said to-day."

"I won't," she declared.

"You will," said he. And then he dropped a very buttery piece of buttered toast on the carpet and, picking it up, said "damn" under his breath; and then they both laughed, and Zora found him human.

"Why are you so bent on educating me?" she asked.

"Because," said he, "I am one of the few men of your acquaintance who doesn't want to marry you."

"Indeed?" said Zora sarcastically, yet hating herself for feeling a little pang of displeasure. "May I ask why?"

"Because," said he, "I've a wife and five children already."

On the top of her matchmaking and her reflections on Truth in the guise of the Veiled Prophet of Khorasan, came Clem Sypher to take possession of his new house. Since Zora had seen him in Monte Carlo he had been to New York, Chicago, and San Francisco, fighting the Jebusa Jones dragon in its lair. He had written Zora stout dispatches during the campaign. Here a victory. There a defeat. Everywhere a Napoleonic will to conquer—but everywhere also an implied admission of the almost invulnerable strength of his enemy.

"I'm physically tired," said he, on the first day of his arrival, spreading his large frame luxuriously among the cushions of Mrs. Oldrieve's chintz-covered Chesterfield. "I'm tired for the only time in my life. I wanted you," he added, with one of his quick, piercing looks. "It's a curious thing, but I've kept saying to myself for the last month, 'If I could only come into Zora Middlemist's presence and drink in some of her vitality, I should be a new man.' I've never wanted a human being before. It's strange, isn't it?"

Zora came up to him, tea in hand, a pleasant smile on her face.

"The Nunsmere air will rest you," she said demurely.

"I don't think much of the air if you're not in it. It's like whiskey-less soda water." He drew a long breath. "My God! It's good to see you again. You're the one creature on this earth who believes in the Cure as I do myself."

Zora glanced at him guiltily. Her enthusiasm for the Cure as a religion was tepid. In her heart she did not believe in it. She had tried it a few weeks before on the sore head of a village baby, with disastrous results; then the mother had called in the doctor, who wrote out a simple prescription which healed the child immediately. The only real evidence of its powers she had seen was on Septimus's brown boots. Humanity, however, forbade her to deny the faith with which Clem Sypher credited her; also a genuine feeling of admiration mingled with pity for the man.

"Do you find much scepticism about?" she asked.

"It's lack of enthusiasm I complain of," he replied. "Instead of accepting it as the one heaven-sent remedy, people will use any other puffed and advertised stuff. Chemists are even lukewarm. A grain of mustard seed of faith among them would save me thousands of pounds a year.

6

Not that I want to roll in money, Mrs. Middlemist. I'm not an avaricious man. But a great business requires capital—and to spend money merely in flogging the invertebrate is waste—desperate waste."

It was the first time that Zora had heard the note of depression.

"Now that you are here, you must stay for a breathing space," she said kindly. "You must forget it, put it out of your mind, take a holiday. Strong as you are, you are not cast iron, and if you broke down, think what a disaster it would be for the Cure."

"Will you help me to have a holiday?"

She laughed. "To the best of my ability—and provided you don't want to make me shock Nunsmere too much."

He waved his hand in the direction of the village and said, Napoleonically:

"I'll look after Nunsmere. I have the motor here. We can go all over the country. Will you come?"

"On one condition."

"And that?"

"That you won't spread the Cure among our Surrey villages, and that you'll talk of something else all the time."

He rose and put out his hand. "I accept," he cried frankly. "I'm not a fool. I know you're right. When are you coming to see Penton Court? I will give a house-warming. You say that Dix has settled down here. I'll look him up. I'll be glad to see the muddle-headed seraph again. I'll ask him to come, too, so there will be you and he—and perhaps your sister will honor me, and your mother, Mrs. Oldrieve?"

"Mother doesn't go out much nowadays," said Zora. "But Emmy will no doubt be delighted to come."

"I have a surprise for you," said Sypher. "It's a brilliant idea—have had it in my head for months—you must tell me what you think of it."

The entrance of Mrs. Oldrieve and Emmy put an end to further talk of an intimate nature, and as Mrs. Oldrieve preferred the simple graces of stereotyped conversation, the remainder of Sypher's visit was uneventful. When he had taken his leave she remarked that he seemed to be a most superior person.

"I'm so glad he has made a good impression on mother," said Zora afterwards.

"Why?" asked Emmy.

"It's only natural that I should be glad."

"Oho!" said Emmy.

"What do you mean?"

"Nothing, dear."

"Look here, Emmy," said Zora, half laughing, half angry. "If you say or think such a thing I'll—I'll slap you. Mr. Sypher and I are friends. He hasn't the remotest idea of our being anything else. If he had, I would never speak to him again as long as I live."

Emmy whistled a comedy air, and drummed on the window-pane.

"He's a very remarkable man," said Zora.

"A most superior person," mimicked Emmy.

"And I don't think it's very good taste in us to discuss him in this manner."

"But, my dear," said Emmy, "it's you that are discussing him. I'm not. The only remark I made about him was a quotation from mother."

"I'm going up to dress for dinner," said Zora.

She was just a little indignant. Only into Emmy's fluffy

head could so preposterous an idea have entered. Clem Sypher in love with her? If so, why not Septimus Dix? The thing thus reduced itself to an absurdity. She laughed to herself, half ashamed of having allowed Emmy to see that she took her child's foolishness seriously, and came down to dinner serene and indulgent.

CHAPTER VII

"ARE you going to have your bath first, or your breakfast?" asked Wiggleswick, putting his untidy gray head inside the sitting-room door.

Septimus ran his ivory rule nervously through his hair.

"I don't know. Which would you advise?"

"What?" bawled Wiggleswick.

Septimus repeated his remark in a louder voice.

"If I had to wash myself in cold water," said Wiggleswick contemptuously, "I'd do it on an empty stomach."

"But if the water were warm?"

"Well, the water ain't warm, so it's no good speculating."

"Dear me," said Septimus. "Now that's just what I enjoy doing."

Wiggleswick grunted. "I'll turn on the tap and leave it."

The door having closed behind his body servant, Septimus laid his ivory rule on the portion of the complicated diagram of machinery which he had been measuring off, and soon became absorbed in his task. It was four o'clock in the afternoon. He had but lately risen, and sat in pyjamas and dressing-gown over his drawing. A bundle of proofs and a jam-pot containing a dissipated looking rosebud lay on that space of the table not occupied by the double-elephant sheet of paper. By his side was a manuscript covered with calculations to which he referred or added from time to time. A bleak November light came in through the window, and Septimus's chair was on the right-hand side of the table. It was characteristic of him to sit unnecessarily in his own light.

Presently a more than normal darkening of the room caused him to look at the window. Clem Sypher stood outside, gazing at him with amused curiosity. Hospitably, Septimus rose and flung the casement window open.

"Do come in."

As the aperture was two feet square, all of Clem Sypher that could respond to the invitation was his head and shoulders.

"Is it good morning, good afternoon, or good night?" he asked, surveying Septimus's attire.

"Morning," said Septimus. "I've just got up. Have some breakfast."

He moved to a bell-pull by the fireplace, and the tug was immediately followed by a loud report.

"What the devil's that?" asked Sypher, startled.

"That," said Septimus mildly, "is an invention. I pull the rope and a pistol is fired off in the kitchen. Wiggleswick says he can't hear bells. What's for breakfast?" he asked, as Wiggleswick entered.

"Haddock. And the bath's running over."

Septimus waved him away. "Let it run." He turned to Sypher. "Have a haddock?"

"At four o'clock in the afternoon? Do you want me to be sick?"

"Good heavens, no!" cried Septimus. "Do come in and I'll give you anything you like."

He put his hand again on the bell-pull. A hasty exclamation from Sypher checked his impulse.

"I say, don't do that again. If you'll open the front door for me," he added, "I may be able to get inside."

A moment or two later Sypher was admitted, by the orthodox avenues, into the room. He looked around him, his hands on his hips.

"I wonder what on earth this would have been like if our dear lady hadn't had a hand in it."

As Septimus's imagination was entirely scientific he could furnish no solution to the problem. He drew a chair to the fire and bade his guest sit down, and handed him a box of cigars which also housed a pair of compasses, some stamps, and a collar stud. Sypher selected and lit a cigar, but declined the chair for the moment.

"You don't mind my looking you up? I told you yesterday I would do it, but you're such a curious creature there's no knowing at what hour you can receive visitors. Mrs. Middlemist told me you were generally in to lunch at half-past four in the morning. Hello, an invention?"

"Yes," said Septimus.

Sypher pored over the diagram. "What on earth is it all about?"

"It's to prevent people getting killed in railway collisions," replied Septimus. "You see, the idea is that every compartment should consist of an outer shell and an inner case in which passengers sit. The roof is like a lid. When there's a collision this series of levers is set in motion, and at once the inner case is lifted through the roof and the people are out of the direct concussion. I haven't quite worked it out yet," he added, passing his hand through his hair. "You see, the same thing might happen when they're just coupling some more carriages on to a train at rest, which would be irritating to the passengers."

"Very," said Sypher, drily. "It would also come rather expensive, wouldn't it?"

"How could expense be an object when there are human lives to be saved?"

"I think, my friend Dix," said Sypher, "you took the wrong turning in the Milky Way before you were born. You were destined for a more enlightened planet. If they won't pay thirteen pence halfpenny for Sypher's Cure, how can you expect them to pay millions for your inventions? That Cure—but I'm not going to talk about it. Mrs. Middlemist's orders. I'm here for a rest. What are these? Proofs? Writing a novel?"

He held up the bundle with one of his kindly smiles and one of his swift glances at Septimus.

"It's my book on guns."

"Can I look?"

"Certainly."

Sypher straightened out the bundle—it was in page-proof —and read the title:

"A Theoretical Treatise on the Construction of Guns of Large Caliber. By Septimus Dix, M.A." He looked through the pages. "This seems like sense, but there are text-books, aren't there, giving all this information?"

"No," said Septimus modestly. "It begins where the text-books leave off. The guns I describe have never been cast."

"Where on earth do you get your knowledge of artillery?"

Septimus dreamed through the mists of memory.

"A nurse I once had married a bombardier," said he.

Wiggleswick entered with the haddock and other breakfast appurtenances, and while Septimus ate his morning meal Sypher smoked and talked and looked through the pages of the Treatise. The lamps lit and the curtains drawn, the room had a cosier appearance than by day. Sypher stretched himself comfortably before the fire.

"I'm not in the way, am I?"

"Good heavens, no!" said Septimus. "I was just thinking how pleasant it was. I've not had a man inside my rooms since I was up at Cambridge—and then they didn't come often, except to rag."

"What did they do?"

Septimus narrated the burnt umbrella episode and other social experiences.

"So that when a man comes to see me who does not throw my things about, he is doubly welcome," he explained. "Besides," he added, after a drink of coffee, "we said something in Monte Carlo about being friends."

"We did," said Sypher, "and I'm glad you've not forgotten it. I'm so much the Friend of Humanity in the bulk that I've somehow been careless as to the individual."

"Have a drink," said Septimus, filling his after-breakfast pipe.

The pistol shot brought Wiggleswick, who, in his turn, brought whiskey and soda, and the two friends finished the afternoon in great amity. Before taking his departure Sypher asked whether he might read through the proofs of the gun book at home.

"I think I know enough of machinery and mathematics to understand what you're driving at, and I should like to examine these guns of yours. You think they are going to whip creation?"

"They'll make warfare too dangerous to be carried on. At present, however, I'm more interested in my railway carriages."

"Which will make railway traveling too dangerous to be carried on!" laughed Sypher, extending his hand. "Goodby."

When he had gone, Septimus mused for some time in happy contentment over his pipe. He asked very little of the world, and oddly enough the world rewarded his modesty by giving him more than he asked for. To-day he had seen Sypher in a new mood, sympathetic, unegotistical, nonrobustious, and he felt gratified at having won a man's friendship. It was an addition to his few anchorages in life. Then, in a couple of hours he would sun himself in the smiles of his adored mistress, and listen to the prattle of his other friend, Emmy. Mrs. Oldrieve would be knitting by the lamp, and probably he would hold her wool, drop it, and be scolded as if he were a member of the family; all of which was a very gracious thing to the sensitive, lonely man, warming his heart and expanding his nature. It filled his head with dreams: of a woman dwelling by right in this house of his, and making the air fragrant by her presence. But as the woman—although he tried his utmost to prevent it and to conjure up the form of a totally different type—took the shape of Zora Middlemist, he discouraged such dreams as making more for mild unhappiness than for joy, and bent his thoughts to his guns and railway carriages and other world-upheaving inventions. The only thing that caused him any uneasiness was an overdraft at his bank due to cover which he had to pay on shares purchased for him by a circularizing bucket-shop keeper. It had seemed so simple to write Messrs. Shark & Co., or whatever alias the philanthropic financier assumed, a check for a couple of hundred pounds, and receive Messrs. Shark's check for two thousand in a fortnight, that he had wondered why other people did not follow this easy road to fortune. Perhaps they did, he reflected: that was how they managed to keep a large family of daughters and a motor car. But when the shark conveyed to him in unintelligible terms the fact that unless he wrote a check for two or three hundred pounds more his original stake would be lost, and when these also fell through the bottomless bucket of Messrs. Shark & Co. and his bankers called his attention to an overdrawn account, it began to dawn upon him that these were not the methods whereby a large family of daughters and a motor car were unprecariously maintained. The loss did not distress him to the point of sleeplessness; his ideas as to the value of money were as vague as his notions on the rearing of babies; but he was publishing his book at his own expense, and was concerned at not being in a position to pay the poor publisher immediately.   .

At Mrs. Oldrieve's he found his previsions nearly all fulfilled. Zora, with a sofa-ful of railway time-tables and ocean-steamer handbooks, sought his counsel as to a voyage round the world which she had in contemplation; Mrs. Oldrieve impressed on his memory a recipe for an omelette which he was to convey verbally to Wiggleswick, although he confessed that the only omelette that Wiggleswick had tried to make they had used for months afterwards as a kettle-holder; but Emmy did not prattle. She sat in a corner, listlessly turning over the leaves of a novel and taking an extraordinary lack of interest in the general conversation. The usual headache and neuralgia supplied her excuse. She looked pale, ill, and worried; and worry on a baby face is a lugubrious and pitiful spectacle.

After Mrs. Oldrieve had retired for the night, and while

Zora happened to be absent from the room in search of an atlas, Septimus and Emmy were left alone for a moment.

"I'm so sorry you have a headache," said Septimus sympathetically. "Why don't you go to bed?"

"I hate bed. I can't sleep," she replied, with an impatient shake of the body. "You mustn't mind me. I'm sorry I'm so rotten—ah! well then—such an uninspiring companion, if you like," she added, seeing that the word had jarred on him. Then she rose. "I suppose I bore you. I had better go, as you suggest, and get out of the way."

He intercepted her petulant march to the door.

"I wish you'd tell me what's the matter. It isn't only a headache."

"It's Hell and the Devil and all his angels," said Emmy. "and I'd like to murder somebody."

"You can murder me, if it would do you any good," said Septimus.

"I believe you'd let me," she said, yielding. "You're a good sort." She turned, with a short laugh, her novel held in both hands behind her back, one finger holding the place. A letter dropped from it. Septimus picked it up and handed it to her. It bore an Italian stamp and the Naples postmark.

"Yes. That's from him," she said resentfully. "I've not had a letter for a week, and now he writes to say he has gone to Naples on account of his health. You had better let me go, my good Septimus; if I stay here much longer I'll be talking slush and batter. I've got things on my nerves."

"Why don't you talk to Zora?" he suggested. "She is so wonderful."

"She's the last person in the world that must know anything. Do you understand? The very last."

"I'm afraid I don't understand," he replied ruefully.

"She doesn't know anything about Mordaunt Prince. She must never know. Neither must mother. They don't often talk much about the family; but they're awfully proud of it. Mother's people date from before Noah, and they look down on the Oldrieves because they sprang up like mushrooms just after the Flood. Prince's real name is Huzzle, and his father kept a boot shop. I don't care a hang, because he's a gentleman, but they would."

"But yet you're going to marry him. They must know sooner or later. They ought to know."

"Time enough when I'm married. Then nothing can be done and nothing can be said."

"Have you ever thought whether it wouldn't be well to give him up?" said Septimus, in his hesitating way.

"I can't, I can't!" she cried. Then she burst into tears, and, afraid lest Zora should surprise her, left the room without another word.

On such occasions the most experienced man is helpless. He shrugs his shoulders, says "Whew!" and lights a cigarette. Septimus, with an infant's knowledge of the ways of young women, felt terribly distressed by the tragedy of her tears. Something must be done to stop them. He might start at once for Naples, and, by the help of strong gendarmes whom he might suborn, bring back Mordaunt Prince presently to London. Then he remembered his overdrawn banking account, and sighfully gave up the idea. If only he were not bound to secrecy and could confide in Zora. This a sensitive honor forbade. What could he do? As the fire was getting low he mechanically put on a lump of coal with the pincers. When Zora returned with the atlas she found him rubbing them through his hair, and staring at vacancy.

"If I do go round the world," said Zora, a little while later, when they had settled on which side of South America Valparaiso was situated—and how many nice and clever people could tell you positively, offhand?—"if I go round the world, you and Emmy will have to come too. It would do her good. She has not been looking well lately."

"It would be the very thing for her," said he.

"And for you too, Septimus," she remarked, with a quizzical glance and smile.

"It's always good for me to be where you are."

"I was thinking of Emmy and not of myself," she laughed. "If you could take care of her, it would be an excellent thing for you."

"She wouldn't even trust me with her luggage," said Septimus, miles away from Zora's meaning. "Would you?"

She laughed again. "I'm different. I should really have to look after the two of you. But you could pretend to be taking care of Emmy."

"I would do anything that gave you pleasure."

"Would you?" she asked.

They were sitting by the table—the atlas between them. She moved her hand and touched his. The light of the lamp shone through her hair, turning it to luminous gold. Her arm was bare to the elbow, and the warm fragrance of her nearness overspread him. The touch thrilled him to the depths, and he flushed to his upstanding Struwel Peter hair. He tried to say something—he knew not what; but his throat was smitten with sudden dryness. It seemed to him that he had sat there, for the best part of an hour, tongue-

NOT UNPICTURESQUELY, HE KISSED HER FINGER TIPS.

(page 95)

tied, looking stupidly at the confluence of the blue veins on her arm, longing to tell her that his senses swam with the temptation of her touch and the rise and fall of her bosom, through the great love he had for her, and yet terror-stricken lest she might discover his secret, and punish his audacity according to the summary methods of Juno, Diana, and other offended goddesses whom mortals dared to love. It could only have been a few seconds, for he heard her voice in his ears, at first faint and then gathering distinctness, continuing in almost the same breath as her question.

"Would you? Do you know the greatest pleasure you could give me? It would be to become my brother—my real brother."

He turned bewildered eyes upon her.

"Your brother?"

She laughed, half impatiently, half gaily, gave his hand a final tap and rose. He stood, too, mechanically.

"I think you're the obtusest man I've ever met. Any-one else would have guessed long ago. Don't you see, you dear, foolish thing"—she laid her hands on his shoulders and looked with agonizing deliciousness into his face— "don't you see that you want a wife to save you from ome-lettes that you have to use as kettle-holders, and to give you a sense of responsibility? And don't you see that Emmy, who is never happier than when—oh!" she broke off im-patiently, "don't you see?"

He had built for himself no card house of illusion, so it did not come toppling down with dismaying clatter. But all the same he felt as if her kind hands had turned death cold and were wringing his heart. He took them from his shoulders, and, not unpicturesquely, kissed her finger-tips. Then he dropped them and walked to the fire and, with his back to the room, leaned on the mantelpiece. A little china dog fell with a crash into the fender.

"Oh, I'm so sorry—" he began piteously.

"Never mind," said Zora, helping him to pick up the pieces. "A man who can kiss a woman's hands like that is at liberty to clear the whole house of gimcrackery."

"You are a very gracious lady. I said so long ago," replied Septimus.

"I think I'm a fool," said Zora.

His face assumed a look of horror. His goddess a fool? She laughed gaily.

"You look as if you were about to remark, 'If any man had said that, the word would have been his last'! But I am, really. I thought there might be something between you and Emmy and that a little encouragement might help you. Forgive me. You see," she went on, a trace of dewiness in her frank eyes, "I love Emmy dearly, and in a sort of way I love you, too. And need I give any more explanation?"

It was an honorable amends, royally made. Zora had a magnificent style in doing such things: an indiscreet, venturesome, meddlesome princess she might be, if you will; somewhat unreserved, somewhat too conscious of her own Zoraesque sufficiency to possess the true womanly intuition and sympathy; but still a princess who had the grand manner in her scorn of trivialities. Septimus's hand shook a little as he fitted the tail to the hollow bit of china dog-end. It was sweet to be loved, although it was bitter to be loved in a sort of way. Even a man like Septimus Dix has his feelings. He had to hide them.

"You make me very happy," he said. "Your caring so much for me as to wish me to marry your sister, I shall never forget it. You see, I've never thought of her in that way. I suppose I don't think of women at all in that way," he went on, with a certain splendid mendacity. "It's a case of cog-wheels instead of corpuscles. I'm just a heathen bit of machinery, with my head full of diagrams."

"You're a tender-hearted baby," said Zora. "Give me those bits of dog."

She took them from his hand and threw the mutilated body into the fire.

"See," she said, "let us keep tokens. I'll keep the head and you the tail. If ever you want me badly send me the tail, and I'll come to you from any distance—and if I want you I'll send you the head."

"I'll come to you from the ends of the earth," said Septimus.

So he went home a happy man, with his tail in his pocket.

The next morning, about eight o'clock, just as he was sinking into his first sleep, he was awakened through a sudden dream of battle by a series of revolver shots. Wondering whether Wiggleswick had gone mad or was attempting an elaborate and painful mode of suicide, he leaped out of bed and rushed to the landing.

"What's the matter?"

"Hello! You're up at last!" cried Clem Sypher, appearing at the bottom of the stairs, sprucely attired for the city, and wearing a flower in the buttonhole of his overcoat. "I've had to break open the front door in order to get in at all, and then I tried shooting the bell for your valet. Can I come up?"

"Do," said Septimus, shivering. "Do you mind if I go back to bed?"

7

"Do anything, except go to sleep," said Sypher. "Look here. I'm sorry if I disturbed you, but I couldn't wait. I'm off to the office and heaven knows when I shall be back. I want to talk to you about this."

He sat on the foot of the bed and threw the proofs of the gun book on to Septimus's body, vaguely outlined beneath the clothes. In the gray November light—Zora's carefully chosen curtains and blinds had not been drawn—Sypher, pink and shiny, his silk hat (which he wore) a resplendent miracle of valetry, looked an urban yet roseate personification of Dawn. He seemed as eager as Septimus was supine.

"I've sat up half the night over this thing," said he, "and I really believe you've got it."

"Got what?" asked Septimus.

"*It*. The biggest thing on earth, bar Sypher's Cure."

"Wait till I've worked out my railway carriages," said Septimus.

"Your railway carriages! Good gracious! Haven't you any sense of what you're doing? Here you've worked out a scheme that may revolutionize naval gunnery, and you talk rot about railway carriages."

"I'm glad you like the book," said Septimus.

"Are you going to publish it?"

"Of course."

"Ask your publisher how much he'll take to let you off your bargain."

"I'm publishing it at my own expense," said Septimus, in the middle of a yawn.

"And presenting it gratis to the governments of the world?"

"Yes. I might send them copies," said Septimus. "It's a good idea."

Clem Sypher thrust his hat to the back of his head, and paced the room from the wash-stand past the dressing-table to the wardrobe and back again.

"Well, I'm hanged!" said he.

Septimus asked why.

"I thought I was a philanthropist," said Sypher, "but by the side of you I'm a vulture. Has it not struck you that, if the big gun is what I think, any government on earth would give you what you like to ask for the specification?"

"Really? Do you think they would give me a couple of hundred pounds?" asked Septimus, thinking vaguely of Mordaunt Prince in Naples and his overdrawn banking account. The anxiety of his expression was not lost on Sypher.

"Are you in need of a couple of hundred pounds?" he asked.

"Until my dividends are due. I've been speculating, and I'm afraid I haven't a head for business."

"I'm afraid you haven't," grinned Sypher, leaning over the footrail of the bed. "Next time you speculate come to me first for advice. Let me be your agent for these guns, will you?"

"I should be delighted," said Septimus, "and for the railway carriages too. There's also a motor car I've invented which goes by clockwork. You've got to wind it by means of a donkey engine. It's quite simple."

"I should think it would be," said Sypher drily. "But I'll only take on the guns just for the present."

He drew a check book from one pocket and a fountain pen from another.

"I'll advance you two hundred pounds for the sole right

to deal with the thing on your behalf. My solicitors will send you a document full of verbiage which you had better send off to your solicitor to look through before you sign it. It will be all right. I'm going to take the proofs. Of course this stops publishing," he remarked, looking round from the dressing-table where he was writing the check.

Septimus assented and took the check wonderingly, remarking that he didn't in the least know what it was for.

"For the privilege of making your fortune. Good-by," said he. "Don't get up."

"Good night," said Septimus, and the door having closed behind Clem Sypher, he thrust the check beneath the bed-clothes, curled himself up and went to sleep like a dormouse.

CHAPTER VIII

CLEM SYPHER stood at the front door of Penton Court a day or two afterwards, awaiting his guests and taking the air. The leaves of the oaks that lined the drive fell slowly under the breath of a southwest wind, and joined their sodden brethren on the path. The morning mist still hung around the branches. The sky threatened rain.

A servant came from within the house, bringing a telegram on a tray. Sypher opened it, and his strong, pink face became as overcast as the sky. It was from the London office of the Cure, and contained the information that one of his largest buyers had reduced his usual order by half. The news was depressing. So was the prospect before him, of dripping trees and of evergreens on the lawn trying to make the best of it in forlorn bravery. Heaven had ordained that the earth should be fair and Sypher's Cure invincible. Something was curiously wrong in the execution of Heaven's decrees. He looked again at the preposterous statement, knitting his brow. Surely this was some base contrivance of the enemy. They had been underselling and outadvertising him for months, and had ousted him from the custom of several large firms already. Something had to be done. As has been remarked before, Sypher was a man of Napoleonic methods. He called for a telegraph form, and wrote as he stood, with the tray as a desk:

"If you can't buy advertising rights on St. Paul's Cathedral or Westminster Abbey, secure outside pages of usual dailies for Thursday. Will draw up 'ad' myself."

He gave it to the servant, smiled in anticipation of the battle, and felt better. When Zora, Emmy, and Septimus appeared at the turn of the drive, he rushed to meet them, beaming with welcome and exuberant in phrase. This was the best housewarming that could be imagined. Just three friends to luncheon—three live people. A gathering of pale-souled folk would have converted the house into a chilly barn. They would warm it with the glow of friendship. Mrs. Middlemist, looking like a rose in June, had already irradiated the wan November garden. Miss Oldrieve he likened to a spring crocus, and Septimus (with a slap on the back) could choose the vegetable he would like to resemble. They must look over the house before lunch. Afterwards, outside, the great surprise awaited them. What was it? Ah! He turned laughing eyes on them, like a boy.

The great London firm to whom he had entrusted the furniture and decoration had done their splendid worst. The drawing-room had the appearance of an hotel sitting-room trying to look coy. An air of factitious geniality pervaded the dining-room. An engraving of Frans Hals's "Laughing Cavalier" hung with too great a semblance of jollity over the oak sideboard. Everything was too new, too ordered, too unindividual; but Sypher loved it, especially the high-art wall-paper and restless frieze. Zora, a woman of instinctive taste, who, if she bought a bedroom water-bottle, managed to identify it with her own personality, professed her admiration with a woman's pitying mendacity, but resolved to change many things for the good of Clem Sypher's soul. Emmy, still pale and preoccupied, said little. She was not in a mood to appreciate Clem

Sypher, whose loud voice and Napoleonic manners jarred upon her nerves. Septimus thought it all prodigiously fine, whereat Emmy waxed sarcastic.

"I wish I could do something for you," he said, heedless of her taunts, during a moment when they were out of ear-shot of the others. He had already offered to go to Naples and bring back Mordaunt Prince, and had received instant orders not to be a fool. "I wish I could make you laugh again."

"I don't want to laugh," she replied impatiently. "I want to sit on the floor and howl."

They happened to be in the hall. At the farther end Septimus caught sight of a fluffy Persian kitten playing with a bit of paper, and guided by one of his queer intuitions he went and picked it up and laid its baby softness against the girl's cheek. Her mood changed magically.

"Oh, the darling!" she cried, and kissed its tiny, wet nose.

She was quite polite to Sypher during luncheon, and laughed when he told her that he called the kitten Jebusa Jones. She asked why.

"Because," said he, showing his hand covered with scratches, "she produces on the human epidermis the same effect as his poisonous cuticle remedy."

Whereupon Emmy decided that the man who could let a kitten scratch his hand in that fashion had elements of good in his nature.

"Now for the surprise," said Sypher, when Septimus and he joined the ladies after lunch. "Come."

They followed him outside, through the French windows of the drawing-room. "Other people," said he, "want houses with lawns reaching down to the side of the river or the Menai Straits or Windermere. I'm the only person, I think, who has ever sought for a lawn running down to a main line of railway."

"That's why this house was untenanted so long," said Zora.

A row of trees separated the small garden from the lawn in question. When they passed through this screen, the lawn and the line of railway and the dreamy, undulating Surrey country came into view. Also an enormous board. Why hadn't he taken it down, Zora asked.

"That's the surprise!" exclaimed Sypher eagerly. "Come round to the front."

He led the way, striding some yards ahead. Presently he turned and struck a dramatic attitude, as a man might do who had built himself a new wonder house. And then on three astonished pairs of eyes burst the following inscription in gigantic capitals which he who flew by in an express train could read:

SYPHER'S CURE!
Clem Sypher.   Friend of Humanity!
I LIVE HERE!

"Isn't that great?" he cried. "I've had it in my mind for years. It's the personal note that's so valuable. This brings the whole passing world into personal contact with me. It shows that Sypher's Cure isn't a quack thing run by a commercial company, but the possession of a man who has a house, who lives in the very house you can see through the trees. 'What kind of a man is he?' they ask.

"ISN'T THAT GREAT? . . . . IT'S THE PERSONAL NOTE
THAT'S SO INVALUABLE."

(page 104)

'He must be a nice man to live in such a nice house. I almost feel I know him. *I'll try his Cure.*' Don't you think it's a colossal idea?"

He looked questioningly into three embarrassed faces. Emmy, in spite of her own preoccupation, suppressed a giggle. There was a moment's silence, which was broken by Septimus's mild voice:

"I think, by means of levers running down to the line and worked by the trains as they passed, I could invent a machine for throwing little boxes of samples from the board into the railway carriage windows."

Emmy burst out laughing. "Come and show me how you would do it."

She linked her arm in his and dragged him down to the line, where she spoke with mirthful disrespect of Sypher's Cure. Meanwhile Zora said nothing to Sypher.

"Don't you like it?" he asked at last, disconcerted.

"Do you want me to be the polite lady you've asked to lunch or your friend?"

"My friend and my helper," said he.

"Then," she replied, touching his coat sleeve, "I must say that I don't like it. I hate it. I think it's everything that is most abominable."

The board was one pride of his heart, and Zora was another. He looked at them both alternately in a piteous, crestfallen way.

"But why?" he asked.

Zora's eyes filled with tears. She saw that her lack of appreciation had hurt him to the heart. She was a generous woman, and did not convict him, as she would have done another man, of blatant vulgarity. Yet she felt preposterously pained. Why could not this great, single-minded creature, with ideas as high as they were queer, perceive the board's rank abomination?

"It's unworthy of you," she said bravely. "I want everyone to respect you as I do. You see the Cure isn't everything. There's a man behind it."

"That's the object of the board," said Sypher. "To show the man."

"But it doesn't show the chivalrous gentleman that I think you are," she replied quickly. "It gives the impression of some one quite different—a horrid creature who would sell his self-respect for money. Oh, don't you understand? It's as bad as walking through the streets with 'Sypher's Cure' painted on your hat."

"What can I do about it?" he asked.

"Take it down at once," said Zora.

"But to exhibit the board was my sole reason for buying the place."

"I'm very sorry," she said gently, "but I can't change my opinion."

He cast a lingering glance at the board, and then turned.

"Let us go back to the house," he said.

They walked a little way in silence. As they passed by the shrubbery at the side of the house, he gravely pushed aside a wet, hanging branch for her to proceed dry. Then he joined her again.

"You are angry with me for speaking so," said Zora.

He stopped and looked at her, his eyes bright and clear.

"Do you think I'm a born fool? Do you think I can't tell loyalty when I see it, and am such an ass as not to prize it above all things? It cost you a lot to say that to me. You're right. I suppose I've lost sense of myself in the Cure. When I think of it, I seem just to be the machine that is distributing it over the earth. And that, too, I suppose, is why I want you. The board is an abomination that cries to heaven. It shall be instantly removed. There!"

He held out his hand. She gave him hers and he pressed it warmly.

"Are you going to give up the house now that it's useless?" she asked.

"Do you wish me to?"

"What have I to do with it?"

"Zora Middlemist," said he, "I'm a superstitious man in some things. You have everything to do with my success. Sooner than forfeit your respect I would set fire to every stick I possessed. I would give up everything I had in the world except my faith in the Cure."

"Wouldn't you give up that—if it were necessary so as to keep my respect?" she asked, prompted by the insane devil that lurks in the heart of even the most sainted of women and does not like its gracious habitat to be reckoned lower than a quack ointment. It is the same little devil that makes a young wife ask her devoted husband which of the two he would save if she and his mother were drowning. It is the little devil that is responsible for infinite mendacity on the part of men. "Have you ever said that to another woman?" No; of course he hasn't; and the wretch is instantly perjured. "Would you sell your soul for me?" "My immortal soul," says the good fellow, instantaneously converted into an atrocious liar; and the little devil coos with satisfaction and curls himself up snugly to sleep.

But on this occasion the little devil had no success.

"I would give up my faith in the Cure for nothing in the wide world," said Sypher gravely.

"I'm very glad to hear it," said Zora, in her frankest tone. But the little devil asked her whether she was quite sure; whereupon she hit him smartly over the head and bade him lie down. Her respect, however, for Sypher increased.

They were joined by Emmy and Septimus.

"I think I could manage it," said the latter, "if I cut a hole a foot square in the board and fixed a magazine behind it."

"There will be no necessity," returned Sypher. "Mrs. Middlemist has ordered its immediate removal."

That was the end of the board episode. The next day he had it taken down and chopped into fire-wood, a cartload of which he sent with his humble compliments to Mrs. Middlemist. Zora called it a burnt offering. She found more satisfaction in the blaze that roared up the chimney than she could explain to her mother; perhaps more than she could explain to herself. Septimus had first taught her the pleasantness of power. But that was nothing to this. Anybody, even Emmy, curly-headed baby that she was, could turn poor Septimus into a slave. For a woman to impose her will upon Clem Sypher, Friend of Humanity, the Colossus of Curemongers, was no such trumpery achievement.

Emmy, when she referred to the matter, expressed the hope that Zora had rubbed it into Clem Sypher. Zora deprecated the personal bearing of the slang metaphor, but admitted, somewhat grandly, that she had pointed out the error in taste.

"I can't see, though, why you take all this trouble over Mr. Sypher," said Emmy.

"I value his friendship," replied Zora, looking up from a letter she was reading.

This was at breakfast. When the maid had entered with the post Emmy had gripped the table and watched with hungry eyes, but the only letter that had come for her had been on theatrical business. Not the one she longed for. Emmy's world was out of joint.

"You've changed your opinion, my dear, as to the value of men," she sneered. "There was a time when you didn't want to see them or speak to them or have anything to do with them. Now it seems you can't get on without them."

"My dear Emmy," said Zora calmly, "men as possible lovers and men as staunch friends are two entirely different conceptions."

Emmy broke a piece of toast viciously.

"I think they're beasts," she exclaimed.

"Good heavens! Why?"

"Oh, I don't know. They are."

Then, after the quick, frightened glance of the woman who fears she has said too much, she broke into a careless half-laugh.

"They are such liars. Fawcett promised me a part in his new production and writes to-day to say I can't have it."

As Emmy's professional disappointments had been many, and as Zora in her heart of hearts did not entirely approve of her sister's musical-comedy career, she tempered her sympathy with philosophic reflections. She had never taken Emmy seriously. All her life long Emmy had been the kitten sister, with a kitten's pretty but unimportant likes, dislikes, habits, occupations, and aspirations. To regard her as being under the shadow of a woman's tragedy had never entered her head. The kitten playing Antigone, Ophelia, or such like distressed heroines, in awful, grim earnest is not a conception that readily occurs even to the most affectionate and imaginative of kitten owners. Zora accepted Emmy's explanation of her petulance with a spirit entirely unperturbed, and resumed the perusal of her letter. It was from the Callenders, who wrote from California. Zora must visit them on her way round the world.

She laid down the letter and stirred her tea absently, her mind full of snow-capped sierras, and clear blue air, and peach forests, and all the wonders of that wonderland. And Emmy stirred her tea, too, in an absent manner, but her mind was filled with the most terrible thoughts where-with a woman's mind can be haunted.

CHAPTER IX

SEPTIMUS had never seen a woman faint before. At first he thought Emmy was dead, and rubbed agonized hands together like a fly. When he realized what had happened, he produced a large jack-knife which he always carried in his trousers pocket—for the purpose, he explained, of sharpening pencils—and offered it to Zora with the vague idea that the first aid to fainting women consisted in cutting their stay-laces. Zora rebuked him for futility, and bade him ring the bell for the maid.

It was all very sudden. The scene had been one that of late had grown so familiar: Zora and Septimus poring over world itineraries, the latter full of ineffectual suggestion and irrelevant reminiscence, and Emmy reading by the fire. On this occasion it was the *Globe* newspaper which Septimus, who had spent the day in London on an unexecuted errand to his publisher, had brought back with him. Evening papers being luxuries in Nunsmere, he had hidden it carefully from Wiggleswick, in order to present it to the ladies. Suddenly there was a rustle and a slither by the fire-place, and Emmy, in a dead faint, hung over the arm of the chair. In her hand she grasped the outer sheet of the paper. The inner sheet, according to the untidy ways of women with newspapers, lay discarded on the floor.

With Septimus's help Zora and the maid carried her to the sofa; they opened the window and gave her smelling salts. Septimus anxiously desired to be assured that she was not dying, and Zora thanked heaven that her mother had gone to bed. Presently Emmy recovered consciousness.

"I must have fainted," she said in a whisper.

"Yes, dear," said Zora, kneeling by her side. "Are you better?"

Emmy stared past Zora at something unseen and terrifying.

"It was foolish. The heat, I suppose. Mr. Sypher's burning board." She turned an appealing glance to Septimus. "Did I say anything silly?"

When he told her that she had slipped over the arm of the chair without a word, she looked relieved and closed her eyes. As soon as she had revived sufficiently she allowed herself to be led up-stairs; but before going she pressed Septimus's hand with feverish significance.

Even to so inexperienced a mind as his the glance and the hand-shake conveyed a sense of trust, suggested dimly a reason for the fainting fit. Once more he stood alone and perplexed in the little drawing-room. Once more he passed his long fingers through his Struwel Peter hair and looked about the room for inspiration. Finding none, he mechanically gathered up the two parts of the newspaper, with a man's instinct for tidiness in printed matter, and smoothed out the crumples that Emmy's hand had made on the outer sheet. Whilst doing so, a paragraph met his eye, causing him to stare helplessly at the paper.

It was the announcement of the marriage of Mordaunt Prince at the British Consulate in Naples.

The unutterable perfidy of man! For the first time in his guileless life Septimus met it face to face. To read of human depravity in the police reports is one thing, to see it fall like a black shadow across one's life is another. It

horrified him. Mordaunt Prince had committed the un-
forgivable sin. He had stolen a girl's love, and basely,
meanly, he had slunk off, deceiving her to the last. To
Septimus the lover who kissed and rode away had ever appeared a despicable figure of romance. The fellow who
did it in real life proclaimed himself an unconscionable
scoundrel. The memory of Emmy's forget-me-not blue
eyes turning into sapphires as she sang the villain's praises
smote him. He clenched his fists and put to incoherent
use his limited vocabulary of anathema. Then fearing, in
his excited state, to meet Zora, lest he should betray the
miserable secret, he stuffed the newspaper into his pocket,
and crept out of the house.

Before his own fire he puzzled over the problem. Something must be done. But what? Hale Mordaunt Prince
from his bride's arms and bring him penitent to Nunsmere?
What would be the good of that, seeing that polygamy is
not openly sanctioned by Western civilization? Proceed to
Naples and chastise him? That were better. The monster deserved it. But how are men chastised? Septimus
had no experience. He reflected vaguely that people did
this sort of thing with a horsewhip. He speculated on the
kind of horsewhip that would be necessary. A hunting
crop with no lash would not be more effective than an ordinary walking stick. With a lash it would be cumbrous,
unless he kept at an undignified distance and flicked at his
victim as the ring-master in the circus flicks at the clown.
Perhaps horsewhips for this particular purpose could be
obtained from the Army and Navy Stores. It should be
about three feet long, flexible and tapering to a point. Unconsciously his inventive faculty began to work. When he
had devised an adequate instrument, made of fine steel

8

wires ingeniously plaited, he awoke, somewhat shame-facedly, to the commonplaces of the original problem. What was to be done?

He pondered for some hours, then he sighed and sought consolation in his bassoon; but after a few bars of "Annie Laurie" he put the unedifying instrument back in its corner and went out for a walk. It was a starry night of frost. Nunsmere lay silent as Bethlehem; and a star hung low in the east. Far away across the common gleamed one soli-tary light in the vicarage windows; the Vicar, good gentle-man, finishing his unruffled sermon while his parish slept. Otherwise darkness spread over everything save the sky. Not a creature on the road, not a creature on the common, not even the lame donkey. Incredibly distant the faint sound of a railway whistle intensified the stillness. Septi-mus's own footsteps on the crisp grass rang loud in his ears. Yet both stillness and darkness felt companionable, in har-mony with the starlit dimness of the man's mind. His soul was having its adventure while mystery filled the outer air. He walked on, wrapped in the nebulous fantasies which passed with him for thought, heedless, as he always was, of the flight of time. Once he halted by the edge of the pond, and, sitting on a bench, lit and smoked his pipe until the cold forced him to rise. With an instinctive desire to hear some earthly sound, he picked up a stone and threw it into the water. He shivered at the ghostly splash and moved away, himself an ineffectual ghost wandering aimlessly in the night.

The Vicar's lamp had been extinguished long ago. A faint breeze sprang up. The star sank lower in the sky. Suddenly, as he turned back from the road to cross the common for the hundredth time, he became aware that he was not alone. Footsteps rather felt than heard were in front of him. He pressed forward and peered through the darkness, and finally made out a dim form some thirty yards away. Idly he followed and soon recognized the figure as that of a woman hurrying fast. Why a woman should be crossing Nunsmere Common at four o'clock in the morning passed his power of conjecture. She was going neither to nor from the doctor, whose house lay behind the vicarage on the right. All at once her objective became clear to him. He thought of the splash of the stone. She was making straight for the pond. He hastened his pace, came up within a few yards of her and then stopped dead. It was Emmy. He recognized the zibeline toque and coat edged with the same fur which she often wore. She carried something in her hand, he could not tell what.

She went on, unconscious of his nearness. He followed her, horror-stricken. Emmy, a new Ophelia, was about to seek a watery grave for herself and her love sorrow. Again came the problem which in moments of emergency Septimus had never learned to solve. What should he do? Across the agony of his mind shot a feeling of horrible indelicacy in thrusting himself upon a woman at such a moment. He was half tempted to turn back and leave her to the sanctity of her grief. But again the splash echoed in his ears and again he shivered. The water was so black and cold. And what could he say to Zora? The thought lashed his pace to sudden swiftness and Emmy turned with a little scream of fear.

"Who are you?"

"It's I, Septimus," he stammered, taking hold of his cap. "For God's sake, don't do it."

"I shall. Go away. How dare you spy on me?"

She stood and faced him, and her features were just discernible in the dim starlight. Anger rang in her voice. She stamped her foot.

"How dare you?"

"I haven't been spying on you," he explained. "I only recognized you a couple of minutes ago. I was walking about—taking a stroll before breakfast, you know."

"Oh!" she said, stonily.

"I'm dreadfully sorry to have intruded upon you," he continued, twirling his cap nervously in his fingers while the breeze played through his upstanding hair. "I didn't mean to—but I couldn't stand by and let you do it. I couldn't, really."

"Do what?" she asked, still angry. Septimus did not know that beneath the fur-lined jacket her heart was thumping madly.

"Drown yourself," said Septimus.

"In the pond?" she laughed hysterically. "In three feet of water? How do you think I was going to manage it?"

Septimus reflected. He had not thought of the pond's inadequate depth.

"You might have lain down at the bottom until it was all over," he remarked in perfect seriousness. "I once heard of a servant girl who drowned herself in a basin of water."

Emmy turned impatiently and, walking on, waved him away; but he accompanied her mechanically.

"Oh, don't follow me," she cried in a queer voice. "Leave me alone, for God's sake. I'm not going to commit suicide. I wish to heaven I had the pluck."

"But if you're not going to do that, why on earth are you here?"

"I'm taking a stroll before breakfast—just like yourself.

Why am I here? If you really want to know," she added defiantly, "I'm going to London—by the early train from Hensham—the milk train. See, I'm respectable. I have my luggage." She swung something in the dark before him and he perceived that it was a handbag. "Now are you satisfied? Or do you think I was going to take a handkerchief and a powder puff into the other world with me? I'm just simply going to London—nothing more."

"But it's a seven-mile walk to Hensham."

She made no reply, but quickened her pace. Septimus, in a whirl of doubt and puzzledom, walked by her side, still holding his cap in his hand. Even the intelligence of the local policeman would have connected her astounding appearance on the common with the announcement in the *Globe*. He took that for granted. But if she were not about to destroy herself, why this untimely flight to London? Why walk seven miles in wintry darkness when she could have caught a train at Ripstead (a mile away) a few hours later, in orthodox comfort? It was a mystery, a tragic and perplexing mystery.

They passed by the pond in silence, crossed the common and reached the main road.

"I wish I knew what to do, Emmy," he said at last. "I hate forcing my company upon you, and yet I feel I should be doing wrong to leave you unprotected. You see, I should not be able to face Zora."

"You had better face her as late as possible," she replied quickly. "Perhaps you had better walk to the station with me. Would you?"

"It would ease my mind."

"All right. Only, for God's sake, don't chatter. I don't want you of all people to get on my nerves."

"Let me carry your bag," said Septimus, "and you had better have my stick."

The process of transference brought to his consciousness the fact of his bareheadedness.   He put on his cap and they trudged along the road like gipsy man and wife, saying not a word to each other.   For two miles they proceeded thus, sometimes in utter blackness when the road wound between thick oak plantations, sometimes in the lesser dimness of the open when it passed by the rolling fields; and not a sign of human life disturbed the country stillness.   Then they turned into the London road and passed through a village.   Lights were in the windows.   One cottage door stood open.   A shaft of light streamed across Emmy's face, and Septimus caught a glimpse of drawn and haggard misery.   They went on for another mile.   Now and then a laborer passed them with an unsurprised greeting.   A milk-cart rattled by and then all was silence again.   Gradually the stars lost brilliance.

All of a sudden, at the foot of a rise crowned by a cottage looming black against the sky, Emmy broke down and cast herself on a heap of stones by the side of the road, a help-less bundle of sobs and incoherent lamentations.   She could bear it no longer.   Why had he not spoken to her? She could go no further.   She wished she were dead. What was going to become of her?   How could he walk by her side saying nothing, like a dumb jailer?   He had better go back to Nunsmere and leave her to die by the wayside. It was all she asked of Heaven.

"Oh, God have pity on me," she moaned, and rocked herself to and fro.

Septimus stood for a time tongue-tied in acute distress. This was his first adventure in knight-errantry and he had

served before neither as page nor squire. He would have
given his head to say the unknown words that might comfort her. All he could do was to pat her on the shoulder
in a futile way and bid her not to cry, which, as all the world
knows, is the greatest encouragement to further shedding
of tears a weeping woman can have. Emmy sobbed more
bitterly than ever. Once more on that night of agonizing
dubiety, what was to be done? He looked round desperately for guidance, and, as he looked, a light appeared in
the window of the hilltop cottage.

"Perhaps," said he, "if I knock at the door up there,
they can give you a glass of milk. Or a cup of tea," he
added, brightening with the glow of inspiration. "Or they
may be able to let you lie down for a while."

But Emmy shook her head miserably. Milk, tea, recumbent luxury were as nothing to her. Neither poppy
nor mandragora (or words to that effect) could give her
ease again. And she couldn't walk four miles, and she
must catch the morning train.

"If you'll tell me what I can do," said Septimus, "I'll
do it."

A creaky rumble was heard in the distance and presently
they made out a cart coming slowly down the hill. Septimus had another brilliant idea.

"Let me put you into that and take you back to Nunsmere."

She sprang to her feet and clutched his arm.

"Never. Never, do you hear? I couldn't bear it.
Mother, Zora—I couldn't see them again. Last night they
nearly drove me into hysterics. What do you suppose I
came out for at this hour, if it wasn't to avoid meeting them?
Let us go on. If I die on the road, so much the better."

"Perhaps," said Septimus, "I could carry you."

She softened, linked her arm in his, and almost laughed, as they started up the hill.

"What a good fellow you are, and I've been behaving like a beast. Anyone but you would have worried me with questions—and small wonder. But you haven't even asked me——"

"Hush," said Septimus. "I know. I saw the paragraph in the newspaper. Don't let's talk of it. Let us talk of something else. Do you like honey? The Great Bear put me in mind. Wiggleswick wants to keep bees. I tell him, if he does, I'll keep a bear. He could eat the honey, you see. And then I could teach him to dance by playing the bassoon to him. Perhaps he would like the bassoon," he continued, after a pause, in his wistful way. "Nobody else does."

"If you had it with you now, I should love it for your sake," said Emmy with a sob.

"If you would take my advice and rest in the cottage, I could send for it," he replied unsmilingly.

"We must catch the train," said Emmy.

In Wirley, half a mile further, folks were stirring. A cart laden with market produce waited by a cottage door for the driver who stood swallowing his final cup of tea. A bare-headed child clung round his leg, an attendant Hebe. The wanderers halted.

"If the other cart could have taken us back to Nunsmere," said Septimus, with the air of a man who has arrived at Truth, "this one can carry us to the station."

And so it fell out. The men made Emmy as comfortable as could be among the cabbages, with some sacks for rugs, and there she lay drowsy with pain and weariness until they came to the end of their journey.

A gas-light or two accentuated the murky dismalness of the little station. Emmy sank exhausted on a bench in the booking hall, numb with cold, and too woebegone to think of her hair, which straggled limply from beneath the zibe-line toque. Septimus went to the booking office and asked for two first-class tickets to London. When he joined her again she was crying softly.

"You're coming with me? It is good of you."

"I'm responsible for you to Zora."

A shaft of jealousy shot through her tears.

"You always think of Zora."

"To think of her," replied Septimus, vaguely allusive, "is a liberal education."

Emmy shrugged her shoulders. She was not of the type that makes paragons out of her own sex, and she had also a sisterly knowledge of Zora unharmonious with Septimus's poetic conception. But she felt too miserable to argue. She asked him the time.

At last the train came in. There was a great rattling of milk-cans on the gloomy platform, and various slouching shapes entered third-class carriages. The wanderers had the only first-class compartment to themselves. It struck cold and noisome, like a peculiarly unaired charnel-house. A feeble lamp, whose effect was dimmed by the swishing dirty oil in the bottom of the globe, gave a pretense at illumination. The guard passing by the window turned his lantern on them and paused for a wondering moment. Were they a runaway couple? If so, thought he, they had arrived at quick repentance. As they looked too dismal for tips, he concerned himself with them no more. The train started. Emmy shook with cold, in spite of her fur-lined jacket. Septimus took off his overcoat and spread it over their two bodies as they huddled together for warmth. After a while her head drooped on his shoulder and she slept, while Septimus sucked his empty pipe, not daring to light it lest he should disturb her slumbers. For the same reason he forbore to change his original awkward attitude, and in consequence suffered agonies of pins and needles. To have a solid young woman asleep in your arms is not the romantic pleasure the poets make out; for comfort, she might just as well stand on your head. Also, as Emmy unconsciously drew the overcoat away from him, one side of his body perished with cold; and a dinner suit is not warm enough for traveling on a frosty morning.

The thought of his dinner jacket reminded him of his puzzledom. What were Emmy and himself doing in that galley of a railway carriage when they might have been so much more comfortable in their own beds in Nunsmere? It was an impenetrable mystery to which the sleeping girl who was causing him such acute though cheerfully borne discomfort alone had the key. In vain did he propound to himself the theory that such speculation betokened an in-delicate mind; in vain did he ask himself with unwonted severity what business it was of his; in vain did he try to hitch his thoughts to Patent Safety Railway Carriages, which were giving him a great deal of trouble; in vain did he try to sleep. The question haunted him. So much so that when Emmy awoke and rubbed her eyes, and in some confusion apologized for the use to which she had put his shoulder, he was almost ashamed to look her in the face.

"What are you going to do when you get to Victoria?" Emmy asked.

Septimus had not thought of it. "Go back to Nunsmere, I suppose, by the next train—unless you want me?"

"No, I don't want you," said Emmy absently. "Why should I?"

And she gazed stonily at the suburban murk of the great city until they reached Victoria. There, a dejected four-wheeled cab with a drooping horse stood solitary on the rank—a depressing object. Emmy shivered at the sight.

"I can't stand it. Drive me to my door. I know I'm a beast, Septimus dear, but I am grateful. I am, really."

The cab received them into its musty interior and drove them through the foggy brown of a London winter dawn. Unimaginable cheerlessness enveloped them. The world wore an air of disgust at having to get up on such a morning. The atmosphere for thirty yards around them was clear enough, with the clearness of yellow consommé, but ahead it stood thick, like a purée of bad vegetables. They passed through Belgravia, and the white-blinded houses gave an impression of universal death, and the empty streets seemed waiting for the doors to open and the mourners to issue forth. The cab, too, had something of the sinister, in that it was haunted by the ghosts of a fourpenny cigar and a sixpenny bottle of scent which continued a lugubrious flirtation; and the windows rattled a *danse macabre*. At last it pulled up at the door of Emmy's Mansions in Chelsea.

She looked at him very piteously, like a frightened child. Her pretty mouth was never strong, but when the corners drooped it was babyish. She slipped her hand in his.

"Don't leave me just yet. It's silly, I know—but this awful journey has taken everything out of me. Every bit of it has been worse than the last. Edith—that's my maid

—will light a fire—you must get warm before you start—
and she'll make some coffee. Oh, do come. You can
keep the cab."

"But what will your maid think?" asked Septimus, who
for all his vagueness had definite traditions as to the proprieties of life.

"What does it matter? What does anything in this
ghastly world matter? I'm frightened, Septimus, horribly
frightened. I daren't go up by myself. Oh! Come!"

Her voice broke on the last word. Saint Anthony would
have yielded; also his pig. Septimus handed her out of
the cab, and telling the cabman to wait, followed her through
the already opened front door of the Mansions up to her
flat. She let herself in with her latchkey and showed him
into the drawing-room, turning on the electric light as he
entered.

"I'll go and wake Edith," she said. "Then we can have
some breakfast. The fire's laid. Do you mind putting a
match to it?"

She disappeared and Septimus knelt down before the
grate and lit the paper. In a second or two the flame caught
the wood, and, the blower being down, it blazed fiercely.
He spread his ice-cold hands out before it, incurious of the
futile little room whose draperies and fripperies and inconsiderable flimsiness of furniture proclaimed its owner, intent only on the elemental need of warmth. He was disturbed by the tornadic entrance of Emmy.

"She's not here!" she exclaimed tragically. Her baby
face was white and there were dark shadows under the eyes
which stared at him with a touch of madness. "She's not
here!"

"Perhaps she has gone out for a walk," Septimus suggested, as if London serving-maids were in the habit of taking the air at eight o'clock on a foggy morning.

But Emmy heard him not. The dismaying sense of utter loneliness smote her down. It was the last straw. Edith, on whom she had staked all her hopes of physical comfort, was not there. Overstrained in body, nerves, and mind, she sank helplessly in the chair which Septimus set out for her before the fire, too exhausted to cry. She began to speak in a queer, toneless voice:

"I don't know what to do. Edith could have helped me. I want to get away and hide. I can't stay here. It's the first place Zora will come to. She mustn't find me. Edith has been through it herself. She would have taken me somewhere abroad or in the country where I could have stayed in hiding till it was over. It was all so sudden— the news of his marriage. I was half crazy, I couldn't make plans. I thought Edith would help me. Now she has gone, goodness knows where. My God, what shall I do?"

She went on, looking at him haggardly, a creature driven beyond the reticence of sex, telling her inmost secret to a man as if it were a commonplace of trouble. It did not occur to her distraught mind that he was a man. She spoke to herself, without thought, uttering the cry for help that had been pent within her all that awful night.

The puzzledom of Septimus grew unbearable in its intensity; then suddenly it burst like a skyrocket and a blinding rain of fire enveloped him. He stood paralyzed with pain and horror.

The sullen morning light diffused itself through the room, mingling ironically with the pretty glow cast by the pink-shaded electric globes, while the two forlorn grotesques regarded each other, unconscious of each other's grotesque-

ness, the girl disheveled and haggard, the man with rough
gray coat unbuttoned, showing the rumpled evening dress;
her toque miserably awry, his black tie riding above his
collar, the bow somewhere behind his ear. And the tragedy
of tragedies of a young girl's life was unfolded.

"My God, what am I to do?"

Septimus stared at her, his hands in his trousers pockets.
In one of them his fingers grasped a folded bit of paper.
He drew it out unthinkingly—a very dirty bit of paper.
In his absent-minded way he threw it towards the fire, but
it fell on the tiled hearth. In moments of great strain the
mind seizes with pitiful eagerness on the trivial. Emmy
looked at the paper. Something familiar about its shape
struck her. She leaned forward, picked it up and unfolded
it.

"This is a check," she said in a matter-of-fact tone.
"Did you mean to throw it away?"

He took it from her and, looking at it, realized that it
was Clem Sypher's check for two hundred pounds.

"Thanks," said he, thrusting it into his overcoat pocket.

Then his queerly working brain focused associations.

"I know what we can do," said he. "We can go to Naples."

"What good would that be?" she asked, treating the
preposterous question seriously.

He was taken aback by her directness, and passed his
fingers through his hair.

"I don't know," said he.

"The first thing we must do," said Emmy—and her voice
sounded in her own ears like someone else's—"is to get
away from here. Zora will be down by the first train after
my absence is discovered. You quite see that Zora mustn't
find me, don't you?"

"Of course," said Septimus, blankly. Then he brightened. "You can go to an hotel. A Temperance Hotel in Bloomsbury. Wiggleswick was telling me about one the other day. A friend of his burgled it and got six years. A man called Barkus."

"But what was the name of the hotel?"

"Ah! that I forget," said Septimus. "It had something to do with Sir Walter Scott. Let me see. Lockhart—no, Lockhart's is a different place. It was either the Bride of Lammermoor or—yes," he cried triumphantly, "it was the Ravenswood, in Southampton Row."

Emmy rose. The switch off onto the trivial piece of paper had braced her unstrung nerves for a final effort: that, and the terror of meeting Zora.

"You'll take me there. I'll just put some things together."

He opened the door for her to pass out. On the threshold she turned.

"I believe God sent you to Nunsmere Common last night."

She left him, and he went back to the fire and filled and lit his pipe. Her words touched him. They also struck a chord of memory. His ever-wandering mind went back to a scene in undergraduate days. It was the Corn Exchange at Cambridge, where the most famous of all American evangelists was holding one of a series of revivalist meetings. The great bare hall was packed with youths, who came, some to scoff and others to pray. The coarse-figured, bald-headed, brown-bearded man in black on the platform, with his homely phrase and (to polite undergraduate ears) terrible Yankee twang, was talking vehemently of the trivial instruments the Almighty used to effect His purposes. Moses's rod, for instance. "You can imagine

Pharaoh," said he—and the echo of the great voice came to Septimus through the years—"you can imagine Pharaoh walking down the street one day and seeing Moses with a great big stick in his hand. 'Hallo, Moses,' says he, 'where are you going?' 'Where am I going?' says Moses. 'I guess I'm going to deliver the Children of Israel out of the House of Bondage and conduct them to a land flowing with milk and honey.' 'And how are you going to do it, Moses?' '*With this rod, sir, with this rod!*'"

Septimus remembered how this bit of unauthenticated history was greeted with derision by the general, and with a shocked sense of propriety by the cultivated—and young men at the university can be very cultivated indeed on occasion. But the truth the great preacher intended to convey had lingered at the back of his own mind and now came out into the light. Perhaps Emmy had spoken more truly than she thought. In his simple heart he realized himself to be the least effectual of men, apparently as unhelpful towards a great deliverance as the walking stick used by Moses. But if God had sent him to Nunsmere Common and destined him to be the mean instrument of Emmy's deliverance? He rubbed the warm pipe bowl against his cheek and excogitated the matter in deep humility. Yes, perhaps God had sent him. His religious belief was nebulous, but up to its degree of clarity it was sincere.

A few minutes later they were again in the cab jogging wearily across London to Southampton Row; and the little empty drawing-room with all its vanities looked somewhat ghostly, lit as it was by the day and by the frivolously shaded electric light which they had forgotten to switch off.

CHAPTER X

When Septimus had seen Emmy admitted to the Ravens-wood Hotel, he stood on the gloomy pavement outside wondering what he should do. Then it occurred to him that he belonged to a club—a grave, decorous place where the gay pop of a champagne cork had been known to produce a scandalized silence in the luncheon-room, and where serious-minded members congregated to scowl at one another's unworthiness from behind newspapers. A hansom conveyed him thither. In the hall he struggled over two telegrams which had caused him most complicated thought during his drive. The problem was to ease Zora's mind and to obtain a change of raiment without disclosing the whereabouts of either Emmy or himself. This he had found no easy matter, diplomacy being the art of speaking the truth with intent to deceive, and so finely separated from sheer lying as to cause grave distress to Septimus's candid soul. At last, after much wasting of telegraph forms, he decided on the following:

To Zora: "Emmy safe in London. So am I. Don't worry. Devotedly, Septimus."

To Wiggleswick: "Bring clothes and railway carriage diagrams secretly to Club."

Having dispatched these, he went into the coffee-room and ordered breakfast. The waiters served him in horrified silence. A gaunt member, breakfasting a few tables off, asked for the name of the debauchee, and resolved to write to the Committee. Never in the club's history had a member breakfasted in dress clothes—and in such disreputably disheveled dress clothes! Such dissolute mohocks were a stumbling-block and an offense, and the gaunt member, who had prided himself on going by clockwork all his life, felt his machinery in some way dislocated by the spectacle. But Septimus ate his food unconcernedly, and afterwards, mounting to the library, threw himself into a chair before the fire and slept the sleep of the depraved till Wiggleswick arrived with his clothes. Then, having effected an outward semblance of decency, he went to the Ravenswood Hotel. Wiggleswick he sent back to Nunsmere.

Emmy entered the prim drawing-room where he had been waiting for her, the picture of pretty flower-like misery, her delicate cheeks white, a hunted look in her baby eyes. A great pang of pity went through the man, hurting him physically. She gave him a limp hand, and sat down on a saddle-bag sofa, while he stood hesitatingly before her, balancing himself first on one leg and then on the other.

"Have you had anything to eat?"

Emmy nodded.

"Have you slept?"

"That's a thing I shall never do again," she said querulously. "How can you ask?"

"If you don't sleep, you'll get ill and die," said Septimus.

"So much the better," she replied.

"I wish I could help you. I do wish I could help you."

"No one can help me. Least of all you. What could a man do in any case? And, as for you, my poor Septimus, you want as much taking care of as I do."

The depreciatory tone did not sting him as it would have done another man, for he knew his incapacity. He had also gone through the memory of Moses's rod the night before.

"I wonder whether Wiggleswick could be of any use?" he said, more brightly.

Emmy laughed dismally. Wiggleswick! To no other mind but Septimus's could such a suggestion present itself.

"Then what's to be done?"

"I don't know," said Emmy.

They looked at each other blankly, two children face to face with one of the most terrible of modern social problems, aghast at their powerlessness to grapple with it. It is a situation which wrings the souls of the strong with an agony worse than death. It crushes the weak, or drives them mad, and often brings them, fragile wisps of human semblance, into the criminal dock. Shame, disgrace, social pariahdom; unutterable pain to dear ones; an ever-gaping wound in fierce family pride; a stain on two generations; an incurable malady of a once blithe spirit; woe, disaster, and ruin—such is the punishment awarded by men and women to her who disobeys the social law and, perhaps with equal lack of volition, obeys the law physiological. The latter is generally considered the greater crime.

These things passed through Septimus's mind. His ignorance of the ways of what is, after all, an indifferent, self-centered world exaggerated them.

"You know what it means?" he said tonelessly.

"If I didn't, should I be here?"

He made one last effort to persuade her to take Zora into her confidence. His nature abhorred deceit, to say nothing of the High Treason he was committing; a rudiment of common sense also told him that Zora was Emmy's natural helper and protector. But Emmy had the obstinacy of a weak nature. She would die rather than Zora should know. Zora would never understand, would never forgive her. The disgrace would kill her mother.

"If you love Zora, as you say you do, you would want to save her pain," said Emmy finally.

So Septimus was convinced. But once more, what was to be done?

"You had better go away, my poor Septimus," she said, bending forward listlessly, her hands in her lap. "You see you're not a bit of use now. If you had been a different sort of man—like anyone else—one who could have helped me—I shouldn't have told you anything about it. I'll send for my old dresser at the theater. I must have a woman, you see. So you had better go away."

Septimus walked up and down the room deep in thought. A spinster-looking lady in a cheap blouse and skirt, an inmate of the caravanserai, put her head through the door and, with a disapproving sniff at the occupants, retired. At length Septimus broke the silence:

"You said last night that you believed God sent me to you. I believe so too. So I'm not going to leave you."

"But what can you do?" asked Emmy, ending the sentence on a hysterical note which brought tears and a fit of sobbing. She buried her head in her arms on the sofa-end, and her young shoulders shook convulsively. She was an odd mixture of bravado and baby helplessness. To leave her to fight her terrible battle with the aid only of a theater dresser was an impossibility. Septimus looked at her with mournful eyes, hating his futility. Of what use was he to any God-created being? Another man, strong and capable, any vital, deep-chested fellow that was passing along Southampton Row at that moment, would have known how to take her cares on his broad shoulders and ordain, with kind imperiousness, a course of action. But he—he could only clutch his fingers nervously and shuffle with his feet, which of itself must irritate a woman with nerves on edge. He could do nothing. He could suggest nothing save that he should follow her about like a sympathetic spaniel. It was maddening. He walked to the window and looked out into the unexhilarating street, all that was man in him in revolt against his ineffectuality.

Suddenly came the flash of inspiration, swift, illuminating, such as happened sometimes when the idea of a world-upsetting invention burst upon him with bewildering clearness; but this time more radiant, more intense than he had ever known before; it was almost an ecstasy. He passed both hands feverishly through his hair till it could stand no higher.

"I have it!" he cried; and Archimedes could not have uttered his famous word with a greater thrill.

"Emmy, I have it!"

He stood before her gibbering with inspiration. At his cry she raised a tear-stained face and regarded him amazedly.

"You have what?"

"The solution. It is so simple, so easy. Why shouldn't we have run away together?"

"We did," said Emmy.

"But really—to get married."

"Married?"

She started bolt upright on the sofa, the feminine ever on the defensive.

"Yes," said Septimus quickly. "Don't you see? If you will go through the form of marriage with me—oh, just the form, you know—and we both disappear abroad somewhere for a year—I in one place and you in another, if you like—then we can come back to Zora, nominally married, and—and——"

"And what?" asked Emmy, stonily.

"And then you can say you can't live with me any longer. You couldn't stand me. I don't think any woman could. Only Wiggleswick could put up with my ways."

Emmy passed her hands across her eyes. She was somewhat dazed.

"You would give me your name—and shield me—just like that!" Her voice quavered.

"It isn't much to give. It's so short," he remarked absently. "I've always thought it such a silly name."

"You would tie yourself for life to a girl who has disgraced herself, just for the sake of shielding her?"

"Why, it's done every day," said Septimus.

"Is it? Oh, God! You poor innocent!" and she broke down again.

"There, there," said Septimus kindly, patting her shoulder. "It's all settled, isn't it? We can get married by special license—quite soon. I've read of it in books. Perhaps the Hall Porter can tell me where to get one. Hall Porters know everything. Then we can write to Zora and tell her it was a runaway match. It's the easiest thing in the world. I'll go and see after it now."

He left her prostrate on the sofa, her heart stone cold, her body lapped in flame from feet to hair. It was not given to him to know her agony of humiliation, her agony of temptation. He had but followed the message which his simple faith took to be divine. The trivial name of Dix would be the instrument wherewith the deliverance of Emmy from the House of Bondage should be effected. He went out

cheerily, stared for a moment at the Hall Porter, vaguely
associating him with the matter in hand, but forgetting
exactly why, and strode into the street, feeling greatly up-
lifted. The broad-shouldered men who jostled him as he
pursued his absent-minded and therefore devious course no
longer appeared potential champions to be greatly envied.
He felt that he was one of them, and blessed them as they
jostled him, taking their rough manners as a sign of kin-
ship. The life of Holborn swallowed him. He felt glad
who once hated the dismaying bustle. His heart sang for
joy. Something had been given him to do for the sake of
the woman he loved. What more can a man do than lay
down his life for a friend? Perhaps he can do a little more
for a loved woman: marry somebody else.

Deep down in his heart he loved Zora. Deep down in his
heart, too, dwelt the idiot hope that the miracle of miracles
might one day happen. He loved the hope with a mother's
passionate love for a deformed and imbecile child, knowing
it unfit to live among the other healthy hopes of his con-
ceiving. At any rate, he was free to bring her his daily
tale of worship, to glean a look of kindness from her clear
eyes. This was his happiness. For her sake he would
sacrifice it. For Zora's sake he would marry Emmy. The
heart of Septimus was that of a Knight-Errant confident in
the righteousness of his quest. The certainty had come
all at once in the flash of inspiration. Besides, was he not
carrying out Zora's wish? He remembered her words. It
would be the greatest pleasure he could give her—to become her brother, her real brother. She would approve.
And beyond all that, deep down also in his heart he knew
it was the only way, the wise, simple, Heaven-directed way.

The practical, broad-shouldered, common-sense children

of this world would have weighed many things one against the other. They would have taken into account sentimentally, morally, pharisaically, or cynically, according to their various attitudes towards life, the relations between Emmy and Mordaunt Prince which had led to this tragic situation. But for Septimus her sin scarcely existed. When a man is touched by an angel's feather he takes an angel's view of mortal frailties.

He danced his jostled way up Holborn till the City Temple loomed through the brown air. It struck a chord of association. He halted on the edge of the curb and regarded it across the road, with a forefinger held up before his nose as if to assist memory. It was a church. People were apt to be married in churches. Sometimes by special license. That was it! A special license. He had come out to get one. But where were they to be obtained? In a properly civilized country, doubtless they would be sold in shops, like boots and hair-brushes, or even in post-offices, like dog licenses. But Septimus, aware of the deficiencies of an incomplete social organization, could do no better than look wistfully up and down the stream of traffic, as it roared and flashed and lumbered past. A policeman stopped beside him. He appeared so lost, he met the man's eyes with a gaze so questioning, that the policeman paused.

"Want to go anywhere, sir?"

"Yes," said Septimus. "I want to go where I can get a special license to be married."

"Don't you know?"

"No. You see," said Septimus confidentially, "marriage has been out of my line. But perhaps you have been married, and might be able to tell me."

"Look here, sir," said the policeman, eyeing him kindly, but officially. "Take my advice, sir; don't think of getting married. You go home to your friends."

The policeman nodded knowingly and stalked away, leaving Septimus perplexed by his utterance. Was he a Socrates of a constable with a Xantippe at home, or did he regard him as a mild lunatic at large? Either solution was discouraging. He turned and walked back down Holborn somewhat dejected. Somewhere in London the air was thick with special licenses, but who would direct his steps to the desired spot? On passing Gray's Inn one of his brilliant ideas occurred to him. The Inn suggested law; the law, solicitors, who knew even more about licenses than Hall Porters and Policemen. A man he once knew had left him one day after lunch to consult his solicitors in Gray's Inn. He entered the low, gloomy gateway and accosted the porter.

"Are there any solicitors living in the Inn?"

"Not so many as there was. They're mostly architects. But still there's heaps."

"Will you kindly direct me to one?"

The man gave him two or three addresses, and he went comforted across the square to the east wing, whose Georgian mass merged without skyline into the fuliginous vapor which Londoners call the sky. The lights behind the blindless windows illuminated interiors and showed men bending over desks and drawing-boards, some near the windows with their faces sharply cut in profile. Septimus wondered vaguely whether any one of those visible would be his solicitor.

A member of the first firm he sought happened to be disengaged, a benevolent young man wearing gold spectacles, who received his request for guidance with sympathetic interest and unfolded to him the divers methods whereby British subjects could get married all over the world, including the High Seas on board one of His Majesty's ships of the Mercantile Marine. Solicitors are generally bursting with irrelevant information. When, however, he elicited the fact that one of the parties had a flat in London which would technically prove the fifteen days' residence, he opened his eyes.

"But, my dear sir, unless you are bent on a religious ceremony, why not get married at once before the registrar of the Chelsea district? There are two ways of getting married before the registrar—one by certificate and one by license. By license you can get married after the expiration of one whole day next after the day of the entry of the notice of marriage. That is to say, if you give notice tomorrow you can get married not the next day, but the day after. In this way you save the heavy special license fee. How does it strike you?"

It struck Septimus as a remarkable suggestion, and he admired the lawyer exceedingly.

"I suppose it's really a good and proper marriage?" he asked.

The benevolent young man reassured him; it would take all the majesty of the Probate, Divorce and Admiralty division of the High Court of Justice to dissolve it. Septimus agreed that in these circumstances it must be a capital marriage. Then the solicitor offered to see the whole matter through and get him married in the course of a day or two. After which he dismissed him with a professional blessing which cheered Septimus all the way to the Ravenswood Hotel.

CHAPTER XI

Good heavens, mother, they're married!" cried Zora, staring at a telegram she had just received.

Mrs. Oldrieve woke with a start from her after-luncheon nap.

"Who, dear?"

"Why, Emmy and Septimus Dix. Read it."

Mrs. Oldrieve put on her glasses with faltering fingers, and read aloud the words as if they had been in a foreign language: "Septimus and I were married this morning at the Chelsea Registrar's. We start for Paris by the 2.30. Will let you know our plans. Love to mother from us both. Emmy."

"What does this mean, dear?"

"It means, my dear mother, that they're married," said Zora; "but why they should have thought it necessary to run away to do it in this hole-and-corner fashion I can't imagine."

"It's very terrible," said Mrs. Oldrieve.

"It's worse than terrible. It's idiotic," said Zora.

She was mystified, and being a woman who hated mystification, was angry. Her mother began to cry. It was a disgraceful thing; before a registrar, too.

"As soon as I let her go on the stage, I knew something dreadful would happen to her," she wailed. "Of course Mr. Dix is foolish and eccentric, but I never thought he could do anything so irregular."

"I have no patience with him!" cried Zora. "I told

139

him only a short while ago that both of us would be delighted if he married Emmy."

"They must come back, dear, and be married properly. Do make them," urged Mrs. Oldrieve. "The Vicar will be so shocked and hurt—and what Cousin Jane will say when she hears of it——"

She raised her mittened hands and let them fall into her lap. The awfulness of Cousin Jane's indignation transcended the poor lady's powers of description. Zora dismissed the Vicar and Cousin Jane as persons of no account. The silly pair were legally married, and she would see that there was a proper notice put in *The Times*. As for bringing them back—she looked at the clock.

"They are on their way now to Folkestone."

"It wouldn't be any good telegraphing them to come back and be properly married in church?"

"Not the slightest," said Zora; "but I'll do it if you like."

So the telegram was dispatched to "Septimus Dix, Boulogne Boat, Folkestone," and Mrs. Oldrieve took a brighter view of the situation.

"We have done what we can, at any rate," she said by way of self-consolation.

Now it so happened that Emmy, like many another person at their wits' end, had given herself an amazing amount of unnecessary trouble. Her flight had not been noticed till the maid had entered her room at half-past eight. She had obviously packed up some things in a handbag. Obviously again she had caught the eight-fifteen train from Ripstead, as she had done once or twice before when rehearsals or other theatrical business had required an early arrival in London. Septimus's telegram had not only allayed no apprehension, but it had aroused a mild curiosity. Septimus was master of his own actions. His going up to London was no one's concern. If he were starting for the Equator a telegram would have been a courtesy. But why announce his arrival in London? Why couple it with Emmy's? And why in the name of guns and musical comedies should Zora worry? But when she reflected that Septimus did nothing according to the orthodox ways of men, she attributed the superfluous message to his general infirmity of character, smiled indulgently, and dismissed the matter from her mind. Mrs. Oldrieve had nothing to dismiss, as she had been led to believe that Emmy had gone up to London by the morning train. She only bewailed the flighty inconsequence of modern young women, until she reflected that Emmy's father had gone and come with disconcerting unexpectedness from the day of their wedding to that of his death on the horns of a buffalo; whereupon she fatalistically attributed her daughter's ways to heredity. So while the two incapables were sedulously covering up their tracks, the most placid indifference as to their whereabouts reigned in Nunsmere.

The telegram, therefore, announcing their marriage found Zora entirely unprepared for the news it contained. What a pitiful tragedy lay behind the words she was a million miles from suspecting. She walked with her head above such clouds, her eyes on the stars, taking little heed of the happenings around her feet—and, if the truth is to be known, finding mighty little instruction or entertainment in the firmament. The elopement, for it was nothing more, brought her eyes, however, earthwards. "Why?" she asked, not realizing it to be the most futile of questions when applied to human actions. To every such "Why?"

there are a myriad answers. When a mysterious murder is committed, everyone seeks the motive. Unless circumstance unquestionably provides the key of the enigma, who can tell? It may be revenge for the foulest of wrongs. It may be that the assassin objected to the wart on the other man's nose—and there are men to whom a wart is a Pelion of rank offense, and who believe themselves heaven-appointed to cut it off. It may be for worldly gain. It may be merely for amusement. There is nothing so outrageous, so grotesque, which, if the human brain has conceived it, the human hand has not done. Many a man has taken a cab, on a sudden shower, merely to avoid the trouble of unrolling his umbrella, and the sanest of women has been known to cheat a 'bus conductor of a penny, so as to wallow in the gratification of a crossing-sweeper's blessing. When the philosopher asks the Everlasting Why, he knows, if he be a sound philosopher—and a sound philosopher is he who is not led into the grievous error of taking his philosophy seriously—that the question is but the starting point of the entertaining game of Speculation.

To this effect spake the Literary Man from London, when next he met Zora. Nunsmere was in a swarm of excitement and the alien bee had, perforce, to buzz with the rest.

"The interesting thing is," said he, "that the thing has happened. That while the inhabitants of this smug village kept one dull eye on the decalogue and another on their neighbors, Romance on its rosy pinions was hovering over it. Two people have gone the right old way of man and maid. They have defied the paralyzing conventions of the engagement. Oh! the unutterable, humiliating, deadening period! When each young person has to pass the in-

spection of the other's relations. When simpering friends
maddeningly leave them alone in drawing-rooms and con-
servatories so that they can hold each other's hands.
When they are on probation *coram publico*. Our friends
have defied all this. They have defied the orange blos-
soms, the rice, the wedding presents, the unpleasant public affidavits, the whole indecent paraphernalia of an
orthodox wedding—the bridal veil—a survival from the
barbaric days when a woman was bought and paid for
and a man didn't know what he had got until he had
married her and taken her home—the senseless new
clothes which brand them immodestly wherever they go.
Two people have had the courage to avoid all this, to treat
marriage as if it really concerned themselves and not Tom,
Dick, and Harry. They've done it. Why, doesn't matter.
All honor to them."

He waved his stick in the air—they had met on the common—and the lame donkey, who had strayed companion-
ably near them, took to his heels in fright.

"Even the donkey," said Zora, "Mr. Dix's most intimate
friend, doesn't agree with you."

"The ass will agree with the sage only in the millen-
nium," said Rattenden.

But Zora was not satisfied with the professional philosopher's presentation of the affair. She sought Wiggleswick,
whom she found before a blazing fire in the sitting-room,
his feet on the mantelpiece, smoking a Havana cigar. On
her approach he wriggled to attention, and extinguishing
the cigar by means of saliva and a horny thumb and forefinger, put the stump into his pocket.

"Good morning, Wiggleswick," said Zora cheerfully.

"Good morning, ma'am," said Wiggleswick.

"You seem to be having a good time."

Wiggleswick gave her to understand that, thanks to his master's angelic disposition and his own worthiness, he always had a good time.

"Now that he's married there will have to be a few changes in household arrangements," said Zora.

"What changes?"

"There will be a cook and parlor maid and regular hours, and a mistress to look after things."

Wiggleswick put his cunning gray head on one side.

"I'm sure they'll make me very comfortable, ma'am. If they do the work, I won't raise no manner of objection."

Zora, regarding the egoist with mingled admiration and vexedness, could only say, "Oh!"

"I never raised no objection to his marriage from the first," said Wiggleswick.

"Did he consult you about it?"

"Of course he did," he replied with an indulgent smile, while the light of sportive fancy gleamed behind his blear eyes. "He looks on me as a father, he does, ma'am. 'Wiggleswick,' says he, 'I'm going to be married.' 'I'm delighted to hear it, sir,' says I. 'A man needs a woman's 'and about him,' says I."

"When did he tell you this?"

Wiggleswick searched his inventive memory.

"About a fortnight ago. 'If I may be so bold, sir, who is the young lady?' I asks. 'It's Miss Emily Oldrieve,' says he, and I said, 'A nicer, brighter, prettier bit of goods' —I beg your pardon, ma'am—'young lady, you couldn't pick up between here and Houndsditch.' I did say that, ma'am, I tell you straight." He looked at her keenly to see whether this expression of loyal admiration of his new mistress had taken effect, and then continued. "And then he says to me, 'Wiggleswick, there ain't going to be no grand wedding. You know me.'—And I does, ma'am. The outlandish things he does, ma'am, would shock an alligator.—'I should forget the day,' says he. 'I should lose the ring. I should marry the wrong party. I should forget to kiss the bridesmaids. Lord knows what I shouldn't do. So we're going up to London to be married on the Q. T., and don't you say nothing to nobody.'"

"So you've been in this conspiracy for a fortnight," said Zora severely, "and you never thought it your duty to stop him doing so foolish a thing?"

"As getting married, ma'am?"

"No. Such a silly thing as running away."

"Of course I did, ma'am," said Wiggleswick, who went on mendaciously to explain that he had used every means in his power to prevail on his master to submit to the orthodox ceremony for the sake of the family.

"Then you might have given me a hint as to what was going on."

Wiggleswick assumed a shocked expression. "And disobey my master? Orders is orders, ma'am. I once wore the Queen's uniform."

Zora, sitting on the arm of a chair, half steadying herself with her umbrella, regarded the old man standing respectfully at attention before her with a smile whose quizzicality she could not restrain. The old villain drew himself up in a dignified way.

"I don't mean the government uniform, ma'am. I've had my misfortunes like anyone else. I was once in the army—in the band."

"Mr. Dix told me that you had been in the band," said

Zora with all her graciousness, so as to atone for the smile. "You played that instrument in the corner."

"I did, ma'am," said Wiggleswick.

Zora looked down at the point of her umbrella on the floor. Having no reason to disbelieve Wiggleswick's circumstantial though entirely fictitious story, and having by the smile put herself at a disadvantage, she felt uncomfortably routed.

"Your master never told you where he was going or how long he was likely to be away?" she asked.

"My master, ma'am," replied Wiggleswick, "never knows where he is going. That's why he wants a wife who can tell him."

Zora rose and looked around her. Then, with a sweep of her umbrella indicating the general dustiness and untidiness of the room:

"The best thing you can do," said she, "is to have the house thoroughly cleaned and put in order. They may be back any day. I'll send in a charwoman to help you."

"Thank you, ma'am," said Wiggleswick, somewhat glumly. Although he had lied volubly to her for his own ends, he stood in awe of her commanding personality, and never dreamed of disregarding her high behests. But he had a moral disapproval of work. He could see no nobility in it, having done so much enforced labour in his time.

"Do you think we need begin now, ma'am?" he asked anxiously.

"At once," said Zora. "It will take you a month to clean the place. And it will give you something to do."

She went away femininely consoled by her exercise of authority—a minor victory covering a retreat. But she still felt very angry with Septimus.

When Clem Sypher came down to Penton Court for the week-end, he treated the matter lightly.

"He knew that he was acceptable to your mother and yourself, so he has done nothing dishonorable. All he wanted was your sister and the absence of fuss. I think it sporting of him. I do, truly."

"And I think you're detestable!" cried Zora. "There's not a single man that can understand."

"What do you want me to understand?"

"I don't know," said Zora, "but you ought to understand it."

A day or two later, meeting Rattenden again, she found that he comprehended her too fully.

"What would have pleased you," said he, "would have been to play the *sœur noble*, to have gathered the young couple in your embrace, and magnanimously given them to each other, and smiled on the happiness of which you had been the bounteous dispenser. They've cheated you. They've cut your part clean out of the comedy, and you don't like it. If I'm not right will you kindly order me out of the room? Well?" he asked, after a pause, during which she hung her head.

"Oh, you can stay," she said with a half-laugh. "You're the kind of man that always bets on a certainty."

Rattenden was right. She was jealous of Emmy for having unceremoniously stolen her slave from her service —that Emmy had planned the whole conspiracy she had not the slightest doubt—and she was angry with Septimus for having been weak enough to lend himself to such duplicity. Even when he wrote her a dutiful letter from Paris—to the telegram he had merely replied, "Sorry; impossible"—full of everything save Emmy and their plans for the future, she did not forgive him. How dared he consider himself fit to travel by himself? His own servant qualified his doings as outlandish.

"They'll make a terrible mess of their honeymoon," she said to Clem Sypher. "They'll start for Rome and find themselves in St. Petersburg."

"They'll be just as happy," said Sypher. "If I was on my honeymoon, do you think I'd care where I went?"

"Well, I wash my hands of them," said Zora with a sigh, as if bereft of dear responsibilities. "No doubt they're happy in their own way."

And that, for a long time, was the end of the matter. The house, cleaned and polished, glittered like the instrument room of a man-of-war, and no master or mistress came to bestow on Wiggleswick's toil the meed of their approbation. The old man settled down again to well-earned repose, and the house grew dusty and dingy again, and dustier and dingier as the weeks went on.

It has been before stated that things happen slowly in Nunsmere, even the reawakening of Zora's nostalgia for the Great World and Life and the Secrets of the Earth. But things do happen there eventually, and the time came when Zora found herself once again too big for the little house. She missed Emmy's periodical visits. She missed the regulation of Septimus. She missed her little motor expeditions with Sypher, who had sold his car and was about to sell "The Kurhaus, Kilburn Priory." The Cure seemed to have transformed itself from his heart to his nerves. He talked of it—or so it appeared to her—with more braggadocio than enthusiasm. He could converse of little else. It was going to smash Jebusa Jones's Cuticle Remedy to the shreds of its ointment boxes. The deepening vertical line between the man's brows she did not notice, nor did she interpret the wistful look in his eyes when he claimed her help. She was tired of the Cure and the Remedy and Sypher's fantastic need of her as ally. She wanted Life, real, quivering human Life. It was certainly not to be found in Nunsmere, where faded lives were laid away in lavender. For sheer sensations she began to tolerate the cynical analysis of the Literary Man from London. She must go forth on her journeyings again. She had already toyed with the idea when, with Septimus's aid, she had mapped out voyages round the world. Now she must follow it in strenuous earnest. The Callenders had cabled her an invitation to come out at once to Los Angeles. She cabled back an acceptance.

"So you're going away from me?" said Sypher, when she announced her departure.

There was a hint of reproach in his voice which she resented.

"You told me in Monte Carlo that I ought to have a mission in life. I can't find it here, so I'm going to seek one in California. What happens in this Sleepy Hollow of a place that a live woman can concern herself with?"

"There's Sypher's Cure——"

"My dear Mr. Sypher!" she laughed protestingly.

"Oh," said he, "you are helping it on more than you imagine. I'm going through a rough time, but with you behind me, as I told you before, I know I shall win. If I turn my head round, when I'm sitting at my desk, I have a kind of fleeting vision of you hovering over my chair. It puts heart and soul into me, and gives me courage to make desperate ventures."

"As I'm only there in the spirit, it doesn't matter whether the bodily I is in Nunsmere or Los Angeles."

"How can I tell?" said he, with one of his swift, clear glances. "I meet you in the body every week and carry back your spirit with me. Zora Middlemist," he added abruptly, after a pause, "I implore you not to leave me."

He leaned his arm on the mantelpiece from which Septimus had knocked the little china dog, and looked down earnestly at her, as she sat on the chintz-covered sofa behind the tea-table. At her back was the long casement window, and the last gleams of the wintry sun caught her hair. To the man's visionary fancy they formed an aureole.

"Don't go, Zora."

She was silent for a long, long time, as if held by the spell of the man's pleading. Her face softened adorably and a tenderness came into the eyes which he could not see. A mysterious power seemed to be lifting her towards him. It was a new sensation, pleasurable, like floating down a stream with the water murmuring in her ears. Then, suddenly, as if startled to vivid consciousness out of a dream, she awakened, furiously indignant.

"Why shouldn't I go? Tell me once and for all, why?"

She expected what any woman alive might have expected save the chosen few who have the great gift of reading the souls of the poet and the visionary; and Clem Sypher, in his way, was both. She braced her nerves to hear the expected. But the poet and the visionary spoke.

It was the old story of the Cure, his divine mission to spread the healing unguent over the suffering earth. Voices had come to him as they had come to the girl at Domrémy, and they had told him that through Zora Middlemist, and no other, was his life's mission to be accomplished.

To her it was anticlimax. Reaction forced a laugh against her will. She leaned back among the sofa cushions.

"Is that all?" she said, and Sypher did not catch the significance of the words. "You seem to forget that the rôle of Mascotte is not a particularly active one. It's all very well for you, but I have to sit at home and twirl my thumbs. Have you ever tried that by way of soul-satisfying occupation? Don't you think you're just a bit—egotistical?"

He relaxed the tension of his attitude with a sigh, thrust his hands into his pockets and sat down.

"I suppose I am. When a man wants something with all the strength of his being and thinks of nothing else day or night, he develops a colossal selfishness. It's a form of madness, I suppose. There was a man called Bernard Palissy who had it, and made everybody sacrifice themselves to his idea. I've no right to ask you to sacrifice yourself to mine."

"You have the right of friendship," said Zora, "to claim my interest in your hopes and fears, and that I've given you and shall always give you. But beyond that, as you say, you have no right."

He rose, with a laugh. "I know. It's as logical as a proposition of Euclid. But all the same I feel I have a higher right, beyond any logic. There are all kinds of phenomena in life which have nothing whatsoever to do with reason. You have convinced my reason that I'm an egotistical dreamer. But nothing you can do or say will ever remove the craving for you that I have here"—and he thumped his big chest—"like hunger."

When he had gone Zora thought over the scene with more disturbance of mind than she appreciated. She laughed to herself at Sypher's fantastic claim. To give up the great things of the world, Life itself, for the sake of a quack ointment! It was preposterous. Sypher was as crazy as Septimus; perhaps crazier, for the latter did not thump his chest and inform her that his guns or his patent convertible bed-razor-strop had need of her "here." Decidedly, the results of her first excursion into the big world had not turned out satisfactorily. Her delicate nose sniffed at them in disdain. The sniff, however, was disappointingly unconvincing. The voices of contemptible people could not sound in a woman's ears like the drowsy murmuring of waters. The insane little devil that had visited her in Clem Sypher's garden whispered her to stay.

But had not Zora, in the magnificence of her strong womanhood, in the hunger of her great soul, to find somewhere in the world a Mission in Life, a fulness of existence which would accomplish her destiny? Down with the insane little devil and all his potential works! Zora laughed and recovered her serenity. Cousin Jane, who had had much to write concerning the elopement, was summoned, and Zora, with infinite baggage in the care of Turner, set sail for California.

The New World lay before her with its chances of real, quivering, human Life. Nunsmere, where nothing ever happened, lay behind her. She smiled graciously at Sypher, who saw her off at Waterloo, and said nice things to him about the Cure, but before her eyes danced a mirage in which Clem Sypher and his Cure were not visible. The train steamed out of the station. Sypher stood on the edge of the platform and watched the end buffers until they were out of sight; then he turned and strode away, and his face was that of a man stricken with great loneliness.

CHAPTER XII

IT never occurred to Septimus that he had done a quixotic thing in marrying Emmy, any more than to pat himself on the back for a monstrously clever fellow when he had completed a new invention. At the door of the Registry Office he took off his hat, held out his hand, and said good-by.

"But where are you going?" Emmy asked in dismay.

Septimus didn't know. He waved his hand vaguely over London, and said, "Anywhere."

Emmy began to cry. She had passed most of the morning in tears. She felt doubly guilty now that she had accepted the sacrifice of his life; an awful sense of loneliness also overwhelmed her.

"I didn't know that you hated me like that," she said.

"Good heavens!" he cried in horror. "I don't hate you. I only thought you had no further use for me."

"And I'm to be left alone in the street?"

"I'll drive you anywhere you like," said he.

"And then get rid of me as soon as possible? Oh! I know what you must be feeling."

Septimus put his hand under her arm, and led her away, in great distress.

"I thought you wouldn't be able to bear the sight of me."

"Oh, don't be silly!" said Emmy.

Her adjuration was on a higher plane of sentiment than expression. It comforted Septimus.

"What would you like me to do?"

"Anything except leave me to myself—at any rate for the present. Don't you see, I've only you in the world to look to."

"God bless my soul," said he, "I suppose that's so. It's very alarming. No one has ever looked to me in all my life. I'd wander barefoot for you all over the earth. But couldn't you find somebody else who's more used to looking after people? It's for your own sake entirely," he hastened to assure her.

"I know," she said. "But you see it's impossible for me to go to any of my friends, especially after what has happened." She held out her ungloved left hand. "How could I explain?"

"You must never explain," he agreed, sagely. "It would undo everything. I suppose things are easy, after all, when you've set your mind on them—or get some chap that knows everything to tell you how to do them—and there's lots of fellows about that know everything—solicitors and so forth. There's the man who told me about a Registrar. See how easy it was. Where would you like to go?"

"Anywhere out of England." She shuddered. "Take me to Paris first. We can go on from there anywhere we like."

"Certainly," said Septimus, and he hailed a hansom.

Thus it fell out that the strangely married pair kept together during the long months that followed. Emmy's flat in London had been rented furnished. The maid Edith had vanished, after the manner of many of her kind, into ancillary space. The theater and all it signified to Emmy became a past dream. Her inner world was tragical enough, poor child. Her outer world was Septimus. In

Paris, as she shrank from meeting possible acquaintances, he found her a furnished *appartement* in the Boulevard Raspail, while he perched in a little hotel close by. The finding of the *appartement* was an illustration of his newly invented, optimistic theory of getting things done.

He came back to the hotel where he had provisionally lodged her and informed her of his discovery. She naturally asked him how he had found it.

"A soldier told me," he said.

"A soldier?"

"Yes. He had great baggy red trousers and a sash around his waist and a short blue jacket braided with red and a fez with a tassel and a shaven head. He saved me from being run over by a cab."

Emmy shivered. "Oh, don't talk of it in that calm way —suppose you had been killed!"

"I suppose the Zouave would have buried me—he's such a helpful creature, you know. He's been in Algiers. He says I ought to go there. His name is Hégisippe Cruchot."

"But what about the flat?" asked Emmy.

"Oh, you see, I fell down in front of the cab and he dragged me away and brushed me down with a waiter's napkin—there was a café within a yard or two. And then I asked him to have a drink and gave him a cigarette. He drank absinthe, without water, and then I began to explain to him an idea for an invention which occurred to me to prevent people from being run over by cabs, and he was quite interested. I'll show you——"

"You won't," said Emmy, with a laugh. She had her lighter moments. "You'll do no such thing—not until you've told me about the flat."

"Oh! the flat," said Septimus in a disappointed tone, as

if it were a secondary matter altogether. "I gave him another absinthe and we became so friendly that I told him that I wanted a flat and didn't in the least know how to set about finding one. It turned out that there was an *appartement* vacant in the house of which his mother is concierge. He took me along to see it, and introduced me to Madame, his mother. He has also got an aunt who can cook."

"I should like to have seen you talking to the Zouave," said Emmy. "It would have made a pretty picture—the two of you hobnobbing over a little marble table."

"It was iron, painted yellow," said Septimus. "It wasn't a resplendent café."

"I wonder what he thought of you."

"Well, he introduced me to his mother," replied Septimus gravely, whereat Emmy broke into merry laughter, for the first time for many days.

"I've taken the *appartement* for a month and the aunt who can cook," he remarked.

"What!" cried Emmy, who had not paid very serious regard to the narrative. "Without knowing anything at all about it?"

She put on her hat and insisted on driving there incontinently, full of misgivings. But she found a well-appointed house, a deep-bosomed, broad-beamed concierge, who looked as if she might be the mother of twenty helpful Zouaves, and an equally matronly and kindly-faced sister, a Madame Bolivard, the aunt aforesaid who could cook.

Thus, as the ravens fed Elijah, so did Zouaves and other casual fowl aid Septimus on his way. Madame Bolivard in particular took them both under her ample wing, to the girl's unspeakable comfort. A *brav' femme*, Madame Bolivard, who not only could cook, but could darn stockings and mend linen, which Emmy's frivolous fingers had never learned to accomplish. She could also prescribe miraculous *tisanes* for trivial ailments, could tell the cards, and could converse volubly on any subject under heaven; the less she knew about it, the more she had to say, which is a great gift. It spared the girl many desolate and despairing hours.

It was a lonely, monotonous life. Septimus she saw daily. Now and then, if Septimus were known to be upstairs, Hégisippe Cruchot, coming to pay his filial respects to his mother and his mother's *bouillabaisse* (she was from Marseilles) and her *matelote* of eels, luxuries which his halfpenny a day could not provide, would mount to inquire dutifully after his aunt and incidentally after the *belle dame du troisième*. He was their only visitor from the outside world, and as he found a welcome and an ambrosial form of alcohol compounded of Scotch whiskey and Maraschino (whose subtlety Emmy had learned from an eminent London actor-manager at a far-away supper party), he came as often as his respectful ideas of propriety allowed.

They were quaint gatherings, these, in the stiffly furnished little salon: Emmy, fluffy-haired, sea-shell-cheeked, and softly raimented, lying indolently on the sofa amid a pile of cushions—she had sent Septimus out to "La Samaritaine" to buy some (in French furnished rooms they stuff the cushions with cement), and he had brought back a dozen in a cab, so that the whole room heaved and swelled with them; Septimus, with his mild blue eyes and upstanding hair, looking like the conventional picture of one who sees a ghost; Hégisippe Cruchot, the outrageousness of whose piratical kit contrasted with his suavity of manner, sitting with military precision on a straight-backed chair; and Madame Bolivard standing in a far corner of the room, her bare arms crossed above her blue apron, and watching the scene with an air of kindly proprietorship. They spoke in French, for only one word of English had Hégisippe and his aunt between them, and that being "Howdodogoddam" was the exclusive possession of the former. Emmy gave utterance now and then to peculiar vocables which she had learned at school, and which Hégisippe declared to be the purest Parisian he had ever heard an Englishwoman use, while Septimus spoke very fair French indeed. Hégisippe would twirl his little brown mustache—he was all brown, skin and eyes and close-cropped hair, and even the skull under the hair—and tell of his military service and of the beautiful sunshine of Algiers and, when his aunt was out of the room, of his Arcadian love affairs. She served in a wine shop in the Rue des Francs-Bouchers. When was he going to get married? At Emmy's question he laughed, with a wave of his cigarette, and a clank of his bayonet against the leg of the chair. On a sou a day? Time enough for that when he had made his fortune. His mother then would doubtless find him a suitable wife with a dowry. When his military service was over he was going to be a waiter. When he volunteered this bit of information Emmy gave a cry of surprise. This dashing, swaggering desperado of a fellow a waiter!

"I shall never understand this country!" she cried.

"When one has good introductions and knows how to comport oneself, one makes much"—and he rubbed his thumb and fingers together, according to the national code of pantomime.

And then his hosts would tell him about England and the

fogs, wherein he was greatly interested; or Septimus would discourse to him of inventions, the weak spot in which his shrewd intelligence generally managed to strike, and then Septimus would run his fingers through this hair and say, "God bless my soul, I never thought of that," and Emmy would laugh; or else they talked politics. Hégisippe, being a Radical, *fiché*'d himself absolutely of the Pope and the priests. To be kind to one's neighbors and act as a good citizen summed up his ethical code. He was as moral as any devout Catholic.

"What about the girl in the Rue des Francs-Bouchers?" asked Emmy.

"If I were a good Catholic, I would have two, for then I could get absolution," he cried gaily, and laughed immoderately at his jest.

The days of his visits were marked red in Emmy's calendar.

"I wish I were a funny beggar, and had lots of conversation like our friend Cruchot, and could make you laugh," said Septimus one day, when the *tædium vitæ* lay heavy on her.

"If you had a sense of humor you wouldn't be here," she replied, with some bitterness.

Septimus rubbed his thin hands together thoughtfully.

"I don't know why you should say that," said he. "I never heard a joke I didn't see the point of. I'm rather good at it."

"If you don't see the point of this joke, I can't explain it, my dear. It has a point the size of a pyramid."

He nodded and looked dreamily out of the window at the opposite houses. Sometimes her sharp sayings hurt him. But he understood all, in his dim way, and pardoned all. He never allowed her to see him wince. He stood so long silent that Emmy looked up anxiously at his face, dreading the effect of her words. His hand hung by his side—he was near the sofa where she lay. She took it gently, in a revulsion of feeling, kissed it, and, as he turned, flung it from her.

"Go, my dear; go. I'm not fit to talk to you. Yes, go. You oughtn't to be here; you ought to be in England in your comfortable home with Wiggleswick and your books and inventions. You're too good for me, and I'm hateful. I know it, and it drives me mad."

He took her hand in his turn and held it for a second or two in both of his and patted it kindly.

"I'll go out and buy something," he said.

When he returned she was penitent and glad to see him; and although he brought her as a present a hat—a thing of purple feathers and green velvet and roses, in which no self-respecting woman would be seen mummified a thousand years hence—she neither laughed at it nor upbraided him, but tried the horror on before the glass and smiled sweetly while the cold shivers ran down her back.

"I don't want you to say funny things, Septimus," she said, reverting to the starting point of the scene, "so long as you bring me such presents as this."

"It's a nice hat," he admitted modestly. "The woman in the shop said that very few people could wear it."

"I'm so glad you think I'm an exceptional woman," she said. "It's the first compliment you have ever paid me."

She shed tears, though, over the feathers of the hat, before she went to bed, good tears, such as bring great comfort and cleanse the heart. She slept happier that night;

SHE NEITHER LAUGHED AT IT NOR UPBRAIDED HIM, BUT TRIED THE
HORROR ON AND SMILED SWEETLY WHILE THE COLD SHIVERS
RAN DOWN HER BACK.

(page 160)

and afterwards, whenever the devils entered her soul and the pains of hell got hold upon her, she recalled the tears, and they became the holy water of an exorcism.

Septimus, unconscious of this landmark in their curious wedded life, passed tranquil though muddled days in his room at the Hôtel Godet. A gleam of sunlight on the glazed hat of an omnibus driver, the stick of the whip and the horse's ear, as he was coming home one day on the *impériale*, put him on the track of a new sighting apparatus for a field gun which he had half invented some years before. The working out of this, and the superintendence of the making of the model at some works near Vincennes, occupied much of his time and thought. In matters appertaining to his passion he had practical notions of procedure; he would be at a loss to know where to buy a tooth-brush, and be dependent on the ministrations of a postman or an old woman in a charcoal shop, but to the place where delicate instruments could be made he went straight, as instinctively and surely as a buffalo heads for water. Many of his books and papers had been sent him from time to time by Wiggleswick, who began to dread the post, the labor of searching and packing and dispatching becoming too severe a tax on the old villain's leisure. These lay in promiscuous heaps about the floor of his bedroom, stepping-stones amid a river of minor objects, such as collars and bits of india rubber and the day before yesterday's *Petit Journal*. The *femme de chambre* and the dirty, indeterminate man in a green baize apron, who went about raising casual dust with a great feather broom, at first stowed the litter away daily, with jackdaw ingenuity of concealment, until Septimus gave them five francs each to desist; whereupon they desisted with alacrity, and the books became the stepping-stones aforesaid, stepping-stones to higher things. His only concern was the impossibility of repacking them when the time should come for him to leave the Hôtel Godet, and sometimes the more academic speculation as to what Zora would say should some miracle of levitation transport her to the untidy chamber. He could see her, radiant and commanding, dispelling chaos with the sweep of her parasol.

There were few moments in the day when he did not crave her presence. It had been warmth and sunshine and color to him for so long that now the sun seemed to have disappeared from the sky, leaving the earth a chill monochrome. Life was very difficult without her. She had even withdrawn from him the love "in a sort of way" to which she had confessed. The goddess was angry at the slight cast on her by his secret marriage. And she was in California, a myriad of miles away. She could not have been more remote had she been in Saturn. When Emmy asked him whether he did not long for Wiggleswick and the studious calm of Nunsmere, he said, "No." And he spoke truly; for wherein lay the advantage of one spot on the earth's surface over another, if Zora were not the light thereof? But he kept his reason in his heart. They rarely spoke of Zora.

Of the things that concerned Emmy herself so deeply, they never spoke at all. Of her hopes and fears for the future he knew nothing. For all that was said between them, Mordaunt Prince might have been the figure of a dream that had vanished into the impenetrable mists of dreamland. To the girl he was a ghastly memory which she strove to hide in the depths of her soul. Septimus saw that she suffered, and went many quaint and irrelevant ways to alleviate her misery. Sometimes they got on her nerves; more often they made the good tears come. Once she was reading a tattered volume of George Eliot which she had picked up during a stroll on the quays, and calling him over to her side pointed out a sentence: "Dogs are the best friends, they are always ready with their sympathy and they ask no questions."

"That's like you," she said; "but George Eliot had never met a man like you, poor thing, so she had to stick the real thing down to dogs."

Septimus reddened. "Dogs bark and keep one from sleeping," he said. "My next-door neighbor at the Hôtel Godet has two. An ugly man with a beard comes and takes them out in a motor car. Do you know, I'm thinking of growing a beard. I wonder how I should look in it?"

Emmy laughed and caught his sleeve. "Why won't you even let me tell you what I think of you?"

"Wait till I've grown the beard, and then you can," said Septimus.

"That will be never," she retorted; "for if you grow a beard, you'll look a horror, like a Prehistoric Man—and I sha'n't have anything to do with you. So I'll never be able to tell you."

"It would be better so," said he.

They made many plans for settling down in some part of rural France or Switzerland—they had the map of Europe to choose from—but Septimus's vagueness and a disinclination for further adventure on the part of Emmy kept them in Paris. The winter brightened into spring, and Paris, gay in lilac and sunshine, held them in her charm. There were days when they almost forgot, and became the light-hearted companions of the lame donkey on Nunsmere Common.

A day on the Seine, for instance, in a steamboat, when the water was miraculously turned to sparkling wine and the great masses of buildings were bathed in amber and the domes of the Pantheon and the Invalides and the cartouches and bosses of the Pont Alexandre III shone burnished gold. There was Auteuil, with its little open-air restaurants, rustic trellis and creepers, and its *friture* of gudgeon and dusty salt and cutlery and great yards of bread, which Emmy loved to break with Septimus, like Christmas crackers. Then, afterwards, there was the winding Seine again, Robinson Crusoe's Island in all its greenery, and St. Cloud with its terrace looking over the valley to Paris wrapped in an amethyst haze, with here and there a triumphant point of glory.

A day also in the woods of Bas Meudon, alone beneath the trees, when they talked like children, and laughed over the luncheon basket which Madame Bolivard had stuffed full of electrifying edibles; when they lay on their backs and looked dreamily at the sky through the leaves, and listened to the chirrup of insects awakening from winter and the strange cracklings and tiny voices of springtide, and gave themselves up to the general vibration of life which accompanies the working of the sap in the trees.

Days, too, in mid-Paris, in the Luxembourg Gardens, among the nursery maids and working folk; at cafés on the remoter boulevards, where the kindly life of Paris, still untouched by touristdom, passes up and down, and the spring gets into the step of youth and sparkles in a girl's eyes. At the window even of the *appartement* in the Boulevard Raspail, when the air was startlingly clear and scented and brought the message of spring from far lands, from the golden shores of the Mediterranean, from the windy mountain tops of Auvergne, from the broad, tender green fields of Central France, from every heart and tree and flower, from Paris itself, quivering with life. At such times they would not talk, both interpreting the message in their own ways, yet both drawn together into a common mood in which they vaguely felt that the earth was still a Land of Romance, that the mystery of rebirth was repeating itself according to unchanging and perpetual law; that inconsiderable, forlorn human atoms though they were, the law would inevitably affect them too, and cause new hopes, new desires, and new happiness to bud and flower in their hearts.

During these spring days there began to dawn in the girl's soul a knowledge of the deeper meaning of things. When she first met Septimus and delightedly regarded him as a new toy, she was the fluffy, frivolous little animal of excellent breeding and half education, so common in English country residential towns, with the little refinements somewhat coarsened, the little animalism somewhat developed, the little brain somewhat sharpened, by her career on the musical-comedy stage. Now there were signs of change. A glimmering notion of the duty of sacrifice entered her head. She carried it out by appearing one day, when Septimus was taking her for a drive, in the monstrous nightmare of a hat. It is not given to breathing male to appreciate the effort it cost her. She said nothing; neither did he. She sat for two hours in the victoria, enduring the tortures of the uglified, watching him out of the tail of her eye and waiting for a sign of recognition. At last she could endure it no longer.

"I put this thing on to please you," she said.

"What thing?"

"The hat you gave me."

"Oh! Is that it?" he murmured in his absent way. "I'm so glad you like it."

He had never noticed it. He had scarcely recognized it. It had given him no pleasure. She had made of herself a sight for gods and men to no earthly purpose. All her sacrifice had been in vain. It was then that she really experienced the disciplinary irony of existence. She never wore the hat again; wherein she was blameless.

The spring deepened into summer, and they stayed on in the Boulevard Raspail until they gave up making plans. Paris baked in the sun, and theaters perished, and riders disappeared from the Acacias, and Cook's brakes replaced the flashing carriages in the grand Avenue des Champs Elysées, and the great Anglo-Saxon language resounded from the Place de la Bastille to the Bon Marché. The cab horses drooped as if drugged by the vapor of the melting asphalt beneath their noses. Men and women sat by doorways, in front of little shops, on the benches in wide thoroughfares. The Latin Quarter blazed in silence and the gates of the great schools were shut. The merchants of lemonade wheeled their tin vessels through the streets and the bottles crowned with lemons looked pleasant to hot eyes. For the dust lay thick upon the leaves of trees and the lips of men, and the air was heavy with the over-fulfilment of spring's promise.

Septimus was sitting with Hégisippe Cruchot outside the little café of the iron tables painted yellow where first they had consorted.

"*Mon ami,*" said he, "you are one of the phenomena that make me believe in the *bon Dieu*. If you hadn't dragged me from under the wheels of the cab, I should have been killed, and if I had been killed you wouldn't have introduced me to your aunt who can cook, and what I should have done without your aunt heaven only knows. I owe you much."

"*Bah, mon vieux,*" said Hégisippe, "what are you talking about? You owe me nothing."

"I owe you three lives," said Septimus.

CHAPTER XIII

HÉGISIPPE CRUCHOT laughed and twirled his little brown mustache.

"If you think so much of it," said he, "you can acquit your debt in full by offering me another absinthe to drink the health of the three."

"Why, of course," said Septimus.

Hégisippe, who was sitting next the door, twisted his head round and shouted his order to those within. It was a very modest little café; in fact it was not a café at all, but a *Marchand des vins* with a zinc counter inside, and a couple of iron tables outside on the pavement to convey the air of a *terrasse*. Septimus, with his genius for the inharmonious, drank tea; not as the elegant nowadays drink at Colombin's or Rumpelmayer's, but a dirty, gray liquid served with rum, according to the old French fashion, before *five-o'cloquer* became a verb in the language. When people ask for tea at a *Marchand des vins*, the teapot has to be hunted up from goodness knows where; and as for the tea . . . ! Septimus, however, sipped the decoction of the dust of ages with his usual placidity. He had poured himself out a second cup and was emptying into it the remainder of the carafe of rum, so as to be ready for the toast as soon as Hégisippe had prepared his absinthe, when a familiar voice behind him caused him to start and drop the carafe itself into the teacup.

"Well, I'm blessed!" said the voice.

It was Clem Sypher, large, commanding, pink, and smiling. The sight of Septimus hobnobbing with a Zouave outside a humble wine merchant's had drawn from him the exclamation of surprise. Septimus jumped to his feet.

"My dear fellow, how glad I am to see you. Won't you sit down and join us? Have a drink."

Sypher took off his gray Homburg hat for a moment, and wiped a damp forehead.

"Whew! How anybody can stay in Paris this weather unless they are obliged to is a mystery."

"Why do you stay?" asked Septimus.

"I'm not staying. I'm passing through on my way to Switzerland to look after the Cure there. But I thought I'd look you up. I was on my way to you. I was in Nunsmere last week and took Wiggleswick by the throat and choked your address out of him. The Hôtel Godet. It's somewhere about here, isn't it?"

"Over there," said Septimus, with a wave of the hand. He brought a chair from the other table. "Do sit down."

Sypher obeyed. "How's the wife?"

"The—what?" asked Septimus.

"The wife—Mrs. Dix."

"Oh, very well, thank you," he said hurriedly. "Let me introduce you to my good friend Monsieur Hégisippe Cruchot of the Zouaves—Monsieur Cruchot—Monsieur Clem Sypher."

Hégisippe saluted and declared his enchantment according to the manners of his country. Sypher raised his hat politely.

"Of Sypher's Cure—Friend of Humanity. Don't forget that," he said laughingly in French.

"*Qu'est ce que c'est que ça?*" asked Hégisippe, turning to Septimus. Septimus explained.

"Ah-h!" cried Hégisippe, open-mouthed, the light of recognition in his eyes. "*La Cure Sypher!*" He made it rhyme with "prayer." "But I know that well. And it is Monsieur who fabricates *ce machin-là?*"

"Yes; the Friend of Humanity. What have you used it for?"

"For my heels when they had blisters after a long day's march."

The effect of these words on Sypher was electrical. He brought both hands down on the table, leaned back in his chair, and looked at Septimus.

"Good heavens!" he cried, changing color, "it never occurred to me."

"What?"

"Why—blistered heels—marching. Don't you see? It will cure the sore feet of the Armies of the World. It's a revelation! It will be in the knapsack of every soldier who goes to manœuvers or to war! It will be a jolly sight more useful than a marshal's bâton! It will bring soothing comfort to millions of brave men! Why did I never think of it? I must go round to all the War Offices of the civilized globe. It's colossal. It makes your brain reel. Friend of Humanity? I shall be the Benefactor of the Human Race."

"What will you have to drink?" asked Septimus.

"Anything. *Donnez-moi un bock,*" he said impatiently, obsessed by his new idea. "Tell me, Monsieur Cruchot, you who have used the *Cure Sypher*. It is well known in the French army is it not? You had it served out from the regimental medical stores?"

"Ah, no, Monsieur. It is my mother who rubbed it on my heels."

Sypher's face expressed disappointment, but he cheered up again immediately.

"Never mind. It is the idea that you have given me. I am very grateful to you, Monsieur Cruchot."

Hégisippe laughed. "It is to my mother you should be grateful, Monsieur."

"I should like to present her with a free order for the Cure for life—if I knew where she lived."

"That is easy," said Hégisippe, "seeing that she is concierge in the house where the *belle dame* of Monsieur has her *appartement*."

"Her *appartement?*" Sypher turned sharply to Septimus. "What's that? I thought you lived at the Hôtel Godet."

"Of course," said Septimus, feeling very uncomfortable. "I live in the hotel, and Emmy lives in a flat. She couldn't very well stay in the Hôtel Godet, because it isn't a nice place for ladies. There's a dog in the courtyard that howls. I tried to throw him some cold ham the other morning about six o'clock to stop him; but it hit a sort of dustman, who ate it and looked up for more. It was very good ham, and I was going to have it for supper."

"But, my dear man," said Sypher, laying his hand on his friend's shoulder, and paying no heed to the dog, ham, and dustman story, "aren't you two living together?"

"Oh, dear, no!" said Septimus, in alarm, and then, catching at the first explanation—"you see, our hours are different."

Sypher shook his head uncomprehendingly. The proprietor of the establishment, in dingy shirt-sleeves, set down the beer before him. Hégisippe, who had mixed his absinthe and was waiting politely until their new friend should be served, raised his glass.

"Just before you came, Monsieur," said he, "I was about to drink to the health——"

"Of *L'Armée-Française*," interrupted Septimus, reaching out his glass.

"But no," laughed Hégisippe. "It was to Monsieur, Madame, et Bébé."

"Bébé?" cried Sypher, and Septimus felt his clear, swift glance read his soul.

They clinked glasses. Hégisippe, defying the laws governing the absorption of alcohols, tossed off his absinthe in swashbuckler fashion, and rose.

"Now I leave you. You have many things to talk about. My respectful compliments to Madame. Messieurs, au revoir."

He shook hands, saluted and swaggered off, his chechia at the very back of his head, leaving half his shaven crown uncovered in front.

"A fine fellow, your friend, an intelligent fellow——" said Sypher, watching him.

"He's going to be a waiter," said Septimus.

"Now that he has had his heels rubbed with the cure he may be more ambitious. A valuable fellow, for having given me a stupendous idea—but a bit indiscreet, eh? Never mind," he added, seeing the piteous look on Septimus's face. "I'll have discretion for the two of us. I'll not breathe a word of it to anybody."

"Thank you," said Septimus.

There was an awkward silence. Septimus traced a diagram on the table with the spilled tea. Sypher lighted a cigar, which he smoked in the corner of his mouth, American fashion.

"Well, I'm damned!" he muttered below his breath.

He looked hard at Septimus, intent on his tea drawing. Then he shifted his cigar impatiently to the other side of his mouth. "No, I'm damned if I am. I can't be."

"You can't be what?" asked Septimus, catching his last words.

"Damned."

"Why should you be?"

"Look here," said Sypher, "I've rushed in rather unceremoniously into your private affairs. I'm sorry. But I couldn't help taking an interest in the two of you, both for your own sake and that of Zora Middlemist."

"I suppose you would do anything for her."

"Yes."

"So would I," said Septimus, in a low voice. "There are some women one lives for and others one dies for."

"She is one of the women for whom one would live."

Septimus shook his head. "No, she's the other kind. It's much higher. I've had a lot of time to think the last few months," he continued after a pause. "I've had no one but Emmy and Hégisippe Cruchot to talk to—and I've thought a great deal about women. They usedn't to come my way, and I didn't know anything at all about them."

"Do you now?" asked Sypher, with a smile.

"Oh, a great deal," replied Septimus seriously. "It's astonishing what a lot of difference there is between them and between the ways men approach different types. One woman a man wants to take by the hand and lead, and another—he's quite content if she makes a carpet of his body and walks over it to save her feet from sharp stones. It's odd, isn't it?"

"Not very," said Sypher, who took a more direct view of things than Septimus. "It's merely because he has got a kindly feeling for one woman and is desperately in love with the other."

"Perhaps that's it," said Septimus.

Sypher again looked at him sharply, as a man does who thinks he has caught another man's soul secret. It was only under considerable stress of feeling that such coherence of ideas could have been expressed by his irrelevant friend. What he had learned the last few minutes had been a surprise, a pain, and a puzzle to him. The runaway marriage held more elements than he had imagined. He bent forward confidentially.

"You would make a carpet of your body for Zora Middlemist?"

"Why, of course," replied the other in perfect simplicity.

"Then, my friend, you're desperately in love with her."

There was kindness, help, sympathy in the big man's voice, and Septimus, though the challenge caused him agonies of shyness, did not find it in his heart to resent Sypher's logic.

"I suppose every man whom she befriends must feel the same towards her. Don't you?"

"I? I'm different. I've got a great work to carry through. I couldn't lie down for anybody to walk over me. My work would suffer—but in this mission of mine Zora Middlemist is intimately involved. I said it when I first saw her, and I said it just before she left for California. She is to stand by my side and help me. How, God knows." He laughed, seeing the bewildered face of Septimus, who had never heard of this transcendental connection of Zora with the spread of Sypher's Cure. "You seem to think I'm crazy. I'm not. I work everything on the most hard and fast common-sense lines. But when a voice inside you tells you a thing day and night, you must believe it."

Said Septimus: "If you had not met her, you wouldn't have met Hégisippe Cruchot, and so you wouldn't have got the idea of Army blisters."

Sypher clapped him on the shoulder and extolled him as a miracle of lucidity. He explained magniloquently. It was Zora's unseen influence working magnetically from the other side of the world that had led his footsteps towards the Hôtel Godet on that particular afternoon. She had triumphantly vindicated her assertion that geographical location of her bodily presence could make no difference.

"I asked her to stay in England, you know," he remarked more simply, seeing that Septimus lagged behind him in his flight.

"What for?"

"Why, to help me. For what other reason?"

Septimus took off his hat and laid it on the chair vacated by Hégisippe, and ran his fingers reflectively up his hair. Sypher lit another cigar. Their side of the little street was deep in shade, but on half the road and on the other side of the way the fierce afternoon sunlight blazed. The merchant of wine, who had been lounging in his dingy shirt-sleeves against the door-post, removed the glasses and wiped the table clear of the spilled tea. Sypher ordered two more bocks for the good of the house, while Septimus, still lost in thought, brought his hair to its highest pitch of Struwel Peterdom. Passers-by turned round to look at them, for well-dressed Englishmen do not often sit outside a *Marchand des vins*, especially one with such hair. But passers-by are polite in France and do not salute the unfamiliar with ribaldry.

"Well," said Sypher, at last.

"We've been speaking intimately," said Septimus. He paused, then proceeded with his usual diffidence. "I've never spoken intimately to a man before, and I don't quite know how to do it—it must be just like asking a woman to marry you—but don't you think you were selfish?"

"Selfish? How?"

"In asking Zora Middlemist to give up her trip to California, just for the sake of the Cure."

"It's worth the sacrifice," Sypher maintained.

"To you, yes; but it mayn't be so to her."

"But she believes in the thing as I do myself!" cried Sypher.

"Why should she, any more than I, or Hégisippe Cruchot? If she did, she would have stayed. It would have been her duty. You couldn't expect a woman like Zora Middlemist to fail in her duty, could you?"

Sypher rubbed his eyes, as if he saw things mistily. But they were quite clear. It was really Septimus Dix who sat opposite, concentrating his discursive mind on Sypher's Cure and implicitly denying Zora's faith. A simple-minded man in many respects, he would not have scorned to learn wisdom out of the mouths of babes and sucklings; but out of the mouth of Septimus what wisdom could possibly proceed? He laughed his suggestion away somewhat blusteringly and launched out again on his panegyric of the Cure. But his faith felt a quiver all through its structure, just as a great building does at the first faint shock of earthquake.

"What made you say that about Zora Middlemist?" he asked when he had finished.

"I don't know," replied Septimus. "It seemed to be right to say it. I know when I get things into my head there appears to be room for nothing else in the world. One takes things for granted. When I was a child my father took it for granted that I believed in predestination. I couldn't; but I did not dare tell him so. So I went about with a load of somebody else's faith on my shoulders. It became intolerable; and when my father found out he beat me. He had a bit of rope tied up with twine at the end for the purpose. I shouldn't like this to happen to Zora."

This ended the discussion. The landlord at his doorpost drew them into talk about the heat, the emptiness of Paris and the happy lot of those who could go into villeggiatura in the country. The arrival of a perspiring cabman in a red waistcoat and glazed hat caused him to retire within and administer to the newcomer's needs.

"One of my reasons for looking you up," said Sypher, "was to make my apologies."

"Apologies?"

"Yes. Haven't you thought about the book on guns and wondered at not hearing from me?"

"No," said Septimus. "When I've invented a thing the interest has gone. I've just invented a new sighting apparatus. I'll show you the model if you'll come to the hotel."

Sypher looked at his watch and excused himself on the ground of business engagements. Then he had to dine and start by the nine o'clock train.

"Anyhow," said he, "I'm ashamed at not having done anything with the guns. I did show the proofs to a naval expert, but he made all sorts of criticisms which didn't help. Experts know everything that is known and don't want to know anything that isn't. So I laid it aside."

"It doesn't matter in the least," said Septimus eagerly, "and if you want to break the contract you sent me, I can pay you back the two hundred pounds." But Sypher assured him that he had never broken a contract in his life, and they shook hands and went their respective ways, Septimus to the *appartement* in the Boulevard Raspail, and Sypher thoughtfully in the direction of the Luxembourg.

He was sorry, very sorry for Septimus Dix. His kindness of heart had not allowed him to tell the brutal truth about the guns. The naval expert had scoffed in the free manner of those who follow the sea and declared the great guns a mad inventor's dream. The Admiralty was overwhelmed with such things. The proofs were so much waste paper. Sypher had come prepared to break the news as gently as he could; but after all their talk it was not in his heart to do so. And the two hundred pounds—he regarded it as money given to a child to play with. He would never claim it. He was sorry, very sorry for Septimus. He looked back along the past year and saw the man's dog-like devotion to Zora Middlemist. But why did he marry Emmy, loving the sister as he did? Why live apart from her, having married her? And the child? It was all a mystery in which he did not see clear. He pitied the ineffectuality of Septimus with the kind yet half-contemptuous pity of the strong man with a fine nature. But as for his denial of Zora's faith, he laughed it away. Egotistical, yes. Zora had posed the same question as Septimus and he had answered it. But her faith in the Cure itself, his mission to spread it far and wide over the earth, and to save the nations from vulgar competitors who thought of nothing but sordid gain—that, he felt sure, remained unshaken.

Yet as he walked along, in the alien though familiar city, he was smitten, as with physical pain, by a craving for her presence, for the gleam of her eyes, for the greatness of sympathy and comprehension that inhabited her generous and beautiful frame. The need of her was imperious. He stopped at a café on the Boulevard Saint-Michel, called for the wherewithal to write, and like a poet in the fine frenzy of inspiration, poured out his soul to her over the heels of the armies of the world.

He had walked a great deal during the day. When he stepped out of the cab that evening at the Gare de Lyon, he felt an unfamiliar stinging in his heel. During the process of looking after his luggage and seeking his train he limped about the platform. When he undressed for the night in his sleeping compartment, he found that a ruck in his sock had caused a large blister. He regarded it with superstitious eyes, and thought of the armies of the world. *In hoc signo vinces!* The message had come from heaven.

He took a sample box of Sypher's Cure from his handbag, and, almost with reverence, anointed his heel.

CHAPTER XIV

CLEM SYPHER slept the sleep of the warrior preparing for battle. When he awoke at Lyons he had all the sensations of a wounded Achilles. His heel smarted and tingled and ached, and every time he turned over determined on a continuation of slumber, his foot seemed to occupy the whole width of the berth. He reanointed himself and settled down again. But wakefulness had gripped him. He pulled up the blinds of the compartment and let the dawn stream in, and, lying on his back, gave himself up to the plans of his new campaign. The more he thought out the scheme the simpler it became. He had made it his business to know personages of high influence in every capital in Europe. Much of his success had already been gained that way. The methods of introduction had concerned him but little. For social purposes they could have been employed only by a pushing upstart; but in the furtherance of a divine mission the apostle does not bind his inspired feet with the shackles of ordinary convention. Sypher rushed in, therefore, where the pachyderms of Park Lane would have feared to tread. Just as the fanatical evangelist has no compunction in putting to an entire stranger embarrassing questions as to his possession of the Peace of God, so had Sypher no scruple in approaching any foreigner of distinguished mien in an hotel lounge and converting him to the religion of Sypher's Cure. In most cosmopolitan resorts his burly figure and pink face were well known. Newspapers paragraphed his arrival and departure. People pointed him out to one another in promenades. Distinguished personages to whom he had casually introduced himself introduced him to other distinguished personages. When he threw off the apostle and became the man, his simple directness and charm of manner caused him to be accepted pleasurably for his own sake. Had he chosen to take advantage of his opportunities he might have consorted with very grand folks indeed; at a price, be it said, which his pride refused to pay. But he had no social ambitions. The grand folks therefore respected him and held out a cordial hand as he passed by. That very train was carrying to Switzerland a Russian Grand Duke who had greeted him with a large smile and a "*Ah! ce bon Sypher!*" on the platform of the Gare de Lyon, and had presented him as the Friend of Humanity to the Grand Duchess.

To Sypher, lying on his back and dreaming of the days when through him the forced marches of weary troops would become light-hearted strolls along the road, the jealously guarded portals of the War Offices of the world presented no terrors. He ticked off the countries in his mind until he came to Turkey. Whom did he know in Turkey? He had once given a certain Musurus Bey a light for his cigarette in the atrium of the Casino at Monte Carlo; but that could scarcely be called an introduction. No matter; his star was now in the ascendant. The Lord would surely provide a Turk for him in Geneva. He shifted his position in the berth, and a twinge of pain passsed through his foot, hurting horribly.

When he rose to dress, he found some difficulty in putting on his boot. On leaving the train at Geneva he could scarcely walk. In his room at the hotel he anointed his heel again with the Cure, and, glad to rest, sat by the window looking at the blue lake and Mont Blanc white-capped in the quivering distance, his leg supported on a chair.

Then his traveler, who had arranged to meet him by appointment, was shown into the room. They were to lunch together. To ease his foot Sypher put on an evening slipper and hobbled downstairs.

The traveler told a depressing tale. Jebusa Jones had got in everywhere and was underselling the Cure. A new German skin remedy had insidiously crept on to the market. Wholesale houses wanted impossible discounts, and retail chemists could not be inveigled into placing any but the most insignificant orders. He gave dismaying details, terribly anxious all the while lest his chief should attribute to his incompetence the growing unpopularity of the Cure. But to his amazement Sypher listened smilingly to his story of disaster, and ordered a bottle of champagne.

"All that is nothing!" he cried. "A flea bite in the ocean. It will right itself as the public realize how they are being taken in by these American and German impostors. The Cure can't fail. And let me tell you, Dennymede, my son, the Cure is going to flourish as it has never flourished before. I've got a scheme that will take your breath away."

The glow of inspiration in Sypher's blue eyes and the triumph written on his resolute face brought the features of the worried traveler for the first time into an expression of normal satisfaction with the world.

"I will stagger you to your commercial depths, my boy," Sypher continued. "Have a drink first before I tell you."

He raised his champagne glass. "To Sypher's Cure!" They drank the toast solemnly.

And then Sypher unfolded to his awe-stricken subordinate the scheme for deblistering the heels of the armies of the world. Dennymede, fired by his enthusiasm, again lifted his brimming glass.

"By God, sir, you are a conqueror, an Alexander, a Hannibal, a Napoleon! There's a colossal fortune in it."

"And it will give me enough money," said Sypher, "to advertise Jebusa Jones and the others off the face of the earth."

"You needn't worry about them, sir, when you've got the army contracts," said the traveler.

He could not follow the spirituality underlying his chief's remark. Sypher laid down the peach he was peeling and looked pityingly at Dennymede as at one of little faith, one born to the day of small things.

"It will be all the more my duty to do so," said he, "when the instruments are placed in my hands. What, after all, is the healing of a few blistered feet, compared with the scourge of leprosy, eczema, itch, psoriasis, and what not? And, as for the money itself, what is it?"

He preached his sermon. The securing of the world's army contracts was only a means towards the shimmering ideal. It would clear the path of obstacles and leave the Cure free to pursue its universal way as *consolatrix afflictorum*.

The traveler finished his peach, and accepted another which his host hospitably selected for him.

"All the same, sir," said he, "this is the biggest thing you've struck. May I ask how you came to strike it?"

"Like all great schemes, it had humble beginnings," said Sypher, in comfortable postprandial mood, unconsciously flattered by the admiration of his subordinate. "Newton saw an apple drop to the ground: hence the theory of gravitation. The glory of Tyre and Sidon arose from the purple droppings of a little dog's mouth who had been eating shellfish. The great Cunarders came out of the lid of Stephenson's family kettle. A soldier happened to tell me that his mother had applied Sypher's Cure to his blistered heels—and that was the origin of the scheme."

He leaned back in his chair, stretched out his legs and put one foot over the other. He immediately started back with a cry of pain.

"I was forgetting my own infernal blister," said he. "About a square inch of skin is off and all the flesh round it is as red as a tomato."

"You'll have to be careful," advised the traveler. "What are you using for it?"

"Using for it? Why, good heavens, man, the Cure! What else?"

He regarded Dennymede as if he were insane, and Dennymede in his confusion blushed as red as the blistered heel.

They spent the afternoon over the reports and figures which had so greatly depressed the traveler. He left his chief with hopes throbbing in his breast. He had been promised a high position in the new Army Contract Department. As soon as he had gone Sypher rubbed in more of the Cure.

He passed a restless night. In the morning he found the ankle considerably swollen. He could scarcely put his foot to the ground. He got into bed again and rang the bell for the valet de chambre. The valet entered. Sypher explained. He had a bad foot and wanted to see a doctor. Did the valet know of a good doctor? The valet not only knew of a good doctor, but an English doctor resident in Geneva who was always summoned to attend English and American visitors at the hotel; furthermore, he was in the hotel at that very moment.

"Ask him if he would kindly step up," said Sypher.

He looked ruefully at his ankle, which was about the size of his calf, wondering why the Cure had not effected its advertised magic. The inflammation, however, clearly required medical advice. In the midst of his ruefulness the doctor, a capable-looking man of five and thirty, entered the room. He examined the heel and ankle with professional scrutiny. Then he raised his head.

"Have you been treating it in any way?"

"Yes," said Sypher, "with the Cure."

"What Cure?"

"Why, Sypher's Cure."

The doctor brought his hand down on the edge of the footboard of the bed, with a gesture of impatience.

"Why on earth do people treat themselves with quack remedies they know nothing about?"

"Quack remedies!" cried Sypher.

"Of course. They're all pestilential, and if I had my way I'd have them stacked in the market place and burned by the common hangman. But the most pestilential of the lot is Sypher's Cure. You ought never to have used it."

Sypher had the sensation of the hotel walls crashing down upon his head, falling across his throat and weighing upon his chest. For a few instants he suffered a nightmare paralysis. Then he gasped for breath. At last he said very quietly:

"Do you know who I am?"

"I have not the pleasure," said the doctor. "They only gave me your room number."

"I am Clem Sypher, the proprietor of Sypher's Cure."

The two men stared at one another, Sypher in a blue-striped pyjama jacket, supporting himself by one elbow on the bed, the doctor at the foot.   The doctor spread out his hands.

"It's the most horrible moment of my life.   I am at your mercy.   I only gave you my honest opinion, the result of my experience.   If I had known your name—naturally——"

"You had better go," said Sypher in a queer voice, digging the nails into the palms of his hands.   "Your fee—?"

"There is no question of it.   I am only grieved to the heart at having wounded you.   Good morning."

The door closed behind him, and Sypher gave himself up to his furious indignation.

This soothed the soul but further inflamed the ankle. He called up the manager of the hotel and sent for the leading medical man in Geneva.   When he arrived he took care to acquaint him with his name and quality.   Dr. Bourdillot, professor of dermatology in the University of Geneva, made his examination, and shook a tactful head. With all consideration for the many admirable virtues of *la cure Sypher*, yet there were certain maladies of the skin for which he personally would not prescribe it.   For this, for that—he rattled off half a dozen of learned diseases— it might very well be efficacious.   Its effect would probably be benign in a case of elephantiasis.   But in a case of abrasion of the cuticle, where there was a large surface of raw flesh laid bare, perhaps a simpler treatment might be more desirable.

His tone was exquisite, and he chose his language so that not a word could wound.   Sypher listened to him with a sinking heart.

"In your opinion then, doctor," said he, "it isn't a good thing for blistered heels?"

"You ask for my opinion," replied the professor of dermatology at the University of Geneva. "I give it you. No."

Sypher threw out a hand, desperately argumentative.

"But I know of a case in which it has proved efficacious. A Zouave of my acquaintance——"

Dr. Bourdillot smiled. "A Zouave? Just as nothing is sacred to a sapper, so is nothing hurtful to a Zouave. They have hides like hippopotamuses, those fellows. You could dip them in vitriol and they wouldn't feel it."

"So his heels recovered in spite of the Cure?" said Sypher, grimly.

"Evidently," said Dr. Bourdillot.

Sypher sat in his room for a couple of days, his leg on a chair, and looked at Mont Blanc, exquisite in its fairy splendor against the far, pale sky. It brought him no consolation. On the contrary it reminded him of Hannibal and other conquerors leading their footsore armies over the Alps. When he allowed a despondent fancy to wander uncontrolled, he saw great multitudes of men staggering shoeless along with feet and ankles inflamed to the color of tomatoes. Then he pulled himself together and set his teeth. Dennymede came to visit him and heard with dismay the verdict of science, which crushed his hope of a high position in the new Army Contract Department. But Sypher reassured him as to his material welfare by increasing his commission on foreign sales; whereupon he began to take a practical view of the situation.

"We can't expect a patent medicine, sir, to do everything."

"I quite agree with you," said Sypher. "It can't make two legs grow where one grew before, but it ought to cure blisters on the heel. Apparently it won't. So we are where we were before I met Monsieur Hégisippe Cruchot. The only thing is that we mustn't now lead people to suppose that it's good for blisters."

"They must take their chance," said Dennymede. He was a sharp, black-haired young man, with a worried brow and a bilious complexion. The soothing of the human race with Sypher's Balm of Gilead mattered nothing to him. His atrabiliar temperament rendered his attitude towards humanity rather misanthropic than otherwise. "Indeed," he continued, "I don't see why you shouldn't try for the army contracts without referring specifically to sore feet."

"*Caveat emptor*," said Sypher.

"I beg your pardon?" said Dennymede, who had no Latinity.

"It means, let the buyer beware; it's up to the buyer to see what stuff he's buying."

"Naturally. It's the first principle of business."

Sypher turned his swift clear glance on him and banged the window-ledge with his hand.

"It's the first principle of damned knavery and thieving," he cried, "and if I thought anyone ran my business on it, they'd go out of my employ at once! It's at the root of all the corruption that exists in modern trade. It salves the conscience of the psalm-singing grocer who puts ground beans into his coffee. It's a damnable principle."

He thumped the window-ledge again, very angry. The traveler hedged.

"Of course it's immoral to tell lies and say a thing is what it isn't. But on the other hand no one could run a patent medicine on the lines of warning the public as to what it isn't good for. You say on the wrapper it will cure gout and rheumatism. If a woman buys a bottle and gives it to her child who has got scarlet fever, and the child dies from it, it's her lookout and not yours. When a firm does issue a warning such as 'Won't Wash Clothes,' it's a business proceeding for the firm's own protection."

"Well, we'll issue a warning, 'Won't Cure Blisters,'" said Sypher. "I advertise myself as the Friend of Humanity. I am, according to my lights. If I let poor fellows on the march reduce their feet to this condition I should be the scourge of mankind like"—he snapped his fingers trying to recall the name—"like Atlas—no it wasn't Atlas, but no matter. Not a box of the Cure has been sold without the guarantee stamp of my soul's conviction on it."

"The Jebusa Jones people aren't so conscientious," said Dennymede. "I bought a pot of their stuff this morning. They've got a new wrapper. See." He unfolded a piece of paper and pointed out the place to his chief. "They have a special paragraph in large print: 'Gives instant relief to blistered feet. Every mountaineer should carry it in his gripsack.'"

"They're the enemies of God and man," said Sypher, "and sooner than copy their methods I would close down the factory and never sell another box as long as I lived."

"It's a thousand pities, sir, anyhow," said Dennymede, trying to work back diplomatically, "that the army contract scheme has to be thrown overboard."

"Yes, it's a nuisance," said Sypher.

When he had dismissed the traveler he laughed grimly. "A nuisance!"

The word was a grotesque anticlimax.

He sat for a long while with his hands blinding his eyes, trying to realize what the abandonment of the scheme meant to him.   He was a man who faced his responsibilities squarely.   For the first time in his life he had tried the Cure seriously on himself—chance never having given him cause before—and it had failed.   He had heard the Cure which he regarded as a divine unction termed a pestilential quackery; the words burned red-hot in his brain.   He had heard it depreciated, with charming tact and courtesy, by a great authority on diseases of the skin.   One short word, "no," had wiped out of existence his Napoleonic scheme for the Armies of the World—for putting them on a sound footing.   He smiled bitterly as the incongruous jest passed through his mind.

He had been fighting for months, and losing ground; but this was the first absolute check that his faith had received. He staggered under it, half wonderingly, like a man who has been hit by an unseen hand and looks around to see whence the blow came.   Why should it come now?   He looked back along the years.   Not a breath of disparagement had touched the Cure's fair repute.   His files in London were full of testimonials honorably acquired.   Some of these, from lowly folk, were touching in their simple gratitude.   It is true that his manager suggested that the authors had sent them in the hope of gain and of seeing their photographs in the halfpenny papers.   But his manager, Shuttleworth, was a notorious and dismal cynic who believed in nothing save the commercial value of the Cure. Letters had come with coroneted flaps to the envelopes. The writers certainly hoped neither for gain nor for odd notoriety.   He had never paid a fee for a testimonial throughout his career; every one that he printed was genuine and unsolicited. He had been hailed as the Friend of Humanity by all sorts and conditions of men. Why suddenly should he be branded as a dealer in pestilence?

His thought wandered back to the beginning of things. He saw himself in the chemist's shop in Bury Saint Edmunds—a little shop in a little town, too small, he felt, for the great unknown something within him that was craving for expansion. The dull making up of prescriptions, the selling of tooth powder and babies' feeding bottles—the deadly mechanical routine—he remembered the daily revolt against it all. He remembered his discovery of the old herbalists; his delight in their quaint language; the remedies so extraordinary and yet so simple; his first idea of combining these with the orthodox drugs of the British Pharmacopœia; his experiments; his talks with an aged man who kept a dingy little shop of herbs on the outskirts of the town, also called a pestilential fellow by the medical faculty of the district, but a learned ancient all the same, who knew the qualities of every herb that grew, and with some reeking mess of pulp was said to have cured an old woman's malignant ulcer given up as incurable by the faculty. He remembered the night when the old man, grateful for the lad's interest in his learning, gave him under vows of secrecy the recipe of this healing emulsion, which was to become the basis of Sypher's Cure. In those days his loneliness was cheered by a bulldog, an ugly, faithful beast whom he called Barabbas—he sighed to think how many Barabbases had lived and died since then—and who, contracting mange, became the *corpus vile* of many experiments—first with the old man's emulsion, then with the emulsion mixed with other drugs, all bound together in pure animal fat, until at last he found a mixture which to his joy made the sores heal and the skin harden and the hair sprout and Barabbas grow sleek as a swell mobsman in affluent circumstances. Then one day came His Grace of Suffolk into the shop with a story of a pet of the Duchess's stricken with the same disease. Sypher modestly narrated his own experience and gave the mighty man a box of the new ointment. A fortnight afterwards he returned. Not only had it cured the dog, but it must have charmed away the eczema on his ducal hands. Full of a wild surmise he tried it next on his landlady's child, who had a sore on its legs, and lo! the sore healed. It was then that the Divine Revelation came to him; it was then that he passed his vigil, as he had told Zora, and consecrated himself and his Cure to the service of humanity.

The steps, the struggles, the purchase of the chemist's business, the early exploitation of the Cure, its gradual renown in the district, the first whisperings of its fame abroad, thanks to His Grace of Suffolk, the early advertising, the gradual growth, the sale of the chemist's business, the establishment of "Sypher's Cure" as a special business in the town, the transference to London, the burst into world-wide fame—all the memories came back to him, as he sat by the window of the Hôtel de l'Europe and blinded his face with his hands.

He dashed them away, at last, with a passionate gesture.

"It can't be! It can't be!" he cried aloud, as many another man has cried in the righteous rebellion of his heart against the ironical decrees of the high gods whom his simple nature has never suspected of their eternal and inscrutable irony.

CHAPTER XV

If you travel on the highroad which skirts the cliff-bound coast of Normandy you may come to a board bearing the legend "Hottetôt-sur-Mer" and a hand pointing down a narrow gorge. If you follow the direction and descend for half a mile you come to a couple of villas, a humble café, some fishermen's cottages, one of which is also a general shop and a *débit de tabac*, a view of a triangle of sea, and eventually to a patch of shingly beach between two great bastions of cliffs. The beach itself contains a diminutive jetty, a tiny fleet of fishing smacks, some nets, three bathing machines joined together by ropes on which hang a few towels and bathing costumes, a dog, a child or so with spade and bucket, two English maiden ladies writing picture post-cards, a Frenchman in black, reading a Rouen newspaper under a gray umbrella, his wife and daughter, and a stall of mussels presided over by an old woman with skin like seaweed. Just above the beach, on one side of the road leading up the gorge, is a miniature barn with a red cupola, which is the Casino, and, on the other, a long, narrow, blue-washed building with the words written in great black letters across the façade, "Hôtel de la Plage."

As soon as Emmy could travel, she implored Septimus to find her a quiet spot by the sea whither the fashionable do not resort. Septimus naturally consulted Hégisippe Cruchot. Hégisippe asked for time to consult his comrades. He returned with news of an ideal spot. It was a village in the Pyrenees about six thousand feet up in the air and forty miles from a railway station. They could shoot bears all day long. When Emmy explained that a village on the top of the Pyrenees was not by the seaside, and that neither she nor his aunt, Madame Bolivard, took any interest in the destruction of bears, he retired somewhat crestfallen and went with his difficulties to Angélique, the young lady in the wine shop in the Rue des Francs-Bouchers. Angélique informed him that a brave sailor on leave from his torpedo boat was in the habit of visiting the wine shop every evening. He ought to know something of the sea. A meeting was arranged by Angélique between Hégisippe, Septimus and the brave sailor, much to Emmy's skeptical amusement; and the brave sailor, after absorbing prodigious quantities of alcohol and reviewing all the places on the earth's coastline from Yokohama to Paris-Plage, declared that the veritable Eden by the Sea was none other than his native village of Hottetôt-sur-Mer. He made a plan of it on the table, two square packets of tobacco representing the cliffs, a pipe stem the road leading up the gorge, some tobacco dust the beach, and some coffee slops applied with the finger the English Channel.

Septimus came back to Emmy. "I have found the place. It is Hottetôt-sur-Mer. It has one hotel. You can catch shrimps, and its mussels are famous all over the world."

After consultation of a guide to Normandy, on which Emmy's prudence insisted, they found the brave sailor's facts mainly correct, and decided on Hottetôt-sur-Mer.

"I will take you there, see that you are comfortably settled, and then come back to Paris," said Septimus. "You'll be quite happy with Madame Bolivard, won't you?"

"Of course," said Emmy, looking away from him. "What are you going to do in Paris, all by yourself?"

"Guns," he replied. Then he added reflectively: "I also don't see how I can get out of the Hôtel Godet. I've been there some time, and I don't know how much to give the servants in tips. The only thing is to stay on."

Emmy sighed, just a bit wistfully, and made no attempt to prove the futility of his last argument. The wonderfully sweet of life had come to her of late mingled with the unutterably bitter. She was in the state of being when a woman accepts, without question. Septimus then went to the St. Lazare station to make arrangements and discovered an official who knew a surprising amount about railway traveling and the means of bringing a family from domicile to station. He entered Septimus's requirements in a book and assured him that at the appointed hour an omnibus would be waiting outside the house in the Boulevard Raspail. Septimus thought him a person of marvelous intellect and gave him five francs.

So the quaint quartette started in comfort: Septimus and Emmy and Madame Bolivard and the little lump of mortality which the Frenchwoman carried in her great motherly arms. Madame Bolivard, who had not been out of Paris for twenty years, needed all her maternal instincts to subdue her excitement at the prospect of seeing the open country and the sea. In the railway carriage she pointed out cattle to the unconscious infant with the tremulous quiver of the traveler who espies a herd of hippogriffin.

"Is it corn that, Monsieur? *Mon Dieu*, it is beautiful. Regard then the corn, my cherished one."

But the cherished one cared not for corn or cattle. He preferred to fix his cold eyes on Septimus, as if wondering what he was doing in that galley. Now and again Septimus would bend forward and, with a vague notion of the way to convey one's polite intentions to babies, would prod him gingerly in the cheek and utter an insane noise and then surreptitiously wipe his finger on his trousers. When his mother took him she had little spasms of tenderness during which she pressed him tightly to her bosom and looked frightened. The child was precious to her. She had paid a higher price than most women, and that perhaps enhanced its value.

At Fécamp a rusty ramshackle diligence awaited them. Their luggage, together with hen-coops, baskets, bundles, packing-cases, were piled on top in an amorphous heap. They took their places inside together with an old priest and a peasant woman in a great flapping cap. The old priest absorbed snuff in great quantities and used a red handkerchief. The closed windows of the vehicle rattled, it was very hot, and the antiquated cushions smelled abominably. Emmy, tired of the railway journey and suffocated by the heat, felt inclined to cry. This was her first step into her newly conditioned world, and her heart sank. She regretted her comfortable rooms in Paris and the conditions of existence there of which Septimus was an integral part. She had got used to them, to his forced association with the intimate details of her life, to his bending over the child like a grotesque fairy godfather and making astonishing suggestions for its upbringing. She had regarded him less as a stranger to be treated with feminine reserve than the doctor. Now it was different. She was about to take up her own life again, with new responsibilities, and the dearly loved creature whom she had bullied and laughed at and leaned on would go away to take up his own queer way of life, and the relations between them could not possibly be the same again. The diligence was taking her on the last stage of her journey towards the new conditions, and it jolted and bumped and smelled and took an interminable time.

"I'm sure," said she woefully, "there's no such place as Hottetôt-sur-Mer, and we are going on forever to find it."

Presently Septimus pointed triumphantly through the window.

"There it is!"

"Where?" cried Emmy, for not a house was in sight. Then she saw the board.

The old diligence turned and creaked and swung and pitched down the gorge. When they descended at the Hôtel de la Plage, the setting sun blazed on their faces across the sea and shed its golden enchantment over the little pebbly beach. At that hour the only living thing on it was the dog, and he was asleep. It was a spot certainly to which the fashionable did not resort.

"It will be good for baby."

"And for you."

She shrugged her shoulders. "What is good for one is not always—" She paused, feeling ungrateful. Then she added, "It's the best place you could have brought us to."

After dinner they sat on the beach and leaned against a fishing-boat. It was full moon. The northern cliff cast its huge shadow out to sea and half way across the beach. A knot of fisher folk sat full in the moonlight on the jetty and sang a song with a mournful refrain. Behind them in the square of yellow light of the salon window could be seen the figures of the two English maiden ladies apparently still addressing picture post-cards. The luminous picture stood out sharp against the dark mass of the hotel. Beyond the shadow of the cliff the sea lay like a silver mirror in the windless air. A tiny border of surf broke on the pebbles. Emmy drew a long breath and asked Septimus if he smelled the seaweed. The dog came and sniffed at their boots; then from the excellent leather judging them to be persons above his social station, he turned humbly away. Septimus called him, made friends with him—he was a smooth yellow dog of no account—and eventually he curled himself up between them and went to sleep. Septimus smoked his pipe. Emmy played with the ear of the dog and looked out to sea. It was very peaceful. After a while she sighed.

"I suppose this must be our last evening together."

"I suppose it must," said Septimus.

"Are you quite sure you can afford all the money you're leaving with me?"

"Of course. It comes out of the bank."

"I know that, you stupid," she laughed. "Where else could it come from unless you kept it in a stocking? But the bank isn't an unlimited gold-mine from which you can draw out as many handfuls as you want."

Septimus knocked the ashes out of his pipe.

"People don't get sovereigns out of gold-mines. I wish they did. They extract a bit of gold about the size of this pebble out of a ton of quartz. I once bought shares in a gold-mine and there wasn't any gold in it at all. I always used to be buying things like that. People sold them to me. I was like Moses."

"Moses?"

"Oh, not *that* Moses. He could get anything out of anything. He got water out of a rock. I mean the son of the Vicar of Wakefield, who bought the green spectacles."

"Oh," said Emmy, who after the way of her generation had never heard of him.

"I don't do it—let people sell me things—any more, now," he said gravely. "I seem to have got wise. Perhaps it has come through having had to look after you. I see things much clearer."

He filled and lit another pipe and began to talk about Orion just visible over the shoulder of the cliff. Emmy, whose interests were for the moment terrestrial, interrupted him:

"There's one thing I want you to see clearly, my dear, and that is that I owe you a frightful lot of money. But I'm sure to get something to do when I'm back in London and then I can repay you by instalments. Remember, I'm not going to rest until I pay you back."

"I sha'n't rest if you do," said Septimus, nervously. "Please don't talk of it. It hurts me. I've done little enough in the world, God knows. Give me this chance of —the Buddhists call it 'acquiring merit.'"

This was not a new argument between them. Emmy had a small income under her father's will, and the prospect of earning a modest salary on the stage. She reckoned that she would have sufficient to provide for herself and the child. Hitherto Septimus had been her banker. Neither of them had any notion of the value of money, and Septimus had a child's faith in the magic of the drawn check. He would as soon have thought of measuring the portion of whisky he poured out for a guest as of counting the money he advanced to Emmy.

She took up his last words, and speaking in a low tone, as a woman does when her pride has gone from her, she said:

"Haven't you acquired enough merit already, my dear?

Don't you see the impossibility of my going on accepting things from you? You seem to take it for granted that you're to provide for me and the child for the rest of our lives. I've been a bad, unprincipled fool of a girl, I know—yes, rotten bad; there are thousands like me in London——"

Septimus rose to his feet.

"Oh, don't, Emmy, don't! I can't stand it."

She rose too and put her hands on his shoulders.

"You must let me speak to-night—our last night before we part. It isn't generous of you not to listen."

The yellow dog, disturbed in his slumbers, shook himself, and regarding them with an air of humble sympathy turned and walked away discreetly into the shadow. The fisher folk on the jetty still sang their mournful chorus.

"Sit down again."

Septimus yielded. "But why give yourself pain?" he asked gently.

"To ease my heart. The knife does good. Yes, I know I've been worthless. But I'm not as bad as that. Don't you see how horrible the idea is to me? I must pay you back the money—and of course not come on you for any more. You've done too much for me already. It sometimes stuns me to think of it. It was only because I was in hell and mad—and grasped at the hand you held out to me. I suppose I've done you the biggest wrong a woman can do a man. Now I've come to my senses, I shudder at what I've done."

"Why? Why?" said Septimus, growing miserably unhappy.

"How can you ever marry, unless we go through the vulgarity of a collusive divorce?"

"My dear girl," said he, "what woman would ever marry a preposterous lunatic like me?"

"There's not a woman living who ought not to have gone down on her bended knees if she had married you."

"I should never have married," said he, laying his hand for a moment reassuringly on hers.

"Who knows?" She gave a slight laugh. "Zora is only a woman like the rest of us."

"Why talk of Zora?" he said quickly. "What has she to do with it?"

"Everything. You don't suppose I don't know," she replied in a low voice. "It was for her sake and not for mine."

He was about to speak when she put out her hand and covered his mouth.

"Let me talk for a little."

She took up her parable again and spoke very gently, very sensibly. The moonlight peacefulness was in her heart. It softened the tone of her voice and reflected itself in unfamiliar speech.

"I seem to have grown twenty years older," she said.

She desired on that night to make her gratitude clear to him, to ask his pardon for past offenses. She had been like a hunted animal; sometimes she had licked his hand and sometimes she had scratched it. She had not been quite responsible. Sometimes she had tried to send him away, for his own sake. For herself, she had been terrified at the thought of losing him.

"Another man might have done what you did, out of chivalry; but no other man but you would not have despised the woman. I deserved it; but I knew you didn't despise me. You have been just the same to me all through as you were in the early days. It braced me up and helped me to keep some sort of self-respect. That was the chief reason why I could not let you go. Now all is over. I am quite sane and as happy as I ever shall be. After to-night it stands to reason we must each lead our separate lives. You can't do anything more for me, and God knows, poor dear, I can't do anything for you. So I want to thank you."

She put her arm around his shoulder and kissed his cheek.

Septimus flushed. Her lips were soft and her breath was sweet. No woman save his mother had ever kissed him. He turned and took her hands.

"Let me accept that in full payment for everything. You want me to go away happy, don't you?"

"My dear," she said, with a little catch in her voice, "if there was anything in the world I could do to make you happy, short of throwing baby to a tiger, I would do it."

Septimus took off his cap and brought his hair to its normal perpendicularity. Emmy laughed.

"Dear me! What are you going to say?"

Septimus reflected for a moment.

"If I dine off a bloater in a soup-plate in the drawing-room, or if my bed isn't made at six o'clock in the evening, and my house is a cross between a pigsty and an ironmonger's shop, nobody minds. It is only Septimus Dix's extraordinary habits. But if the woman who is my wife in the eyes of the world——"

"Yes, yes, I see," she said hurriedly. "I hadn't looked at it in that light."

"The boy is going to Cambridge," he murmured. "Then I should like him to go into Parliament. There are deuced

"MY DEAR, IF THERE WAS ANYTHING IN THE WORLD I COULD DO TO
MAKE YOU HAPPY, SHORT OF THROWING BABY TO A TIGER,
I WOULD DO IT."

(page 202)

clever fellows in Parliament. I met one in Venice two or three years ago. He knew an awful lot of things. We spent an evening together on the Grand Canal and he talked all the time most interestingly on the drainage system of Barrow-in-Furness. I wonder how fellows get to know about drains."

Emmy said: "Would it make you happy?"

From her tone he gathered that she referred to the subject of contention between them and not to his thirst for sanitary information.

"Of course it would."

"But how shall I ever repay you?"

"Perhaps once a year," he said. "You can settle up in full, as you did just now."

There was a long silence and then Emmy remarked that it was a heavenly night.

CHAPTER XVI

In the course of time Sypher returned to London to fight a losing battle against the Powers of Darkness and derive whatever inspiration he could from Zora's letters. He also called dutifully at "The Nook" during his week-end visits to Penton Court, where he found restfulness in the atmosphere of lavender. Mrs. Oldrieve continued to regard him as a most superior person. Cousin Jane, as became a gentlewoman of breeding, received him with courtesy—but a courtesy marked by that shade of reserve which is due from a lady of quality to the grandfatherless. If she had not striven against the unregeneracy of mortal flesh she would have disapproved of him offhand because she disapproved of Zora; but she was a conscientious woman, and took great pride in overcoming prejudices. She also collected pewter, the history of which Sypher, during his years of self-education, had once studied, in the confused notion that it was culture. All knowledge is good; from the theory of quaternions to the way to cut a ham-frill. It is sure to come in useful, somehow. An authority on Central African dialects has been known to find them invaluable in altercations with cabmen, and a converted burglar has, before now, become an admirable house-agent. What Sypher, therefore, had considered merely learned lumber in his head cemented his friendship with Cousin Jane— or rather, to speak by the book, soldered it with pewter. As for the Cure, however, she did not believe in it, and told him so, roundly. She had been brought up to believe in doctors, the Catechism, the House of Lords, the inequality of the sexes, and the Oldrieve family, and in that faith she would live and die. Sypher bore her no malice. She did not call the Cure pestilential quackery. He was beginning not to despise the day of small things.

"It may be very good in its way," she said, "just as Liberalism and Darwinism and eating in restaurants may be good things. But they are not for me."

Cousin Jane's conversation provided him with much innocent entertainment. Mrs. Oldrieve was content to talk about the weather, and what Zora and Emmy used to like to eat when they were little girls: subjects interesting in themselves but not conducive to discussion. Cousin Jane was nothing if not argumentative. She held views, expounded them, and maintained them. Nothing short of a declaration from Jehovah bursting in glory through the sky could have convinced her of error. Even then she would have been annoyed. She profoundly disapproved of Emmy's marriage to Septimus, whom she characterized as a doddering idiot. Sypher defended his friend warmly. He also defended Wiggleswick at whose ways and habits the good lady expressed unrestrained indignation. She could not have spoken more disrespectfully of Antichrist.

"You mark my words," she said, "he'll murder them both in their sleep."

Concerning Zora, too, she was emphatic.

"I am not one of those who think every woman ought to get married; but if she can't conduct herself decently without a husband, she ought to have one."

"But surely Mrs. Middlemist's conduct is irreproachable," said Sypher.

"Irreproachable? Do you think trapesing about alone all over the earth—mixing with all sorts of people she doesn't know from Adam, and going goodness knows where and doing goodness knows what, and idling her life away, never putting a darn in her stockings even—is irreproachable conduct on the part of a young woman of Zora's birth and appearance? The way she dresses must attract attention, wherever she goes. It's supposed to be 'stylish' nowadays. In my time it was immodest. When a young woman was forced to journey alone she made herself as inconspicuous as possible. Zora ought to have a husband to look after her. Then she could do as she liked—or as he liked, which would be much the best thing for her."

"I happen to be in Mrs. Middlemist's confidence," said Sypher. "She has told me many times that she would never marry again. Her marriage——"

"Stuff and rubbish!" cried Cousin Jane. "You wait until the man comes along who has made up his mind to marry her. It must be a big strong man who won't stand any nonsense and will take her by the shoulders and shake her. She'll marry him fast enough. We'll see what happens to her in California."

"I hope she won't marry one of those dreadful creatures with lassos," said Mrs. Oldrieve, whose hazy ideas of California were based on hazier memories of Buffalo Bill's Wild West Show which she had seen many years ago in London.

"I hope Mrs. Middlemist won't marry at all," said Sypher, in a tone of alarm.

"Why?" asked Cousin Jane.

She shot the question at him with almost a snarl. Sypher paused for a moment or two before replying.

"I should lose a friend," said he.

"Humph!" said Cousin Jane.

If the late Rev. Laurence Sterne had known Cousin Jane, "Tristram Shandy" would have been the richer by a chapter on "Humphs." He would have analyzed this particular one with a minute delicacy beyond the powers of Clem Sypher through whose head rang the echo of the irritating vocable for some time afterwards. It meant something. It meant something uncomfortable. It was directly leveled at himself and yet it seemed to sum up her previous disparaging remarks about Zora. "What the dickens *did* she mean by it?" he asked himself.

He came down to Nunsmere every week now, having given up his establishment at Kilburn Priory and sold the house—"The Kurhaus," as he had named it in his pride. A set of bachelor's chambers in St. James's sheltered him during his working days in London. He had also sold his motor-car; for retrenchment in personal expenses had become necessary, and the purchase-money of house and car were needed for the war of advertising which he was waging against his rivals. These were days black with anxiety and haunting doubt, illuminated now and then by Zora, who wrote gracious letters of encouragement. He carried them about with him like talismans.

Sometimes he could not realize that the great business he had created could be on the brink of failure. The routine went on as usual. At the works at Bermondsey the same activity apparently prevailed as when the Cure had reached the hey-day of its fortune some five years before. In the sweet-smelling laboratory gleaming with white tiles and copper retorts, the white-aproned workmen sorted and weighed and treated according to the secret recipe the bundles of herbs that came in every day and were stacked in pigeon-holes along the walls. In the boiling-sheds, not so sweet-smelling, the great vats of fat bubbled and ran, giving out to the cooling-troughs the refined white cream of which the precious ointment was made. Beyond there was another laboratory vast and clean and busy, where the healing ichor of the herbs was mixed with the drugs and the cream. Then came the work-rooms where rows of girls filled the celluloid boxes, one dabbing in the well-judged quantity, another cutting it off clean to the level of the top with a swift stroke of the spatula, another fitting on the lid, and so on, in endless but fascinating monotony until the last girl placed on the trolley by her side, waiting to carry it to the packing-shed, the finished packet of Sypher's Cure as it would be delivered to the world. Then there were the packing-sheds full of deal cases for despatching the Cure to the four quarters of the globe, some empty, some being filled, others stacked in readiness for the carriers: a Babel of sounds, of hammering clamps, of creaking barrows, of horses by the open doors rattling their heavy harness and trampling the flagstones with their heavy hoofs; a ceaseless rushing of brawny men in sackcloth aprons, of dusty men with stumps of pencils and note-books and crumpled invoices, counting and checking and reporting to other men in narrow glass offices against the wall. Outside stood the great wagons laden with the white deal boxes bound with iron hoops and bearing in vermilion letters the inscription of Sypher's Cure.

Every detail of this complicated hive was as familiar to him as his kitchen was to his cook. He had planned it all, organized it all. Every action of every human creature in the place from the skilled pharmaceutist responsible for the preparation of the ointment to the grimy boy who did odd jobs about the sheds had been pre-conceived by him, had had its mainspring in his brain. Apart from idealistic aspirations concerned with the Cure itself, the perfecting of this machinery of human activity had been a matter of absorbing interest, its perfection a subject of honorable pride.

He walked through the works day after day, noting the familiar sights and sounds, pausing here and there lovingly, as a man does in his garden to touch some cherished plant or to fill himself with the beauty of some rare flower. The place was inexpressibly dear to him. That those furnaces should ever grow cold, that those vats should ever be empty, that those two magic words should cease to blaze on the wooden boxes, should fade from the sight of man, that those gates should ever be shut, seemed to transcend imagination. The factory had taken its rank with eternal, unchanging things, like the solar system and the Bank of England. Yet he knew only too well that there had been change in the unchanging and in his soul dwelt a sickening certainty that the eternal would be the transient. Gradually the staff had been reduced, the output lessened. Already two of the long tables once filled with girls stood forlornly empty.

His comfortably appointed office in Moorgate Street told the same story. Week after week the orders slackened and gradually the number of the clerks had shrunk. Gloom settled permanently on the manager's brow. He almost walked on tiptoe into Sypher's room and spoke to him in a hushed whisper, until rebuked for dismalness.

"If you look like that, Shuttleworth, I shall cry."

On another occasion Shuttleworth said:

14

"We are throwing money away on advertisements. The concern can't stand it."

Sypher turned, blue pencil in hand, from the wall where draft proofs of advertisements were pinned for his correction and master's touch. This was a part of the business that he loved. It appealed to the flamboyant in his nature. It particularly pleased him to see omnibuses pass by bearing the famous "Sypher's Cure," an enlargement of his own handwriting, in streaming letters of blood.

"We're going to double them," said he; and his air was that of the racing Mississippi captains of old days who in response to the expostulation of their engineers sent a little nigger boy to sit on the safety-valve.

The dismal manager turned up his eyes to heaven with the air of the family steward in Hogarth's "Mariage à la Mode." He had not his chief's Napoleonic mind; but he had a wife and a large family. Clem Sypher also thought of that—not only of Shuttleworth's wife and family, but also of the wives and families of the many men in his employ. It kept him awake at nights.

In the soothing air of Nunsmere, however, he slept, in long dead stretches, as a tired man sleeps, in spite of trains which screeched past the bottom of his lawn. Their furious unrest enhanced the peace of village things. He began to love the little backwater of the earth whose stillness calmed the fever of life. As soon as he stepped out on to the platform at Ripstead a cool hand seemed to touch his forehead, and charm away the cares that made his temples throb. At Nunsmere he gave himself up to the simplicities of the place. He took to strolling, like Septimus, about the common and made friends with the lame donkey. On Sunday mornings he went to church. He had first found himself there out of curiosity, for, though not an irreligious man, he was not given to pious practices; but afterwards he had gone on account of the restfulness of the rural service. His mind essentially reverend took it very seriously, just as it took seriously the works of a great poet which he could not understand or any alien form of human aspiration; even the parish notices and the publication of banns he received with earnest attention. His intensity of interest as he listened to the sermon sometimes flattered the mild vicar, and at other times—when thinness of argument pricked his conscience—alarmed him considerably. But Sypher would not have dared enter into theological disputation. He took the sermon as he took the hymns, in which he joined lustily. Cousin Jane, whom he invariably met with Mrs. Oldrieve after the service and escorted home, had no such scruples. She tore the vicar's theology into fragments and scattered them behind her as she walked, like a hare in a paper chase.

Said the Literary Man from London, who had strolled with them on one of these occasions:

"The good lady's one of those women who speak as if they had a relation who had married a high official in the Kingdom of Heaven and now and then gave them confidential information."

Sypher liked Rattenden because he could often put into a phrase his own unformulated ideas. He also belonged to a world to which he himself was a stranger, the world of books and plays and personalities and theories of art. Sypher thought that its denizens lived on a lofty plane.

"The atmosphere," said Rattenden, "is so rarified that the kettle refuses to boil properly. That is why we always have cold tea at literary gatherings. My dear fellow, it's a damned world. It talks all day and does nothing all night. The ragged Italian in front of the fresco in his village church or at the back of the gallery at the opera of his town knows more essentials of painting and music than any of us. It's a hollow sham of a world filled with empty words. I love it."

"Then why abuse it?" laughed Sypher.

"Because it's a wanton and the wanton angers you and fascinates you at the same time. You never know how to take her. You are aware she hasn't got a heart, but her lips are red. She is unreal. She holds views in defiance of common sense. Which is the nobler thing to do—to dig potatoes or paint a man digging potatoes? She swears to you that the digger is a clod of earth and the painter a handful of heaven. She is talking rot. You know it. Yet you believe her."

Sypher was not convinced by the airy paradoxician. He had a childish idea that painters and novelists and actors were superior beings. Rattenden found this Arcadian and cultivated Sypher's society. They took long walks together on Sunday afternoons.

"After all," said Rattenden, "I can speak freely. I am a pariah among my kind."

Sypher asked why.

"Because I don't play golf. In London it is impossible to be seriously regarded as a literary man unless you play golf."

He found Sypher a good listener. He loved to catch a theory of life, hold it in his hand like a struggling bird while he discoursed about it, and let it go free into the sunshine again. Sypher admired his nimbleness of mind.

"You juggle with ideas as the fellows on the stage do with gilt balls."

"It's a game I learned," said Rattenden. "It's very useful. It takes one's mind off the dull question of earning bread and butter for a wife and five children."

"I wish you'd teach it to me," said Sypher. "I've many wives and many children dependent on me for bread and butter!"

Rattenden was quick to note the tone of depression. He laughed kindly.

"Looking on is just as good. When you're worried in London why don't you look me up? My wife and I will play the game for you. She's an amusing body. Heaven knows how I should have got through without her. She also swears by Sypher's Cure.

So they became friends. Sypher, since the blistered heel episode, had lost his fearless way of trumpeting the Cure far and wide, having a nervous dread of seeing the p and q of the hateful words form themselves on the lips of a companion. He became subdued, and spoke only of travel and men and things, of anything but the Cure. He preferred to listen and, as Rattenden preferred to talk, he found conversation a simple matter. Rattenden was an amusing anecdotist and had amassed a prodigious amount of raw material for his craft. To the collector, by some unknown law of attraction, come the objects which he collects. Everywhere he goes he finds them to his hand, as Septimus's friend found the Toby jugs. Wherever Rattenden turned, a bit of gossip met his ear. Very few things, therefore, happened in literary and theatrical London which did not come inevitably to his knowledge. He could have wrecked many homes and pricked many reputations. As a man of the world, however, he used his knowledge with discretion, and as an artist in anecdote he selected fastidiously. He seldom retailed a bit of gossip for its own sake; when he did so he had a purpose.

One evening they dined together at Sypher's club, a great semi-political institution with many thousand members. He had secured, however, a quiet table in a corner of the dining-room which was adorned with full-length portraits of self-conscious statesmen. Sypher unfolded his napkin with an air of satisfaction.

"I've had good news to-day. Mrs. Middlemist is on her way home."

"You have the privilege of her friendship," said Rattenden. "You're to be envied. *O fortunate nimium.*"

He preserved some of the Oxford tradition in tone and manner. He had brown hair turning gray, a drooping mustache and wore pince-nez secured by a broad black cord. Being very short-sighted his eyes seen through the thick lenses were almost expressionless.

"Zora Middlemist," said he, squeezing lemon over his oysters, "is a grand and splendid creature whom I admire vastly. As I never lose an opportunity of telling her that she is doing nothing with her grand and splendid qualities, I suffer under the ban of her displeasure."

"What do you think she ought to do with them?" asked Sypher.

"It's a difficult and delicate matter to discuss a woman with another man; especially—" he waved a significant hand. "But I, in my little way, have written a novel or two—studies of women. I speak therefore as an expert. Now, just as a painter can't correctly draw the draped figure unless he has an anatomical knowledge of the limbs beneath, so is a novelist unable to present the character of a woman with sincerity and verisimilitude unless he has taken into account all the hidden physiological workings of that woman's nature. He must be familiar with the workings of the sex principle within her, although he need not show them in his work, any more than the painter shows the anatomy. Analyzing thus the imaginary woman, one forms a habit of analyzing the real woman in whom one takes an interest—or rather one does it unconsciously." He paused. "I told you it was rather delicate. You see what I'm trying to get at? Zora Middlemist is driven round the earth like Io by the gadfly of her temperament. She's seeking the Beauty or Meaning or Fulfilment, or whatever she chooses to call it, of Life. What she's really looking for is Love."

"I don't believe it," said Sypher.

Rattenden shrugged his shoulders. "It's true all the same. But in her case it's the great love—the big thing for the big man—the gorgeous tropical sunshine in which all the splendor of her can develop. No little man will move her. She draws them all round her—that type has an irresistible atmosphere—but she passes them by with her magnificent head in the air. She is looking all the time for the big man. The pathetic comedy of it is that she is as innocent and as unconscious of the object of her search as the flower that opens its heart to the bee bearing the pollen on its wings. I'm not infallible as a general rule. In this case I am."

He hastened to consume his soup which had got cold during his harangue.

"You've mixed much with women and studied them," said Sypher. "I haven't. I was engaged to a girl once, but it was a tepid affair. She broke it off because it was much more vital to me to work in my laboratory than to hold her hand in her mother's parlor. No doubt she was right. This was in the early days when I was experimenting with the Cure. Since then I've been a man of one idea. It has absorbed all my soul and energies, so that I've had none to spare for women. Here and there, of course——"

"I know. The trifling things. They are part of the banquet of life. One eats and forgets."

Sypher glanced at him and nodded his appreciation of the Literary Man's neat way of putting things. But he did not reply. He ate his fish in silence, hardly tasting it, his mind far away following Zora Middlemist across the seas. A horrible, jealous hatred of the big man for whom she sought sprang up in his heart. His pink face flushed red.

"This *sole bonne femme* is excellent," said Rattenden.

Sypher started in confusion, and praised the chef, and talked gastronomy while his thoughts were with Zora. He remembered the confession of Septimus Dix in Paris. Septimus had been caught in the irresistible atmosphere. He loved her, but he was one of the little men and she had passed him by with her magnificent head in the air. The gastronomic talk languished. Presently Rattenden said:

"One of the feminine phenomena that has puzzled me most of late has been the marriage of her sister to Septimus Dix."

Sypher laid down his knife and fork.

"How extraordinary that you should mention it! He was in my mind as you spoke."

"I was thinking of the sister," said Rattenden. "She has Mrs. Middlemist's temperament without her force of character—the sex without the splendor. I heard a very curious thing about her only yesterday."

"What was it?"

"It was one of those things that are not told."

"Tell me," said Sypher, earnestly. "I have reasons for asking. I am convinced there are circumstances of which neither Mrs. Dix's mother nor sister know anything. I'm a loyal man. You may trust me."

"Very well," said Rattenden. "Have you ever heard of a man called Mordaunt Prince? Yes—a well-known actor —about the biggest blackguard that disgraces the stage. He was leading man at the theater where she last played. They were doing 'The Widow of Ware.' They were about a great deal together. It was common gossip at the time."

"Gossip is notoriously uncharitable," said Sypher.

"If charity covers a multitude of sins, uncharitableness has the advantage of uncovering them. The *pudor britannicus*, however, is responsible for uncovering the one I am going to tell you of. About two or three months before the marriage, Emmy Oldrieve and Mordaunt Prince were staying together at an hotel in Tunbridge Wells. There was no mistake about it. There they were. They had a motor with them. A week before the Dix marriage was announced Mordaunt Prince married a Mrs. Morris—old Sol Morris, the money-lender's widow."

Sypher stared at him.

"It's one of the least amazing of human phenomena," said Rattenden, cynically. "I'm only puzzled at Calypso being so soon able to console herself for the departure of Ulysses, and taking up with such a dreamy-headed shadow of a man as our friend Dix. The end of the Mordaunt Prince story is that he soon grew too much for the widow, who has pensioned him off, and now he is drinking himself to death in Naples."

"Emmy Oldrieve! Good God, is it possible?" cried Sypher, absently pushing aside the dish the waiter handed him.

Rattenden carefully helped himself to partridge and orange salad.

"It's not only possible, but unquestionable fact. You see," he added complacently, "nothing can happen without its coming sooner or later to me. My informant was staying at the hotel all the time. You will allow me to vouch absolutely for her veracity."

Sypher did not speak for some moments. The large dining-room with its portraits of self-conscious statesmen faded away and became a little street in Paris, one side in shade and the other baking in the sun; and at a little iron table sat a brown and indiscreet Zouave and Septimus Dix, pale, indecisive, with a wistful appeal in his washed-out blue eyes. Suddenly he regained consciousness, and, more for the sake of covering his loss of self-possession than for that of eating, he recalled the waiter and put some partridge on his plate. Then he looked across the table at his guest and said very sternly:

"I look to you to prevent this story going any further."

"I've already made it my duty to do so," said Rattenden.

Sypher helped his guest to wine.

"I hope you like this Roederer," said he. "It's the only exquisite wine in the club, and unfortunately there are not more than a few bottles left. I had seven dozen of the same *cuvée* in my cellar at Priory Park—if anything, in better condition. I had to sell it with the rest of the things when I gave up the house. It went to my heart. Champagne is the only wine I understand. There was a time when it stood as a symbol to me of the unattainable. Now that I can drink it when I will, I know that all the laws of philosophy forbid its having any attraction for me. Thank heaven I'm not dyspeptic enough in soul to be a philosopher and I'm grateful for my aspirations. I cultivated my taste for champagne out of sheer gratitude."

"Any wise man," said Rattenden, "can realize his dreams. It takes something much higher than wisdom to enjoy the realization."

"What is that?"

"The heart of a child," said Rattenden. He smiled in his inscrutable way behind his thick lenses, and sipped his champagne. "Truly a delicious wine," said he.

Sypher said good-by to his guest on the steps of the club, and walked home to his new chambers in St. James's deep in thought. For the first time since his acquaintance with Rattenden, he was glad to part from him. He had a great need of solitude. It came to him almost as a shock to realize that things were happening in the world round about him quite as heroic, in the eyes of the High Gods, as the battle between Sypher's Cure and Jebusa Jones's Cuticle Remedy. The curtain of life had been lifted, and a flash of its inner mysteries had been revealed. His eyes still were dazed. But he had received the gift of vision. He had seen beyond doubt or question the heart of Septimus Dix. He knew what he had done, why he had done it.

Zora Middlemist had passed Septimus by with her magnificent head in the air. But he was not one of the little men.

"By God, he is not!" he cried aloud, and the cry came from his depths.

Zora Middlemist had passed him, Clem Sypher, by with her magnificent head in the air.

He let himself into his chambers; they struck him as being chill and lonely, the casual, uncared-for hiding-place of one of the little men. He stirred the fire, almost afraid to disturb the cold silence by the rattle of the poker against the bars of the grate. His slippers were set in readiness on the hearth-rug, and the machine who valeted him had fitted them with boot-trees. He put them on, and unlocking his desk, took out the letter which he had received that morning from Zora.

"For you," she wrote, "I want victory all along the line —the apotheosis of Sypher's Cure on Earth. For myself, I don't know what I want. I wish you would tell me."

Clem Sypher sat in an arm-chair and looked into the fire until it went out. For the first time in his life he did not know what he wanted.

CHAPTER XVII

THE days that followed were darkened by overwhelming anxieties, so that he speculated little as to the Ultimately Desired. A chartered accountant sat in the office at Moorgate Street and shed around him the gloom of statistics. Unless a miracle happened the Cure was doomed.

It is all very well to seat a little nigger on the safety-valve if the end of the journey is in sight. The boiler may just last out the strain. But to suppose that he will sit there in permanent security to himself and the ship for an indefinite time is an optimism unwarranted by the general experience of this low world. Sypher's Cure could not stand the strain of the increased advertisement. Shuttleworth found a dismal pleasure in the fulfilment of his prophecy. A reduction in price had not materially affected the sales. The Jebusa Jones people had lowered the price of the Cuticle Remedy and still undersold the Cure. During the year the Bermondsey works had been heavily mortgaged. The money had all been wasted on a public that had eyes and saw not, that had ears and heard not the simple gospel of the Friend of Humanity—"Try Sypher's Cure." In the midst of the gloom Shuttleworth took the opportunity of deprecating the unnecessary expense of production, never having so greatly dared before. Only the best and purest materials had been possible for the divine ointment. By using second qualities, a great saving could be effected without impairing the efficacy of the Cure. Thus Shuttleworth.   Sypher blazed into holy anger, as if he had been counseled to commit sacrilege.

Radical reforms were imperative, if the Cure was to be saved.   He spent his nights over vast schemes only to find the fatal flaw in the cold light of the morning.   This angered him.   It seemed that the sureness of his vision had gone.   Something strange, uncanny had happened within him, he knew not what.   It had nothing to do with his intellectual force, his personal energy.   It had nothing to do with his determination to win through and restore the Cure to its former position in the market.   It was something subtle, spiritual.

The memory of the blistered heel lived with him.   The slight doubt cast by Septimus on Zora's faith remained disturbingly at the back of his mind.   Yet he clung passionately to his belief.   If it were not Heaven-sent, then was he of men most miserable.

Never had he welcomed the sight of Nunsmere more than the next Saturday afternoon when the trap turned off the highroad and the common came into view.   The pearls and faint blues of the sky, the tender mist softening the russet of the autumn trees, the gray tower of the little church, the red roofs of the cottages dreaming in their old-world gardens, the quiet green of the common with the children far off at play and the lame donkey watching them in philosophic content—all came like the gift of a very calm and restful God to the tired man's eyes.

He thought to himself: "It only lacks one figure walking across the common to meet me."   Then the thought again: "If she were there would I see anything else?"

At Penton Court the maid met him at the door.

"Mr. Dix is waiting to see you, sir."

"Mr. Dix! Where is he?"

"In the drawing-room. He has been waiting a couple of hours."

He threw off his hat and coat, delighted, and rushed in to welcome the unexpected guest. He found Septimus sitting in the twilight by the French window that opened on the lawn, and making elaborate calculations in a note-book.

"My dear Dix!" He shook him warmly by the hand and clapped him on the shoulder. "This is more than a pleasure. What have you been doing with yourself?"

Septimus said, holding up the note-book:

"I was just trying to work out the problem whether a boy's expenses from the time he begins feeding-bottles to the time he leaves the University increases by arithmetical or geometrical progression."

Sypher laughed. "It depends, doesn't it, on his taste for luxuries?"

"This one is going to be extravagant, I'm afraid," said Septimus. "He cuts his teeth on a fifteenth-century Italian ivory carving of St. John the Baptist—I went into a shop to buy a purse and they gave it to me instead—and turns up his nose at coral and bells. There isn't much of it to turn up. I've never seen a child with so little nose. I invented a machine for elongating it, but his mother won't let me use it."

Sypher expressed his sympathy with Mrs. Dix, and inquired after her health. Septimus reported favorably. She had passed a few weeks at Hottetôt-sur-Mer, which had done her good. She was now in Paris under the mothering care of Madame Bolivard, where she would stay until she cared to take up her residence in her flat in Chelsea, which was now free from tenants.

"And you?" asked Sypher.

"I've just left the Hôtel Godet and come back to Nuns-mere. Perhaps I'll give up the house and take Wiggles-wick to London when Emmy returns. She promised to look for a flat for me. I believe women are rather good at finding flats."

Sypher handed him a box of cigars. He lit one and held it awkwardly with the tips of his long, nervous fingers. He passed the fingers of his other hand, with the familiar gesture, up his hair.

"I thought I'd come and see you," he said hesitatingly, "before going to 'The Nook.' There are explanations to be made. My wife and I are good friends, but we can't live together. It's all my fault. I make the house intoler-able. I—I have an ungovernable temper, you know, and I'm harsh and unloving and disagreeable. And it's bad for the child. We quarrel dreadfully—at least, she doesn't."

"What about?" Sypher asked gravely.

"All sorts of things. You see, if I want breakfast an hour before dinner-time, it upsets the household. Then there was the nose machine—and other inventions for the baby, which perhaps might kill it. You can ex-plain all this and tell them that the marriage has been a dreadful mistake on poor Emmy's side, and that we've decided to live apart. You will do this for me, won't you?"

"I can't say I'll do it with pleasure," said Sypher, "for I'm more than sorry to hear your news. I suspected as much when I met you in Paris. But I'll see Mrs. Oldrieve as soon as possible and explain."

"Thank you," said Septimus; "you don't know what a service you would be rendering me."

He uttered a sigh of relief and relit his cigar which had gone out during his appeal. Then there was a silence. Septimus looked dreamily out at the row of trees that marked the famous lawn reaching down to the railway line. The mist had thickened with the fall of the day and hung heavy on the branches, and the sky was gray. Sypher watched him, greatly moved; tempted to cry out that he knew all, that he was not taken in by the simple legend of his ungovernable temper and unlovely disposition. His heart went out to him, as to a man who dwelt alone on lofty heights, inaccessible to common humanity. He was filled with pity and reverence for him. Perhaps he exaggerated. But Sypher was an idealist. Had he not set Sypher's Cure as the sun in his heaven and Zora as one of the fixed stars?

It grew dark. Sypher rang for the lamp and tea.

"Or would you like breakfast?" he asked laughingly.

"I've just had supper," said Septimus. "Wiggleswick found some cheese in a cupboard. I buried it in the front garden." A vague smile passed on his face like a pale gleam of light over water on a cloudy day. "Wiggleswick is deaf. He couldn't hear it."

"He's a lazy scoundrel," said Sypher. "I wonder you don't sack him."

Septimus licked a hanging strip of cigar-end into position —he could never smoke a cigar properly—and lit it for the third time.

"Wiggleswick is good for me," said he. "He keeps me human. I am apt to become a machine. I live so much among them. I've been working hard on a new gun—or rather an old gun. It's field artillery, quick-firing. I got on to the idea again from a sighting apparatus I invented.

15

I have the specification in my pocket. The model is at home. I brought it from Paris."

He fetched a parcel of manuscript from his pocket and unrolled it into flatness.

"I should like to show it to you. Do you mind?"

"It would interest me enormously," said Sypher.

"I invent all sorts of things. I can't help it. But I always come back to guns—I don't know why. I hope you've done nothing further with the guns of large caliber. I've been thinking about them seriously, and I find they're all moonshine."

He smiled with wan cheerfulness at the waste of the labor of years. Sypher, on whose conscience the guns had laid their two hundred ton weight, felt greatly relieved. Their colossal scale had originally caught his imagination which loved big conceptions. Their working had seemed plausible to his inexpert eye. He had gone with confidence to his friend, the expert on naval gunnery, who had reported on them in breezy, sea-going terms of disrespect. Since then he had shrunk from destroying his poor friend's illusions.

"Yes, they're all unmanageable. I see what's wrong with them—but I've lost my interest in naval affairs." He paused and added dreamily: "I was horribly seasick crossing the Channel this time.

"Let us have a look at the field-gun," said Sypher encouragingly. Remembering the naval man's language, he had little hope that Septimus would be more successful by land than by sea; but his love and pity for the inventor compelled interest. Septimus's face brightened.

"This," said he, "is quite a different thing. You see I know more about it."

"That's where the bombardier comes in," laughed Sypher.

"I shouldn't wonder," replied Septimus.

He spread the diagram on a table, and expounded the gun. Absorbed in his explanation he lost the drowsy incertitude of his speech and the dreaminess of his eyes. He spoke with rapidity, sureness, and a note of enthusiasm rang oddly in his voice. On the margins he sketched illustrations of the Gatling, the Maxim, and the Hotchkiss and other guns, and demonstrated the superior delicate deadliness of his own. It could fire more rounds per minute than any other piece of artillery known to man. It could feed itself automatically from a magazine. The new sighting apparatus made it as accurate as a match rifle. Its power of massacre was unparalleled in the history of wholesale slaughter. A child might work it.

Septimus's explanation was too lucid for a man of Sypher's intelligence not to grasp the essentials of his invention. To all his questions Septimus returned satisfactory answers. He could find no flaw in the gun. Yet in his heart he felt that the expert would put his finger on the weak spot and consign the machine to the limbo of phantasmagoric artillery.

"If it is all you say, there's a fortune in it," said he.

"There's no shadow of doubt about it," replied Septimus. "I'll send Wiggleswick over with the model to-morrow, and you can see for yourself."

"What are you going to do with it?"

"I don't know," said Septimus, in his usual manner. "I never know what to do with things when I invent them. I once knew a man in the Patent Office who patented things for me. But he's married now and gone to live in Balham."

"But he's still at the Patent Office?"

"Perhaps he is," said Septimus. "It never occurred to me. But it has never done me any good to have things patented. One has to get them taken up. Some of them are drunk and disorderly enough for them to be taken up at once," he added with his pale smile. He continued: "I thought perhaps you would replace the big-caliber guns in our contract by this one."

Sypher agreed with pleasure to the proposal. He knew a high military official in the Ordnance Department of the War Office who would see that the thing was properly considered. "If he's in town I'll go and see him at once."

"There's no hurry," said Septimus. "I shouldn't like you to put yourself out. I know you're a very busy man. Go in any time you happen to be passing. You are there pretty often now, I suppose."

"Why?"

"My friend Hégisippe Cruchot gave you an idea in Paris —about soldiers' feet. How is it developing?"

Sypher made a wry face. "I found, my dear Dix, it was like your guns of large caliber." He rose and walked impatiently about the room. "Don't let us talk about the Cure, there's a dear fellow. I come down here to forget it."

"Forget it?"

Septimus stared at him in amazement.

"Yes. To clear my mind and brain of it. To get a couple of nights' sleep after the rest of the week's nightmare. The concern is going to hell as fast as it can, and"—he stopped in front of Septimus and brought down his hands in a passionate gesture—"I can't believe it. I can't believe it! What I'm going through God only knows."

"I at least had no notion," said Septimus. "And I've

been worrying you with my silly twaddle about babies and guns."

"It's a godsend for me to hear of anything save ruin and the breaking up of all that was dear to me in life. It's not like failure in an ordinary business. It has been infinitely more than a business to me. It has been a religion. It is still. That's why my soul refuses to grasp facts and figures."

He went on, feeling a relief in pouring out his heart to one who could understand. To no one had he thus spoken. With an expansive nature he had the strong man's pride. To the world in general he turned the conquering face of Clem Sypher, the Friend of Humanity, of Sypher's Cure. To Septimus alone had he shown the man in his desperate revolt against defeat. The lines around his mouth deepened into lines of pain, and pain lay behind his clear eyes and in the knitting of his brows.

"I believed the Almighty had put an instrument for the relief of human suffering into my hands. I dreamed great dreams. I saw all the nations of the earth blessing me. I know I was a damned fool. So are you. So is every visionary. So are the apostles, the missionaries, the explorers —all who dream great dreams—all damned fools, but a glorious company all the same. I'm not ashamed to belong to it. But there comes a time when the apostle finds himself preaching to the empty winds, and the explorer discovers his El Dorado to be a barren island, and he either goes mad or breaks his heart, and which of the two I'm going to do I don't know. Perhaps both."

"Zora Middlemist will be back soon," said Septimus. "She is coming by the White Star line, and she ought to be in Marseilles by the end of next week."

"She writes me that she may winter in Egypt. That is why she chose the White Star line," said Sypher.

"Have you told her what you've told me?"

"No," said Sypher, "and I never shall while there's a hope left. She knows it's a fight. But I tell her—as I have told my damned fool of a soul—that I shall conquer. Would you like to go to her and say, 'I'm done—I'm beaten'? Besides, I'm not."

He turned and poked the fire, smashing a great lump of coal with a stroke of his muscular arm as if it had been the skull of the Jebusa Jones dragon. Septimus twirled his small mustache and his hand inevitably went to his hair. He had the scared look he always wore at moments when he was coming to a decision.

"But you would like to see Zora, wouldn't you?" he asked.

Sypher wheeled round, and the expression on his face was that of a prisoner in the Bastille who had been asked whether he would like a summer banquet beneath the trees of Fontainebleau.

"You know that very well," said he.

He laid down the poker and crossed the room to a chair.

"I've often thought of what you said in Paris about her going away. You were quite right. You have a genius for saying and doing the simple right thing. We almost began our friendship by your saying it. Do you remember? It was in Monte Carlo. You remember that you didn't like my looking on Mrs. Middlemist as an advertisement. Oh, you needn't look uncomfortable, my dear fellow. I loved you for it. In Paris you practically told me that I oughtn't to regard her as a kind of fetich for the Cure, and claim her bodily presence. You also put before me the fact that there was no more reason for her to believe in the Cure than yourself or Hégisippe Cruchot. If you could tell me anything more," said he earnestly, "I should value it."

What he expected to learn from Septimus he did not know. But once having exalted him to inaccessible heights, the indomitable idealist was convinced that from his lips would fall words of gentle Olympian wisdom. Septimus, blushing at his temerity in having pointed out the way to the man whom he regarded as the incarnation of force and energy, curled himself up awkwardly in his chair, clasping his ankles between his locked fingers. At last the oracle spoke.

"If I were you," he said, "before going mad or breaking my heart, I should wait until I saw Zora."

"Very well. It will be a long time. Perhaps so much the better. I shall remain sane and heart-whole all the longer."

After dinner Sypher went round to "The Nook," and executed his difficult mission as best he could. To carry out Septimus's wishes, which involved the vilification of the innocent and the beatification of the guilty, went against his conscience. He omitted, therefore, reference to the demoniac rages which turned the home into an inferno, and to the quarrels over the machine for elongating the baby's nose. Their tempers were incompatible; they found a common life impossible; so, according to the wise modern view of things, they had decided to live apart while maintaining cordial relations.

Mrs. Oldrieve was greatly distressed. Tears rolled down her cheeks on to her knitting. The old order was changing too rapidly for her and the new to which it was giving place seemed anarchy to her bewildered eyes. She held up tremulous hands in protest. Husband and wife living apart so cheerfully, for such trivial reasons! Even if one had suffered great wrong at the hands of the other it was their duty to remain side by side. "Those whom God had joined together——"

"He didn't," snapped Cousin Jane. "They were joined together by a scrubby man in a registry office."

This is the wild and unjust way in which women talk. For aught Cousin Jane knew the Chelsea Registrar might have been an Antinous for beauty.

Mrs. Oldrieve shook her head sadly. She had known how it would be. If only they had been married in church by their good vicar, this calamity could not have befallen them.

"All the churches and all the vicars and all the archbishops couldn't have made that man anything else than a doddering idiot! How Emmy could have borne with him for a day passes my understanding. She has done well to get rid of him. She has made a mess of it, of course. People who marry in that way generally do. It serves her right."

So spoke Cousin Jane, whom Sypher found, in a sense, an unexpected ally. She made his task easier. Mrs. Oldrieve remained unconvinced.

"And the baby just a month or so old. Poor little thing! What's to become of it?"

"Emmy will have to come here," said Cousin Jane firmly, "and I'll bring it up. Emmy isn't fit to educate a rabbit. You had better write and order her to come home at once."

"I'll write to-morrow," sighed Mrs. Oldrieve.

Sypher reflected on the impossibilities of the proposition and on the reasons Emmy still had for remaining in exile in Paris. He also pitied the child that was to be brought up by Cousin Jane. It had extravagant tastes. He smiled.

"My friend Dix is already thinking of sending him to the University; so you see they have plans for his education."

Cousin Jane sniffed. She would make plans for them! As for the University—if it could turn out a doddering idiot like Septimus, it was criminal to send any young man to such a seat of unlearning. She would not allow him to have a voice in the matter. Emmy was to be summoned to Nunsmere.

Sypher was about to deprecate the idea when he reflected again, and thought of Hotspur and the spirits from the vasty deep. Cousin Jane could call, and so could Mrs. Oldrieve. But would Emmy come? As the answer to the question was in the negative he left Cousin Jane to her comfortable resolutions.

"You will no doubt discuss the matter with Dix," he said.

Cousin Jane threw up her hands. "Oh, for goodness' sake, don't let him come here! I couldn't bear the sight of him."

Sypher looked inquiringly at Mrs. Oldrieve.

"It has been a great shock to me," said the gentle lady. "It will take time to get over it. Perhaps he had better wait a little."

Sypher walked home in a wrathful mood. Ostracism was to be added to Septimus's crown of martyrdom.

Perhaps, on the other hand, the closing of "The Nook" doors was advantageous. He had dreaded the result of

Cousin Jane's cross-examination, as lying was not one of his friend's conspicuous accomplishments. Soothed by this reflection he smoked a pipe, and took down Bunyan's "Pilgrim's Progress" from his shelves.

While he was deriving spiritual entertainment from the great battle between Christian and Apollyon and consolation from the latter's discomfiture, Septimus was walking down the road to the post-office, a letter in his hand. The envelope was addressed to "Mrs. Middlemist, White Star Co.'s S. S. *Cedric*, Marseilles." It contained a blank sheet of headed note-paper and the tail of a little china dog.

CHAPTER XVIII

As soon as a woman knows what she wants she generally gets it. Some philosophers assert that her methods are circuitous; others, on the other hand, maintain that she rides in a bee line toward the desired object, galloping ruthlessly over conventions, susceptibilities, hearts, and such like obstacles. All, however, agree that she is unscrupulous, that the wish of the woman is the politely insincere wish of the Deity, and that she pursues her course with a serene sureness unknown to man. It is when a woman does not know what she wants that she baffles the philosopher just as the ant in her aimless discursiveness baffles the entomologist. Of course, if the philosopher has guessed her unformulated desire, then things are easy for him, and he can discourse with certitude on feminine vagaries, as Rattenden did on the journeyings of Zora Middlemist. He has the word of the enigma. But to the woman herself her state of mind is an exasperating puzzle, and to her friends, philosophic or otherwise, her consequent actions are disconcerting.

Zora went to California, where she was hospitably entertained, and shown the sights of several vast neighborhoods. She peeped into the Chinese quarter at San Francisco, and visited the Yosemite Valley. Attentive young men strewed her path with flowers and candy. Young women vowed her eternal devotion. She came into touch with the intimate problems of the most wonderful social organism the world has ever seen, and was confronted with stupendous works of nature and illimitable solitudes wherein the soul stands appalled. She also ate a great quantity of peaches. When her visit to the Callenders had come to an end she armed herself with introductions and started off by herself to see America. She traveled across the Continent, beheld the majesty of Niagara and the bewildering life of New York. She went to Washington and Boston. In fact, she learned many things about a great country which were very good for her to know, receiving impressions with the alertness of a sympathetic intellect, and pigeonholing them with feminine conscientiousness for future reference.

It was all very pleasant, healthful, and instructive, but it no more helped her in her quest than gazing at the jewelers' windows in the Rue de la Paix. Snow-capped Sierras and crowded tram-cars were equally unsuggestive of a mission in life. In the rare moments which activity allowed her for depression she began to wonder whether she was not chasing the phantom of a wild goose. A damsel to whom in a moment of expansion she revealed the object of her journeying exclaimed: "What other mission in life has a woman than to spend money and look beautiful?"

Zora laughed incredulously.

"You've accomplished half already, for you do look beautiful," said the damsel. "The other half is easy."

"But if you haven't much money to spend?"

"Spend somebody else's. Lord! If I had your beauty I'd just walk down Wall Street and pick up a millionaire between my finger and thumb, and carry him off right away."

When Zora suggested that life perhaps might have some deeper significance, the maiden answered:

"Life is like the school child's idea of a parable—a

heavenly story (if you've lots of money) with no earthly meaning."

"Don't you ever go down beneath the surface of things?" asked Zora.

"If you dig down far enough into the earth," replied the damsel, "you come to water. If you bore down deep enough into life you come to tears. My dear, I'm going to dance on the surface and have a good time as long as I can. And I guess you're doing the same."

"I suppose I am," said Zora. And she felt ashamed of herself.

At Washington fate gave her an opportunity of attaining the other half of the damsel's idea. An elderly senator of enormous wealth proposed marriage, and offered her half a dozen motor-cars, a few palaces and most of the two hemispheres. She declined.

"If I were young, would you marry me?"

Zora's beautiful shoulders gave the tiniest shrug of uncertainty. Perhaps her young friend was right, and the command of the earth was worth the slight penalty of a husband. She was tired and disheartened at finding herself no nearer to the heart of things than when she had left Nunsmere. Her attitude toward the once unspeakable sex had imperceptibly changed. She no longer blazed with indignation when a man made love to her. She even found it more agreeable than looking at cataracts or lunching with ambassadors. Sometimes she wondered why. The senator she treated very tenderly.

"I don't know. How can I tell?" she said a moment or two after the shrug.

"My heart is young," said he.

Zora met his eyes for the millionth part of a second and

turned her head away, deeply sorry for him. The woman's instinctive look dealt instantaneous death to his hopes. It was one more enactment of the tragedy of the bald head and the gray beard. He spoke with pathetic bitterness. Like Don Ruy Gomez da Silva in "Hernani," he gave her to understand that now, when a young fellow passed him in the street, he would give up all his motor-cars and all his colossal canned-salmon business for the young fellow's raven hair and bright eyes.

"Then you would love me. I could make you."

"What is love, after all?" asked Zora.

The elderly senator looked wistfully through the years over an infinite welter of salmon-tins, seeing nothing else.

"It's the meaning of life," said he. "I've discovered it too late."

He went away sorrowful, and Zora saw the vanity of great possessions.

On the homeward steamer she had as a traveling companion a young Englishman whom she had met at Los Angeles, one Anthony Dasent, an engineer of some distinction. He was bronzed and healthy and lithe-limbed. She liked him because he had brains and looked her squarely in the face. On the first evening of the voyage a slight lurch of the vessel caused her to slip, and she would have fallen had he not caught her by the arms. For the first time she realized how strong a man could be. It was a new sensation, not unpleasurable, and in thanking him she blushed. He remained with her on deck, and talked of their California friends and the United States. The next day he established himself by her side, and discoursed on the sea and the sky, human aspirations, the discomforts of his cabin, and a belief in eternal punishment. The day after that he told her of his ambitions, and showed her photographs of his mother and sisters. After that they exchanged views on the discipline of loneliness. His profession, he observed, took him to the waste places of the earth, where there was never a woman to cheer him, and when he came back to England he returned to a hearth equally unconsoled. Zora began to pity his forlorn condition. To build strong bridges and lay down railroads was a glorious thing for a man to do; to do it without sweetheart or wife was nothing less than heroic.

In the course of time he told her that she was the most beautiful woman he had ever met. He expressed his admiration of the gold flecks in her brown eyes and the gleams of gold in her hair when it was caught by the sun. He also wished that his sisters could have their skirts cut like hers and could learn the art of tying a veil over a hat. Then he took to scowling on inoffensive young men who fetched her wraps and lent her their binoculars. He declared one of them to be an unmitigated ass to throw whom overboard would be to insult the Atlantic. And then Zora recognized that he was stolidly in love with her after the manner of his stolid kind. She felt frightened, and accused herself of coquetry. Her sympathy with his barren existence had perhaps overstepped the boundaries of polite interest. She had raised false hopes in a young and ingenuous bosom. She worked herself up to a virtuous pitch of self-reprobation and flagellated herself soundly, taking the precaution, however, of wadding the knots of the scourge with cotton-wool. After all, was it her fault that a wholesome young Briton should fall in love with her? She remembered Rattenden's uncomfortable words on the eve of her first pilgrimage:

"Beautiful women like yourself, radiating feminine magnetism, worry a man exceedingly. You don't let him go about in peace, so why should he let you?"

So Zora came face to face with the eternal battle of the sexes. She stamped her foot in the privacy of her cabin, and declared the principle to be horrid and primeval and everything that was most revolting to a woman who had earnestly set forth to discover the highest things of life. For the remainder of the voyage she avoided Anthony Dasent's company as much as possible, and, lest he should add jealousy to the gloom in which he enveloped himself, sought unexciting joys in the society of a one-eyed geologist who discoursed playfully on the foraminifera of the Pacific slope.

One day Dasent came on her alone, and burst out wrathfully:

"Why are you treating me like this?"

"Like what?"

"You are making a fool of me. I'm not going to stand it."

Then she realized that when the average man does not get what he wants exactly when he wants it he loses his temper. She soothed him according to the better instincts of her sex, but resolved to play no more with elementary young Britons. One-eyed geologists were safer companions. The former pitched their hearts into her lap; the latter, like Pawkins, the geologist of the Pacific slope, gave her boxes of fossils. She preferred the fossils. You could do what you liked with them: throw them overboard when the donor was not looking, or leave them behind in a railway carriage, or take them home and present them to the vicar who collected butterflies, beetles, ammonites, and tobacco stoppers. But an odd assortment of hearts to a woman who does not want them is really a confounded nuisance. Zora was very much relieved when Dasent, after eating an enormous breakfast, bade her a tragic farewell at Gibraltar.

It was a cloudless afternoon when she steamed into Marseilles. The barren rock islands on the east rose blue-gray from a blue sea. To the west lay the Isles of Frioul and the island of the Château d'If, with its prison lying grim and long on the crest; in front the busy port, the white noble city crowned by the church of Notre Dame de la Garde standing sentinel against the clear sky.

Zora stood on the crowded deck watching the scene, touched as she always was by natural beauty, but sad at heart. Marseilles, within four-and-twenty hours of London, meant home. Although she intended to continue her wanderings to Naples and Alexandria, she felt that she had come to the end of her journey. It had been as profitless as the last. Pawkins, by her side, pointed out the geological feature of the rocks. She listened vaguely, and wondered whether she was to bring him home tied to her chariot as she had brought Septimus Dix and Clem Sypher. The thought of Sypher drew her heart to Marseilles.

"I wish I were landing here like you, and going straight home," she said, interrupting the flow of scientific information. "I've already been to Naples, and I shall find nothing I want at Alexandria."

"Geologically, it's not very interesting," said Pawkins.

"I'm afraid prehistoric antiquity doesn't make my pulses beat faster."

"That's the advantage of it."

16

"One might just as well be a fossil oneself."

"Much better," said Pawkins, who had read Schopenhauer.

"You are not exhilarating to a depressed woman," said Zora with a laugh.

"I am sorry," he replied stiffly. "I was trying to entertain you."

He regarded her severely out of his one eye and edged away, as if he repented having wasted his time over so futile an organism as a woman. But her feminine magnetism drew him back.

"I'm rather glad you are going on to Alexandria," he remarked in a tone of displeasure, and before she could reply he marched off to look after his luggage.

Zora's eyes followed him until he disappeared, then she shrugged her shoulders. Apparently one-eyed geologists were as unsafe as elementary young Britons and opulent senators. She felt unfairly treated by Providence. It was maddening to realize herself as of no use in the universe except to attract the attention of the opposite sex. She clenched her hands in impotent anger. There was no mission on earth which she could fulfil. She thought enviously of Cousin Jane.

The steamer entered the harbor; the passengers for Marseilles landed, and the mail was brought aboard. There was only one letter for Mrs. Middlemist. It bore the Nunsmere postmark. She opened it and found the tail of the little china dog.

She looked at it for a moment wonderingly as it lay absurdly curled in the palm of her hand, and then she burst into tears. The thing was so grotesquely trivial. It meant so much. It was a sign and a token falling, as it were, from the sky into the midst of her despairing mood, rebuking her, summoning her, declaring an unknown mission which she was bound to execute. It lay in her hand like a bit of destiny, inexorable, unquestionable, silently compelling her forthwith to the human soul that stood in great need of her. Fate had granted the wish she had expressed to the one-eyed geologist. She landed at Marseilles, and sped homeward by the night train, her heart torn with anxiety for Septimus.

All night long the rhythmic clatter of the train shaped itself into the burden of her words to him: "If ever you want me badly, send me the tail, and I'll come to you from any distance." She had spoken then half jestingly, all tenderly. That evening she had loved him "in a sort of way," and now that he had sent for her, the love returned. The vivid experiences of the past months which had blinded her to the quieter light of home faded away into darkness. Septimus in urgent need, Emmy and Clem Sypher filled her thoughts. She felt thankful that Sypher, strong and self-reliant, was there to be her ally, should her course with Septimus be difficult. Between them they could surely rescue the ineffectual being from whatever dangers assailed him. But what could they be? The question racked her. Did it concern Emmy? A child, she knew, had just been born. A chill fear crept on her lest some tragedy had occurred through Septimus's folly. From him any outrageous senselessness might be expected, and Emmy herself was scarcely less irresponsible than her babe. She reproached herself for having suggested his marriage with Emmy. Perhaps in his vacant way he had acted entirely on her prompting. The marriage was wrong. Two helpless children should never have taken on themselves the

graver duties of life toward each other and future generations.

If it were a case in which a man's aid were necessary,
there stood Sypher, a great pillar of comfort.   Unconsciously
she compared him with the men with whom she had come
in contact during her travels—and she had met many of
great charm and strength and knowledge.   For some strange
reason which she could not analyze, he towered above them
all, though in each separate quality of character others
whom she could name surpassed him far.   She knew his
faults, and in her lofty way smiled at them.   Her character
as goddess or guardian angel or fairy patroness of the Cure
she had assumed with the graciousness of a grown-up lady
playing charades at a children's party.   His occasional
lapses from the traditions of her class jarred on her fine
susceptibilities.   Yet there, in spite of all, he stood rooted
in her life, a fact, a puzzle, a pride and a consolation.   The
other men paled into unimportant ghosts before him, and
strayed shadowy through the limbo of her mind.   Till now
she had not realized it.   Septimus, however, had always
dwelt in her heart like a stray dog whom she had rescued
from vagrancy.   He did not count as a man.   Sypher did.

Thus during the long, tedious hours of the journey home
the two were curiously mingled in her anxious conjectures,
and she had no doubt that Sypher and herself, the strong
and masterful, would come to the deliverance of the weak.

Septimus, who had received a telegram from Marseilles,
waited for her train at Victoria.   In order to insure being
in time he had arrived a couple of hours too soon, and patiently wandered about the station.   Now and then he
stopped before the engines of trains at rest, fascinated, as

he always was, by perfect mechanism. A driver, dismounting from the cab, and seeing him lost in admiration of the engine, passed him a civil word, to which Septimus, always courteous, replied. They talked further.

"I see you're an engineer, sir," said the driver, who found himself in conversation with an appreciative expert.

"My father was," said Septimus. "But I could never get up in time for my examinations. Examinations seem so silly. Why should you tell a set of men what they know already?"

The grimy driver expressed the opinion that examinations were necessary. He who spoke had passed them.

"I suppose you can get up at any time," Septimus remarked enviously. "Somebody ought to invent a machine for those who can't."

"You only want an alarm-clock," said the driver.

Septimus shook his head. "They're no good. I tried one once, but it made such a dreadful noise that I threw a boot at it."

"Did that stop it?"

"No," murmured Septimus. "The boot hit another clock on the mantelpiece, a Louis Quinze clock, and spoiled it. I did get up, but I found the method too expensive, so I never tried it again."

The engine of an outgoing train blew off steam, and the resounding din deafened the station. Septimus held his hands to his ears. The driver grinned.

"I can't stand that noise," Septimus explained when it was over. "Once I tried to work out an invention for modifying it. It was a kind of combination between a gramaphone and an orchestrion. You stuck it inside somewhere, and instead of the awful screech a piece of music would come out of the funnel. In fact, it might have gone on playing all the time the train was in motion. It would have been so cheery for the drivers, wouldn't it?"

The unimaginative mechanic whose wits were scattered by this fantastic proposition used his bit of cotton waste as a handkerchief, and remarked with vague politeness that it was a pity the gentleman was not an engineer. But Septimus deprecated the compliment. He looked wistfully up at the girders of the glass roof and spoke in his gentle, tired voice.

"You see," he concluded, "if I had been in practice as an engineer I should never have designed machinery in the orthodox way. I should have always put in little things of my own—and then God knows what would have happened."

He brought his eyes to earth with a wan smile, but his companion had vanished. A crowd had filled the suburban platform at the end of which he stood, and in a few moments the train clattered off. Then, remembering that he was hungry, he went to the refreshment-room, where, at the suggestion of the barmaid, he regaled himself on two hard-boiled eggs and a glass of sherry. The meal over, he loitered palely about the busy station, jostled by frantic gentlemen in silk hats rushing to catch suburban trains, and watched grimly by a policeman who suspected a pocket-picking soul beneath his guileless exterior.

At last, by especial grace of heaven, he found himself on the platform where the custom-house barrier and the long line of waiting porters heralded the approach of the continental train. Now that only a few moments separated him from Zora, his heart grew cold with suspense. He had not seen her since the night of Emmy's fainting fit. Her letters, though kind, had made clear to him her royal displeasure at his unceremonious marriage. For the first time he would look into her gold-flecked eyes out of a disingenuous soul. Would she surprise his guilty secret? It was the only thing he feared in a bewildering world.

The train came in, and as her carriage flashed by Zora saw him on the platform with his hat off, passing his fingers nervously through his Struwel Peter hair. The touch of the familiar welcoming her brought moisture to her eyes. As soon as the train stopped she alighted, and leaving Turner (who had accompanied her on the pilgrimage, and from Dover had breathed fervent thanks to Heaven that at last she was back in the land of her fathers) to look after her luggage, she walked down the platform to meet him.

He was just asking a porter at frantic grapple with the hand baggage of a large family whether he had seen a tall and extraordinarily beautiful lady in the train, when she came up to him with outstretched hands and beaming eyes. He took the hands and looked long at her, unable to speak. Never had she appeared to him more beautiful, more gracious. The royal waves of her hair beneath a fur traveling-toque invested her with queenliness. The full youth of her figure not hidden by a fur jacket brought to him the generous woman. A bunch of violets at her bosom suggested the fragrant essence of her.

"Oh, it's good to see you, Septimus. It's good!" she cried. "The sight of you makes me feel as if nothing mattered in the world except the people one cares for. How are you?"

"I'm very well indeed," said Septimus. "Full of inventions."

She laughed and guided him up the platform through

the cross-traffic of porters carrying luggage from train to cabs.

"Is mother all right?" she asked anxiously.

"Oh, yes," said Septimus.

"And Emmy and the baby?"

"Remarkably well. Emmy has had him christened. I wanted him to be called after you. Zoroaster was the only man's name I could think of, but she did not like it, and so she called it Octavius after me. Also Oldrieve after the family, and William."

"Why William?"

"After Pitt," said Septimus in the tone of a man who gives the obvious answer.

She halted for a moment, perplexed.

"Pitt?"

"Yes; the great statesman. He's going to be a member of Parliament, you know."

"Oh," said Zora, moving slowly on.

"His mother says it's after the lame donkey on the common. We used to call it William. He hasn't changed a bit since you left."

"So the baby's full name is—" said Zora, ignoring the donkey.

"William Octavius Oldrieve Dix. It's so helpful to a child to have a good name."

"I long to see him," said Zora.

"He's in Paris just now."

"Paris?" she echoed.

"Oh, he's not by himself, you know," Septimus hastened to reassure her, lest she might think that the babe was alone among the temptations and dissipations of the gay city. "His mother's there, too."

She shook him by the coat-sleeve.

"What an exasperating thing you are! Why didn't you tell me? I could have broken my journey or at least asked them to meet me at the Gare du Nord. But why aren't they in England?"

"I didn't bring them with me."

She laughed again at his tone, suspecting nothing.

"You speak as if you had accidentally left them behind, like umbrellas. Did you?"

Turner came up, attended by a porter with the hand baggage.

"Are you going on to Nunsmere to-night, ma'am?"

"Why should you?" asked Septimus.

"I had intended to do so. But if mother is quite well, and Emmy and the baby are in Paris, and you yourself are here, I don't quite see the necessity."

"It would be much nicer if you remained in London," said he.

"Very well," said Zora, "we shall. We can put up at the Grosvenor Hotel here for the night. Where are you staying?"

Septimus murmured the name of his sedate club, where his dissolute morning appearance was still remembered against him.

"Go and change and come back and dine with me in an hour's time."

He obeyed the command with his usual meekness, and Zora followed the porter through the subway to the hotel.

"We haven't dined together like this," she said, unfolding her napkin an hour afterwards, "since Monte Carlo. Then it was hopelessly unconventional. Now we can dine in the strictest propriety. Do you understand that you're my brother-in-law?"

She laughed, radiant, curiously happy at being with him. She realized, with a little shock of discovery, the restfulness that was the essential quality of his companionship. He was a quiet haven after stormy seas; he represented something intimate and tender in her life.

They spoke for a while of common things: her train journey, the crossing, the wonders she had seen. He murmured incoherent sketches of his life in Paris, the new gun, and Hégisippe Cruchot. But of the reason for his summons he said nothing. At last she leaned across the table and said gently:

"Why am I here, Septimus? You haven't told me."

"Haven't I?"

"No. You see, the little dog's tail brought me post-haste to you, but it gave me no inkling why you wanted me so badly."

He looked at her in his scared manner.

"Oh, I don't want you at all; at least, I do—most tremendously—but not for myself."

"For whom, then?"

"Clem Sypher," said Septimus.

She paled slightly, and looked down at her plate and crumbled bread. For a long time she did not speak. The announcement did not surprise her. In an inexplicable way it seemed natural. Septimus and Sypher had shared her thoughts so oddly during her journey. An unaccountable shyness had checked her impulse to inquire after his welfare. Indeed, now that the name was spoken she could scarcely believe that she had not expected to hear it.

"What is the matter?" she asked at length.

"The Cure has failed."

"Failed?"

She looked up at him half incredulously. The very last letter she had received from Sypher had been full of the lust of battle. Septimus nodded gloomily.

"It was only a silly patent ointment like a hundred others, but it was Sypher's religion. Now his gods have gone, and he's lost. It's not good for a man to have no gods. I didn't have any once, and the devils came in. They drove me to try haschisch. But it must have been very bad haschisch, for it made me sick, and so I was saved."

"What made you send for me so urgently? The dog's tail—you knew I had to come."

"Sypher wanted you—to give him some new gods."

"He could have sent for me himself. Why did he ask you?"

"He didn't," cried Septimus. "He doesn't know anything about it. He hasn't the faintest idea that you're in London to-night. Was I wrong in bringing you back?"

To Zora the incomprehensible aspect of the situation was her own attitude. She did not know whether Septimus was wrong or not. She told herself that she ought to resent the summons which had caused her such needless anxiety as to his welfare, but she could feel no resentment. Sypher had failed. The mighty had fallen. She pictured a broken-hearted man, and her own heart ached for him.

"You did right, Septimus," she said very gently. "But of what use can I be to him?"

Septimus said: "He's the one to tell you that."

"But do you think he knows? He didn't before. He wanted me to stay as a kind of Mascotte for the Cure—simply sit still while he drew influence out of me or something. It was absurd."

It was on this occasion that Septimus made his one contribution to pessimistic philosophy.

"When you analyze anything in life," said he, "don't you think that you always come down to a *reductio ad absurdum?*"

CHAPTER XIX

" I'M very sorry to leave you, Mr. Sypher," said Shuttle-worth, "but my first duty is to my wife and family."

Clem Sypher leaned back in his chair behind his great office desk and looked at his melancholy manager with the eyes of a general whose officers refuse the madness of a forlorn hope.

"Quite so," he said tonelessly. "When do you want to go?"

"You engaged me on a three-months' notice, but——"

"But you want to go now?"

"I have a very brilliant position offered me if I can take it up in a fortnight."

"Very well," said Sypher.

"You won't say it's a case of rats deserting a sinking ship, will you, sir? As I say, my wife and family——"

"The ship's sinking. You're quite right to leave it. Is the position offered you in the same line of business?"

"Yes," said Shuttleworth, unable to meet his chief's clear, unsmiling eyes.

"One of the rival firms?"

Shuttleworth nodded, then broke out into mournful as-severations of loyalty. If the Cure had flourished he would have stayed with Mr. Sypher till the day of his death. He would have refused the brilliant offer. But in the cir-cumstances——"

"*Sauve qui peut*," said Sypher. "Another month or two and Sypher's Cure becomes a thing of the past. Nothing can pull it through. I was too sanguine. I wish I had taken your advice oftener, Shuttleworth."

Shuttleworth thanked him for the compliment.

"One learns by experience," said he modestly. "I was born and bred in the patent-medicine business. It's very risky. You start a thing. It catches on for a while. Then something else more attractive comes on the market. There's a war of advertising, and the bigger capital wins. The wise man gets out of it just before the rival comes. If you had taken my advice five years ago, and turned it into a company, you'd have been a rich man now, without a care in the world. Next time you will."

"There'll be no next time," said Sypher gravely.

"Why not? There's always money in patent medicines. For instance, in a new cure for obesity if properly worked. A man like you can always get the money together."

"And the cure for obesity?"

Shuttleworth's dismal face contracted into the grimace which passed with him for a smile.

"Any old thing will do, so long as it doesn't poison people."

Uncomfortable under his chief's silent scrutiny, he took off his spectacles, breathed on them, and wiped them with his handkerchief.

"The public will buy anything, if you advertise it enough."

"I suppose they will," said Sypher. "Even Jebusa Jones's Cuticle Remedy."

Shuttleworth started and put on his spectacles.

"Why shouldn't they buy the Remedy, after all?"

"*You* ask me that?" said Sypher. All through the interview he had not shifted his position. He sat fixed like a florid ghost.

The manager shuffled uneasily in his chair beside the desk, and cleared his throat nervously.

"I'm bound to," said he, "in self-defense. I know what you think of the Cure—but that's a matter of sentiment. I've been into the thing pretty thoroughly, and I know that there's scarcely any difference in the composition of the Remedy and the Cure. After all, any protecting grease that keeps the microbes in the air out of the sore place does just as well—sometimes better. There's nothing in patent ointment that really cures. Now is there?"

"Are you going to the Jebusa Jones people?" asked Sypher.

"I have my wife and family," the manager pleaded. "I couldn't refuse. They've offered me the position of their London agent. I know it must pain you," he added hurriedly, "but what could I do?"

"Every man for himself and the devil take the hindmost. So you will give me what they used to call my *coup de grâce*. You'll just stab me dead as I lie dying. Well, in a fortnight's time you can go."

The other rose. "Thank you very much, Mr. Sypher. You have always treated me generously, and I'm more than sorry to leave you. You bear me no ill will?"

"For going from one quack remedy to another? Certainly not."

It was only when the door closed behind the manager that Sypher relaxed his attitude. He put both hands up to his face, and then fell forward on to the desk, his head on his arms.

The end had come. To that which mattered in the man, the lingering faith yet struggling in the throes of dissolution, Shuttleworth had indeed given the *coup de grâce*.

That he had joined the arch-enemy who in a short time would achieve his material destruction signified little. When something spiritual is being done to death, the body and mind are torpid. Even a month ago, had Shuttleworth uttered such blasphemy within those walls Clem Sypher would have arisen in his wrath like a mad crusader and have cloven the blasphemer from skull to chine. To-day, he had sat motionless, petrified, scarcely able to feel. He knew that the man spoke truth. As well put any noxious concoction of drugs on the market and call it a specific against obesity or gravel or deafness as Sypher's Cure. Between the heaven-sent panacea which was to cleanse the skin of the nations and send his name ringing down the centuries as the Friend of Humanity and the shiveringly vulgar Jebusa Jones's Cuticle Remedy there was not an atom of important difference. One was as useful or as useless as the other. The Cure was pale green; the Remedy rose pink. Women liked the latter best on account of its color. Both were quack medicaments.

He raised a drawn and agonized face and looked around the familiar room, where so many gigantic schemes had been laid, where so many hopes had shone radiant, and saw for the first time its blatant self-complacency, its piteous vulgarity. Facing him was the artist's original cartoon for the great poster which once had been famous all over the world, and now, for lack of money, only lingered in shreds on a forgotten hoarding in some Back of Beyond. It represented the Friend of Humanity, in gesture, white beard, and general appearance resembling a benevolent minor prophet, distributing the Cure to a scrofulous universe. In those glorified days, he had striven to have his own lineaments depicted above the robe of the central figure, but the artist had declared them to be unpictorial, and clung to the majesty of the gentleman in the white beard. Around the latter's feet were gathered a motley crew—the fine lady in her ball dress, the shoeblack, the crowned king, the red Indian in Fenimore Cooper feathers, the half-naked negro, the wasted, ragged mother with her babe, the jockey, the Syrian leper, and a score of other types of humans, including in the background a hairy-faced creature, the "dog-faced man" of Barnum's show. They were well grouped, effective, making the direct appeal to an Anglo-Saxon populace, which in its art must have something to catch hold of, like the tannin in its overdrawn tea. It loved to stand before this poster and pick out the easily recognized characters and argue (as Sypher, whose genius had suggested the inclusion of the freak had intended) what the hairy creature could represent, and, as it stood and picked and argued, the great fact of Sypher's Cure sank deep into their souls. He remembered the glowing pride with which he had regarded this achievement, the triumphal progress he made in a motor-car around the London hoardings the day after the poster had been pasted abroad. And now he knew it in his heart to be nothing but a tawdry, commercial lie.

Framed in oak on his walls hung kindly notes relating to the Cure from great personages or their secretaries. At the bottom of one ran the sprawling signature of the Grand Duke who had hailed him as "*ce bon Sypher*" at the Gare de Lyon when he started on the disastrous adventure of the blistered heel. There was the neatly docketed set of pigeonholes containing the proofs of all the advertisements he had issued. Lying before him on his desk was a copy, resplendently bound in morocco for his own gratification, of the forty-page, thin-paper pamphlet which was wrapped, a miracle of fine folding, about each packet of the Cure. On each page the directions for use were given in a separate language. French, Fijian, Syrian, Basque were there——forty languages—so that all the sons of men could read the good tidings and amuse themselves at the same time by trying to decipher the message in alien tongues.

Wherever he looked, some mockery of vain triumph met his eye: an enlargement of a snapshot photograph of the arrival of the first case of the Cure on the shores of Lake Tchad; photographs of the busy factory, now worked by a dwindling staff; proofs of full-page advertisements in which "Sypher's Cure" and "Friend of Humanity" figured in large capitals; the model of Edinburgh Castle, built by a grateful inmate of a lunatic asylum out of the red celluloid boxes of the Cure.

He shuddered at all these symbols and images of false gods, and bowed his head again on his arms. The abyss swallowed him. The waters closed over his head.

How long he remained like this he did not know. He had forbidden his door. The busy life of the office stood still. The dull roar of Moorgate Street was faintly heard, and now and then the windows vibrated faintly. The sprawling, gilt, mid-Victorian clock on the mantelpiece had stopped.

Presently an unusual rustle in the room caused him to raise his head with a start. Zora Middlemist stood before him. He sprang to his feet.

"You? You?"

"They wouldn't let me in. I forced my way. I said I must see you."

He stared at her, open-mouthed. A shivering thrill

passed through him, such as shakes a man on the verge of a great discovery.

"You, Zora? You have come to me at this moment?"

He looked so strange and staring, so haggard and disheveled, that she moved quickly to him and laid both her hands on his.

"My dear friend, my dearest friend, is it as bad as that?"

A throb of pain underlay the commonplace words. The anguish on his face stirred the best and most womanly in her. She yearned to comfort him. But he drew a pace or two away, and held up both hands as if warding her off, and stared at her still, but with a new light in his clear eyes that drank in her beauty and the sorcery of her presence.

"My God!" he cried, in a strained voice. "My God! What a fool I've been!"

He swerved as if he had received a blow and sank into his office chair, and turned his eyes from her to the ground, and sat stunned with joy and wonder and misery. He put out a hand blindly, and she took it, standing by his side. He knew now what he wanted. He wanted her, the woman. He wanted her voice in his ears, her kiss on his lips, her dear self in his arms. He wanted her welcome as he entered his house, her heart, her soul, her mind, her body, everything that was hers. He loved her for herself, passionately, overwhelmingly, after the simple way of men. He had raised his eyes from the deeps of hell, and in a flash she was revealed to him—incarnate heaven.

He felt the touch of her gloved hand on his, and it sent a thrill through his veins which almost hurt, as the newly coursing blood hurts the man that has been revived from torpor. The mistiness that serves a strong man for tears clouded his sight. He had longed for her; she had come. From their first meeting he had recognized, with the visionary's glimpse of the spiritual, that she was the woman of women appointed unto him for help and comfort. But then the visionary had eclipsed the man. Destiny had naught to do with him but as the instrument for the universal spreading of the Cure. The Cure was his life. The woman appointed unto him was appointed unto the Cure equally with himself. He had violently credited her with his insane faith. He had craved her presence as a mystical influence that in some way would paralyze the Jebusa Jones Dragon and give him supernatural strength to fight. He had striven with all his power to keep her radiant like a star, while his own faith lay dying.

He had been a fool. All the time it was the sheer woman that had held him, the sheer man. And yet had not destiny fulfilled itself with a splendid irony in sending her to him then, in that moment of his utter anguish, of the utter annihilation of the fantastic faith whereby he had lived for years? From the first he had been right, though with a magnificent lunacy. It was she, in very truth, who had been destined to slay his dragon. It was dead now, a vulgar, slimy monster, incapable of hurt, slain by the lightning flash of love, when his eyes met hers, a moment or two ago. In a confused way he realized this. He repeated mechanically:

"What a fool I've been! What a fool I've been!"

"Why?" asked Zora, who did not understand.

"Because—" he began, and then he stopped, finding no words. "I wonder whether God sent you?"

"I'm afraid it was only Septimus," she said with a smile.

"Septimus?"

He was startled. What could Septimus have to do with her coming? He rose again, and focusing his whirling senses on conventional things, wheeled an armchair to the fire, and led her to it, and took his seat near her in his office chair.

"Forgive me," he said, "but your coming seemed supernatural. I was dazed by the wonderful sight of you. Perhaps it's not you, after all. I may be going mad and have hallucinations. Tell me that it's really you."

"It's me, in flesh and blood—you can touch for yourself —and my sudden appearance is the simplest thing in the world."

"But I thought you were going to winter in Egypt?"

"So did I, until I reached Marseilles. This is how it was."

She told him of the tail of the little china dog, and of her talk with Septimus the night before.

"So I came to you," she concluded, "as soon as I decently could, this morning."

"And I owe you to Septimus," he said.

"Ah, I know! You ought to have owed me to yourself," she cried, misunderstanding him. "If I had known things were so terrible with you I would have come. I would, really. But I was misled by your letters. They were so hopeful. Don't reproach me."

"Reproach you! You who have given this crazy fellow so much! You who come to me all sweetness and graciousness, with heaven in your eyes, after having been dragged across Europe and made to sacrifice your winter of sunshine, just for my sake! Ah, no! It's myself that I reproach."

"For what?" she asked.

"For being a fool, a crazy, blatant, self-centered fool. My God!" he exclaimed, smiting the arm of his chair as a new view of things suddenly occurred to him. "How can you sit there—how have you suffered me these two years—without despising me? How is it that I haven't been the mock and byword of Europe? I must have been!"

He rose and walked about the room in great agitation.

"These things have all come crowding up together. One can't realize everything at once. 'Clem Sypher, Friend of Humanity!' How they must have jeered behind my back if they thought me sincere! How they must have despised me if they thought me nothing but an advertising quack! Zora Middlemist, for heaven's sake tell me what you have thought of me. What have you taken me for—a madman or a charlatan?"

"It is you that must tell me what has happened," said Zora earnestly. "I don't know. Septimus gave me to understand that the Cure had failed. He's never clear about anything in his own mind, and he's worse when he tries to explain it to others."

"Septimus," said Sypher, "is one of the children of God."

"But he's a little bit incoherent on earth," she rejoined, with a smile. "What has really happened?"

Sypher drew a long breath and pulled himself up.

"I'm on the verge of a collapse. The Cure hasn't paid for the last two years. I hoped against hope. I flung thousands and thousands into the concern. The Jebusa Jones people and others out-advertised me, out-manœuvered me at every turn. Now every bit of capital is gone, and I can't raise any more. I must go under."

Zora began, "I have a fairly large fortune——"

He checked her with a gesture, and looked at her clear and full.

"God bless you," he said. "My heart didn't lie to me at Monte Carlo when it told me that you were a great-souled woman. Tell me. Have you ever believed in the Cure in the sense that I believed in it?"

Zora returned his gaze. Here was no rhodomontading. The man was grappling with realities.

"No," she replied simply.

"Neither do I any longer," said Sypher. "There is no difference between it and any quack ointment you can buy at the first chemist's shop. That is why, even if I saw a chance of putting the concern on its legs again, I couldn't use your money. That is why I asked you, just now, what you have thought of me—a madman or a quack?"

"Doesn't the mere fact of my being here show you what I thought of you?"

"Forgive me," he said. "It's wrong to ask you such questions."

"It's worse than wrong. It's unnecessary."

He passed his hands over his eyes, and sat down.

"I've gone through a lot to-day. I'm not quite myself, so you must forgive me if I say unnecessary things. God sent you to me this morning. Septimus was His messenger. If you hadn't appeared just now I think I should have gone into black madness."

"Tell me all about it," she said softly. "All that you care to tell. I am your nearest friend—I think."

"And dearest."

"And you are mine. You and Septimus. I've seen hundreds of people since I've been away, and some seem to have cared for me—but there's no one really in my life but you two."

Sypher thought: "And we both love you with all there is in us, and you don't know it." He also thought jealously: "Who are the people that have cared for you?"

He said: "No one?"

A smile parted her lips as she looked him frankly in the eyes and repeated the negative. He breathed a sigh of relief, for he had remembered Rattenden's prophecy of the big man whom she was seeking, of the love for the big man, the gorgeous tropical sunshine in which all the splendor in her could develop. She had not found him. From the depths of his man's egotism he uttered a prayer of thanksgiving.

"Tell me," she said again.

"Do you remember my letter from Paris in the summer?"

"Yes. You had a great scheme for the armies of the world."

"That was the beginning," said he, and then he told her all the grotesque story to the end, from the episode of the blistered heel. He told her things that he had never told himself; things that startled him when he found them expressed in words.

"In Russia," said he, "every house has its sacred pictures, even the poorest peasant's hut. They call them ikons. These," waving to the walls, "were my ikons. What do you think of them?"

For the first time Zora became aware of the furniture and decoration of the room. The cartoon, the advertisement proofs, the model of Edinburgh Castle, produced on her the same effect as the famous board in the garden at Penton Court. Then, however, she could argue with him on the question of taste, and lay down laws as the arbiter of the elegancies of conduct. Now he viewed the sorry images with her own eyes, and he had gone through fire to attain this clearness of vision. What could be said? Zora the magnificent and self-reliant found not a word, though her heart was filled with pity. She was brought face to face with a ridiculous soul-tragedy, remote from her poor little experience of life. It was no time to act the beneficent goddess. She became self-conscious, fearful to speak lest she might strike a wrong note of sympathy. She wanted to give the man so much, and she could give him so little.

"I'm dying to help you," she said, rather piteously. "But how can I?"

"Zora," he said huskily.

She glanced up at him and he held her eyes with his, and she saw how she could help him.

"No, don't—don't. I can't bear it."

She rose and turned away. "Don't let us change things. They were so sweet before. They were so strange—your wanting me as a sort of priestess—I used to laugh—but I loved it all the time."

"That's why I said I've been a fool, Zora."

The bell of the telephone connected with his manager's office rang jarringly. He seized the transmitter in anger.

"How dare you ring me up when I gave orders I was to be undisturbed? I don't care who wants to see me. I'll see nobody."

He threw down the transmitter. "I'm very sorry," he began. Then he stopped. The commonplace summons from the outer world brought with dismaying suddenness to his mind the practical affairs of life. He was a ruined man. The thought staggered him. How could he say to Zora Middlemist: "I am a beggar. I want to marry you"?

She came to him with both hands outstretched, her instinctive gesture when her heart went out, and used his Christian name for the first time.

"Clem, let us be friends—good friends—true, dear friends, but don't spoil it all for me."

When a woman, infinitely desired, pleads like that with glorious eyes, and her fragrance and her dearness are within arm's length, a man has but to catch her to him and silence her pleadings with a man's strength, and carry her off in triumph. It has been the way of man with woman since the world began, and Sypher knew it by his man's instinct. It was a temptation such as he had never dreamed was in the world. He passed through a flaming, blazing torment of battle.

"Forget what I have said, Zora. We'll be friends, if you so wish it."

He pressed her hands and turned away. Zora felt that she had gained an empty victory.

"I ought to be going," she said.

"Not yet. Let us sit down and talk like friends. It's many weary months since I have seen you."

She remained a little longer and they talked quietly of many things. On bidding her good-by he said half playfully:

"I've often wondered why you have taken up with a fellow like me."

"I suppose it's because you're a big man," said Zora.

CHAPTER XX

SEPTIMUS walked back to his club after his dinner with Zora, blessing his stars for two reasons: first, because a gracious providence had restored him to favor in his goddess's sight, and, secondly, because he had escaped without telling her of the sundered lives of Emmy and himself. By the time he went to bed, however, having pondered for some hours over the interdependent relations between Zora, Sypher, Emmy, and himself, he had entangled his mind into a condition of intricate complication. He longed to continue to sun himself in the presence of his divinity. But being a married man (no matter how nominally), too much sunning appeared reprehensible. He had also arranged for the sunning of Clem Sypher, and was aware of the indelicacy of two going through this delicious process at the same time. He also dreaded the possible incredulity of Zora when he should urge the ferociousness of his domestic demeanor as the reason for his living apart from his wife. The consequence was that after a sleepless night he bolted like a rabbit to his burrow at Nunsmere. At any rate, the mission of the dog's tail was accomplished.

His bolt took place on Friday. On Saturday morning he was awakened by Wiggleswick.

The latter's attire was not that of the perfect valet. He wore an old, colored shirt open at the throat, a pair of trousers hitched up to his shoulder blades by means of a pair of red braces, and a pair of dilapidated carpet slippers.

"Here's a letter."

"Oh, post it," said Septimus sleepily.

"You haven't written it. The missus has written it. It has a French stamp and the Paris postmark. You'd better read it."

He put it on his master's pillow, and went to the window to admire the view. Septimus aroused, read the letter. It was from Emmy. It ran:

"DEAREST SEPTIMUS:

"I can't stand this loneliness in Paris any longer. I can't, I can't. If you were here and I could see you even once a week, I shouldn't mind. But to go on day after day indefinitely without a comforting word from you is more than I can bear. You say the flat is ready. I am coming over at once with baby and Madame Bolivard, who swears she will never leave me. How she is going to get on in London without a word of English, I don't know. I don't mind if I meet Zora. Perhaps it will be better for you that I should. And I think it will be quite safe for me now. Don't hate me and think me horrid and selfish, my dear Septimus, but I do want you. I do. I do. Thanks for the toy train. Baby enjoys the paint on the carriages *so* much; but Madame Bolivard says it isn't good for him. Dear, if I thought you wouldn't forgive me for being such a worry, I wouldn't worry you.

"Your always grateful   EMMY."

Septimus lit the half-smoked pipe of the night before that lay on the coverlet, and becoming aware of Wiggleswick, disturbed his contemplation of nature by asking him if he had ever been married.

"What?" asked Wiggleswick in the unmodulated tone of the deaf.

"Have you ever been married, Wiggleswick?"

"Heaps of times," said the old man.

"Dear me," said Septimus. "Did you commit bigamy?"

"Bigamy? No. I buried 'em all honorable."

"That," said Septimus, "was very kind of you."

"It was out of gratitude."

"For their goodness?"

"No. For being delivered from 'em. I had a lot of experience before I could learn the blessedness of a single life."

Septimus sighed. "Yet it must be very nice to have a wife, Wiggleswick."

"But ain't yer got one?" bawled the disreputable body-servant.

"Of course, of course," said Septimus hurriedly. "I was thinking of the people who hadn't."

Wiggleswick approached his master's bedside, with a mysteriously confidential air.

"Don't you think we're all cosy and comfortable here, sir?"

"Yes," said Septimus dubiously.

"Well, I for one have nothing to complain of. The vittles is good, and one sleeps warm, and one has one's beer and 'baccy regular. What more does a man want? Not women. Women's a regrettable hincident."

"Aren't you cold standing there in your shirt sleeves, Wiggleswick?" asked Septimus, in his hesitating way.

Wiggleswick ignored the delicacy of the suggestion.

"Cold? No. If I was cold, I'd precious soon make myself warm. Which I wish to remark, Mr. Dix, that now you've parted with the missus pro tem., don't you think it's more cosy and comfortable? I don't say but if she came here I'd do my best willingly. I know my duty. But, sir, a woman, what with her dusting and cleaning, and washing of herself in hot water, and putting flowers in mugs do up-set things terrible. I've been married oftener than you. I know 'em. Don't you think we get on better, the two of us, as we are?"

"We get on very nicely," said Septimus politely, "but

I'm afraid you'll have to do some cleaning and dusting
to-day. I'm awfully sorry to trouble you. Mrs. Middlemist has returned to England, and may be down this afternoon."

A look of dismay came over Wiggleswick's crafty,
weather-beaten face.

"Well, I'm jiggered. I'm just jiggered," said he.

"I'm delighted to hear it," murmured Septimus. "Bring
me my shaving-water."

"Are you going to get up?" asked Wiggleswick in a tone
of disgusted incredulity.

"Yes."

"Then you'll be wanting breakfast."

"Oh, no," said Septimus, with the wan smile that sometimes flickered over his features, "afternoon tea will do—
with some bacon and eggs and things."

The old man went out grumbling, and Septimus turned
to his letter. It was very kind of Emmy, he thought, to
write to him so affectionately.

He spent the mild, autumn morning on the common con-
sulting the ducks in the pond, and seeking inspiration from
the lame donkey, his state of mind being still complicated.
The more he reflected on Emmy's letter and on Wiggleswick's views on women the less did he agree with Wiggleswick. He missed Emmy, who had treated him very tenderly since their talk in the moonlight at Hottetôt-sur-Mer;
and he missed the boy who, in the later days in Paris, after
her return, had conceived an infantile infatuation for him,
and would cease crying or go to sleep peacefully if only he
could gather a clump of Septimus's hair in his tiny fingers.
He missed a thousand gossamer trifles—each one so imper-
ceptible, all added together so significant. He was not in

the least cosy and comfortable with his old villain of a serving-man.

Thus he looked forward, in his twilight way, to Emmy's coming. He would live, perhaps, sometimes in Nunsmere and sometimes in London. Quite lately, on visiting his bankers, in order to make arrangements for the disposal of his income, he was surprised to find how rich he was; and the manager, an astoundingly well-informed person, explained that a commercial concern in which he held many shares had reached such a pitch of prosperity as to treble his dividends. He went away with the vague notion that commercial companies were models of altruistic generosity. The main point, however, made clear by the exceptionally intelligent manager, being that he was richer by several hundreds a year, he began to dream of a more resplendent residence for Emmy and the boy than the little flat in Chelsea. He had observed that there were very nice houses in Berkeley Square. He wondered how much a year they were, with rates and taxes. For himself, he could perch in any attic close by. He resolved to discuss Berkeley Square with Emmy as soon as she arrived. William Octavius Oldrieve Dix, Member of Parliament, ought to start life in proper surroundings.

Clem Sypher, down for the week-end at Penton Court, burst in upon him during the afternoon. He came with exciting news. The high official in the Ordnance Department of the War Office had written to him that morning to the effect that he was so greatly impressed by the new quick-firing gun that he proposed to experiment forthwith, and desired to be put into communication with the inventor.

"That's very nice," said Septimus, "but shall I have to go and see him?"

"Of course," cried Sypher. "You'll have to interview boards and gunners and engineers, and superintend experiments. You'll be a person of tremendous importance."

"Oh, dear!" said Septimus, "I couldn't. I couldn't, really."

He was panic-stricken at the notion.

"You'll have to," laughed Sypher.

Septimus clutched at straws. "I'm afraid I shall be too busy. Emmy's coming to London—and there's the boy's education. You see, he has to go to Cambridge. Look here," he added, a brilliant idea occurring to him, "I'm fearfully rich; I don't want any more money. I'll sell you the thing outright for the two hundred pounds you advanced me, and then I shan't have anything more to do with it."

"I think before you make any proposals of the kind you ought to consult Mrs. Dix," said Sypher with a laugh.

"Or Zora."

"Or Zora," said Sypher. "She came down by the same train as I did. I told her the good news. She was delighted."

He did not inform Septimus that, for all her delight, Zora had been somewhat sceptical. She loved Septimus, she admitted, but his effectuality in any sphere of human endeavor was unimaginable. Could anything good come out of Nazareth?

About half an hour later the goddess herself arrived, shown in by Wiggleswick, who had been snatching the pipe of the over-driven by the front-gate. She looked flushed, resolute, indignant, and, on seeing Sypher, she paused for a second on the threshold. Then she entered. Sypher took up his hat and stick.

"No, no. You had better stay. You may help us. I suppose you know all about it."

Septimus's heart sank. He knew what "it" meant.

"Yes, Sypher knows. I told him."

"But why didn't you tell me, dear Septimus, instead of letting me hear of it from mother and Cousin Jane? I don't think it was loyal to me."

"I forgot," said Septimus in desperation. "You see, I sometimes remember it and sometimes forget it. I'm not used to getting married. Wiggleswick has been married several times. He was giving me a lot of advice this morning."

"Anyhow, it's true?" asked Zora, disregarding Wiggleswick.

"Oh, yes! You see, my ungovernable temper——"

"Your what?"

It was no use. On receiving the announcement she looked just as he had expected her to look. He tried to stammer out his catalogue of infamies, but failed. She burst out laughing, and Sypher, who knew all and was anxiously wondering how to save the situation, laughed too.

"My poor, dear Septimus," she said kindly, "I don't believe a word of it. The woman who couldn't get on with you must be a virago. I don't care whether she's my own sister or not, she is treating you abominably."

"But, indeed she's not," pleaded poor Septimus. "We're the best of friends. I really want to live like this. I do. I can't live without Wiggleswick. See how cosy and comfortable he makes me."

Zora looked round, and the cosiness and comfort made her gasp. Cobwebs hung from the old oak beams across the ceiling; a day or two's ashes defiled the grate; the win-

18

dows were splashed with mud and rain. There were no curtains. Her finger drawn along the green baize table-cloth revealed the dust. A pair of silver candlesticks on the mantelpiece were stained an iridescent brown. The mirror was fly-blown. In the corner of the room a tray held the remains of the last meal, and a plate containing broken food had overflowed onto a neighboring chair. An odd, uncleaned boot lay, like a frowsy, drunken visitor, on the floor. The springs of the armchair on which she sat were broken.

"It's not fit for a pig to live in," she declared. "It's a crime to leave you to that worthless old scoundrel. I'll talk to him before I go. He won't like it. And then I'll write to Emmy. If that has no effect, I'll go over to Paris and bring her to her senses."

She had arrived royally indignant, having had a pitched battle with Cousin Jane, who took Emmy's side and alluded to Septimus in terms of withering contempt. Now she was furiously angry. The two men looked at her with wistful adoration, for when Zora was furious in a good cause she was very beautiful. And the adoration in each man's heart was intensified by the consciousness of the pathetic futility of her noble rage. It was for her own sake that the situation had arisen over which she made such a pother, and she was gloriously unconscious of it. Sypher could not speak lest he should betray his knowledge of Septimus's secret, and Septimus could only murmur incoherent ineffectualities concerning the perfection of Emmy, the worthlessness of himself, and the diamond soul that lodged in Wiggleswick's forbidding body. Zora would not listen to unreason. It was Emmy's duty to save her husband from the dust and ashes of his present cosiness, if she could do nothing else for him; and she, Zora, in her magnificence, was going to see that Emmy's duty was performed. Instead of writing she would start the next morning for Paris. It would be well if Septimus could accompany her.

"Mrs. Dix is coming to London, I believe," said Sypher.

Zora looked inquiringly at Septimus, who explained discursively. Zora renounced Paris. She would wait for Emmy. For the time being the incident was closed. Septimus, in his hospitality, offered tea.

"I'll get it for you," said Zora. "It will be a good opportunity to speak sweetly to Wiggleswick."

She swept out of the room; the two men lit cigarettes and smoked for a while in silence. At last Sypher asked:

"What made you send her the tail of the little dog?"

Septimus reddened, and ran two of the fingers of the hand holding the cigarette up his hair, and spilled half an inch of ash on his head.

"I broke the dog, you see," he explained luminously, "I knocked it off the mantelpiece. I'm always doing it. When Emmy has a decent house I'll invent something to keep dogs and things on mantelpieces."

Sypher said: "Do you know you've done me one of those services which one man rarely does for another. I'll never forget it to my dying day. By bringing her to me you've saved my reason. You've made me a different being. I'm Clem Sypher—but, by God! you're the Friend of Humanity."

Septimus looked at him with the terrified expression of a mediæval wrongdoer, writhing under an ecclesiastical curse. He made abject apology.

"It was the only thing I could do," said he.

"Of course it was. And that's why you did it. I never

dreamed when you told me to wait until I saw her before going mad or breaking my heart that you meant to send for her. It has set me in front of a new universe."

He rose and stretched his large limbs and smiled confidently at the world out of his clear blue eyes. Two little words of Zora had inspired him with the old self-reliance and sense of predestination to great things. Out of her own mouth had come the words which, when they had come out of Rattenden's, had made his heart sink in despair. She had called him a "big man." Like many big men, he was superstitious. He believed Rattenden's prophetic utterance concerning Zora. He was, indeed, set in front of a new universe, and Septimus had done it by means of the tail of a little china dog.

As he was stretching himself, Wiggleswick shambled in, with the fear of Zora written on his wrinkled brow, and removed the tray and the plate of broken victuals. What had passed between them neither he nor Zora would afterwards relate; but Wiggleswick spent the whole of that night and the following days in unremitting industry, so that the house became spick and span as his own well-remembered prison cells. There also was a light of triumph in Zora's eyes when she entered a few moments afterwards with the tea-tray, which caused Sypher to smile and a wicked feeling of content to enter Septimus's mild bosom.

"I think it was high time I came home," she remarked, pouring out the tea.

The two men supported the proposition. The western hemisphere, where she had tarried so long, could get on very well by itself. In the meantime the old eastern hemisphere had been going to pieces. They had a gay little meal. Now that Zora had settled Wiggleswick, arranged her plan of campaign against Emmy, and established very agreeable and subtle relations between Sypher and herself, she could afford to shed all her charm and gaiety and graciousness on her subjects. She was infinitely glad to be with them again. Nunsmere had unaccountably expanded; she breathed freely and no longer knocked her head against beams in bedroom ceilings.

She rallied Septimus on his new gun.

"He's afraid of it," said Sypher.

"What! Afraid of its going off?" he laughed.

"Oh, no," said Septimus. "I've heard lots of them go off."

"When?" asked Zora.

Septimus reddened, and for once was at a loss for one of the curiously evasive answers in which his timidity took refuge. He fidgeted in his chair. Zora repeated her jesting question. "Was it when they were firing royal salutes in St. James's Park?"

"No," said Septimus.

His back being against the fading light she could not perceive the discomfiture on his face. She longed to elicit some fantastic irrelevance.

"Well, where was it? Why this mystery?"

"I'll tell you two," said Septimus. "I've never told you before. In fact, I've never told any one—not even Wiggleswick. I don't like to think of it. It hurts. You may have wondered how I ever got any practical acquaintance with gunnery. I once held a commission in the Militia Garrison Artillery. That's how I came to love guns."

"By why should that pain you, my dear Septimus?" asked Zora.

"They said I was incompetent," he murmured, brokenly,

"and took away my commission. The colonel said I was a disgrace to the service."

Clem Sypher smote the arm of his chair and started up in his wrath.

"By heavens! I'll make the blundering idiot eat his words. I'll ram them down his throat with the cleaner of the new gun. I'll make you the biggest ornament the service ever possessed. I'll devote my existence to it! The Dix gun shall wipe humanity off the face of the earth!"

"I don't want it to do that," said Septimus, meekly.

Zora begged his forgiveness very sweetly for her indiscretion, and having comforted him with glowing prophecies of fame and domestic happiness, went home with a full heart. She loved Sypher for his generous outburst. She was deeply touched by Septimus's tragic story, but having a sense of humor she could not repress a smile at the thought of Septimus in uniform, handling a battery of artillery.

CHAPTER XXI

Cousin Jane was for packing her boxes and departing, but Zora bade her remain until her own plans were settled. As soon as Emmy arrived she would have to go to London and play fairy godmother, a proceeding which might take up considerable time. Mrs. Oldrieve commended her beneficent intention, and besought her to bring the irreligiously wedded pair to the Vicar, and have them wedded in a respectable, Anglican way. She was firmly convinced that if this were done, nothing more could possibly be heard of separate lives. Zora promised to do her best, but Cousin Jane continued to sniff. It would be far better, she declared, to shut the man up in an idiot asylum and bring Emmy to Nunsmere, where the child could have a decent upbringing. Zora dissented loftily, but declined to be led into a profitless argument.

"All I ask of you, my dear Jane," said she, "is to take care of mother a little longer while I do what I consider my duty."

She did not inform Cousin Jane that a certain freedom of movements was also rendered desirable by what she considered her duty to Clem Sypher. Cousin Jane lacked the finer threads of apprehension, and her comments might have been crude. When Zora announced her intention to Sypher of leading a migratory existence between London and Nunsmere for the sakes of Emmy and himself, he burst into a panegyric on her angelic nature. Her presence would irradiate these last dark days of disaster, for the time was quickly approaching when the Bermondsey factory would be closed down, and Sypher's Cure would fade away from the knowledge of men.

"Have you thought of the future—of what you are going to do?" she asked.

"No," said he, "but I have faith in my destiny."

Zora felt this to be magnificent, but scarcely practical.

"You'll be without resources?"

"I never realized how full empty pockets could be," he declared.

They were walking across the common, Sypher having lunched at "The Nook." Presently they came across Septimus sitting by the pond. He rose and greeted them. He wore an overcoat buttoned up to the throat and a cloth cap. Zora's quick eyes noted an absence of detail in his attire.

"Why, you're not dressed! Oh, you do want a wife to look after you."

"I've only just got up," he explained, "and Wiggleswick wanted to do out my bedroom, so I hadn't time to find my studs. I was thinking all night, you see, and one can't think and sleep at the same time."

"A new invention?" laughed Zora.

"No. The old ones. I was trying to count them up. I've taken out about fifty patents, and there are heaps of things half worked out which might be valuable. Now I was thinking that if I made them all over to Sypher he might get in some practical fellow to set them right, and start companies and things to work them, and so make a lot of money."

He took off his cap and ran his hand up his hair. "There's also the new gun. I do wish you'd have that, too," he added, anxiously. "In fact, it was our talk yesterday that put the other idea into my head."

Sypher clapped him on the shoulder and called him his dear, generous fellow. But how could he accept?

"They're not all rot," said Septimus pleadingly. "There's a patent corkscrew which works beautifully. Wiggleswick always uses it."

Sypher laughed. "Well, I'll tell you what we can do. We can get a syndicate together to run the Dix inventions, and pay you royalties on sales."

"That seems a very good idea," said Zora judicially.

But Septimus looked dissatisfied. "I wanted to give them to Sypher," said he.

Zora reminded him laughingly that he would have to provide for the future member of Parliament's election expenses. The royalties would come in handy. She could not take Septimus's inventions seriously. But Sypher spoke of them later in his enthusiastic way.

"Who knows? There may be things hidden among his models and specifications of enormous commercial value. Lots of his inventions are crazy, but some are bound to be practical. This field gun, for instance. The genius who could have hit on that is capable of inventing anything. Why shouldn't I devote my life to spreading the Dix inventions over the earth? It's a colossal idea. Not one invention, but fifty—from a corkscrew to a machine gun. It's better than Sypher's Cure, isn't it?"

She glanced swiftly at him to see whether the last words were spoken in bitterness. They were not. His face beamed as it had beamed in the days when he had rhapsodied over the vision of an earth, one scab, to be healed by Sypher's Cure.

"Say you think it's better," he urged.

"Yes. It's better," she assented. "But it's chimerical."

"So are all the dreams ever dreamed by man. I shouldn't like to pass my life without dreams, Zora. I could give up tobacco and alcohol and clean collars and servants, and everything you could think of—but not dreams. Without them the earth is just a sort of backyard of a place."

"And with them?" said Zora.

"An infinite garden."

"I'm afraid you'll be disillusioned over poor Septimus," she said, "but I shouldn't like you to take up anything you didn't believe in. What would be quite honest in another man wouldn't be honest in you."

"That means," said Sypher, "you wouldn't like to see me going on dealing in quack medicines?"

Zora flushed red.

"It was at the back of my mind," she confessed. "But I did put my thoughts into the form of a compliment."

"Zora," said he, "if I fell below what I want to appear in your eyes, I should lose the dearest dream of all."

In the evening came Septimus to Penton Court to discuss the new scheme with Sypher. Wiggleswick, with the fear of Zora heavy upon him, had laid out his master's dinner suit, and Septimus had meekly put it on. He had also dined in a Christian fashion, for the old villain could cook a plain dinner creditably when he chose. Septimus proclaimed the regeneration of his body servant as one of the innumerable debts he owed to Zora.

"Why do you repay them to me?" asked Sypher.

Then he rose, laughed into the distressed face, and put both his hands on Septimus's shoulders.

"No, don't try to answer. I know more about you than

you can possibly conceive, and to me you're transparency itself. But you see that I can't accept your patents, don't you?"

"I shall never do anything with them."

"Have you tried?"

"No."

"Then I will. It will be a partnership between my business knowledge and energy and your brains. That will be right and honorable for the two of us."

Septimus yielded. "If both you and Zora think so, it must be," he said. But in his heart he was disappointed.

A few days afterwards Shuttleworth came into Sypher's office, with an expression of cheerfulness on his dismal countenance.

"Can I have a few moments with you, sir?"

Sypher bade him be seated. Since his defection to the enemy, Shuttleworth had avoided his chief as much as possible, the excess of sorrow over anger in the latter's demeanor toward him being hard to bear. He had slunk about, not daring to meet his eyes. This morning, however, he reeked of conscious virtue.

"I have a proposal to put before you, with which I think you'll be pleased," said he.

"I'm glad to hear it," said Sypher.

"I'm proud to say," continued Shuttleworth, "that it was my suggestion, and that I've carried it through. I was anxious to show you that I wasn't ungrateful for all your past kindnesses, and my leaving you was not as disloyal as you may have thought."

"I never accused you of disloyalty," said Sypher. "You had your wife and children. You did the only thing possible."

"You take a load off my mind," said Shuttleworth.

He drew a long breath, as though relieved from an intolerable burden.

"What is your proposal?" asked Sypher.

"I am authorized by the Jebusa Jones Company to approach you with regard to a most advantageous arrangement for both parties. It's your present intention to close down the factory and shut up this office as soon as things can be wound up."

"That's my intention," said Sypher.

"You'll come out of it solvent, with just a thousand pounds or so in your pocket. The Cure will disappear from the face of the earth."

"Quite so," said Sypher. He leaned back in his chair, and held an ivory paper-knife in both hands.

"But wouldn't that be an enormous pity?" said Shuttleworth. "The Cure is known far and wide. Economically financed, and put, more or less, out of reach of competition it can still be a most valuable property. Now, it occurred to me that there was no reason why the Jebusa Jones Company could not run Sypher's Cure side by side with the Cuticle Remedy. They agree with me. They are willing to come to terms, whereby they will take over the whole concern as it stands, with your name, of course, and advertisements and trade-marks, and pay you a percentage of the profits."

Sypher made no reply. The ivory paper-knife snapped, and he laid the pieces absently on his desk.

"The advantage to you is obvious," remarked Shuttleworth, who was beginning to grow uneasy before the sphinx-like attitude of his chief.

"Quite obvious," said Sypher. Then, after a pause:

"Do they propose to ask me to manage the Sypher Cure branch?"

The irony was lost on Shuttleworth.

"No—well—not exactly—" he stammered.

Sypher laughed grimly, and checked further explanations.

"That was a joke, Shuttleworth. Haven't you noticed that my jokes are always rather subtle? No, of course you are to manage the Cure."

"I know nothing about that, sir," said Shuttleworth hastily.

Sypher rose and walked about the room, saying nothing, and his manager followed him anxiously with his eyes. Presently he paused before the cartoon of the famous poster.

"This would be taken over with the rest?"

"I suppose so. It's valuable—part of the good-will."

"And the model of Edinburgh Castle—and the autograph testimonials, and the 'Clem Sypher. Friend of Humanity'?"

"The model isn't much use. Of course, you could keep that as a curiosity——"

"In the middle of my drawing-room table," said Sypher, ironically.

Shuttleworth smiled, guessing that the remark was humorous.

"Well," he said, "that's as you please. But the name and title naturally are the essence of the matter."

"I see," said Sypher. "'Clem Sypher, Friend of Humanity,' is the essence of the matter."

"With the secret recipe, of course."

"Of course," said Sypher, absently. He paced the room once or twice, then halted in front of Shuttleworth, looked at him fixedly for a second or two out of his clear eyes and resumed his walk; which was disconcerting for Shuttleworth, who wiped his spectacles.

"Do you think we might now go into some details with regard to terms?"

"No," said Sypher, stopping short of the fireplace, "I don't. I've got to agree to the principle first."

"But, surely, there's no difficulty about that!' cried Shuttleworth, rising in consternation. "I can see no earthly reason——"

"I don't suppose you can," said Sypher. "When do you want an answer?"

"As soon as possible."

"Come to me in an hour's time and I'll give it you."

Shuttleworth retired. Sypher sat at his desk, his chin in his hand, and struggled with his soul, which, as all the world knows, is the most uncomfortable thing a man has to harbor in his bosom. After a few minutes he rang up a number on the telephone.

"Are you the Shaftesbury Club? Is Mr. Septimus Dix in?"

He knew that Septimus was staying at the club, as he had come to town to meet Emmy, who had arrived the evening before from Paris.

Mr. Dix was in. He was just finishing breakfast, and would come to the telephone. Sypher waited, with his ear to the receiver.

"Is that you, Septimus? It's Clem Sypher speaking. I want you to come to Moorgate Street at once. It's a matter of immediate urgency. Get into a hansom and tell the man to drive like the devil. Thanks."

He resumed his position and sat motionless until, about

half an hour later, Septimus, very much scared, was shown into the room.

"I felt sure you were in. I felt sure you would come. There's a destiny about all this business, and I seem to have a peep into it. I am going to make myself the damnedest fool of all created beings—the very damnedest."

Septimus murmured that he was sorry to hear it.

"I hoped you might be glad," said Sypher.

"It depends upon the kind of fool you're going to make of yourself," cried Septimus, a ray of wonderful lucidity flashing across his mind. "There's a couplet of Tennyson's—I don't read poetry, you know," he broke off apologetically, "except a little Persian. I'm a hard, scientific person, all machinery. My father used to throw poetry books into the fire if he caught me with one, but my mother used to read to me now and then—oh, yes!—Tennyson. It goes: '*They called me in the public squares, The fool that wears a crown of thorns.*' That's the best kind of a fool to be." He suddenly looked round. "Dear me; I've left my umbrella in the cab. That's the worst kind of a fool to be."

He smiled wanly, dropped his bowler hat on the floor, and eventually sat down.

"I want to tell you something," said Sypher, standing on the hearthrug with his hands on his hips. "I've just had an offer from the Jebusa Jones Company."

Septimus listened intently while he told the story, wondering greatly why he, of all unbusinesslike, unpractical people—in spite of his friendship with Sypher—should be summoned so urgently to hear it. If he had suspected that in reality he was playing the part of an animated conscience, he would have shriveled up through fright and confusion.

Said Sypher: "If I accept this offer I shall have a fair income for the rest of my days. I can go where I like, and do what I like. Not a soul can call my commercial honesty in question. No business man, in his senses, would refuse it. If I decline, I start the world again with empty pockets. What shall I do? Tell me."

"I?" said Septimus, with his usual gesture of diffidence. "I'm such a silly ass in such things."

"Never mind," said Sypher. "I'll do just what you would do."

Septimus reflected, and said, hesitatingly:

"I think I should do what Zora would like. She doesn't mind empty pockets."

Sypher dashed his hand across his forehead, and broke into a loud cry.

"I knew you would say that! I brought you here to say it! Thank God! I love her, Septimus. I love her with every fiber in me. If I had sold my name to these people I should have sold my honor. I should have sold my birthright for a mess of pottage. I couldn't have looked her in the face again. Whether she will marry me or not has nothing to do with it. It would have had nothing to do with it in your case. You would have been the best kind of fool and so shall I."

He swung about the room greatly excited, his ebullient nature finding in words relief from past tension. He laughed aloud, proclaimed his love for Zora, shook his somewhat bewildered friend by the hand, and informed him that he, Septimus, alone of mortals, was responsible for the great decision. And while Septimus wondered what the deuce he meant, he rang the bell and summoned Shuttleworth.

The dismal manager entered the room. On seeing Sypher's cheery face, his own brightened.

"I've thought the matter over, Shuttleworth."

"And you've decided——"

"To refuse the offer, absolutely."

The manager gasped. "But, Mr. Sypher, have you reflected——"

"My good Shuttleworth," said Sypher, "in all the years we've worked together have you ever known me to say I've made up my mind when I haven't?"

Shuttleworth marched out of the room and banged the door, and went forth to declare to the world his opinion of Clem Sypher. He had always been half crazy; now he had gone stick, stark, staring, raving, biting mad. And those to whom he told the tale agreed with him.

But Sypher laughed his great laugh.

"Poor Shuttleworth. He has worked hard to bring off this deal. I'm sorry for him. But one can't serve God and Mammon."

Septimus rose and took his hat. "I think it awfully wonderful of you," he said. "I really do. I should like to talk to you about it—but I must go and see Emmy. She came last night."

Sypher inquired politely after her health, also that of her baby.

"He's taking such a deuce of a time to grow up," said Septimus. "Otherwise he's well. He's got a tooth. I've been wondering why no dentist has ever invented a set of false teeth for babies."

"Then your turn would come," laughed Sypher, "for you would have to invent them a cast-iron inside."

19

Before Septimus went, Sypher thrust a gold-headed umbrella into his hands.

"It's pouring with rain, and you'll wade about and get wet through. I make a rule never to lend umbrellas, so I give you this from a grateful heart. God bless you."

CHAPTER XXII

THE little flat in Chelsea, cleaned, swept and garnished by the wife of the porter of the Mansions, received Emmy, her babe, Madame Bolivard and multitudinous luggage. All the pretty fripperies and frivolities had been freshened and refurbished since their desecration at alien hands, and the place looked cheery and homelike; but Emmy found it surprisingly small, and was amazed to discover the prodigious space taken up by the baby. When she drew Septimus's attention to this phenomenon he accounted for it by saying that it was because he had such a very big name, which was an excellent thing in that it would enable him to occupy a great deal of room in the universe when he grew up.

She busied herself all the morning about the flat, happier than she had been for a whole year. Her days of Hagardom were over. The menacing shadow of the finger of scorn pointing at her from every airt of heaven had disappeared. A clear sky welcomed her as she came back to take up an acknowledged position in the world. The sense of release from an intolerable ban outweighed the bitterness of old associations. She was at home, in London, among dear familiar things and faces. She was almost happy.

When Madame Bolivard appeared with bonnet and basket undismayedly prepared to market for lunch and dinner, she laughed like a schoolgirl, and made her repeat the list of English words she had taught her in view of this contingency. She could say "cabbage," "sugar," "lettuce," and ask for all sorts of things.

"But suppose you lose your way, Madame Bolivard?"

"I shall find it, madame."

"But how will you ask for directions? You know you can't say 'Ecclefechan Mansions.'"

Madame Bolivard made a hopeless, spluttering sound as if she were blowing teeth out of her mouth, which in no wise resembled the name of the place wherein she dwelt. But Madame Bolivard, as has been remarked, was a *brave femme;* and *allons donc!* this was the least of the difficulties she had had to encounter during her life. Emmy bade her godspeed in her perils among the greengrocers.

She went blithely about her household tasks, and sang and cooed deliciously to the child lying in its bassinette. Every now and then she looked at the clock over the mantelpiece, wondering why Septimus had not come. Only in the depths of her heart—depths which humans in their every-day life dare not sound too frequently—did she confess how foolishly she longed for him. He was late. With Emmy, Septimus never broke an appointment. To insure his being at a certain place at a certain time to meet her he took the most ingenious and complicated precautions. Before now he had dressed overnight and gone to sleep in his clothes so as to be ready when the servant called him in the morning. Emmy, knowing this, after the way of women began to grow anxious. When, therefore, she opened the flat door to him she upbraided him with considerable tenderness.

"It was Clem Sypher," he explained, taking off his overcoat. "He sent for me. He wanted me badly. Why, I don't know. At least I do half know, but the other half I don't. He's a magnificent fellow."

A little later, after Septimus had inspected her morning's work in the flat, and the night's progress in the boy's tooth, and the pretty new blouse which she had put on in his honor, and the rose in her bosom taken from the bunch he had sent to greet her arrival in the flat the night before, and after he had heard of the valorous adventure of Madame Bolivard and of a message from Hégisippe Cruchot which she had forgotten to deliver overnight, and of an announcement from Zora to the effect that she would call at Ecclefechan Mansions soon after lunch, and of many things of infinite importance, Emmy asked him what Clem Sypher had been doing, and wherein lay the particular magnificence of character to which Septimus had alluded.

"He's awfully splendid," said Septimus. "He has given up a fortune for the sake of an idea. He also gave me an umbrella and his blessing. Emmy"—he looked at her in sudden alarm—"did I bring an umbrella with me?"

"You did, dear, and you put it in the stand; but what you've done with the blessing, I don't know."

"I've got it in my heart," said he. "He's a tremendous chap."

Emmy's curiosity was excited. She sat on the fender seat and bent forward, her hands on her knees, in a pretty girlish attitude and fixed her forget-me-not eyes on him.

"Tell me all about it."

He obeyed and expounded Sypher's quixotism in his roundabout fashion. He concluded by showing her how it had been done for Zora's sake.

Emmy made a little gesture of impatience.

"Zora!" she exclaimed jealously. "It's always Zora. To see how you men go on, one would think there was no other woman in the world. Every one does crazy things

for her, and she looks on calmly and never does a hand's
turn for anybody. Clem Sypher's a jolly sight too good
for her."

Septimus looked pained at the disparagement of his goddess. Emmy sprang to her feet and put her finger-tips on
his shoulders.

"Forgive me, dear. Women are cats—I've often told
you—and love to scratch even those they're fond of. Sometimes the more they love them the harder they scratch. But
I won't scratch you any more. Indeed I won't."

The sound of the latch-key was heard in the front door.

"There's Madame Bolivard," she cried. "I must see
what miracle of loaves and fishes she has performed. Do
mind baby till I come back."

She danced out of the room, and Septimus sat on a
straight-backed chair beside the bassinette. The baby—
he was a rather delicate child considerably undergrown for
his age, but a placid, uncomplaining little mortal—looked
at Septimus out of his blue and white china eyes and con-
torted his india-rubber features into a muddle indicative of
pleasure, and Septimus smiled cordially at the baby.

"William Octavius Oldrieve Dix," he murmured—an
apostrophe which caused the future statesman a paroxysm
of amusement—"I am exceedingly glad to see you. I hope
you like London. We're great friends, aren't we? And
when you grow up, we're going to be greater. I don't want
you to have anything to do with machinery. It stops your
heart beating and makes you cold and unsympathetic and
prevents women from loving you. You mustn't invent
things. That's why I am going to make you a Member of
Parliament—a Conservative member."

William Octavius, who had been listening attentively,

suddenly chuckled, as if he had seen a joke. Septimus's gaze conveyed sedate reproof.

"When you laugh you show such a deuce of a lot of gum—like Wiggleswick," said he.

The baby made no reply. The conversation languished. Septimus bent down to examine the tooth, and the baby clutched a tiny fistful of upstanding hair as a reaper clutches a handful of wheat. Septimus smiled and kissed the little crinkled, bubbly lips and fell into a reverie. William Octavius went fast asleep.

When Emmy returned she caught an appealing glance from Septimus and rescued him, a new Absalom.

"You dear thing," she cried, "why didn't you do it yourself?"

"I was afraid of waking him. It's dangerous to wake babies suddenly. No, it isn't babies; it's somnambulists. But he may be one, you see, and as he can't walk we can't tell. I wonder whether I could invent an apparatus for preventing somnambulists from doing themselves damage."

Emmy laughed. "You can invent nothing so wonderful as Madame Bolivard," she cried gaily. "She is contemptuous of the dangers of English marketing. 'The people understood me at once,' she said. She evidently has a poor opinion of them."

Septimus stayed to lunch, a pleasant meal which made them bless Hégisippe Cruchot for introducing them to the aunt who could cook. So far did their gratitude go that Septimus remarked that it would only be decent to add "Hégisippe" to the baby's names. But Emmy observed that he should have thought of that before; the boy had already been christened; it was too late. They drank the Zouave's health instead in some fearful and wonderful red wine which Madame Bolivard had procured from heaven knows what purveyor of dangerous chemicals. They thought it excellent.

"I wonder," said Emmy, "whether you know what this means to me."

"It's home," replied Septimus, with an approving glance around the little dining-room. "You must get me a flat just like this."

"Close by?"

"If it's too close I might come here too often."

"Do you think that possible?" she said, with as much wistfulness as she dare allow herself. "Besides, you have a right."

Septimus explained that as a Master of Arts of the University of Cambridge he had a right to play marbles on the Senate House steps, a privilege denied by statute to persons *in statu pupillari*, but that he would be locked up as a lunatic if he insisted on exercising it.

After a pause Emmy looked at him, and said with sudden tragicality:

"I'm not a horrible, hateful worry to you, Septimus?"

"Lord, no," said Septimus.

"You don't wish you had never set eyes on me?"

"My dear girl!" said Septimus.

"And you wouldn't rather go on living quietly at Nunsmere and not bother about me any more? Do tell me the truth."

Septimus's hand went to his hair. He was unversed in the ways of women.

"I thought all that was settled long ago," he said. "I'm such a useless creature. You give me something to think about, and the boy, and his education, and his teeth. And he'll have whooping cough and measles and breeches and things, and it will be frightfully interesting."

Emmy, elbow on table and chin in hand, smiled at him with a touch of audacity in her forget-me-not eyes.

"I believe you're more interested in the boy than you are in me."

Septimus reddened and stammered, unable, as usual, to express his feelings. He kept to the question of interest.

"It's so different," said he. "I look on the boy as a kind of invention."

She persisted. "And what am I?"

He had one of his luminous inspirations.

"You," said he, "are a discovery."

Emmy laughed. "I do believe you like me a little bit, after all."

"You've got such beautiful finger-nails," said he.

Madame Bolivard brought in the coffee. Septimus in the act of lifting the cup from tray to table let it fall through his nervous fingers, and the coffee streamed over the dainty table-cloth. Madame Bolivard appealed fervently to the Deity, but Emmy smiled proudly as if the spilling of coffee was a rare social accomplishment.

Soon after this Septimus went to his club with orders to return for tea, leaving Emmy to prepare for her meeting with Zora. He had offered to be present at this first interview so as to give her his support, and corroborate whatever statement as to his turpitudes she might care to make in explanation of their decision to live apart. But Emmy preferred to fight her battle single-handed. Alone he had saved the situation by his very vagueness. In conjunction with herself there was no knowing what he might do, for she had resolved to exonerate him from all blame and to attribute to her own infirmities of disposition this calamitous result of their marriage.

Now that the hour of meeting approached she grew nervous. Unlike Zora, she had not inherited her father's fearlessness and joy of battle. The touch of adventurous spirit which she had received from him had been her undoing, as it had led her into temptation which the gentle, weak character derived from her mother had been powerless to resist. All her life she had been afraid of Zora, subdued by her splendid vitality, humbled before her more generous accomplishment. And now she was to fight for her honor and her child's and at the same time for the tender chivalry of the odd, beloved creature that was her husband. She armed herself with woman's weapons, and put on a brave face, though her heart thumped like some devilish machine, racking her mercilessly.

The bell rang. She bent over the boy asleep in the bassinette and gave a mother's touch or two to the tiny coverlet. She heard the flat door open and Zora's rich voice inquire for Mrs. Dix. Then Zora, splendid, deep bosomed, glowing with color, bringing with her a perfume of furs and violets, sailed into the room and took her into her arms. Emmy felt fluffy and insignificant.

"How well you're looking, dear. I declare you are prettier than ever. You've filled out. I didn't come the first thing this morning as I wanted to, because I knew you would find everything topsy-turvy in the flat. Septimus is a dear, but I haven't much faith in his domestic capabilities."

"The flat was in perfect order," said Emmy. "Even that bunch of roses in a jar."

"Did he remember to put in the water?"

Zora laughed, meaning to be kind and generous, to make

it evident to Emmy that she had not come as a violent parti-
san of Septimus, and to lay a pleasant, familiar foundation
for the discussion in prospect. But Emmy resented the
note of disparagement.

"Of course he did," she said shortly.

Zora flew to the bassinette and glowed womanlike over
the baby. A beautiful child, one to be proud of indeed.
Why hadn't Emmy dear proclaimed his uniqueness in the
world of infants? From the references in her letters he
might have been the ordinary baby of every cradle.

"Oh, you ought to be such a happy woman!" she cried,
taking off her furs and throwing them over the back of a
chair. "Such a happy woman!"

An involuntary sigh shook her. The first words had
been intended to convey a gentle reproof; nature had compelled the reiteration on her own account.

"I'm happy enough," said Emmy.

"I wish you could say that with more conviction, dear.
'Happy enough' generally means 'pretty miserable.' Why
should you be miserable?"

"I'm not. I have more happiness than I deserve. I
don't deserve much."

Zora put her arm round her sister's waist.

"Never mind, dear. We'll try to make you happier."

Emmy submitted to the caress for a while and then freed
herself gently. She did not reply. Not all the trying of
Zora and all the Ladies Bountiful of Christendom could
give her her heart's desire. Besides, Zora, with her large
air of smiling *dea ex machina* was hopelessly out of tone
with her mood. She picked up the furs.

"How lovely. They're new. Where did you get them?"
The talk turned on ordinary topics. They had not met

for a year, and they spoke of trivial happenings. Emmy touched lightly on her life in Paris. They exchanged information as to their respective journeys. Emmy had had a good crossing the day before, but Madame Bolivard, who had faced the hitherto unknown perils of the deep with unflinching courage, had been dreadfully seasick. The boy had slept most of the time. Awake he had been as good as gold.

"He's the sweetest tempered child under the sun."

"Like his father," said Zora, "who is both sweet tempered and a child."

The words were a dagger in Emmy's heart. She turned away swiftly lest Zora should see the pain in her eyes. The intensity of the agony had been unforeseen.

"I hope the little mite has a spice of the devil from our side of the family," added Zora, "or it will go hard with him. That's what's wrong with poor Septimus."

Emmy turned with a flash. "There's nothing wrong with Septimus. I wouldn't change him for any man in the world."

Zora raised surprised eyebrows and made the obvious retort:

"Then, my dear, why on earth don't you live with him?"

Emmy shrugged her shoulders, and looked out of the window. There was a block of flats over the way, and a young woman at a window immediately opposite was also looking out. This irritated her. She resented being stared at by a young woman in a flat. She left the window and sat on the sofa.

"Don't you think, Zora, you might let Septimus and myself arrange things as we think best? I assure you we are quite capable of looking after ourselves. We meet in the friendliest way possible, but we have decided to occupy separate houses. It's a matter that concerns ourselves entirely."

Zora was prepared for this attitude, which she had resolved not to countenance. She had come, in all her bravery, to bring Emmy to her senses. Emmy should be brought. She left the bassinette and sat down near her sister and smiled indulgently.

"My dearest child, if you were so-called 'advanced people' and held all sorts of outrageous views, I might understand you. But you are two very ordinary folk with no views at all. You never had any in your life, and if Septimus had one he would be so terribly afraid of it that he would chain it up. I'm quite certain you married without any idea save that of sticking together. Now, why haven't you?"

"I make Septimus miserable. I can't help it. Sooner than make him unhappy I insist upon this arrangement. There!"

"Then I think you are very wicked and heartless and selfish," said Zora.

"I am," said Emmy defiantly.

"Your duty is to make him happy. It would take so little to do that. You ought to give him a comfortable home and teach him to realize his responsibilities toward the child."

Again the stab. Emmy's nerve began to give way. For the first time came the wild notion of facing Zora with the whole disastrous story. She dismissed it as crazy.

"I tell you things can't be altered."

"But why? I can't imagine you so monstrous. Give me your confidence, darling."

"There's nothing to give."

"I'm sure I could put things right for you at once if I knew what was wrong. If it's anything to do with Septimus," she added in her unwisdom and with a charming proprietary smile, "why, I can make him do whatever I like."

"Even if we had quarreled," cried Emmy, losing control of her prudence, "do you suppose I would let *you* bring him back to me?"

"But why not?"

"Have you been so blind all this time as not to see?"

Emmy knew her words were vain and dangerous, but the attitude of her sister, calm and confident, assuming her air of gracious patronage, irritated her beyond endurance. Zora's smile deepened into indulgent laughter.

"My dearest Emmy, you don't mean to say that it's jealousy of me? But it's too ridiculous. Do you suppose I've ever thought of Septimus in that way?"

"You've thought of him just as you used to think of the bob-tailed sheep dog we had when we were children."

"Well, dear, you were never jealous of my attachment to Bobbie or Bobbie's devotion to me," said Zora, smilingly logical. "Come, dear, I knew there was only some silly nonsense at the bottom of this. Look. I'll resign every right I have in poor Septimus."

Emmy rose. "If you call him 'poor Septimus' and speak of him in that tone, you'll drive me mad. It's you that are wicked and heartless and selfish."

"I?" cried Zora, aghast.

"Yes, you. You accept the love and adoration of the noblest gentleman that God ever put into the world, and you treat him and talk of him as if he were a creature of no account. If you were worthy of being loved by him, I shouldn't be jealous. But you're not. You've been so wrapped up in your own magnificence that you've not even condescended to notice that he loved you. And even now, when I tell you, you laugh, as if it were preposterous that 'poor Septimus' could ever dare to love you. You drive me mad."

Zora drew herself up angrily. To make allowances for a silly girl's jealousy was one thing; it was another to be accused in this vehement fashion. Conscious of her innocence, she said:

"Your attack on me is entirely unjustifiable, Emmy. I have done nothing."

"That's why," retorted Emmy quickly. "You've done nothing. Men are sacrificing their lives and fortunes for you, and you do nothing."

"Lives and fortunes? What do you mean?"

"I mean what I say," cried Emmy desperately. "Septimus has done everything short of laying down his life for you, and that he would have done if necessary, and you haven't even taken the trouble to see the soul in the man that was capable of it. And now that something has happened which you can't help seeing you come in your grand way to put it all to rights in a minute. You think I've turned him out because he's a good-natured worry like Bobbie, the bob-tailed sheep dog, and you say, 'Poor fellow, see how pitifully he's wagging his tail. It's cruel of you not to let him in.' That's the way you look at Septimus, and I can't stand it and I won't. I love him as I never dreamed a woman could love a man. I could tear myself into little pieces for him bit by bit. And I can't get him. He's as far removed from me as the stars in heaven. You could never understand. I pray every night to God to forgive me, and to work a miracle and bring him to me. But miracles don't happen. He'll never come to me. He can't come to me. While you have been patronizing him, patting him on the head, playing Lady Bountiful to him —as you are doing to the other man who has given up a fortune this very morning just because he loves you—while you've been doing this and despising him—yes, you know you do in your heart, for a simple, good-natured, half-witted creature who amuses himself with crazy inventions, he has done a thing to save you from pain and shame and sorrow—you, not me—because he loved you. And now I love him. I would give all I have in life for the miracle to happen. But it can't. Don't you understand? It can't!"

She stood panting in front of Zora, a passionate woman obeying elemental laws; and when passionate women obey elemental laws they are reckless in speech and overwhelming in assertion and denunciation. Emmy was the first whom Zora had encountered. She was bewildered by the storm of words, and could only say, rather stupidly:

"Why can't it?"

Emmy drew two or three short breaths. The notion had come again. The temptation was irresistible. Zora should know, having brought it on herself. She opened the door.

"Madame Bolivard!" she cried. And when the French-woman appeared she pointed to the bassinette.

"Take baby into the bedroom. It will be better for him there."

"*Bien, madame,*" said Madame Bolivard, taking up the child. And when the door had closed behind her Emmy pointed to it and said:

"That's why."

Zora started forward, horror stricken.

"Emmy, what do you mean?"

"I'll tell you. I couldn't with him in the room. I should always fancy that he had heard me, and I want him to respect and love his mother."

"Emmy!" cried Zora. "Emmy! What are you saying? Your son not respect you—if he knew—do you mean . . . . ?"

"Yes," said Emmy, "I do—Septimus went through the marriage ceremony with me and gave us his name. That's why we are living apart. Now you know."

"My God!" said Zora.

"Do you remember the last night I was at Nunsmere?"

"Yes. You fainted."

"I had seen the announcement of the man's marriage in the newspaper."

She told her story briefly and defiantly, asking for no sympathy, proclaiming it all *ad majorem Septimi gloriam.* Zora sat looking at her paralyzed with helplessness, like one who, having gone lightly forth to shoot rabbits, suddenly comes upon a lion.

"Why didn't you tell me—at the time—before?"

"Did you ever encourage me to give you my confidence? You patted me on the head, too, and never concerned yourself about my affairs. I was afraid of you—deadly afraid of you. It sounds rather silly now, doesn't it? But I was."

Zora made no protest against the accusation. She sat quite still, her eyes fixed on the foot of the bassinette, adjusting her soul to new and startling conceptions. She said in a whisper:

"My God, what a fool I've been!"

The words lingered a haunting echo in her ears. They

20

were mockingly familiar. Where had she heard them recently? Suddenly she remembered. She raised her head and glanced at Emmy in anything but a proud way.

"You said something just now about Clem Sypher having sacrificed a fortune for me. What was it? I had better hear everything."

Emmy sat on the fender stool, as she had done when Septimus had told her the story, and repeated it for Zora's benefit.

"You say he sent for Septimus this morning?" said Zora in a low voice. "Do you think he knows—about you two?"

"It is possible that he guesses," replied Emmy, to whom Hégisippe Cruchot's indiscretion had been reported. "Septimus has not told him."

"I ask," said Zora, "because, since my return, he has seemed to look on Septimus as a sort of inspired creature. I begin to see things I never saw before."

There was silence. Emmy gripped the mantelpiece and, head on arm, looked into the fire. Zora sat lost in her expanding vision. Presently Emmy said without turning round:

"You mustn't turn away from me now—for Septimus's sake. He loves the boy as if he were his own. Whatever wrong I've done I've suffered for it. Once I was a frivolous, unbalanced, unprincipled little fool. I'm a woman now—and a good woman, thanks to him. To live in the same atmosphere as that exquisite delicacy of soul is enough to make one good. No other man on earth could have done what he has done and in the way he has done it. I can't help loving him. I can't help eating my heart out for him. That's my punishment."

This time the succeeding silence was broken by a half-checked sob. Emmy started round, and beheld Zora crying silently to herself among the sofa cushions. Emmy was amazed. Zora, the magnificent, had broken down, and was weeping like any silly fool of a girl. It was real crying; not the shedding of the tears of sensibility which often stood in her generous eyes. Emmy moved gently across the room—she was a soft-hearted, affectionate woman—and knelt by the sofa.

"Zora, dear."

Zora, with an immense longing for love, caught her sister in her arms, and the two women wept very happily together.

It was thus that Septimus, returning for tea, as he was bidden, found them some while afterwards.

Zora rose, her lashes still wet, and whipped up her furs.

"But you're not going?"

"Yes. I'll leave you two together. I'll do what I can. Septimus—" She caught him by the arm and drew him a step or two towards the door. "Emmy has told me everything. Oh, you needn't look frightened, dear. I'm not going to thank you—" Her voice broke on the laugh. "I should only make a fool of myself. Some other time. I only want to say, don't you think you would be more—more cosy and comfortable if you let her take care of you altogether? She's breaking her heart for love of you, Septimus, and she would make you happy."

She rushed out of the room, and before the pair could recover from their confusion they heard the flat door slam behind her.

Emmy looked at Septimus with a great scare in her blue eyes. She said something about taking no notice of what Zora said.

"But is it true?" he asked.

She said with her back against the wall:

"Do you think it very amazing that I should care for you?"

Septimus ran his hands vehemently up his hair till it reached the climax of Struwel Peterdom. The most wonderful thing in his life had happened. A woman loved him. It upset all his preconceived notions of his place in the universe.

"Yes, I do," he answered. "It makes my head spin round." He found himself close to her. "Do you mean that you love me"—his voice grew tremulous—"as if I were an ordinary man?"

"No," she cried, with a half laugh. "Of course I don't. How could I love an ordinary man as I love you?"

Neither could tell afterwards how it happened. Emmy called the walls to witness that she did not throw herself into his arms, and Septimus's natural timidity precluded the possibility of his having seized her in his; but she stood for a long, throbbing time in his embrace, while he kissed her on the lips and gave all his heart into her keeping.

They sat down together on the fender seat.

"When a man does that," said Septimus, as if struck by a luminous idea, "I suppose he asks the girl to marry him."

"But we are married already," she cried joyously.

"Dear me," said Septimus, "so we are. I forgot. It's very puzzling, isn't it? I think, if you don't mind, I'll kiss you again."

CHAPTER XXIII

ZORA went straight back to her hotel sitting-room. There, without taking off her hat or furs, she wrote a swift, long letter to Clem Sypher, and summoning the waiter, ordered him to post it at once. When he had gone she reflected for a few moments and sent off a telegram. After a further brief period of reflection she went down-stairs and rang up Sypher's office on the telephone.

The mere man would have tried the telephone first, then sent the telegram, and after that the explanatory letter. Woman has her own way of doing things.

Sypher was in. He would have finished for the day in about twenty minutes. Then he would come to her on the nearest approach to wings London locomotion provided.

"Remember, it's something most particular that I want to see you about," said Zora. "Good-by."

She rang off, and went up-stairs again, removed the traces of tears from her face and changed her dress. For a few moments she regarded her outward semblance somewhat anxiously in the glass, unconscious of a new coquetry. Then she sat down before the sitting-room fire and looked at the inner Zora Middlemist.

There was never woman, since the world began, more cast down from her high estate. Not a shred of magnificence remained. She saw herself as the most useless, vaporing and purblind of mortals. She had gone forth from the despised Nunsmere, where nothing ever happened, to travel the world over in search of realities, and had returned to find that Nunsmere had all the time been the center of the realities that most deeply concerned her life. While she had been talking others had been living. The three beings whom she had honored with her royal and somewhat condescending affection had all done great things, passed through flames and issued thence purified with love in their hearts. Emmy, Septimus, Sypher, all in their respective ways, had grappled with essentials. She alone had done nothing—she the strong, the sane, the capable, the magnificent. She had been a tinsel failure. So far out of touch had she been with the real warm things of life which mattered that she had not even gained her sister's confidence. Had she done so from her girlhood up, the miserable tragedy might not have happened. She had failed in a sister's elementary duty.

As a six weeks' wife, what had she done save shiver with a splendid disgust? Another woman would have fought and perhaps have conquered. She had made no attempt, and the poor wretch dead, she had trumpeted abroad her crude opinion of the sex to which he belonged. At every turn she had seen it refuted. For many months she had known it to be vain and false; and Nature, who with all her faults is at least not a liar, had spoken over and over again. She had raised a fine storm of argument, but Nature had laughed. So had the Literary Man from London. She had a salutary vision of herself as the common geck and gull of the queerly assorted pair. She recognized that in order to work out any problem of life one must accept life's postulates and axioms. Even her mother, from whose gentle lips she rarely expected to hear wisdom, had said: "I don't see how you're going to 'live,' dear, without a man to take care of you." Her mother was right, Nature was right, Rattenden was right. She, Zora Middlemist, had been hopelessly wrong.

When Sypher arrived she welcomed him with an unaccustomed heart-beat. The masterful grip of his hands as they held hers gave her a new throb of pleasure. She glanced into his eyes and saw there the steady love of a strong, clean soul. She glanced away and hung her head, feeling unworthy.

"What's this most particular thing you have to say to me?" he asked, with a smile.

"I can't tell it to you like this. Let us sit down. Draw up that chair to the fire."

When they were seated, she said:

"I want first to ask you a question or two. Do you know why Septimus married my sister? Be quite frank, for I know everything."

"Yes," he said gravely, "I knew. I found it out in one or two odd ways. Septimus hasn't the faintest idea."

Zora picked up an illustrated weekly from the floor and used it as a screen, ostensibly from the fire, really from Sypher.

"Why did you refuse the Jebusa Jones offer this morning?"

"What would you have thought of me if I had accepted? But Septimus shouldn't have told you."

"He didn't. He told Emmy, who told me. You did it for my sake?"

"Everything I do is for your sake. You know that well enough."

"Why did you send for Septimus?"

"Why are you putting me through this interrogatory?" he laughed.

"You will learn soon," said Zora. "I want to get every-thing clear in my mind. I've had a great shock. I feel as if I had been beaten all over. For the first time I recognize the truth of the proverb about a woman, a dog, and a walnut tree. Why did you send for Septimus?"

Sypher leaned back in his chair, and as the illustrated paper prevented him from seeing Zora's face, he looked reflectively at the fire.

"I've always told you that I am superstitious. Septimus seems to be gifted with an unconscious sense of right in an infinitely higher degree than any man I have ever known. His dealings with Emmy showed it. His sending for you to help me showed it. He has shown it in a thousand ways. If it hadn't been for him and his influence on my mind I don't think I should have come to that decision. When I had come to it, I just wanted him. Why, I can't tell you."

"I suppose you knew that he was in love with me?" said Zora in the same even tone.

"Yes," said Sypher. "That's why he married your sister."

"Do you know why—in the depths of his heart—he sent me the tail of the little dog?"

"He knew somehow that it was right. I believe it was. I tell you I'm superstitious. But in what absolute way it was right I can't imagine."

"I can," said Zora. "He knew that my place was by your side. He knew that I cared for you more than for any man alive." She paused. Then she said deliberately: "He knew that I loved you all the time."

Sypher plucked the illustrated paper from her hand and cast it across the room, and, bending over the arm of his chair, seized her wrist.

"Zora, do you mean that?"

She nodded, fluttered a glance at him, and put out her free hand to claim a few moments' grace.

"I left you to look for a mission in life. I've come back and found it at the place I started from. It's a big mission, for it means being a mate to a big man. But if you will let me try, I'll do my best."

Sypher thrust away the protecting hand.

"You can talk afterwards," he said.

Thus did Zora come to the knowledge of things real. When the gates were opened, she walked in with a tread not wanting in magnificence. She made the great surrender, which is woman's greatest victory, very proudly, very humbly, very deliciously. She had her greatnesses.

She freed herself, flushed and trembling, throbbing with a strange happiness that caught her breath. This time she believed Nature, and laughed with her in her heart in close companionship. She was mere woman after all, with no mission in life but the accomplishment of her womanhood, and she gloried in the knowledge. This was exceedingly good for her. Sypher regarded her with shining eyes as if she had been an immortal vesting herself in human clay for divine love of him; and this was exceedingly good for Sypher. After much hyperbole they descended to kindly commonplace.

"But I don't see now," he cried, "how I can ask you to marry me. I don't even know how I'm to earn my living."

"There are Septimus's inventions. Have you lost your faith in them?"

He cried with sudden enthusiasm, as who should say, if

an Immortal has faith in them, then indeed must they be divine:

"Do you believe in them now?"

"Utterly. I've grown superstitious, too. Wherever we turn there is Septimus. He has raised Emmy from hell to heaven. He has brought us two together. He is our guardian angel. He'll never fail us. Oh, Clem, thank heaven," she exclaimed fervently, "I've got something to believe in at last."

Meanwhile the guardian angel, entirely unconscious of apotheosis, sat in the little flat in Chelsea blissfully eating crumpets over which Emmy had spread the preposterous amount of butter which proceeds from an overflowing heart. She knelt on the hearth rug watching him adoringly as if he were a hierophant eating sacramental wafer. They talked of the future. He mentioned the nice houses he had seen in Berkeley Square.

"Berkeley Square would be very charming," said Emmy, "but it would mean carriages and motor-cars and powdered footmen and Ascot and balls and dinner parties and presentations at Court. You would be just in your element, wouldn't you, dear?"

She laughed and laid her happy head on his knee.

"No, dear. If we want to have a fling together, you and I, in London, let us keep on this flat as a *pied-à-terre*. But let us live at Nunsmere. The house is quite big enough, and if it isn't you can always add on a bit at the cost of a month's rent in Berkeley Square. Wouldn't you prefer to live at Nunsmere?"

"You and the boy and my workshop are all I want in the world," said he.

"And not Wiggleswick?"

One of his rare smiles passed across his face.

"I think Wiggleswick will be upset."

Emmy laughed again. "What a funny household it will be—Wiggleswick and Madame Bolivard! It will be lovely!"

Septimus reflected for an anxious moment. "Do you know, dear," he said diffidently, "I've dreamed of something all my life—I mean ever since I left home. It has always seemed somehow beyond my reach. I wonder whether it can come true now. So many wonderful things have happened to me that perhaps this, too——"

"What is it, dear?" she asked, very softly.

"I seem to be so marked off from other men; but I've dreamed all my life of having in my house a neat, proper, real parlor maid in a pretty white cap and apron. Do you think it can be managed?"

With her head on his knee she said in a queer voice:

"Yes, I think it can."

He touched her cheek and suddenly drew his hand away.

"Why, you're crying! What a selfish brute I am! Of course we won't have her if she would be in your way."

Emmy lifted her face to him.

"Oh, you dear, beautiful, silly Septimus," she said, "don't you understand? Isn't it just like you? You give every one else the earth, and in return you ask for a parlor maid."

"Well, you see," he said in a tone of distressed apology, "she would come in so handy. I could teach her to mind the guns."

"You dear!" cried Emmy.

THE END

WILLIAM J. LOCKE

The Usurper

"Contains the hall-mark of genius itself. The plot is masterly in conception, the descriptions are all vivid flashes from a brilliant pen. It is impossible to read and not marvel at the skilled workmanship and the constant dramatic intensity of the incident, situations and climax."—*The Boston Herald*.

Derelicts

"Mr. Locke tells his story in a very true, a very moving, and a very noble book. If any one can read the last chapter with dry eyes we shall be surprised. 'Derelicts' is an impressive, an important book. Yvonne is a creation that any artist might be proud of."—*The Daily Chronicle*.

Idols

"One of the very few distinguished novels of this present book season."—*The Daily Mail*.

"A brilliantly written and eminently readable book."
—The London Daily Telegraph.

A Study in Shadows

"Mr. Locke has achieved a distinct success in this novel. He has struck many emotional chords, and struck them all with a firm, sure hand. In the relations between Katherine and Raine he had a delicate problem to handle, and he has handled it delicately."
—The Daily Chronicle.

The White Dove

"It is an interesting story. The characters are strongly conceived and vividly presented, and the dramatic moments are powerfully realized."—*The Morning Post*.

The Demagogue and Lady Phayre

"Think of Locke's clever books. Then think of a book as different from any of these as one can well imagine—that will be Mr. Locke's new book."—*New York World*.

At the Gate of Samaria

"William J. Locke's novels are nothing if not unusual. They are marked by a quaint originality. The habitual novel reader inevitably is grateful for a refreshing sense of escaping the commonplace path of conclusion."—*Chicago Record-Herald*.

ANATOLE FRANCE

Complete Limited Edition in English

Under the general editorship of Frederic Chapman. 8vo., special light-weight paper, wide margins, Caslon type, bound in red and gold, gilt top, and papers from designs by Beardsley, initials by Ospovat. *$2.00 per volume* (except Joan of Arc), *postpaid.*

The Red Lily. Translated by WINIFRED STEPHENS.

" In this great and striking tragedy of a woman's passion for two totally distinct types of men, two things about Mr. France's literary craftsmanship will impress the observant. One is the fine use which has been made of dialogue. The other is the character of Thérèse herself."

Mother of Pearl. Translated by FREDERIC CHAPMAN,
Containing :

The Procurator of Judea	Amycus and Celestine
Our Lady's Juggler	Madame de Luzy
Dawn, etc.	

The Garden of Epicurus. Translated by ALFRED R. ALLINSON, Containing:

In the Elysian Fields	Careers for Women
Card Houses	The Priory, etc.

The Crime of Sylvestre Bonnard. Translated by LAFCADIO HEARN.

This novel was "crowned" by the French Academy in 1881, the author being received into membership in 1896.

" The highest presentation of France's many qualities and gifts is to be found in this exquisite book."

Joan of Arc. Translated by WINIFRED STEPHENS. 2 volumes. *$8.00 net per set. Postage extra.*

" This is an epoch-making book. . . . Beneath the simplicity of the mediæval narrative there may still be discerned the delicious irony and the delicate subtle humor of the novels."
WINIFRED STEPHENS in " *French Novelists of Today.*"

A. C. FOX-DAVIES

The Finances of Sir John Kynnersley
Ornamental cloth.   *12mo.*   *$1.50*

Represents an arch type of the clever swindler. Filled with exciting episodes, worthy of the attention of Sherlock Holmes.

The Dangerville Inheritance   *12mo.*   *$1.50*
A Detective Story
"A detective story of which Gaboriau might be proud."—*London Post.*

"Of the Wilkie Collins pattern."—*New York Times.*

"Plenty of excitement."—*Detroit News-Tribune.*

The Mauleverer Murders   *12mo.*   *$1.50*
A Detective Story
"As an inventor of puzzles the author of 'The Mauleverer Murders' is entitled to honorable rank. We have not, in a long time, read a detective story in which the crucial secret was better kept than in this tale. Decidedly, this is a detective story to make the jaded connoisseur of clever sensationalism 'sit up.'"

—*New York Tribune*

THOMAS COBB

The Chichester Intrigue
Ornamental cloth   12mo $1.50

A love-story with a good plot based upon the accidental discovery of a package of love-letters, which came into hands of one for whom they were not intended.

J. M. DIVER

Captain Desmond, V.C.
Ornamental cloth   12mo $1.50

"A story of the Punjab frontier. The theme is that of Kipling's 'Story of the Gadsbys'—a brilliant and convincing study of an undying problem."—*London Post.*

The Great Amulet   *12mo.*   *$1.50*

A love-story dealing with army life in India.

EMERY POTTLE

Handicapped.   An American Love-story.
Ornamental cloth.   12mo. $1.50.

*** A stirring romance dealing with fashionable life in New York and the hunting set in the country. A strong love-story based upon an unusual theme.

GERTRUDE ATHERTON

Patience Sparhawk and Her Times   *12mo.*   *$1.50*
   " Reached a genuine height in American fiction.   Powerful."
                                       —*Town Topics.*

A Daughter of the Vine   *12mo.*   *$1.50*

The Californians: A Novel   *12mo.*   *$1.50*
   " Her Californians are studies from life."—*The Dial.*

Senator North   *Decorative cloth.*   *12mo.*   *$1.50*
   " Has genuine historical value."—*Outlook.*

His Fortunate Grace   *12mo.*   *$1.25*

The Aristocrats   *Decorative cloth.*   *12mo.*   *$1.50*
   " Deserves more than one reading."—*New York Mail.*

HENRY HARLAND

The Cardinal's Snuff-Box   *12mo.*   *$1.50*

Grey Roses   *12mo.*   *$1.25*

Comedies and Errors   *12mo.*   *$1.50*

The Lady Paramount   *12mo.*   *$1.50*

Mademoiselle Miss, and Other Stories   *12mo.*   *$1.25*

HENRY SUDERMANN

The Undying Past   *12mo.*   *$1.50*
   " A romance of profound and absorbing interest—a transcript of
life, sentiment and passion that holds true in all tongues and times."
                                   —*Philadelphia North American.*

Regina; or The Sins of the Father   *12mo.*   *$1.50*
   " It is a powerful work of fiction, imbued with the Nietzschean
scorn of conventional morality that sweeps like a wind-storm
through so much of recent German literature."—*The Dial.*

RICHARD LE GALLIENNE

The Quest of the Golden Girl   *12mo.*   *$1.50*
   " Charm is the word which best describes the pervading quality of
this book."—*Critic.*

VERNON LEE

Uniform sets boxed. *8 vols. Cloth. $12.00 net. Express extra. $1.50 net each. Postage 10 cents.*

Limbo and Other Essays: "Ariadne in Mantua"
Pope Jacynth, and Other Fantastic Tales
Hortus Vitæ, or the Hanging Gardens
The Sentimental Traveller
The Enchanted Woods
The Spirit of Rome
Genius Loci
Hauntings

** "If we were asked to name the three authors writing in English to-day to whom the highest rank of cleverness and brilliancy might be accorded, we would not hesitate to place among them VERNON LEE."—*Baltimore Sun.*

ELIZABETH BISLAND

The Secret Life. Being the Book of a Heretic.
12mo. $1.50 net. Postage 10 cents

"A book of untrammelled thought on living topics . . . extraordinarily interesting."—*Philadelphia Press.*
"Excellent style, quaint humor, and shrewd philosophy."
—*Review of Reviews.*

W. COMPTON LEITH

Apologia Diffidentis. An intimate personal book.
Cloth. 8vo. $2.50 net. Postage 15 cents.

** "Mr. LEITH formulates the anatomy of diffidence as Burton did of melancholy; and it might almost be said that he has done it with equal charm. The book surpasses in beauty and distinction of style any other prose work of the past few years. Its charm is akin to that of Mr. A. C. Benson's earlier books, yet Mr. Benson at his best has never equalled this. . . . A human document as striking as it is unusual. . . . The impress of truth and wisdom lies deep upon every page."—*The Dial.*

GILBERT K. CHESTERTON

Heretics. Essays. *12mo.* *$1.50 net. Postage 12 cents.*
"Always entertaining."—*New York Evening Sun*
"Always original."—*Chicago Tribune.*

Orthodoxy. Uniform with "Heretics."
12mo. $1.50 net. Postage 12 cents.
"Here is a man with something to say."—*Brooklyn Life.*

All Things Considered. Essays on various subjects, such as :

Conceit and Caricature ; Spiritualism ; Science and Religion ; Woman, etc.
12mo. $1.50 net. Postage 12 cents.

The Napoleon of Notting Hill. *12mo. $1.50.*
"A brilliant piece of satire, gemmed with ingenious paradox."
—*Boston Herald.*

CHARLES H. SHERRILL

Stained Glass Tours in France. How to reach the examples of XIIIth XIVth, XVth and XVIth Century Stained Glass in France (with maps and itineraries) and what they are. *Ornamental cloth. 12mo. Profusely illustrated. $1.50 net. Postage 14 cents.*

*** "The author wastes no time on technicalities, and it will be hard for the reader not to share the author's enthusiasm."—*New York Sun.*

FRANK RUTTER

The Path to Paris. The Record of a Riverside Journey from Le Havre to Paris. 62 Illustrations. *Cloth. 8vo. $5.00 net. Postage 20 cents.*

*** A delightful account of a journey along the banks of the Seine. Impressions and adventures. Descriptions of historic and artistic associations. Of special value are the remarkable illustrations by Hanslip Fletcher.

POEMS WORTH HAVING

Stephen Phillips

NEW POEMS, including IOLE: A Tragedy in One Act; LAUNCELOT AND GUINEVERE, ENDYMION, and many other hitherto unpublished poems.

Cloth, 12mo $1.25 net Half morocco, $4.00 net Postage 10 cents

"I have read the 'New Poems' of Stephen Phillips with the greatest interest. In my judgment it is the best volume that he has ever published."—Wm. Lyon Phelps of Yale University.

Uniform Sets. 4 volumes, including NEW POEMS, POEMS, PAOLO AND FRANCESCA, HEROD.

Cloth, $5.00 net Half morocco, $15.00 net Express 50 cents

Laurence Hope

COMPLETE WORKS. Uniform Edition 3 volumes. 12mo. Bound in red cloth, in box.

India's Love Lyrics, including "The Garden of Kama."
Stars of the Desert
Last Poems. Translations from the Book of Indian Love.

*Cloth, $4.50 net Postage 35 cents Half morocco, $12.00
Postage 50 cents*

"The comparison of Laurence Hope to Sappho readily suggested itself to the admiring reviewers of her first book of poems. . . . The compliment was fully deserved. . . . As a singer of the melancholy of love and passion, Laurence Hope surpasses Swinburne in intensity of feeling and beauty of thought."
—*New York Evening Mail.*

The Poems of Arthur Symons

A Collected Edition of the Poet's works issued in two volumes with a Photogravure Portrait as Frontispiece.

8vo $3.00 net Half morocco, $10.00 Postage 24 cents

The Fool of the World, and Other Poems
BY ARTHUR SYMONS

12mo $1.50 net Half morocco, $5.00 Postage 15 cents

"Stands at the head of all British poets of his generation."—*New York Evening Post.*

The Poems of William Watson

Edited and arranged with an introduction by J. A. SPENDER.

*In 2 volumes 12mo cloth, $2.50 net Half morocco, $7.50 net
Photogravure Portrait Postage 20 cents*

"The lover of poetry cannot fail to rejoice in this handsome edition."—*Philadelphia Press.*

"Work which will live, one may venture to say, as long as the language."—*Philadelphia Public Ledger.*

The
International Studio

An Illustrated Magazine of Fine and Applied Art

PUBLISHED BY JOHN LANE COMPANY
THE BODLEY HEAD
110-114 West Thirty-second Street : NEW YORK CITY

50 *cents* *per month*

Annual Subscription *$5.00*

Three Months' Trial Subscription, $1.00

¶ One Specimen Back Number of the Magazine will be sent to any Address in the United States on Receipt of Ten Cents

IT is the aim of "THE INTERNATIONAL STUDIO" to treat of every Art and Craft—Architecture, Sculpture, Painting, Ceramics, Metal, Glass, Furniture, House Decoration, Design, Bookbinding, Illustrating, Photography, Lithography, Enamel, Jewelry, Needlework, Landscape Gardening, etc. The principal writers on art are contributors to its pages. Many original illustrations, reproduced in every variety of black and white process, half-tone, line, photogravure, etc., are to be found in each number. Color plates of real value are to be found in every issue.